ARTHUR AND EXCALIBUR

THE SWORD OF WISDOM AND LIGHT

The Untold Story

GORDON ETHERINGTON

Order this book online at www.trafford.com
or email orders@trafford.com

Most Trafford titles are also available at major online book retailers.

Cover Design by Scott Spiers.

Note for Librarians: A cataloguing record for this book is available from Library and Archives Canada at www.collectionscanada.ca/amicus/index-e.html

Printed in Victoria, BC, Canada.

ISBN: 978-1-4251-6038-8 (soft)
ISBN: 978-1-4251-6039-5 (e-book)

 www.trafford.com

North America & International
toll-free: 1 888 232 4444 (USA & Canada)
phone: 250 383 6864 ♦ fax: 250 383 6804 ♦ email: info@trafford.com

The United Kingdom & Europe
phone: +44 (0)1865 487 395 ♦ local rate: 0845 230 9601
facsimile: +44 (0)1865 481 507 ♦ email: info.uk@trafford.com

10 9 8 7 6 5 4 3 2

DEDICATION

MY ETERNAL GRATITUDE AND THANKS to Carol Green, International Medium and Spiritual Teacher extraordinaire, for her guidance, dedication and perseverance in teaching all her students, including me, how to connect with our inner self so that everything just flowed naturally. Aiding my development by showing me how to unlock a wealth of knowledge and distant memories that I appeared to possess, that helped make this book possible.

Te anu Carol
In Love, Light and Truth

TABLE OF CONTENTS

ACKNOWLEDGEMENTS

MENTION MUST BE MADE OF MY 'TEAM,' whose varied contribution helped keep me on track through the long hours of writing.

My daughter Mel, who kept demanding more chapters to read as she became engrossed in the story, indicating where she felt words or phrases were too modern and needed amending. Scott, my son-in-law, who helped with the design of the book cover. Jacqui, my volunteer editor, who read and corrected my errors, commenting that she could feel the underlying tension flowing through the story, bless her. Sandy who provided welcome guidance when I was trying to do too many other things, and brought me back to reality and the need to stay focussed on the book. Lauren for her encouragement, compliments and constructive comments, using the draft version of the book as an editing project for her University degree in Journalism. All my friends and colleagues that I haven't the space to mention, that gave me the support and inspiration to finish the task, whilst also working full time.

I travelled extensively around the west country as I took time out for writing this book and met some lovely people that gave me encouragement, especially those at the Camelot Castle Hotel in Tintagel with its wonderful ambience of a bygone era. The modern perfectly matched with the old and where this story really begins with the conception of Arthur.

Last but by no means least, I extend my thanks to those mystical friends of mine from the other side, that I believe shared that time with me long ago. Encouraging, cajoling and guiding me through the sequence of some of the events that I was not a party too at that time. There appeared to be a time limit set in which to finish this book, but I still do not know why, maybe at some point I will, as it is part of a 'quest' that is still ongoing.

AUTHOR'S NOTE

MUCH HAS BEEN WRITTEN ABOUT ARTHUR OVER MANY CENTURIES, but unfortunately what little that might have been written at the time has been lost and does not exist today, even the annals of Gildas, Nennius and Bede have been so widely copied and translated as to leave them suspect. Most were written many years after the events, often with the biased viewpoint of the author. Stories were handed down by word of mouth and developed into myth and legend over time, but most tales tend to have an element of truth in them initially, that are later embroidered upon by each storyteller to enhance the tale. The French romancers were masters in the art of intrigue, introducing new characters and quests to hold the reader's interest and further develop a story. Some of the characters were perhaps real people from other eras, some total fiction, such is the way of a storyteller in developing a legend or sequence of tales. You will not find the likes of Lancelot or Galahad, or indeed many of the other 'knights' in this story, nor the many quests that they were supposedly involved in.

This is the story of the troubled times that this country faced after the Romans had left. How Arthur, following in Uther's footsteps, set out to stop the infighting between rival kings and bring peace and order to a country that was disintegrating and in danger of being overrun by the Saxons.

Christianity had been established for some while and although the Celtic influence was still strong in many areas there was general acceptance of both ways of life by the people. However the Saxons were still pagans and their conversion to Christianity would take several more generations. The task that Arthur set himself was not an easy one in the circumstances, but he persevered and many of the foundations that he laid for a better life survived for many generations, and in some cases were improved upon. It is an important part of the history of this country in its evolution, and showed the world what could be accomplished by working together to stem the flow of the Germanic tribes. Britain was the last outpost then, and history has a tendency to repeat itself, and usually produces the right leader at the right time, just as it did with Arthur.

This story is perhaps best described as a recollection from deep in my memory of what happened in that time, I feel as though I was there and had a part to play in events. Through various unexplained 'coincidences' in the last few years I felt as if I was being directed to write this story and some of the words that I have written are not words that I would use. On occasion I needed to check their meaning, and always it was the correct word.

Whatever your thoughts, I hope you enjoy reading the story as much as I did in writing it.

INTRODUCTION

A TRULY REMARKABLE TALE OF LOVE AND ENDURANCE through the battles and struggles of the world's best loved King - Arthur, as he strove to bring peace and prosperity to Britain by stopping the incessant infighting and uniting the country against the Saxon hordes. Laying the foundations of a better way of life for his people and the country that would last for many years. A man of passion and foresight, a born leader and diplomat who devoted his life, and eventually gave it, as he battled against internal strife and the ever present Saxon threat. He continued the task that Uther had started, but he was a far better King than his father, their characters differed greatly. Arthur was a man of the people and for the people, seeking to ease their burden in life and to be proud of their heritage, working together for the benefit of all. As King he let it be widely known that he was approachable by anyone, whatever their rank and station in life and would seek to resolve their problems or mediate on their behalf. Young or old they were all of equal importance in his eyes, the young because they were the future of his country and the old for their wisdom and advice. No stone was left unturned as he sought to bring his vision into reality, admitting that he was only human and would make mistakes, but he would quickly learn from them. A great exponent of 'service to others, before service to self,' that contributed much to his success throughout his life.

The tension is there as this remarkable young boy, turned King, left his mark on history as he pursued his destiny with compassion and total commitment, losing his wife Gwenhwyfar in the process. He could not have done it alone, and in this respect much was due to Merlin and the other Elders that secretly prepared him for his life as High King, and continued to advise him until the end. His sword Excalibur, given to him by the Lady of the Lake, gave him the protection that he needed, put fear into the hearts of his enemies and aided him in many mystical ways. This is a magical insight into his real life as it happened, not just another mystical fantasy. I feel as if I knew him well.

Chapter 1
THE CONCEPTION OF ARTHUR

THE RIDERS APPROACHED THE TOP OF THE GRASSY KNOLL, soon they would be in sight of their destination on the far side, as the lush green valley dropped slowly towards the shoreline. Only to climb steeply to the narrow causeway that connected the mainland to the fort, clinging precariously to the promontory jutting out into the wild sea way below. *An easy place to defend with a small force,* thought Uther as he paused to survey the rugged beauty of what lay before them. Glancing round at his men he could see in every face the relaxation and mirth returning as each turned their thoughts to the evening ahead and left behind the horrors of earlier. The day had been long and the fighting fierce, but now they could look forward to relaxation and merriment at the court of Gorlois, Duke of Cornwall. A large force of Picts had landed on the coast in the Severn Estuary and struck inland, killing and wreaking havoc on the way, then turned south towards Cornwall.

Gorlois had sent word to the High King, Uther Pendragon, who was camped near Caer Baddon [Bath] at the time, requesting assistance, and the two forces had trapped the Picts in a pincer movement. Gorlois brought his men up from the south and west, whilst Uther moved in from the north and east. Ensnaring the marauding Picts between them, slaughtering every one of them they caught, although they suffered heavy casualties themselves, as the Picts with their painted faces were fierce fighters. Now with the main body of his men encamped for the night, Uther with 30 of his knights was approaching the gates of the fort at Tintagel to be received by the Duke for a night of celebration and undoubted debauchery.

Uther, at the battle hardened age of 26, his red hair blowing in the gentle sea breeze as they descended into the valley, was pleased with himself and as he had more than a passing fancy for Igraine, the beautiful young wife of the middle aged Duke. He was determined to make the most of this visit to satisfy his lust for her. His loins were already singing with fire at the thought of her and he hoped that the opportunity would present itself later to satisfy his lust. Which he was sure it would as he had been pondering on the problem during the ride and had come to several solutions. Now it was just a case of waiting his chance and taking advantage of any situation that arose during the evening, as there would be plenty of wine flowing freely. Unlike most this did not seem to affect him, except to increase his lustful desires. His reputation for the ladies was well known. He fought hard and played hard, such was his appetite for the pleasures of life, but he was always mindful of the lady's reputation and was consequently discreet in his conquests.

The evening was progressing well with a plentiful supply of food and wine being served, the minstrels and jesters providing entertainment, often mocking their fallen foes, causing much laughter and merriment as scenes from the fighting were re-enacted. These scenes were either portrayed as a tragedy or a comedy depending whether it was the demise of friend or foe and were always grossly exaggerated for effect.

The Duke and Uther were in heated debate concerning how many of the Picts had been slain and whose men had done the deed, and this had been going on since the festivities had begun. Each had consumed great quantities of wine and were in good spirits as well as voice, but Igraine and the ladies were beginning to show signs of wear as they repeatedly had their goblets refilled by various knights around the long table, no doubt with nefarious intent. Uther was aware of the state they were getting in, even though he was in constant argument with Gorlois over details of the battle and could see an opportunity arising that he could take advantage of and satisfy his lust for Igraine.

Uther suggested to Gorlois that the ladies be excused as the conversation was becoming too bloodthirsty for their delicate ears and the men had more business to discuss that would keep them busy for some while yet. Gorlois had been unaware that they were still there, being in such deep debate with Uther and promptly excused them. Igraine smiled a thank you to Uther, which set his loins on fire. The ladies departed holding each other for support until a couple of gallant knights offered their services, which two of the ladies eagerly accepted and hung on to them so they had no chance of escaping, even if they had wished too. Uther smiled to himself knowing that those knights would be rather busy until the morning just like he hoped to be later but he needed to keep Gorlois in conversation for another hour at least before he made his move.

Argument continued on the finer points of the battle and who did what and to whom and many of the other knights from both sides joined in to clarify a comment or challenge it as being incorrect. Uther was waving his hands around and in the process knocked over the Duke's wine. Apologising profusely he summoned another into which, as no-one was watching, he poured a small amount of liquid into the goblet that was hidden in a phial in his hand. This was a sleeping draught that he had asked Merlin for on the pretext of not being able to sleep, with the stipulation that it would knock him out for half a day, for Uther obviously did not want to be disturbed when he seduced Igraine. Uther passed the goblet to the Duke and to make sure he drank it and nobody else did he proposed a toast to all the good men that had fallen that day. Everyone who could staggered to their feet and downed their wine, such was the custom on those occasions, then all the

GORDON ETHERINGTON

goblets were refilled, not that there were many now left drinking as the majority had fallen asleep where they sat.

Conversation had all but lapsed although Gorlois tried to get it going again he was falling asleep as the potion took affect and Uther suggested that they retire and carry on the celebrations the following day when they were all refreshed. The Duke thought that would be a good idea and stood up, only to collapse in a heap as his legs gave way as the sleeping draught took effect. Uther bent down and picked him up commenting that he would take him to his quarters as it was not fitting that he should sleep on the floor like one of his men.

Gorlois was not a light man but Uther carried him easily, despite the amount of wine that he had drunk, and made his way to the Duke's bed Chamber where he hoped to find Igraine sleeping deeply. Sure enough in the light of the moon he could see her sleeping soundly beneath the bed robes and his lust for her began to rise. Letting Gorlois slip gently to the floor Uther made his way to the bed and drew back the covers. Even in her night attire Igraine looked beautiful as he bent forward and kissed her gently on the lips, to which she made no response. Good thought Uther, she is overtaken with drink and sleeping deeply and not likely to awaken shouting the place down, thereby bringing others running to see what the fuss might be about. Gorlois was on the floor snoring gently in a deep sleep and if Merlin was right would stay like that for many hours.

Uther undressed and slipped into bed beside Igraine, barely able to control himself as he was hard with passion for her, even when he slipped her night attire off she hardly moved. Uther kissed and caressed her body but then could contain himself no longer, mounted her and possessed her with all his passion to which she started to respond. He took her again and again such was his pent up desire for her as she began to moan and respond very actively although she was still asleep, muttering, 'husband you excel yourself tonight.'

Such was the noise that she was making that her maid came to the bed chamber thinking that Igraine was having a bad dream. Knocking loudly and calling out, but receiving no answer she entered the bed chamber, catching Uther in full flight of his passion. Uttering a cry she stepped forward, tripped over the Duke asleep on the floor, as she had not seen him and fell on the bed, whereupon Uther grabbed her and held her until he had finished and told her to be quiet otherwise he would slit her throat. He detached himself from Igraine and put the bed robes back over with one last look at her voluptuous body and still holding the girl he gathered up his clothes and dragged her from the bed chamber towards his own with continued threats of slitting her throat if she made a noise of any kind. The girl was wise enough to know that he meant what he said, having been caught in the act of seducing her mistress, although she was not sure who he was at that moment.

Once in his own bed chamber he wasted no time in stripping the clothes of her and she made no resistance as he was much stronger than her. It was an accepted way of life at court that knights could take a woman if they chose to, she had little say in it. He told her that if she ever told the Duke about what she had seen then she would suffer a very nasty death and with that proceeded to seduce her too as Uther had a great appetite and stamina for the ladies. For the next four hours he seduced her continuously until she had to ask him to stop as she was exhausted. It was then that she realised who she was sharing a bed with as it was beginning to get light. The King bade her get dressed and return to her own quarters with a reminder not to say a word to the Duke about what she saw in Igraine's bed chamber upon pain of death. The girl departed and although afraid because of the King's warning about what took place, he had not told her that she could not mention being seduced by the King himself, and that brought a smile to her face as she saw that there might be some advantage to be had from that at some point, especially with the other ladies in waiting.

It was several hours after the day had dawned before any real movement appeared in the confines of the fort and one of the first to awake was Igraine who was surprised to find herself under the bed robes without any clothing on at all and even more surprised to see her husband fully clothed asleep on the floor. She summoned her ladies in waiting to see if they could throw any light on the situation, but to no avail although she sensed that one or more of them knew more than they were willing to say at that moment. She was still feeling a bit heady and the lower half of her body was aching as if she had been out riding for many hours, but she had not done that for several days. As her ladies helped her dress she started to have small flashbacks of the dream she had when asleep, a very nice dream, but she dismissed it as her husband was flat out on the floor and still snoring gently, but why did she have no clothing on when she awoke, perhaps it wasn't a dream. Igraine decided that she would have to speak to her ladies privately one at a time and find out the truth, but first she would make her husband comfortable and have them lift him on to the bed which after several abortive attempts they managed to do.

Uther meanwhile was just coming out of his slumber and feeling very pleased with himself and the night's events. He had waited a long time for the opportunity to seduce Igraine and all had gone to plan, except for that silly little girl interrupting the proceeding before he was finished, still he had given her an experience of a lifetime too, especially as he had not released all his passion for Igraine when she disturbed him. Not every young girl gets the chance to be seduced by the King and no doubt she will brag about it to the other girls, who probably wont believe her or anything else that she might let slip. The King is surrounded by many ladies of rank why would he want to dally with a maid they would say. Yes Uther was pleased with himself for making the most of a rare opportunity.

Igraine had gathered from her ladies in waiting that they had prepared her for bed in the normal manner although she had been quite drunk and kept collapsing. They had seen her to bed and then retired themselves although the two older ones were waylaid by a couple of knights and taken to the men's chamber where they stayed the night. Rowena, her maid and the youngest of the ladies, appeared to be the one hiding something, but would not at first say anything until pressed very hard by Igraine, with threats of having her lovely head removed from her body. Only then did Rowena recount what she had seen and what the King was doing when she burst in, and had been for some while by the noise that was being made, that she had decided that Igraine must be having nightmares as the noise never went on that long when she was coupling with her husband. She said that she was shocked and froze as the King grabbed her and threatened her to stay quiet, then took her to his own quarters and seduced her for hours until she became exhausted and begged him to stop. He said he would have her killed if she spoke of this to his Lordship. Rowena then broke down and swooned and collapsed onto the floor. Igraine smiled to herself, *that was no dream I had that was Uther seducing me, what a man, no wonder I ache if he went on that long and then to take this young girl for hours too, coupling with a man will never be the same for either of us now my girl.* Igraine pulled Rowena gently to her feet and told her now that the truth had come out it must be forgotten and never spoken about again, otherwise great trouble would ensue for everyone involved and if that happened death might be a blessing. Igraine told her to go about her business and keep out of sight until the King and his party had left.

Uther Pendragon had hoped to stay with the Duke for a few days with the chance of seducing Igraine again but it was not to be as word had come from the main camp that a request for the King's help had just arrived that would require several days hard riding north to Glevum [Gloucester]. Uther gathered his men and bade Gorlois farewell and good hunting, deer or Picts it didn't matter except they could only eat one of them, at which comment there was a roar of laughter. As he turned to go Uther caught sight of Igraine and was sure she blew him a kiss, well perhaps she wasn't asleep after all, and he smiled to himself as the urge in his loins had finally subsided, for now, and he broke into song as they headed back to the main camp and then north to whatever lay before them.

Five days hard riding brought them to Glevum where they found it was being attacked by remnants of the Picts that had escaped previously, who seemed to have joined up with others, and with Saxons attacking from the east. Uther and his men, together with those loyal to the Duke of Gloucester pushed them northwards and pursued them relentlessly. The fighting lasted sporadically for several weeks as they were hunted down and killed. Many men fell on both sides but Uther's force was much the stronger and they were battle hardened and determined. At last the fighting ceased and Uther decided that they should head eastwards towards Lindinis [Lincoln], only two days ride away, for some well earned rest and recuperation and to catch up on the news and affairs of this area of his kingdom. News of their arrival preceded them and a great banquet was awaiting them on their arrival.

Uther stayed there for many days enjoying the hospitality and the plentiful supply of wine, food and women before deciding, reluctantly, that they should make their way southwards again. The journey south to Caer Baddon [Bath] and thence to Cadbury via Glasteining [Glastonbury] was relatively uneventful and they took their time stopping off at many places on the way, accepting gracefully the hospitality bestowed upon them, even if at times it was given somewhat reluctantly.

* * * * *

Back at Tintagel life was not all that rosy, Gorlois was getting irritable and frustrated as his wife Igraine was not very approachable these days and he was feeling rather bored with the peace and inaction. He wished that he had gone with Uther and was annoyed with himself for not offering at the time. Igraine on the other hand had problems of her own as she was sure that she was with child from the night of passion that Uther had subjected her to and was wondering how long she could keep this from her husband, who would know instantly that it was not his as they had not coupled for some while.

Deliberating on this for several days she decided to seek the advice from that wise counsellor Merlin, whom she had met several times and had taken a liking too. As it was a very delicate matter and only her and the maid Rowena knew of the events that occurred, Igraine decided that she would send Rowena to seek out Merlin and request that he visit her urgently. Summoning the maid, Igraine gave her instructions on what she must do and told her not to divulge anything to Merlin other than to request his urgent attendance at Tintagel to see her and that he must call in as if passing and not as a result of her request, as the Duke must not be aware of anything amiss. As far as Igraine was aware Merlin was most likely at Caer Myrddin [Carmarthen], where he spent a lot of his time, if not Rowena was to do her best to locate him as quickly as possible. She was to go northwards to Beeds Haven, less than half a days ride, and find a fisherman who would be willing to take her across the channel and wait and bring her, and hopefully Merlin, back. Igraine gave her a sum of money and told her to take one of the spare horses. She should not encounter any problems en-route but if there were any was to say that she was on the King's business and that if delayed he would have their head. Rowena, unaware of why Igraine wanted to see Merlin secretly (Igraine had not mentioned that she was with child) grabbed some clothes for the journey and raided the kitchen for food to take with her and then persuaded one of the young lads to prepare a horse, using her Lady's authority. With that she departed and as it was still early knew she could reach her destination well before dark. Igraine meanwhile could only wait and hope that Rowena would locate Merlin and quickly return, as time was running out and in a few weeks she would begin to show a slight bulge where none should be.

* * * * *

Uther arrived in Caer Baddon [Bath] to find that Merlin had been there, but left a few days previously to go on an errand as he called it, no doubt to see that water nymph that he was supposed to hang around with, although nobody could say what she really looked like as she was seldom seen, except from a distance, and then only briefly as she disappeared from sight when observed. The King stayed for nearly a week with the usual round of feasts, good wine and loose women before leaving for Glastonbury and then Cadbury and many were glad to see him go as his appetite for all the pleasures was far beyond what most men could manage, especially the women. It was nothing for Uther to have two or three women in one night and still be up before anyone else and not even a hangover in sight, no wonder a lot of the men were relieved when he moved on, at least they didn't have to worry about their own women so much then, or the amount of wine they had left.

Igraine was beginning to get worried as a week had gone passed and still no Rowena, and Gorlois was getting even more frustrated with his inactivity and obvious lack of attention from his wife, who when challenged on this matter had feigned sickness. This was true in part as she had started to suffer from morning sickness, something that she had not experienced before. Her two ladies in waiting were beginning to wonder what ailment she had, even suggesting that she should call for a physician, which Igraine said was not necessary as it would pass.

At last the following morning Rowena returned, slightly dishevelled looking tired and in need of a good soak, but unable to approach Igraine as the Duke was hanging around, so took herself off to refresh herself and change into more appropriate attire. This delay was extremely frustrating for Igraine but she managed to hide her impatience from her husband until he decided to go out for a ride to overcome his boredom, whereupon she immediately summoned Rowena to her chamber to hear the news. The maid entered and told her that although it had been a long journey it was successful and that Merlin was on his way, but would not arrive until the next morning, as he felt it best that way bearing in mind the cryptic nature of the request. Rowena explained that she was lucky that she had found him as he had only just arrived back from his travels and then there was bad weather in the channel that had delayed them on the return. Igraine thanked her and reminded her that what had happened that night with the King must still remain a secret and she hoped that not a word had been said to Merlin. Rowena assured her that it had not, even though Merlin had asked she had replied that she had only been sent to seek him out and was not privy to her ladyship's reason. The day seemed to drag after her maid departed and she could not even concentrate on her sewing for long but eventually the time passed and the day drew to a close.

Igraine slept soundly and didn't awake till late morning and only then because Gorlois disturbed her saying that an unexpected guest had arrived and that she should prepare herself to greet him. Igraine summoned her ladies and descended to the hall some two hours later, barely able to hide her disappointed at seeing not Merlin, whom she had expected, but Sir Ector, who had called in on his travels to inform the Duke that his wife was with child. and would in a few weeks give birth, that he had been going round making the appropriate arrangements. Igraine felt herself flush but managed to cover it by extending her congratulations with the hope that it would be a boy. At that moment another visitor arrived, and this time it was Merlin and after the usual courtesies and introductions the men disappeared into the courtyard with Gorlois inviting them both to stay the night, which they both gratefully accepted, much to Igraine's relief as it would give her chance to speak to Merlin on his own. The day progressed slowly with the men catching up on the news from afar, especially from Merlin as he travelled widely on what he called his errands.

After several hours Merlin stood up and stretched and said that he was going to walk down to the sea shore for a breath of air and asked Igraine, who was sitting close by sewing with her ladies, if she would care to escort him. She indicated that it would be a pleasure and that she could do with stretching her legs, so they took the long pathway down to the shore with neither saying a word until they arrived, whereupon Merlin asked her what was troubling her so much that she had sent word to him to come quickly and to arrive in such a discreet way. Merlin already knew the reason for the summons, as he was aware of what Uther had planned when he had asked for the sleeping draught because he could not sleep, but he did not wish Igraine to be aware of his pre-knowledge.

Igraine told Merlin the whole story of the night with the King and how he had coupled with her without her knowledge or consent, been discovered by Rowena who he then took to his chamber where he coupled with her for the rest of the night. That she could cope with but the problem was that she was now with child and was beginning to show a little, her husband was not yet aware of what took place, or her condition, The only person aware of her condition was herself, not even Rowena knew, but she would not be able to keep it secret for many more weeks and she feared for her life and that of the child, who could be the King's illegitimate heir if a boy.

Merlin, secretly pleased with the information but not showing it, was deep in thought as he listened and agreed that there was a problem that needed solving. He inquired how Gorlois was these days. She replied that he was bored with little to do and frustrated that she, Igraine, did not appear amenable to him. He would know that the child was not his, as they had not coupled for some while, he had been away for several months and therefore he would know that she had coupled with another. Gorlois had a fearful temper at times and doubted that he would believe that she had succumbed to another without knowing, which was why she feared for her life and Rowena's too for keeping quiet.

Merlin pondered the intricacies of the problem and what might need to be done. It was good that the King had a potential heir in the making, which was what Merlin had hoped would be the outcome of such a liaison, as he had none at present, surprising though that might seem with his reputation. An idea was beginning to germinate but he indicated that he would sleep on it and decide in the morning the plan of action. With that he suggested that they made their way back and joined the others and not to worry as he Merlin would come up with a solution.

The day passed in quiet socialising with one or two other visitors stopping by to congratulate Sir Ector on his news and the evening turned into a small celebration as a result. Merlin, although joining in with the festivities was also formulating a plan in his mind to resolve Igraine's predicament and possibly provide Uther with an heir. Which would help maintain and possibly improve the uneasy stability in the country in the longer term, and as promised he slept on it.

When Igraine appeared the next morning her husband and Merlin were deep in discussion and she left them be until she was invited to join them. Sir Ector had apparently left early to continue his arrangements. Gorlois indicated that Merlin had given him some good news and soon he would see some action at last. Uther was going to mount a campaign in the north of the country and had sent a request out for knights and men from the southern kingdoms to join with him. He Gorlois had been asked to join the King in this endeavour, but was surprised that Uther had not mentioned it himself when he was here last. Although as Merlin had said it was not decided at that time but came from recent information about marauding bands of foreign insurgents causing havoc in northern areas.

As the campaign was likely to be a prolonged one and the Duke would be away for some time Merlin had suggested that she might like a change of scenery for awhile. Igraine agreed that it would be good to have a change and that it might help her health improve as she had been feeling off colour recently, but did not know why. Merlin suggested a healing sanctuary at Lydney near Glevum that would be ideal for her health, she would be able to help the ladies who ran it, if she wished, as they were always in need of willing helpers. When she felt the desire to return home, it could be arranged without a problem. It was agreed that this would be the case and arrangements would be put in place immediately for the transportation of Igraine and whatever she might wish to take with her for a long stay. It would not be necessary for her ladies to go with her, they could stay in Tintagel and look after her son and daughter and take care of any social functions that might be required for visiting dignitaries. Gorlois would arrange with Sir Ector to look after the fort in his absence as he would wish to be close to his wife and her imminent birth and not be chasing round the country with the King's men.

That decided the Duke went to seek out some good wine to celebrate and Merlin had a few moments alone with Igraine to explain that he would now travel to see the King and convince him of the need to mount the campaign that he had just sold to Gorlois. Not that he thought that this would be difficult, as Uther had been thinking along those lines in recent months. Igraine could go to the sanctuary and stay until she had given birth as those maidens that ran it were totally trustworthy and Merlin knew them well. Nothing would be said and nothing asked, all would be discreet and in confidence and after the birth Merlin would arrange for the child to be cared for and brought up according to their standing. Igraine must be prepared to let the child go and not ask where or who with because it would be better that she did not know, it must remain a secret until at least the child was of age. Igraine realised that this must be the way, however painful being parted at birth would be, it had to be for both their sakes and she agreed with Merlin that it would be so. She thanked him for his help, wished him a safe journey and went to seek out her ladies to prepare her requirements for her journey. Gorlois returned with the wine and goblets and they toasted the King and good fortune after which Merlin excused himself that much needed to be done and he must go. He would return in ten days with transport for the Duke's wife and news on the campaign, which would give time for Gorlois to gather sufficient knights and men.

Igraine had much that she could take for a long stay away but decided to try and keep it to the bare minimum as there would be great difference in her size to take into account. She was glad to be busy knowing that she was getting bigger and it would soon be difficult to hide. Her ladies were very happy to be left behind as they would have free reign over what they did, looking forward to this unusual situation and the fun they hoped to have. Just a pity that there would not be many eligible knights left behind, but who knew what visitors that they might have. Her maid Rowena too was glad that the Duke would be away as well as she always felt embarrassed when he was around as she kept thinking back to that fateful night, what stamina the King had, not something you could easily forget. Gorlois was happy now and on the go all the time, sending out request's to knights and men to call on him soonest as he and the King had need of their services and they required the best.

Merlin set out on his travels, sending his thoughts out to Nimue to make the arrangements and despatch a horse and cart with two of the healing ladies on the slow journey to Tintagel to collect Igraine. Merlin would catch up with them before they arrived, after he had sought out Uther and persuaded him to prepare for a northern campaign.

* * * * *

Three days later Merlin arrived in Cadbury and sought a private audience with the King, and perhaps the difficult task of persuading him to raise an army and head to the northern territories, but he need not have worried as Uther was in a fighting mood. After the usual pleasantries the King asked him what news he had from around the country, knowing that Merlin always seemed to have his finger on the pulse and knew what was going on, from his numerous and sometimes mystical sources. Merlin said that the south and west of the country were fairly peaceful at the moment with very little of note happening, the east was suffering minor disturbances, but that was normal with occasional raids from across the sea, but the north was becoming a hot spot and things were getting out of hand. The Picts were pushing further south all the time and the Jutes and Saxons were mounting more frequent raids on the north east coast and increasing their incursions inland and it was time for the King to mount a campaign to purge them from his kingdom. Uther agreed indicating that similar information had been trickling in to him for some time and he was already gathering an army together to shortly move north.

This was excellent news and Merlin advised the King that Gorlois, Duke of Cornwall was in the process of gathering a force together to join with him on such a campaign. This surprised Uther as he had not yet sent word to the south west kingdoms, but Merlin explained that he had recently come from there and arranged it on the King's behalf knowing that it would be most welcome should Uther wished to proceed, and would save time. The King laughed saying that Merlin was always full of surprises and often seemed to second guess him, but he also felt that there was another reason behind this. Merlin was pleased that Uther was aware that there was more and so told him the situation with Igraine and that she had confided in him all that had taken place and wished to find a solution to the problem. Uther was thoughtful and indicated that she was a damned fine woman that he couldn't resist, it was a pity that he could not have her as his queen. Therefore the arrangements that had been made seemed the best solution in the circumstances, especially as no one else was aware of her situation. With Gorlois out of the way and Igraine at Lydney, out of sight of prying eyes, then the secret could be maintained and the child, if it was a boy, would be safe and brought up according to his station, but without knowing who he was until the appropriate time. Uther asked Merlin to give some thought as to who should bring up the boy the right way, knowing that his wise old friend probably had decided who this should be. Emphasising that no one else should be aware of any of the details, not even himself, the King, it had to remain secret to protect both Igraine and the child. The only stipulation that Uther demanded was to know, when the time came, whether he had fathered a boy and consequently an heir and periodic progress on his upbringing. Merlin agreed and the matter was concluded, detailed discussion then took place on the size of the army that was likely to be needed to secure the northern kingdoms.

Merlin departed at first light next morning and headed for Boscastle where he had arranged to meet up with the two healing women and their cart before travelling the final few miles to Tintagel. As usual his timing was good and three days later he caught up with them just before they reached their destination and within a couple of hours they were arriving at Tintagel Fort. Gorlois was out on an errand so Igraine, looking very flushed and pleased, greeted them and showed them to their quarters to freshen up, and then spoke briefly to Merlin advising him of the current situation. Preparations for her departure were complete and although she thought her ladies were beginning to speculate on her slight roundness in shape nothing had been said. The Duke, thankfully, had been too preoccupied to notice anything other than gathering the body of knights and men that he would take with him. Gorlois returned some while later and hearing that Merlin was back, sought him out to go over the final details with him before they wined and feasted. It was agreed that Merlin, the healing women and Igraine would depart northward in the morning and Gorlois would leave the day after and take his force to Uther at Cadbury.

The farewells next morning were a little tearful, with Rowena telling her ladyship to take care and have plenty of rest, which made Igraine more certain that her condition had been discreetly noted, and Gorlois sending her off with his love and he would be back when they had annihilated the troublemakers. With that the cart rumbled forward and they were off on their long slow journey to Lydney, with surprisingly little in the way of luggage for Igraine.

Chapter 2
ARTHUR MEETS THE BEARS

IGRAINE'S TIME AT LYDNEY WAS VERY RELAXING and the healing women certainly knew what they were about. The location was ideal, peace and tranquillity blended in superbly with the surroundings of the flowers, trees and mysterious lake that was close by, reputed to be the domain of the Lady of the Lake, although little was said of her. The whole place had that sense and feeling of calm and wellbeing that was ideal for healing any ailment, as well as inducing a relaxed state of body and mind in preparation for giving birth. This occurred on time and with ease and Igraine gave birth to a healthy baby boy, which delighted her immensely as she had produced an heir for Uther Pendragon, High King of Britain. Although illegitimate it was his only son at the time, however as she was going to have to give him up in a few days she did not name him, as no doubt Merlin would have ideas about that. Psychologically too it would be better for her if he had no name that she could remember him by and hopefully that would make the parting a little easier.

A few days after the arrival of the baby Merlin suddenly appeared and announced that word had reached him of the birth and he had made his way straight here, delighted that it had been a boy. He told Igraine that Uther had been made aware that he had a son an heir and he was very pleased. Igraine wanted to know how Merlin had heard of the birth as it was supposed to be a closely guarded secret known only to the healing women here at the sanctuary. Merlin told her not to worry, that nobody else was aware of her secret and hadn't she realised that this healing sanctuary was under the protection of Nimue, Lady of the Lake, as this was her domain. That she could communicate with Merlin in mystical ways over great distances, and he with her. This came as a complete surprise to Igraine, as although it often appeared that he had mystical powers she had not given much thought to what these actually were. Other than that he was known as a great visionary and on occasion appeared to travel long distances in a short period of time. She knew it was now time for her to return to Tintagel and leave the boy here, whilst Merlin arranged for him to go to a reputable family to bring him up and teach him what he would need to know. Igraine wanted to stay longer but realised that she was already becoming attached to the little lad, like a mother would, delay would make parting even more difficult so she agreed that they should start their long journey back to Tintagel the following day. Merlin told her that the fighting up north appeared to be going well and that the Duke could be returning within the next couple of months if success continued in the same way, that would give her time to re-adjust to life at the fort.

The following morning emotional goodbyes and thanks were said to the healing women and the horse and cart started its long slow journey south. Merlin was staying behind for a day or two but would catch them up later in their journey, he had some important business to attend to he said. This was to visit Nimue and discuss the long term plan for the child's upbringing and the instruction that he would need to make him fit and capable of being a good and strong King. Nimue thought that the lad should stay in the area around Glevum where she could keep an eye on him, but Merlin favoured a different scenario, one that at first seemed totally absurd but one that he felt would benefit the boy. A place where he would be out of harms way and could be given the correct upbringing with a totally reliable and trustworthy knight with much experience, even though it could be said that it was placing him in the lion's den.

After much discussion and debate it was agreed that Arthur, as they had agreed to call the boy, as this was the name that kept appearing in Merlin's visions, would stay at the sanctuary until he was 4 years old. Merlin would then arrange that Sir Ector, by some guise or other, would adopt the boy as companion for his new born son Kay, even though this would be at Padstow, a mere stone's throw from Tintagel. What better place to have him, close to his mother, even though neither would be aware of this. The last place anyone would think of looking if they discovered Uther and Igraine's secret and wished the boy harm. It was also agreed that Sir Ector would not be told of Arthur's true lineage until it became necessary. Merlin stayed for two days as there was much to discuss with Nimue concerning the state of the country and the world in general. Whether they should hold a meeting of the council of Elders soon, but after their mystical telepathic communication with the other Elders it was decided that this was not the right time, events needed to settle more before any full council meeting took place. There was just too much going on for each to leave their area of responsibility for the time necessary to convene what usually turned out to be several days of discussion and decisions, so for the present they would communicate in their usual telepathic way, unless something very major occurred.

Merlin caught up with Igraine as they were approaching Caer Baddon [Bath], where they rested for the night as guests of the bishop, carrying on the long slow journey south the next morning. Merlin passing on the news to Igraine that most of the fighting up north was over and Uther, together with Gorlois, were making their way back southward, mopping up as they went. All had apparently gone well and they had not suffered too many loses, but that they would be stopping off at many places on the way back for the usual festivities and celebrations. *I can just image what Uther will be up to,* thought Igraine, *perhaps he will end up with another son or daughter, or several knowing his sexual appetite, especially after so long on the battlefield.* Listening to Merlin, Igraine wondered where he got all his information from no matter how far away the events, or rather how he received it, as he never seemed to be wrong and it was often within a matter of hours of it happening. An extraordinary man who was always on the go and never seemed to age. She reflected that nobody made any mention of his possible age, they just accepted him for what he was and the way he just seems to pop up at the right time, with hardly a mention of where he had been or what he had been doing, and strangely nobody asked him. They looked upon him as a sage who knew all, saw and heard all, and as he was usually right no-one questioned him, they just accepted what he said. A strange man indeed, full of wisdom and knowledge with an air of authority on him, in a humble way, and with a kindly disposition, but you got the impression that he was not a man to trifle with or to try to get the better of. A rod of iron beneath that becalming exterior that would only be unleashed when absolutely necessary and then beware of the consequences. Igraine began to ponder on whether he had any family, or a wife and children, and decided that when the moment was right she would ask him and maybe at the same time find out how old he really was.

With a start she realised that Merlin had asked her if she was comfortable and she had not replied, apologising she said that she was miles away and that she was feeling alright and no necessity to stop just yet. Merlin gave her a searching look and concluded that wherever her mind had taken her it was not related to the child that she had left behind, and that was good, as the first few days after the parting would be the most difficult for her, but hopefully time would ease her loss. It was good that they would be in Tintagel in a couple of days where Igraine would then be kept busy preparing for the return of her husband. with not much time for other thoughts, with that Merlin turned his mind to other matters that required his attention.

The remainder of the journey passed quite quickly and they arrived to a warm welcome with Sir Ector there to greet them, commenting to Merlin that he was right on time as usual. Igraine was quite surprised but Merlin informed her that he had passed this way a month previous and indicated the day that they should arrive here. *How does Merlin seem to know these things in advance* thought Igraine, *she had not even given birth then, he is definitely a mysterious man with hidden depths, I must engage him in conversation about these matters as soon as is convenient.* The women departed to their quarters to freshen up and Ector and Merlin brought each other up to date on events, although Sir Ector had very little to tell other than a skirmish that they had recently with a small mixed raiding party. Unusually this came as a surprise to Merlin, who seemed to know most things going on. Sir Ector explained that they had come across them whilst out hunting and took sword to them and chased them a good ten miles eastward and not many escaped. A strange bunch of Jutes, Saxons and some of their own kind, not very well dressed but all on horse and obviously up to no good, but they were reluctant to engage with them even though his party was not large, and they took flight. *This is a new development,* thought Merlin, *and was a little worrying as they had been roving so far west, it will need looking into most definitely.* Turning the topic to Sir Ector's family he asked how his wife and young son were and was informed that both were doing well, and the lad was growing fast. They wandered back into the great hall and as the ladies had now returned they partook of some much needed refreshment. Merlin indicated that he would be off the following morning as he had much business to catch up on and he needed to find out more about any mixed raiding parties around this area of the country and because of this he asked Sir Ector if he would provide a small escort for the healing women for their return journey as far as Caer Baddon [Bath] where he would arrange another escort from there to Lydney. Sir Ector readily agreed knowing that his little skirmish had worried Merlin for some reason, more than it seemed to merit.

Merlin had a disturbed night with a recurrence of the dream that he had been having lately. Britain had no High King, Uther was dead and the country was beginning to fall apart with king clashing with king over stupid quarrels, each vying for position and trying to form a greater power base. The country was in chaos and the Saxons, Jutes and Angles were taking every advantage of the situation to extend their influence, by force if necessary. The whole pillar of society that had done so well under the Romans and been mostly held together by the High Kings of Britain after their departure was rapidly crumbling and anarchy was setting in. Amongst the carnage that was happening a few voices were beginning to shout a name and as more took up the chant the noise increased to a crescendo and the name of Arthur was being shouted by thousands of voices in his head. Then the vision appeared and there, to a tremendous cheer stood Arthur, sword raised on high and gleaming in the sunlight. Merlin woke with a start with the sun streaming down on to his face. *We do not have enough time, Arthur has only just been born, we must try and keep things together until it is time but alas I fear that we will not be totally successful, but we must do our best and prepare the little lad as much as possible as I foresee that he will be very young when he becomes High King. He must be strong and fair but ruthless when necessary to bind the country together; otherwise all that we have worked for will be lost. There was much to be done in the meantime,* thought Merlin as he made ready for his departure and sought out Sir Ector and Igraine.

Taking his leave of them he indicated that he had received word that Gorlois would return before the month was out as he was travelling ahead of the King's main army, not wishing to loiter on his return home. Sir Ector excused himself, as he had much to do, and wished Merlin a safe and successful journey leaving Igraine alone with him. Merlin aware that her ladyship had something on her mind asked her if all was well, as she appeared very thoughtful and somewhat distant. Igraine explained that she was puzzled as to how he always knew what was going on and wondered how and where he received all his information from as no messengers were ever seen. Merlin denied knowing everything but said that he had an ability, inherited from his ancestors, that enabled him to see distant places in his mind and converse that way with others of his kind and therefore know of what was happening in many places, without having to be there himself. This might seem very useful but it placed a great burden on those with the gift, as it empowered them with a great responsibility, the information must be used wisely for the greater good of this country and not for personal gain. Igraine thanked him for that honest answer saying that it would put her mind at rest and showed her that he was a very wise and knowledgeable man, far in excess of his apparent years. Merlin laughed saying that was a very polite way of asking his age, but of that he was not sure himself, it was so long ago when he came here, but sometimes it seemed like only yesterday and he still had much to accomplish. Feeling bold now Igraine asked if he had any family, a wife or children. At this Merlin became very sad and quiet as memory took him back to happier times and then the pain appeared on his face with the vision of the butchering that happened to his village and the discovery of the violated remains of his wife and son on his return. The most terrible thing that had happened to him during his time here and it still came back to haunt him once in awhile. Igraine saw the pain in his face and putting her hand on his arm she apologised profusely for bringing back what were obviously unpleasant memories. The moment passed and Merlin regained his composure and smiled at her saying that it was a long time ago, but you never forgot the good or bad memories of life. It was time to take his leave of her now and as he turned to mount his horse she kissed him on his cheek, thanking him for all that he had done and asking that he take good care of her son. *Of course he would, as her son was the future High King of Britain and the country would need him*, with that thought Merlin waved goodbye and set off on his travels.

* * * * *

Young Arthur was doing well, Gwendolyn a young maiden from the village who had recently lost her baby at birth was enlisted to suckle him and give him motherly attention and love. This was beneficial to both, easing the psychological trauma for the woman as it was her first baby and out of wedlock as well as motherly love, stability and a focal point of bonding for Arthur. The healing women at the sanctuary were very good teachers, even with ones so young, as it came naturally to them and was not based on any religious doctrine but on a total understanding of the healing power of nature and its underlying principles that many people had long forgotten. In those first few years Arthur was taught to watch and listen to the birds and animals as they could tell him much by their behaviour and how they inter-reacted with each other. How to tell when everything was peaceful and also the warning signs and sounds when danger was around. Not to show fear towards animals because they would sense it and be on their guard and possibly attack if they felt threatened. The changing colours and types of flowers and trees that were in bloom at different times of the year and how to tell when the weather was changing by all the sounds and colours that were around. By just sitting quietly, listening and observing what was going on around him he would learn and know quite often what was likely to happen next, and he was encouraged to say what he saw and felt. Arthur was very forward for his years and he learnt very quickly and was talking before he was three, asking questions like - why do all animals, people and trees have a mist around them that is often different in colour and size to another. The healing women realised that Arthur was one of those rare people that could see the aura around living things and explained to him that he was seeing the energy of that creature or tree and each one was of a different size and often colour, depending how they were feeling at the time, that the colours changed according to their mood, happy or sad. He wanted to know if everybody could see this mist and was told no, only some people could because they understood nature much more, and before he could ask, yes they could see the same as him. He asked if every living thing had this mist and was told yes, unless they were very ill or just before they died as this mist faded and disappeared. For one so young his questions were quite deep and yet he seemed to understand the answers.

Merlin had called in briefly, on several occasions and was pleased with Arthur's progress and realised it would soon be time to speak to Sir Ector to arrange for the rest of his education. On these visits Arthur would sit and talk to Merlin and ask him questions about what he did and where he had been and what were the people like that he met. Merlin was a little taken aback initially by these direct questions from one so young but realised that there was more to this boy than met the eye and that his curiosity was a very good thing with what lay ahead for him. Merlin told him about different places that he had visited and what the people were like and how they treated each other, as well as strangers, and that there were many people from other lands here, some good and some not very nice. The more that he learnt now at a young age, with the right teaching, the better a High King he would turn out to be, although Arthur was not aware of his probable future and it was necessary that it stayed that way until the time.

As usual whilst he was there Merlin sought out Nimue and they discussed the timing of the lad's move, assuming that there would not be a problem as nothing had been mentioned as yet to Sir Ector, which Merlin would put right in the near future as he would be heading back down that way shortly. To maintain the secrecy of Arthur's parenthood and Merlin's association with him and Igraine it was decided to ask Taliesin, Elder of the South, to deliver Arthur to Sir Ector, as they were good friends. After further discussion they decided that Gwendolyn should accompany them, if she were willing, as a bond had developed between her and young Arthur and he had never questioned if she was his real mother or even asked who his father was. Merlin did not foresee a problem with Sir Ector as he was sure that Gwendolyn could be gainfully employed, as well as providing the motherly love and stability for Arthur, as she had proved very able at doing so far, besides they were both certain that she would want to go. Merlin would explain to Sir Ector as much as was necessary to enlist his help in this matter, without divulging Arthur's true lineage. Telepathic communication was made with Taliesin, who being aware of the situation readily agreed to his part in the proceedings, and a date was arranged for him to collect them from Lydney. A cart would be made available for them that could be left with Sir Ector.

Turning to other matters there did not seem to be any problems around Tintagel and Gorlois had been busy since his return, as Igraine had given birth to a another daughter. She had inquired discreetly as to the welfare of her son when Merlin visited and he assured her that all was fine and he had also kept Uther up to date on the lad's progress as well when passing through Cadbury. Nimue and Merlin were both concerned with the state of unrest that they could detect around the country and expected it to continue to increase as Uther did not seem to have such a strong following as he once had, the rumblings of discontent were growing. There was a general air of tension between him and some of the kings and between some of the kings themselves, which indicated that some were jostling for position. There were various power plays taking place behind the scenes that could soon spill over into open conflict. All Merlin, Nimue and the other Elders could do was watch and wait and use their influence whenever and wherever possible and hope that the simmering fuse would not suddenly flare up and ignite a powder keg of anarchy. Allowing the Saxons and their allies a greater hold in Britain, which at the moment was fairly well contained. Merlin left Nimue a disturbed man as his instincts told him that there was much trouble ahead and there was little he could do to slow it down, but try he must, for the benefit of the country.

* * * * *

Arthur carried on with his learning, always inquisitive and always asking, what were for a young lad very searching questions about many things, including how the plants around him helped to heal sickness and wounds and did the sounds of nature help too. All his questions were answered and he would point out plants when he saw them and say how they helped to heal, such was his quick grasp of what he was taught.

Then one day a nightmare situation happened, for the healing women especially, but young Arthur took it in his stride, either through not understanding his danger or perhaps an inner knowledge that there was nothing to be afraid of, thereby giving an indication of what sort of man he would turn out to be. The three women, Gwendolyn and Arthur were in a small clearing amongst the trees just a short distance from the sanctuary when it happened. Suddenly and silently out of the trees came a fully grown black bear not ten feet from Arthur. Gwendolyn saw him at the same time as the lad did and keeping her voice calm told him to stand perfectly still, which he was, as he was transfixed for a moment never having seen such a large and majestic creature as this before. The bear and Arthur stood looking at each other just as if they were checking each other out, which in fact they were, then the lad smiled and held out his hand towards the bear but still keeping quite still so as not to spook him. There was a gasp from the women as the bear seemed to have decided that there was no danger and slowly moved towards Arthur.

Time seemed to almost stand still as the scene appeared to unfold in slow motion. The women had no option now other than to keep still and quiet and watch, but ever ready to dash to Arthur's aid should he need it. The bear slowly drew closer until they were almost nose to nose and the lad slowly moved his hand to stroke him at the same time talking to him in a low voice saying what a lovely creature he was and that there was nothing to fear (he had never seen a bear before). The bear nuzzled him gently and then turning his face back towards the trees made a slight whining noise, whereupon a young bear came limping out of the trees towards its parent, whimpering as he was obviously in pain and suffering with one of his rear feet as he tried not to put it on the ground. Arthur extended his hand gently towards the young one talking to him as well and the bear nuzzled him just as its parent had done. Then to the astonishment of the women Arthur knelt beside the young one, and then lay down patting the ground beside him for the bear to do the same. The young bear looked at its parent as if to say what do I do now and got a nudge indicating that it should do the same. Arthur could then see that there was a large thorn wedged between its claws that it couldn't get at. Talking to him all the time he gently stroked the front of the paw and with the other hand he was delving beneath the surface leaves on the ground for the damp earth and moist leaves underneath. Still talking gently to the bear he put this compost around where the problem was and then grasping the thorn gently he gave it a quick tug and at the same time with the other hand pressed the compost around the wound to take the pain away. The bear gave a slight roar, shot to his feet and ran off back into the trees. Time for the watchers now returned to its normal speed.

Now was the moment of truth as Arthur was lying on the ground and the adult bear was looming over him. Just as the women were going to yell to frighten off the bear he licked Arthur's face and plodded off after his offspring, turning at the trees to give a short roar before he disappeared from sight. A sigh of relief went up all around which turned to nervous laughter as Arthur rejoined them saying what a beautiful creature he was. But what was it? It was explained to him that he had just seen a bear and normally they were dangerous animals and should not be approached as they could easily kill a person. But perhaps even the animals knew that this was a healing sanctuary and that there was safety and help here, even for them, on the occasions when they could not help themselves. Nobody had ever seen or heard of a bear in that area before so maybe they had travelled some distance to seek help, as animals had a far better instinct and understanding of nature and knowing when they were safe, or those situations to beware of that would bring them into danger. The women praised Arthur and told him that to tune his senses in like the animals did would help him know who were the good people that he met during his life or the ones that would seek to do him harm. It was a good lesson to learn and he had done well but always to be wary and trust his instincts. Arthur was very pleased and talked about the bears for some while after, hoping to see them return, but they had no need to as the treatment was successful, and they were not seen or heard of in that area again. Strange sometimes were the ways of nature to us so-called intelligent beings.

* * * * *

Merlin meanwhile was going about his business and travelling widely throughout the country discovering for himself what he had sensed and already knew about the change coming and violence erupting periodically, albeit over trivial matters. *This is how it always started,* he thought, *before it escalated and eventually got out of hand, unless stamped on at the outset, it was apparent that Uther Pendragon's influence was on the wane, in some places already lost and with it the backing he needed to maintain a semblance of law and order throughout the country. The Saxons were taking advantage of the situation and their area of influence was gradually spreading but so far without violent confrontation. It's surprising how short people's memories are at times, they have already forgotten the problems caused by Vortigen enlisting Saxon aid only to have them turn against him when it suited their agenda. Greed and power were always the downfall of even the strongest man and there were many at the moment who were that short sighted that they could not see beyond the end of their nose. Always pushing for more land, more power, more influence, only to see it disappear before their eyes, to be left wondering why, that is if they were still alive. The country needed a strong leader, a farsighted leader of the people and for the people, who would be respected by all for his fairness, courage and love of his country and not himself. Alas there was no one of that calibre available at present and only time would tell if Arthur could eventually bring peace from chaos, provided he could be instructed in the right ways and even survive until the time was right. All big 'ifs,' but that was all there was.*

Chapter 3
ARTHUR – THE DEVELOPING CHARACTER

MERLIN SPENT SEVERAL MONTHS travelling around the country getting first hand knowledge of the underlying ripple of tension that was spreading across the land. He was not a happy man, and he had much time for thought on his journey. Uther was losing control, slowly but definitely, although there were still many areas where he was still highly regarded his influence and support were under threat. Complacency and apathy were setting in once again, not yet in epidemic proportions, but spreading like any common disease, born on the wind. The wind of change, but this one was not for the better, the dark clouds were beginning to form and were spreading, mainly in the east and north but now gathering pace in the south east too. It would not be very long before most of the country was experiencing the underlying current of unrest, with anarchy raising its ugly head again. *Why do people never seem to learn,* thought Merlin, *what is it in human nature that makes people repeat the same disasters, is their memory that bad or are they that naïve that they don't think it will happen again? Is it impossible for them to live in peace with their neighbours and share in the abundance that this brings or do they want everything for themselves, whatever the consequences, even if they do not live to enjoy the proceeds? The peoples of this world have much to learn and it will take them a very long time to realise the benefits of living in harmony with each other, as opposed to disharmony, much longer than my own people took to learn this lesson. Sometimes I wonder why I agreed to keep on coming here to help move these people forward, when all they appear to want is to undo any of the good things in place and go backwards before they move forwards. Maybe it's just that, they need our help to keep pushing them forward so that one day they will make it, in which case it makes it all worth while. Thankfully our influence is still widespread throughout this world of theirs and many of us still come to help move them forward, albeit slowly.*

Merlin came out of his thoughts with the realisation that he was approaching the healing sanctuary at Lydney, exactly on time as usual. This was something that people often speculated and wondered about, how he always arrived when he said he would. But it was best that they never knew how his people could travel if they wished. It was way in advance of their time and others would undoubtedly want the knowledge for their own ends.

Merlin sought out Nimue to bring her up to date on what he had seen and heard on his travels, although he had already conversed with her telepathically, the same as he had with Taliesin. He had recently visited and spoken to Sir Ector concerning Arthur, who was a little wary of the request at first. Until Merlin explained that he was the son of a very respected knight, who unfortunately was not in a position to care for the boy, but would greatly appreciate him being fostered by an equally respected and erstwhile knight. He would like him brought up in the correct tradition of the chivalry of knighthood as he believed the boy would have great talent when he was of age. If it was possible to accommodate the woman that the boy regarded as his mother that would be greatly appreciated too. Merlin explained that Arthur was almost the same age as Sir Ector's son Kay and that they would be good company for each other as they grew up. At this point Sir Ector agreed to have Arthur as he could see the merits of the situation for his own son as well, and so details were arranged, with Merlin saying that Taliesin would be the one who would bring them to Sir Ector and the date on which they would arrive.

The following day Taliesin arrived at the sanctuary as expected and was introduced to Arthur and Gwendolyn. Arthur took to him immediately and began asking him questions about where they were going, how long would it take to get there, and would they see any bears. Taliesin answered all his questions for the next two hours. Merlin had explained to Gwendolyn what was happening and that it was now time to further Arthur's education and asked if she was happy to go with him.

"Try and leave me behind," she had retorted with a smile.

"Good," replied Merlin, "that's settled then. Sir Ector is expecting you and as far as anyone is concerned you are Arthur's mother and his father was a respected knight whose name you cannot mention as the matter is of a delicate nature. I know that exposes your character to something that you are not, but it is necessary for the boy's sake, besides you do not know his name anyway. Can you do that?"

"Yes to protect Arthur from whatever it is that he needs protecting from, I will do it," she replied.

"Thank you," said Merlin. "Sir Ector will teach Arthur the same as he will be teaching his own son Kay, who is of a similar age, and he will have full responsibility for him. You will continue to have involvement as his mother until such times as he will need to be told the truth, which is a long way off yet."

"Thank you Merlin for letting me go with him as I have become very attached to him and he with me, I think it will benefit both of us and continue the stability in our lives. The healing sisters here helped me when I was in the throes of despair and gave me something to live for in looking after young Arthur and I will be there as long as he needs me. When he eventually grows from me and leads his own life, wherever that takes him, then I shall return here and help other poor souls in need. I have learnt much here of the greater aspects of life and know that I can be of service in helping others leave their hurts behind and move forward to a better life. I am sure that when Arthur needs to know the truth everything will be fine."

With that Merlin expressed his thanks again and took his leave of Gwendolyn and went to rescue Taliesin from Arthur, who was still asking questions.

The next day dawned with a beautiful sunrise and perfect stillness in the air and Arthur was there watching the splendour unfolding, listening to the birds and animals heralding in the new day. The start of a new adventure, as he put it when noticing Taliesin watching him. *This boy has certainly got something about him that is different from the rest,* thought Taliesin. The women came out to say goodbye and Arthur thanked each of them for all they had taught him and said he would come and visit them when he was older and maybe he would see the bears again, which made them all laugh. The cart with Gwendolyn, Taliesin and Arthur slowly rumbled out of the sanctuary gates and started on their long journey south to a new adventure and a new life.

* * * * *

Time passed quickly and Arthur and Gwendolyn were soon settled in with Sir Ector, who was very pleased that his son Kay and Arthur had struck up a friendship straight away and were becoming inseparable. Taliesin had taken them on a long detour, at Merlin's request, to see many places along the way, so that Arthur would have much to talk about, other than the sanctuary at Lydney, which would become a more distant memory, and not be the topic of conversation. This was to protect Arthur in the long run from being identified as Igraine's son if something should be said out of turn and come to her ears and lead her to suspect who he was, not that he knew the name of the sanctuary or even where it was. That was one question that surprisingly he had not asked, but Merlin thought it best not to tempt fate. It was for the same reason that Merlin had arranged to have Taliesin take them to Sir Ector and not himself, as the association would be too obvious, and they had approached from the south and not the north, as an added measure.

Many people knew Taliesin like they did Merlin but very few were aware that they knew each other well or were associated in any way. That was the way they preferred it as this often worked to their advantage, even in the same location they would not always acknowledge each other but converse telepathically and exchange information, which otherwise might not be forthcoming to either one of them. Not many people were aware of this ability that they shared or that others of their kind could do so also, but it was common practice for those of the Elder race to converse in this manner, even over great distances. Both Merlin and Taliesin belonged to the Council of Elders of Britain, a small group trying to bring peace and stability to this country by using their influence in the areas that they looked after. Most people who knew or had heard of them were aware that they appeared to have mystical gifts but none questioned what they were, in case they were turned into something nasty, such was people's superstition at the time. Anyone who appeared to have an ability that was different was classed as mystical, only because people generally didn't understand it, and was someone that it was thought wise not to upset. This generally worked to the advantage to those of the Elder race like Merlin and Taliesin, but not always and sometimes they had to resort to using another of their abilities, that of reading people's thoughts, to get to the truth.

Although the Elders had a mission to bring peace and stability to the areas that they worked in, and they were spread throughout the world, they were not allowed to use their complete powers, which were considerable, otherwise the people would never learn. If they waved the metaphorical magic wand and solved all their problems then the lesson would never be learnt, only delayed, and would end up a much harder lesson next time, almost insurmountable. Slowly did it, but the human species really made it heavy going, such was their character and make up that it would take many centuries before peace and stability became the normal way of life. In the meantime many lessons would have to be learnt and unfortunately learnt again before it would finally sink in and those sent to help this world, like the Elders, could sit back and relax with a job well done. All that could be done was to work with exceptional individuals like Arthur who would help in this long period of transformation, and there would be many like him throughout the world over this period. So that one day in the distant future an enduring peace would prevail and the character of the human race would forever be changed for the better.

* * * * *

Arthur continued to grow and develop alongside Kay, and their friendship blossomed to the point that they were always together. Sir Ector was extremely pleased with their progress in learning the ways of knighthood and chivalry, with both showing exceptional skill and agility with the wooden swords specially made for them, as they were taught to fight on foot. The first foray in being instructed to fight from the back of ponies was a complete disaster as both spent most of the time falling off, such was their exuberance and lack of co-ordination in controlling their pony and engaging with their opponent. Several times swords were broken amidst peels of laughter as one tumbled to the ground, but eventually both got the hang of it and became adept mounted swordsmen and very well matched with each other. Sir Ector would on occasions take them both to tournaments to watch the knights joust and he used those events to test their knowledge of what was going on, explaining that soon they would be able to be a squire to a knight at these events, so they needed to watch carefully.

As Arthur and Kay grew older and stronger and their skills had developed well the wooden swords were replaced with the real thing. Even the blunt practice swords were lethal in untrained hands and of course they were heavier, although two smaller ones had been made for them. Several months practice with these, with only minor accidents, and they were ready to display their talents at one of the tournaments near Tintagel, arranged by Gorlois, Duke of Cornwall. This was an annual three day event with knights from far and wide coming to test their skills and Arthur and Kay were going to give a demonstration in the squires section in the use of the sword, both on foot and mounted, to which although feeling a little nervous they were both looking forward to.

Preparations were made and both had new outfits for the occasion, which certainly increased their feeling of pride, and final instructions were given on how to conduct themselves, with a reminder about the code of chivalry expected of a knight. Although still far too young to be one they were expected to conduct themselves in the same manner, as a reflection of Sir Ector's good training and their understanding of what was expected of them.

The day arrived and they rode the relatively short distance to the venue set in a large meadow close to the fort at Tintagel. Many colourful tents had been erected and already crowds had gathered to gain the best vantage points and fires were going in various places and the smell of cooking wafted on the slight summer breeze. The tournament did not start until midday. In the meantime Sir Ector sought out those that he knew and introduced Arthur and Kay to them, to the boys this seemed to go on for ever, although it was only a couple of hours. By which time the tournament was beginning, with the jesters and jugglers entertaining the crowd as a warm up to the main events. These started with the tests of strength, arm wrestling and tossing the boulder, and to the boys some of these men looked formidable giants with their massive physique, although it was a small wiry man that won the arm wrestling. Following which it was the turn of the young squires to show their various skills, Arthur and Kay watched intently as the younger ones showed their abilities first, then all to soon it was time for them to go into the arena. Dressed in their leather jerkins, leather and iron helms they approached the centre of the arena and acknowledged their hosts with drawn swords, faced each other and similarly raised swords in salute and engaged in combat. First one then the other was on the attack, backwards and forwards they went until Kay put his foot in a hole and went down, Arthur stopped and helped him up, then continued until with an almighty clash Arthur's sword went spinning out of his hand and Kay waited until he had retrieved it. Equally matched the pair showed all the moves that they had been taught, with the crowd shouting encouragement for one or the other, but neither could get the upper hand, even when they began to tire.

Eventually Gorlois called them to halt, thanking them for a marvellous display, but they needed to let others show their skills too, it was obvious that they were so well matched that it had to be a draw. Both were relieved at this as they were certainly feeling weary, but neither would give up as they were on show, in training it didn't matter, but here it was different. They saluted each other with their swords, then their host and left the arena arm in arm to a tremendous round of cheering from the crowd. Others followed into the arena to show their skills but none got the crowd going in the same way that Arthur and Kay had. Sir Ector met them on their return and congratulated them on a rousing and skilful display and commended them for an excellent performance that the crowd appreciated. Many of the knights that had been watching came up to them, introduced themselves and extended their appreciation too, some with the comment that they hoped the mounted display the following day would be just as good. As a reward Sir Ector sent them off to enjoy themselves until the evening feast started. They didn't need telling twice and they were gone in a flash, losing themselves in the crowd.

The next day both the boys were up later than usual feeling quite stiff from the exertion of the previous day. Arthur suggested to Kay that they run to the beach and lay in the surf below Tintagel fort, which they did. The cool water soon eased their young muscles and by the time they had run back both were feeling much refreshed and ready for that day's events.

As their previous day's display had been so good they were given the prime spot of appearing last in the tournament for the younger trainee squires, which meant that they missed most of the earlier action as Sir Ector was giving them last minute instructions, making sure that all was in order. Soon it was their turn and away they went into the arena, paying their respects to their hosts and each other as previously, before showing their skills in mounted combat. All was going well as they demonstrated their turns and twists, trying to get the better of each other, but as before they were equally matched and neither could fault the other. Suddenly in one encounter Kay's pony reared up throwing him heavily to the ground, concussed at least. In a flash Arthur was off his pony sword in the air, and landing on his feet close to Kay he brought the sword flashing down towards Kay's head. The cheering and applause that had been going on turned to gasps of horror from the crowd, this wasn't supposed to happen, it was only a demonstration. The sword bit into the earth, apparently just missing it's target and a huge sigh of relief spontaneously echoed from the crowd. Arthur was kneeling beside Kay, apparently looking for something on his body. Sir Ector rushed out into the arena to check on his son, who was struggling to sit up. Just as he got there Arthur held up what looked like a long stick and gave it to Sir Ector, it was in fact a headless snake. Arthur had seen it just as Kay's pony had reared up, too late to shout a warning. He had fallen right by the side of it and it looked on the point of striking him as Arthur had shot off his pony and despatched it without a moments hesitation, knowing instinctively that he would be accurate with his sword. Sir Ector helped his son, who was still dazed, out of the arena still carrying the dead snake as Arthur gathered the ponies and followed, after acknowledging their hosts with his sword. The crowd realising what had happened on seeing the snake held up cheered them both as they left.

Sir Ector thanked Arthur for his quick thinking and action in saving his son from getting bitten by the snake, which made him feel a little embarrassed, he said it was something that he would do for anyone in the same situation. That was beside the point, as some people would panic and others would do nothing, whereas he had acted immediately without regard for his own safety, indicated Sir Ector. Kay was made to rest for the remainder of the day and Arthur, making sure that he was alright, wandered off still wearing his outfit with his small sword dangling by his side, to see what was going on in the rest of the tented area.

There were fire eaters, jesters and jugglers, whilst others were selling their wares just like on market days. The bright colours glowing in the rays of the sun and the cheerful banter of the people carried on the warm gentle breeze brought a marvellous serenity to the area as everyone relaxed and enjoyed themselves. Several waved or spoke to him as he passed, complimenting him on his performance in the arena, as he drifted leisurely around the tents drinking in the relaxing atmosphere. Full of activity and laughter, the richness of life at its best. *Yet tomorrow could be totally different,* he thought as he drifted away from the crowd, moving passed deserted tents, heading for the open space beyond, *how strange people are, one minute enjoying themselves together, next killing each other, it doesn't make sense to my young mind. What a lot I still have to learn about people and life in general.* He was jolted from his thoughts by the sound of a raised voice, a man's voice, full of anger and hate, then the quieter sobbing and pleading of a lady's voice. Moving quietly closer to where the voices were coming from Arthur saw that it was the Duke and his wife.

"Don't try and deny it you snivelling wretch, I have just come from your maid whose been bragging to her young man about the escapade with the King and your involvement. Not that she wanted to tell me, not until I started to cut her throat that is, then she confessed all, and I mean all."

"What have you done to her, is she still alive?" Igraine sobbed.

"At the moment," and with that Gorlois pushed her to the ground. "now I want the truth from you, all of it, especially your part in it, or do I have to cut your throat too before I get an answer," and to show Igraine that he meant what he said he drew an ornate knife from it's sheath and advanced towards her.

Arthur was horrified at what he saw and visualised the Duke carrying out his threat on his wife. He couldn't just stand there and watch it happen. He had to try and stop it, he didn't even think to run away or get help, he just opened his mouth to speak, but only a faint squeak came out, so he swallowed hard and tried again. Igraine was cowered on the ground with Gorlois bending over her.

"My Lord," the strength of his voice surprised Arthur, "that is not the way a Lord and Knight should treat a Lady, violence will not solve the problem, only cause regret after," where these words came from Arthur had no idea, they just popped into his head. "Problems are often caused by external influences and do not solely relate to one person."

Gorlois, in the act of exposing Igraine's throat to the knife blade, stopped in total surprise and slowly stood up, passing a hand across his brow and shaking his head as if coming out of a dream. He turned to the source of the voice that had penetrated through his blind fury and was astounded to find such a young lad confronting. Recognition slowly dawned on him as to who it was before him and his stance was unmistakable, that of someone prepared for trouble.

"Ah, it is young Arthur," remarked Gorlois. "You are out of your depth here boy, this is no tournament, I've a good mind to take my sword to you my lad and teach you a lesson for interfering in business that does not concern you."

Without thinking Arthur replied, "and I would take my sword to you my Lord to protect the Lady's honour and life, even though I would forfeit my own."

Gorlois burst into a fit of caustic laughter, "her honour, she has lost that my lad, you would die for nothing."

Arthur was ready for the Duke to make his move but he just stood there for a moment looking intensely at him as if making a decision, then turned and walked away.

Igraine cried out, "where are you going husband?"

"To confront the King," was the reply, "then I shall be back to deal with you and your maid," and Gorlois disappeared from sight.

Arthur breathed a tremendous sigh of relief, he wasn't ready to die yet, but couldn't stand by and do nothing, it was not in his nature. He went over to Igraine and helped her up and into a tent, asking if she was alright and did she need anything. She was obviously very shaken by her experience, but said that she was okay and thanked him profusely for being her gallant knight, even at such a young age, but would be obliged if he did not mention the incident to anyone else, as it was a delicate matter. Arthur confirmed that it would remain their secret, as the code of chivalry dictated that a knight should never compromise a lady. Igraine smiled at this and told him that she felt that he would grow up to be a great knight, but now she must go and see if her maid Rowena was alright, after what her husband had said. Arthur took his leave of her and wandered off back towards the noise and frivolity of the main arena, still in a daze over what had happened and the part that he had played. But what surprised him most was that he had not been afraid for one single moment during the whole episode.

Kay was still out of action the next day as Sir Ector insisted that he should rest and so missed the last day of the tournament. Arthur meanwhile decided that a little exploring of the area was warranted before the main events started that day, as he meandered quietly through the meadows on the opposite side from the fort, listening to all the different bird songs and trying to identify them and locate the birds. The different shades of colour were amazing if you looked closely, the lush green of the tall grass, the darker green of the gorse bushes and the many different shades of the leaves on the trees and bushes. Amongst all these greens were sudden islands of reds, yellows and blues of the wild flowers and thistles, a sea of moving colour in the gentle breeze coming off the ocean. Arthur paused often to take it all in as there was so much to see, then climbing up to the top of a rocky mound to survey the scenery all around him he rested for a while, laying down and watching the birds circling high up in the sky, circling, diving and weaving and then climbing again.

Several hours later Arthur awoke with a start, noticing that the sun was beginning to sink slowly towards the horizon, *better be getting back soon,* he thought, *otherwise I will miss the feasting.* Climbing down from the rock he noticed how the colours had changed around it from when he had first arrived, how they seemed stronger and more vibrant. *There is a lot of energy here but you can't see it so well in the bright sunlight. but now that is fading its more obvious,* the thought intrigued him so he moved closer to the rock face and it appeared stronger still. Casting his eyes along the rock he noticed one area that appeared to be a lot different and here the energy seemed to be weaker for some reason. On closer examination it was apparent that there was a recess here. He stared fixedly at it for some while, then ran his hands around the outside of the rock crevice and felt it soft and pliable to his touch. Pushing his hand in further it all felt the same, then his shoulder was in the gap and next minute his whole body was through and he was standing in a dimly lit cave. Where the dim light came from he was not sure but it was just sufficient to see that it was a fairly roomy cave but he could not make out much else. Turning round to look at where he had come in he could not see any chink of light from outside, so decided it was unwise to move from where he was to explore the interior. *What a strange place,* he thought, *I wonder how long it has been here and what it was used for as there was no obvious way in and how he had entered it he wasn't sure, it just happened.* Putting his hand out to touch the rock it seemed solid with no way out and panic started to set in, what if he couldn't get out, he would die a slow horrible death from starvation. Pulling himself together he decided that if he got in then he could get out and he started to think about what he did before he entered. Stare at it and concentrate for awhile noticing any colours or lack of them, so that is exactly what he did, then stretching out his hand as before rubbing it across the rock he felt it become soft and pliable, gradually pushing his hand forward, then his shoulder and next minute he was outside with a great sigh of relief. *Wow whatever happened there, I don't think I want to do that again in a hurry,* he thought, and noticing the sun had sunk a little more started his trek back to the tournament area, puzzling over what had happened but sensing that this was something he had better keep secret, even from Kay.

* * * * *

Ten days later a sombre looking Merlin arrived unexpectedly at the fort. Igraine had heard nothing from her husband since he went to confront Uther about her indiscretion. Welcoming him she took him down to the cove where conversation would be private as on the previous occasion. As they reached the shore she turned to him indicating that she knew that he had come with ill tidings, as no word had reached her from her husband, and by the look on Merlin's face it was obvious that it wouldn't. For once Merlin admitted he was at a loss as to what to say, but what she feared was true, her husband was dead, killed not by Uther, but his guards. Gorlois had arrived at Cadbury in a vile temper and demanded to see Uther, who was otherwise engaged at the time. The guards refused to let him in to see the King until he had relinquished his sword. He refused and attacked the guards, killing one of them, whereupon the others had no choice, as he refused to yield and surrender his weapon. Uther was furious and greatly upset that this should have happened and sends his sincere apologies and as a mark of respect for her loss bequeathed the fort to her for as long as she wished to reside in it. Igraine admitted that she had half expected it since he left in such a murderous mood that day. How ironic life was as she was the one who nearly died and no doubt would have but for the intervention of her young gallant knight. Yet he was not a knight but a very young brave boy who faced her husband down at the crucial moment and stood his ground, willing to die to try and save her, and save her he did without harm befalling himself. Whereupon she told Merlin the whole story and how the young lad had intervened just in time.

This took Merlin by surprise and even more so when asking the lad's name and learning it was Arthur. *Yes,* thought Merlin, *life is ironic, the lad saves his natural mother by his valour but neither is aware of the relationship that binds them together, Arthur is full of surprises that even I did not foresee, I just hope he manages to keep out of trouble and stay alive.* Igraine said she swore him to secrecy concerning the whole episode and smiled when he replied that it was covered by the code of chivalry expected of a knight and that it would be so. There was a good knight in the making there she felt, to which Merlin wholeheartedly agreed and managed a smile, as it was some time since he had heard any good news. *There is hope yet,* he thought, *time is still very much against us, but we cannot give in, good will still prevail in the long run, we must do what we can in the meantime.* Merlin agreed to stay over for the night, saying that the events leading up to her husband's death should be kept secret for all concerned, that her maid's rumour should always be denied as a silly drunken girl causing mischief with her man. He indicated that he would need to see Sir Ector the next day to make him aware of the situation of the Duke's death, without telling him the reasons behind it.

Merlin did not stay long with Sir Ector as he said he had much business to attend to, but felt that he should advise him of recent events concerning the Duke and that he had seen Igraine on Uther's behalf. That she had taken it reasonably well as she knew her husband's temper often got the better of him, but that no one knew what had got into Gorlois that day. He inquired after Ector's wife and asked how the boys were getting on, at which point Sir Ector conveyed to him how well they had done at the tournament and Arthur's quick thinking with the snake. Their progress was remarkable they seemed to bring the best out of each other, such that they were equally matched in whatever they did and were virtually inseparable. It was certainly the hand of providence when he agreed to take on Arthur, even though he had reservations at the time. Their insight, instincts and knowledge seemed way above their years, that he sometimes forgot they were still only children and he admitted that even he, at his age, had learnt from them. They continued to discuss the boys' merits for some while and the instruction that they still needed to become fully fledged squires to a knight. The more Merlin heard about Arthur's exploits the more he looked forward with a renewed sense of hope for the future of the country. *Slowly but surely,* he thought, *that is the only way we can do it, frustrating but necessary. Ensure that the foundations are strong and the benefits will last, to rush would be disaster.*

* * * * *

Time moved slowly on, the fresh crisp colours of spring giving way to the strong vibrant colours of the hot summer that then slowly faded into the chill of autumn, as the cold north wind of winter began to encroach on to the land. This was the time of year that Arthur and Kay liked least as the shorter hours of daylight and bad weather restricted their activities. It was the time of year for the stories of old, the fireside tales of the ancient kings and warriors, of the myths and legends that had been handed down through generations. Stories of distant lands and peoples and catastrophes that had befallen them, old tales of the gods and their demise, the story of Jesus and how the church was expanding its influence throughout many lands as a result. For two young boys those tales were intriguing and full of action and they asked many questions. But a person could only hear a story so many times before it became boring, even when new elements were added to vary the story, so they often used to make themselves scarce for awhile, out into the raw elements of winter.

On one particular day Arthur and Kay had been out making the most of the last remnants of the thin watery sun that had managed somehow to break through the dismal grey sky, before joining the story tellers. There was a chill bite to the wind, but it was just a gentle breeze for most of the day, although in the last hour it had become very still and quiet, even the birds and animals were silent, an eerie feeling pervaded the fading half light of the day. Arthur had stopped and was surveying their surroundings, listening and feeling for some clue as to what was happening, he hadn't encountered this feeling of foreboding before. Something was about to happen, but he was not sure what, whatever it was wouldn't be pleasant. He indicated to Kay, who had been watching him intently, that they should hurry as there was a bad feeling in the air. Kay had never had the same connection to nature that Arthur had, but knew that his friend was usually right in his assumptions and they both set off at a fast trot, as they still had some way to go to reach the safety of the settlement.

They never made it in time, the wind, coming out of nowhere, hit them with such a force that they were bowled over, luckily they were unhurt but found it impossible to stand up in the ferocity of the onslaught. Arthur pointed to a rocky mound off to their right and indicated that they should crawl over to it for shelter. It was hard going, as even on their stomachs the wind was trying to whip them over as they moved. Kay made it first and extended his hand and dragged Arthur into the shelter of a small gulley between the rocks. Thankfully the rocky outcrop was solid with no loose shale to rain down on them, just some earth that whipped up and showered them. Huddled there in their primitive shelter the brunt of the wind passed over them, but the noise was terrible, they had to shout to hear each other and soon gave up trying. Arthur felt something smack him in the back and thinking that a chunk of rock had fallen on him he managed to roll over to remove it, only to discover that it was a bird, a raven, and it appeared to be still alive, although badly concussed. *Must have been blown out of a tree and then hit the rock above,* thought Arthur, gathering him gentle in his hand and placing him under his tunic for warmth and protection, as the wind was likely to whip him away again into oblivion.

Eventually the noise died down as the wind blew itself out and moved on to cause havoc elsewhere. They stood up and were awestruck as each surveyed the devastation around them. Even in the remaining half light they could see that trees had been uprooted, bushes ripped out of the ground and rocks were littered around where there had been none before. Both realised that they had been extremely lucky to survive, then it hit them at the same time, the settlement, how had that fared in the onslaught, they needed to get there as quick as they could. Arthur showed Kay the raven still nestling in his tunic, injured but alive, and said that his friend should go on ahead before darkness fell, as his father would undoubtedly be worried. He would follow at a slower place so as not to jolt the bird. Kay seeing the sense in this agreed and took off at a slow jog, wary of fallen debris that the wind had deposited across the countryside.

The distance was not far, but it took a little while as he was being careful, and as he approached the settlement he saw torches coming towards him. It was a search party sent out by his father when he realised that they were both missing. Kay explained that they were both alright and had taken shelter in time, Arthur was only a short way behind but had sent him on ahead. Some of the party said that they would wait for Arthur as there were some obstacles blocking the way into the village, which had been lucky to escape without too much damage, but two people were missing. Sir Ector was relieved to see his son and glad that Arthur was safe too, as Kay recounted to him what had happened and how they had taken shelter from what must have been the centre of the storm, as the devastation around them was terrible.

Arthur on his return took the raven to his quarters and checked him over to see if he could find anything broken, happy that there wasn't he made a little straw bed for him in the corner and fetched some water and raided the kitchen for some raw meat, as ravens are carrion birds. The bird stayed with Arthur for seven days until it had recovered enough to fly, it had tested its wings on most days but was lacking in strength to go far. Arthur spoke to him quite frequently and he would cock his head as if he understood and on the seventh day he said to the raven that if he felt strong enough he should return to his flock. The raven bobbed his head in answer and flexed his wings, gave a croak and took off climbing high into the sky and disappearing from sight.

* * * * *

Merlin was having that same vision again, where Uther was dead and the country was in turmoil and then the voices start shouting for Arthur. It was becoming a regular occurrence and Merlin knew that the more frequently that he had a dream the closer it was coming to materialising in reality. Many times over the years this pattern had repeated itself with his visions, each time ending exactly as he had foreseen.

He had been doing what Merlin always did well, travelling all over the country, listening, observing, mediating and gauging the strength of opinion concerning Uther and his Kingship, his conclusions did not bode well for the country. Opinion was even less divided now than before, those for Uther were declining rapidly and those against had the majority, but were totally at odds with each other with regard to a successor. Even some of those for Uther were being less than honest and had a foot in both camps, waiting to see what happened before committing themselves. There was much hollow talk on the surface hiding the extent of the discontent and power plays that were unfolding underneath, but Merlin could see through these quite easily. As always time was what Merlin needed, but he had no sway with time, that was outside the scope of what he was allowed to do, even though he had the ability to manipulate the conception of time, his hands were tied. All that Merlin could hope for was that his efforts would delay the inevitable. Hope; such a small word, but such a big responsibility. Alas his vision was getting too frequent - it wouldn't be long before it became reality.

Chapter 4
MERLIN'S VISION

WINTER WAS SLOWLY BEGINNING TO RECEDE and the sweet smell of spring was in the air, wild flowers were beginning to poke through the cold earth and reach up to the light, seeking that extra warmth, the birdsong had a joyous lilt to it, welcoming the new season. Around the sleepy villages and hamlets activity was increasing as they awoke from their long slumber, the sound of happy voices and laughter sweeping away the last remnants of winter. Spring was round the corner, a time of new growth and beginnings, a buzz that went right throughout the land every year without fail. Relief on surviving those harsh barren months, turning to happiness and a light hearted feeling as the warmth bathed the land and regenerated a multitude of colour across the landscape. A time of fun and laughter for all during the transition of the seasons brought out the best in people, with the hope of a good year ahead. A general calm had settled over the country and appeared to be lasting with no trouble in any region, not even a minor squabble. The undercurrent of discontent that had been building up before the turn of the year appeared to have been swept away, a new sense of peace had descended throughout the land, like a gentle wave of contentment.

Arthur and Kay were pleased to be able to get outside at last and carry on with their training and exploring the area in their free time. Sir Ector was glad too, as there was only so much that could be done inside and the boys could be rather a handful when they became bored, now he could keep them busy outside with the many tasks that they needed to learn. Thankfully Gwendolyn had been a blessing throughout those cold dark months, keeping the boys amused and out of mischief, he was glad that Merlin had persuaded him to take her on as well as Arthur. Thinking of which reminded him that Merlin had not been around for some while, and that was a little unusual in itself, but no doubt he would show his face soon, he always did as soon as he was thought about.

Days passed but still no Merlin, and Sir Ector started to feel concerned, as he had never stayed away this long, even if he only stopped by briefly in passing, disappearing as quickly as he had come. Then out of the blue Taliesin arrived early one morning, looking as if he had ridden a great distance in a hurry. Luckily the boys were not around when he sought out Sir Ector and explained in peace and privacy the nature of his visit and the news he brought, before it became common knowledge. Taliesin explained that

Merlin had asked him to come with all speed as he was not in a position to do so himself. Uther, High King of Britain, had decided that he would take the Lady Igraine as his wife and a large troop of his knights were already on their way to escort her and her family to Cadbury Castle, something she was not aware of herself yet. Merlin had gone to see her ahead of the soldiers, to advise her of the King's desire, but would not be there for another day, he did not foresee there being a problem as they were of similar age and well matched and she was a lady of breeding in her own right. Merlin however wished to see the Lady Igraine before her escort arrived as there were several important matters he wished to discuss with her. At the same time the King had sent messengers throughout the country inviting all the kings, lords and knights to his wedding feast, which would be on the day of the summer solstice. Taliesin paused for breath and asked Sir Ector if he was aware of any of this, and on receiving a shake of his head relaxed a little, commenting that he was in time then.

"Merlin has instructed me to warn you that it would be very unwise of you to attend the wedding, in any event the boys must not be allowed to go, even if you do not heed his advice for yourself. He has had a vision, which I am not at liberty to discuss, which leads him to believe that it would be a very dangerous place to be for all those that attend, irrespective of who they were or their standing with the King. Hence his urgent need to see the Lady Igraine before the news reached her, and for me to arrive before any messenger reached you."

Sir Ector could understand now why Taliesin had looked as if he had ridden all day and all night, he probably had. It did not sound very good and he knew enough about Merlin to know that he was usually right, but was intrigued to know what Merlin was expecting to happen, all Taliesin would say however was one word. Treachery. He would not be drawn any more on the subject and with that Sir Ector had to be satisfied.

The problem would be how to decline without offending the King and suffering his wrath, he thought, *this requires some careful deliberation.* Taliesin read his thoughts and offered him the solution, that it would be best to readily accept the invitation and send his congratulations back with the King's messenger, but when the time came just not to go. Both Merlin and Taliesin felt that this would be the wisest and safest course of action, and any excuse for not making it on the day could be made afterwards, if it became necessary in the light of events. Sir Ector pondered on this for a moment and could see the benefit of this, accepting and then not being able to go due to some unforeseen problem, would keep him in good stead with the King. He agreed with Taliesin that he would follow this course of action and thanked him for his advice and wisdom and asked him to convey his gratitude to Merlin, then suggested that he freshen up whilst food and drink was organised, and perhaps a well earned rest before the boys made an appearance.

"That's the best news that I've heard for days," smiled Taliesin.

Hours later two weary boys returned with their cart full of wood, which Sir Ector had sent them to fetch, to get their young muscles working again after the lack of good exercise during the winter. Seeing Taliesin they dashed over to see him, but were reminded by Sir Ector that they had to unload the cart before they did anything else. Weariness deserted Arthur and Kay as they set to removing and stacking the wood in record time, then rejoined Taliesin, plying him with questions about his travels, where he had been and what he had been doing.

Taliesin laughed and said, "one thing at a time boys, I cannot answer all your questions at once, but first tell me what you have been doing, then I will tell you my story."

Time passed all too quickly for Arthur and Kay, the light had begun to fade as the sun sank gently over the horizon in a last blaze of glory, Taliesin remarked that he had done enough talking for one day, any more questions would have to wait. Realising how hungry they were the boys thanked him and took their leave, laughing and smiling as they went in search of food. Taliesin remarked to Sir Ector how well they got on together, being so natural and at ease with each other he felt sure that they would be life long friends and would also be outstanding knights when they were of age, as they were so forward for their young years.

Taliesin stayed until the middle of the following day, being kept busy by never ending questions from Arthur and Kay as usual, but finally he had to bring them to a halt and say that it was time for him to leave, he had many people that he still had to see. Wishing them well he had a few moments alone with Sir Ector advising him to be extra vigilant over the coming months as there was still an underlying undercurrent of unrest lurking beneath all the peace and joviality that had spread across the land. This was the time when complacency set in, unless they were on their guard and aware that events could suddenly take a turn for the worse. It was best to expect the unexpected was Taliesin's farewell comment as he mounted his horse, and waving goodbye headed south to carry word of the King's wedding and Merlin's warning, to several others, that they should be prepared for the worst. Merlin had sent word to all the Elders advising them of the situation so that they might pass the warning on to any that they felt should know. The King's wedding to Igraine would soon be known about throughout the land but Merlin's vision and warning were only for a select few. Time was running out.

* * * * *

Spring slowly meandered into summer and Arthur and Kay were kept very busy with an increased training schedule and didn't have much time for relaxation, but that did not seem to bother them as they enjoyed testing their skills. Sir Ector had taken Merlin's warning to heart, although he did not understand the reason for it, and was keeping the boys close to home, not letting them wander off as they had been known to do before. He was also preparing them as quickly as he could for their young age in the ways of knighthood, lest the country slip into another period of anarchy. Normally they were not bothered too much by outside events in this corner of the country, but times could change and Taliesin's parting comment echoed in his mind. It was best to expect the unexpected and that was what he was doing as each day drew Uther's wedding closer. He had been to see the Lady Igraine the day that her escort had arrived to take her to Cadbury Castle, as she had sent word asking him to call on her urgently. He had extended his congratulations and best wishes on her forthcoming marriage to the King. She had seemed remarkably at ease and laughed at the thought of becoming the Queen. It seemed to amuse her, as although of good breeding, she had always considered herself as a normal country girl and soon she would have to act as the Lady of the Realm. Sir Ector was curious to know what Merlin had wanted to talk to her about, but being a gentlemen he would not raise the subject and Igraine never mentioned that he had called to see her, so he was left wondering.

Two weeks before the big day Merlin finally arrived at Padstow looking extremely tired, just as Taliesin had done on his arrival. *Here is another one who hasn't rested much recently,* thought Sir Ector, as he welcomed him and sent for food and wine. Merlin said he couldn't stay long as he still had much to do but wished to make sure that the boys were alright and that Sir Ector was going to heed his warning and stay away from the wedding. Sir Ector confirmed that he had accepted the invitation as suggested, but that he would not be going, he was curious as to why Merlin thought that it would be so dangerous. Merlin told him that his vision showed that treachery was involved but was not detailed enough to be able to pin point exactly what, but that it would bring great changes to the country after an initial period of mayhem and chaos. The vision had been getting stronger and more frequent as each day passed and Merlin suspected that whatever was going to occur would materialise at Uther's wedding. All the signs pointed to this event, so he was advising all his trusted friends to either go prepared or preferably to find some excuse to stay away, as the innocent were often the victims where treachery was to be found. It saw neither friend nor foe, only the means to and end, in whatever form it took, totally reckless and random. If he knew more then he might be able to stop it or at least minimise its effects, but alas he had not been shown the detail, therefore he had come to the conclusion that this was one occasion when he could not interfere and must let what will be, be. Merlin paused for thought, *we are running out of time and we are not yet fully prepared.*

Looking at Merlin Sir Ector could see that it was affecting him deeply and remained quiet. He had never seen him look so worried in all the time that he had known him, it seemed as if he had aged twenty years since he had last visited. Whatever was going to happen obviously had far reaching consequences that did not bode well for the country or its people, and this had disturbed Merlin greatly. Sir Ector was thankful that he had taken the warning seriously and would need to be constantly vigilant and on his guard until whatever was going to happen had come to pass, then the situation could be assessed.

Merlin gradually surfaced from the grim mood that had enveloped him and offered his apologies for not being able to be any more specific concerning his vision.

"At least we are prepared for something," stated Sir Ector, "even if we are not sure what. Taliesin summed it up with his parting comment, expect the unexpected, that's all we can do."

Merlin agreed, "wait and hope, that is all we can do for now, wait and hope." He excused himself and said that he must be going, as there where still others he needed to see and time was running out for all of them. "Keep the boys close for now," was his parting comment as he wearily departed for his next destination.

Sir Ector watched him go, deep in thought, *there is more to all this than meets the eye and I'm sure Merlin knows what is going to happen even if he does not know how or can even be sure of when, he knows the outcome. Why is he always so concerned about Kay and Arthur and their well being and progression, or is it just Arthur that he is interested in? You never knew with Merlin and what he was thinking unless he told you. What was so special about Arthur I wonder that he was brought here to be educated and cared for away from the centre of court social life, has he a part to play in the future? If so Merlin is keeping close counsel about it. It would be no good questioning his mother Gwendolyn for I doubt that she would know the truth, Merlin is too wise for that.* He paused for a moment as he recollected Merlin's words to him concerning Arthur, '*could he also accommodate the woman that Arthur knows as his mother.*' *Perhaps she is not his natural birth mother at all but has taken on the role for whatever reason, the plot thickens. I could ask her but that is not a gentlemanly question to ask a woman, irrespective of her background, and Merlin would not be happy if I started to pry into his affairs. If or when I need to know then I will be told and it would be best to leave it at that, Merlin always had valid reasons for his actions. A wise and visionary soul who seemed to know so much of what was happening throughout the land and always striving to keep the peace, but this time he was very troubled and no doubt with good reason. Merlin had never been known to be wrong with his visions but was besides himself that on this occasion he could not influence the outcome like he had always done before. This time it was entirely out of his hands and it had affected him greatly, therefore one must assume that whatever was going to happen would have a far reaching effect on everyone's lives.*

* * * * *

Life on Sir Ector's estate continued at its slow meandering pace, even the preparations for the summer solstice fair unwound in a leisurely fashion. Sir Ector was looking after Tintagel Fort for the Lady Igraine, so spent much of his time travelling backwards and forwards and often took Arthur and Kay with him to give them a change of scenery. They always travelled now with a well armed mounted troop and Sir Ector used the opportunity to give the boys training en-route in various methods of combat, in the open country and at times in the woods. They were delighted at this change to their routine, as it had become a little boring not being allowed to wander around the estate at will in their free time, however they were still not allowed to roam around on their own outside the fort. They saw many different animals in the woods and sometimes joined the hunt but as they often joked, no bears.

"That's because you make so much noise," laughed Sir Ector, "they can hear you coming long before you could get close to them, but as it happens no bears have been spotted in these woods for many years, most of them were killed for their fur and any that might remain keep well away from humans now."

The day of the summer solstice fair finally arrived and Arthur and Kay were spending the morning at Padstow with Sir Ector and then they were travelling to Tintagel later in the day to join in the fun there. Sir Ector wondered how the wedding feast was going at Cadbury Castle as the wedding itself was not until noon of the following day, and whether Merlin was there or not, as he had not asked him if he was attending. That was one of his mysterious ways and effects on people, you never remembered to ask him a question until he had gone, unless it was one that he was willing to answer at the time. Sir Ector felt a shiver run through his whole body, from his head to his feet and into the ground and looking around realised that Arthur was watching him. He asked him if he felt it too and Arthur nodded and asked what it was as it did not feel very nice. Something not very nice had happened somewhere and they had felt the energy vibrations from it, perhaps because it directly affected them in some way replied Sir Ector, thinking of Merlin's vision. Kay, looking from one to the other did not know what they were talking about as he had not felt anything, and asked if they were alright. They both nodded as they felt unable to explain that feeling of dread that had passed through them and touched their hearts. *Well,* thought Sir Ector, *whatever has happened I hope that the consequences are not too serious, but going by Merlin's distraught nature on his visit that is probably a false hope.*

* * * * *

Merlin was at Cadbury Castle, and had been for several days, observing, listening and trying to discover if there was an undercurrent of treachery in the air. He was baffled as all was peaceful and jovial with not a hint of anything untoward lurking in the background. Surely he couldn't be wrong, the vision had been that strong and consistent, the regularity increasing as the day approached. Was he missing something, what had he overlooked? Nothing as far as he could see, all the main guests had arrived, with only a few minor stragglers still expected, there were no strange faces amongst them and all around him he could sense and observe only pleasure and excitement as the big day drew closer. Was there to be an attack by the Saxons and their allies? He doubted that as he would have received warning of any build up of hostile forces from his contacts. He had cast his mind and vision around the area and within the castle grounds and could still find nothing but peace and goodwill, he was truly baffled for once in his long life.

At least he had persuaded Uther to send the Lady Igraine to Glastonbury to prepare herself for the wedding in the Abbey the following day, as ladies preferred their preparations to be unhurried. He also reminded the King that a man might wish to complete unfinished business and perhaps tie up a few loose ends before his marriage made that a little difficult. Uther, with a smile on his lips, understood exactly what Merlin was suggesting and saw the merit of his suggestion, as well as the pleasure that he could indulge in and sent one of his guards to Lady Igraine requesting the pleasure of her company. Merlin smiled, *how easy it is to persuade men on a certain course of action by sowing the right seed in their mind and letting it germinate to full bloom within seconds. These people are so easily lead, no wonder they have so much trouble living in peace with one another if a few choice words can alter their thinking so quickly when they see advantage in it for themselves. Its going to be a long hard struggle before they learn the joys of peace and love in the true sense, and experience a far better kind of life in this mixed up and volatile world of theirs. A long hard struggle but well worth the effort, not just for the ambassadors sent to help, like my own people, but for all the people of this world when they eventually discover their own capabilities and the beauty of life that is there for them. But that is a long way off yet, first we need to concentrate on what is happening now and gently lead them forward. I wish I knew what was going to happen to Uther, but then if I did I would do my best to change the course of events and that is not what I am supposed to do, I just have to sit this out and then pick up the pieces. Time has run out for me and for Arthur. All that I can hope for is that my vision is wrong, but in my heart I know that is not so. What will be, will be.* With those thoughts Merlin wandered off to seek out Taliesin who was somewhere amongst the crowd, but he was in no hurry now, the weight of worry had been lifted from his mind to be replaced by an inner peace and calm. The calm before the storm, which he would ride out, then pick up the pieces and carry on as he always did.

Igraine had left for Glastonbury with her entourage and the party atmosphere had moved up a gear as the wine began to flow, the entertainers performed and the feasting started in earnest. It had not taken Uther long to find one of his 'unfinished pieces of business' as Merlin had so delicately put it and was intently whispering in her ear. She gave a long shuddering laugh of pleasure as they walked away together towards the castle chambers oblivious to the knowing stares of those they passed on the way. Uther's reputation and appetite was well known and he wasn't expected back for a couple of hours at least, and then probably to find another conquest knowing him, making the most of his remaining hours before his marriage tomorrow. But would he change, few doubted it, he would just have to be more discreet in future.

As it was a beautifully warm summers day tables had been arranged outside for the main feast, making the most of the long evening of daylight as it was the summer solstice. Uther made his appearance, smiling and with a contented look on his face as the feasting and drinking began in earnest. Merlin and Taliesin had decided to forego the early proceedings and catch up on some well earned rest before putting in an appearance later, as neither were ones for consuming much wine, they had no need of it. Songs were sang, toasts were made and the wine flowed freely and for once it was Uther supplying it all and everyone was making the most of it.

The afternoon progressed slowly into the early evening and still the wine flowed, although some of the guests had consumed too much already and had passed out, sprawled in a variety of positions around the area. Uther was moving from table to table mixing with the guests, laughing and joking and calling for more wine as he went. The wine however did not arrive and people were beginning to voice their disapproval, thinking that Uther had no more, so he sent one of his men to find out what the problem was. Several minutes later he returned stating that there had been a problem opening a barrel, but it was okay now, and saying that the servants appeared bearing huge jugs of wine. Uther shouted to the crowd that there had been a problem locating his best wine but it was now being served, to which there were roars of approval and shouts of 'about time too.' Uther grabbed a couple of jugs with one hand and an attractive lady with another and shouted to the crowd to enjoy it whilst he attended to some urgent business. This brought peels of laughter as everyone knew what sought of business he had in mind, as he disappeared with the young lady.

The wine continued to flow freely, jug after jug, and voices got louder and songs got bawdier as the evening progressed. Then one of the guests gave a strangled cry and pitched forward, foaming at the mouth, then another, and quickly followed by several more. Within minutes there were around thirty or more guests that had collapsed foaming at the mouth. Of those seemingly unaffected some were trying to help those that had collapsed and the others had panicked, dashing around getting in each others way. A cry of 'we've been poisoned' was taken up by many, followed by 'where's the King, he's responsible for this.'

All this commotion brought Merlin and Taliesin out of their slumber with the one thought in their minds, the vision, and they rushed to the feasting area as quickly as they could. The sight that met their eyes was appalling, there were bodies everywhere, some lying very still, others writhing about in agony, whilst some appeared to be trying to help, the rest just sat in stunned silence unable to take in what was happening.

"Poison," muttered Merlin, "we need to find Uther and hope that we are not too late, let us hope that he is running true to form and giving his full attention to some young damsel, instead of the wine."

They searched high and low through all the bed chambers in the castle and although they stumbled across many couples and some groups engaged in compromising positions not a sign of Uther could they find. Returning to the scene of carnage in the feasting area they checked all the bodies on the chance that one might be the King, but alas no, he was nowhere to be found and it was probably too late by now anyway. Stopping to review the scene Merlin cast his minds eye throughout the castle grounds searching for a clue or vision as to the King's location. Slowly combing each area of the castle, - there - something was there, but indistinct. Of course the stables, why didn't he think of that before, the one place that Uther could indulge himself with a lady for a few hours without being disturbed by either the rowdy noise or couples seeking a bed for their passion.

The light was dim in the stables until Merlin delved into the pouch about his waist and produced a crystal wand that he held aloft. Taliesin had done the same and as they both stood quiet for a moment, then uttered an ancient incantation in the elder tongue, the wands burst into light and the whole area was bathed in a soft incandescent glow that illuminated every corner and chased the lurking shadows away.

They found Uther in the hay loft, still coupled in the throes of passion with the young lady, both smiling sweetly at each other, otherwise unmoving. A moment frozen in time, the High King of Britain taking his last journey just as he would have wished, with the empty wine jugs by his side as his epitaph. The first part of Merlin's vision had materialised just as he knew it would, but much too soon. Uther had died from poisoning, accelerated by his passionate exertions, and as the unfortunate lady had not been able to move him she had suffocated under his weight. *Now we have to sort this mess out and make it look respectable for a start,* thought Merlin, and Taliesin reading his mind silently agreed. *It would be too much for Igraine to bear to learn the full circumstances of Uther's last moments, then we need to find out who else has perished in this sorry affair and what repercussions were likely to arise from this turmoil. Take stock of the situation and try and hold everything together for a few more years until Arthur became of age. Much needed to be done and quickly to try and minimise the chaos that was bound to follow. A country without a leader was ripe for plunder and anarchy, just as the next part of his vision portrayed. We will do our best to keep everything together as much as possible by whatever means we can, and hope and pray that we are successful.* He looked at Taliesin who nodded his agreement with Merlin's thoughts as they turned to the grim task of separating the two lovers.

Chapter 5
MERLIN'S PROPHECY

THE NIGHT WAS LONG AND PAINFUL for Merlin and Taliesin as they administered help and potions to those that had not succumbed to the poison, and organising the removal of the dead to the great hall. Merlin had sought out Uther's wise old battle chief Greyfus, who had survived to a good age on his knowledge and wits as he rarely drank, and advised him of the demise of the King and where his body was to be found. He suggested that he take several trusted and discreet men with him as they would also find the body of a lady, as it appeared that the couple were intending to take a ride when they were overcome by the poison. Greyfus looked intently at Merlin but could read nothing in his look, although he suspected that it was only half of the story knowing his King, Uther liked to ride but more often than not the filly only had two legs and not four.

"It wont stop the tales being spread of his last hours though," he commented, "but it will be the only story told by those of us that attend to it, and naturally we will lay them to rest in the great hall separately according to their rank. Leave it to me and I will see that it is done discreetly," with that he went in search of suitable companions for his task, leaving Merlin to save those that he could from the agony of such a death.

Merlin and Taliesin worked for several hours to neutralise the affects of the poison on those still hanging on to life, after which all they could do was wait and hope. Several kings in their own right and many lords owed their lives to Merlin and Taliesin that night, but they both doubted that this fact would be remembered for very long, knowing human nature. Merlin left Taliesin to keep an eye on the patients and went off to the kitchens to question the servants and locate the source of the problem, but as expected there was no sign of anyone. The servants had all made themselves scarce when they discovered what had happened as they knew that they would be blamed for causing so many deaths, and probably forfeit their heads in the process. Merlin began checking the barrels, which had been stacked in rows, working his way towards the rear amazed at how many empty ones there were.

He had counted thirty and still not encountered one that contained any wine, then turning into the next row he almost stumbled over the prone figure of an old man slumped against the barrels. Bending down to check his breathing Merlin realised that he was still alive, but only just, and quickly forced down the old man's throat the remaining potion that he had left. The man coughed and then vomited violently and continued in this way for several minutes before slowly subsiding into a hoarse cough. His eyes rolled and he became aware of someone standing over him and a voice asking him if it was this barrel of wine that he had been drinking. He nodded and a thin whisper emanated from his lips, "couldn't resist it, brought it all the way from Tintagel without touching a drop and then thought why should all the lords have it. Tried to stop the servant girls from taking it, but they just pushed me out of the way in the end saying the King was calling for it as all the rest had gone, think I'd had too much by them anyway to care who drank it."

This was worrying news to Merlin, wine from Tintagel that had been poisoned, by whom and when, was it there or was it here? He needed to know and quickly. Merlin asked the old man if he had been with the wine all the time since it arrived, but received no answer so he bent closer and asked him again shaking him at the same time. No sound came from his lips, but was that a nod, Merlin could not be sure and shook him again but it was too late, the old man had slipped away and with him the answer to a worrying riddle. *Who at Tintagel would want to carry out such an indiscriminate act as this?* thought Merlin, *even the Lady Igraine could have been a victim and she was well liked and respected. Then who was there here who would interfere with this barrel of wine and why this one in particular? It didn't make sense, as nobody could know when or even if this barrel would be drunk and the old man had been protecting it and consuming it himself. He had obviously been here for some while before the servants needed it so it could not have been doctored just before use as one would normally suspect, therefore it indicated that the poison was introduced some while ago. But where and by whom, had a Saxon spy infiltrated Cadbury or Tintagel or maybe somewhere en-route and administered the poison, had Gorlois planned revenge on Uther and Igraine somehow for their suspected indiscretion, knowing the possible outcome of his confrontation with the King, or was there some unknown factor involved? So confusing and so arbitrary in its likely outcome that he could see no reason for it, except that it fulfilled the first part of his vision and at a time that he had recently anticipated. Perhaps we shall never know for sure and that is worrying in itself, we do not even know if it was designed specifically to remove Uther or for other darker reasons by removing many lords and kings. We must be on our guard more than ever now and try and keep it all together until Arthur comes of age.*

Merlin tapped the wine barrel in several places and decided that there was a quarter of it still left and taking the jug that was lying by the old man side he poured some into it and sniffed. He could detect no unusual smell to the wine, but that was not uncommon as there were so many varieties of poison that had no smell when blended with alcohol that he hadn't really expected one, what was obvious though was the taste. A quick acting poison would taste very bitter but a slow acting one would be just slightly sharp and would probably go unnoticed, especially by anyone that had already consumed a large quantity of wine. Merlin tilted the jug and dipped his finger into the wine to moisten it and then placed it on his tongue, not unpleasant but quite a sharp bite to it, much more than he had anticipated. He washed his mouth out several times from the water skin around his waist, a little puzzled by the extra sharpness that he had tasted, but easily masked by previous drinking. If it had been served first then people would have complained but as it was some hours into the feast nobody noticed. However it was plain that whoever had poured the poison into the wine was not skilled in those matters, as too great a quantity was added and many things were left to chance. Thankfully because of this it acted much too quickly and many were saved, whereas a slower acting poison could have killed half the guests overnight during their sleep. Merlin took the stopper out of the barrel and let the remainder pour out onto the dirt floor, whilst he checked that there was no more wine in the store that could cause further problems.

He passed through the great hall on the way back to Taliesin and stopped and viewed the scene. Uther was laid out at the head with three lesser kings, ten lords and twelve knights to his right whilst on his left were two ladies, eight soldiers and two servants. Thirty eight in total plus the old man in the kitchen and any that might still slip away during the night, what a dreadful wedding feast. Merlin stopped, he had forgotten all about the Lady Igraine in all this turmoil, he must go and break the news to her and the bishop before the morning preparations were started. Merlin always seemed to be the bearer of bad news for Igraine, first having to give up her son and not be able to see him, then the news of her husbands death on confronting Uther and now the poisoning of her future husband on the eve of her wedding to the High King of Britain. *If only it had been later,* thought Merlin, *then Arthur would have been the legitimate heir to the throne, but also in more danger until he was of age. Maybe its just as well that events happened when they are meant to and not when we wished them too.*

* * * * *

Merlin arrived at Glastonbury as the warm glow of dawn was breaking and made his way to the bishop's dwelling to advise him of the situation before having to face Igraine and ruin her big day. The bishop as was usual with holy men had already started his day and welcomed Merlin commenting on the fact that he was a little early for the ceremony, but it was as well to be prepared.

"Come break some bread with me you look like you could use some as I fear this early visit is not a good omen. What brings you at the crack of dawn wise one?"

Merlin recounted the events at the wedding feast and the appalling and indiscriminate loss of life that was the outcome and had come as quickly as he could, and as usual the bearer of bad news. The bishop beckoned to one of the nearby brothers and whispered some instructions to him and sent him off to carry them out. He had sent Brother Benedict on an errand to request that the Lady Igraine attended the inner sanctuary at her convenience but as a matter of urgency. He suggested that they wait for her there and offer their prayers to their departed brothers and sisters, also those that might be lingering between both worlds and give thanks for those that were spared.

Igraine appeared within the hour and was most surprised at finding Merlin at prayer with the bishop, then she saw their solemn faces and knew that something terrible had happened.

"Come child, pray with us a moment in the peace of this holy place and let the love of our Lord come upon us and lift our hearts," intoned the bishop in his gentle lilting accent.

For some while they stood in a circle letting that love, peace and tranquillity sweep over them and through them, easing their burdens of life as the bishop said the prayers, then nodded to Merlin to break the news.

Igraine was heartbroken but being a Lady she kept her composure well and thanked them both for their consideration and kindness, then asked if she might be left alone for a few moments to come to terms with the terrible loss on what was to have been her wedding day. *Every time she had seen Merlin in the last few years he had always been the bearer of bad news,* she reflected, *and each time was worse than the time before, would it ever end,* she wondered. *Now that Uther had gone would she be reunited with her son and heir to the throne, wherever he might be, somehow she doubted that Merlin would allow this as he would not be of age yet and perhaps in even more danger if it was known that he existed. Happiness and a good life appeared to slip away from her each time she got close to experiencing it, perhaps that's how her life was supposed to be, always striving for but never attaining the love that she sought. Life can be a hard and cruel struggle but we must not give in, just keep on going and pray that the good times eventually materialise and make all the strife and suffering a thing of the past.* Igraine let her thoughts wander back to Uther and what might have been, letting her heart send out love to him as a final farewell wherever he might be now, and gathering herself she rejoined the bishop and Merlin in the courtyard.

The two of them had been discussing the funeral arrangements for Uther and the other departed souls and had decided that due to the numbers involved the burials would be at Cadbury, unless any kin wished otherwise, and that it would be in four days time. The bishop would attend and Igraine could accompany him if she so wished and afterwards Merlin would see that she had a King's escort back to Tintagel. It was agreed, and Merlin said that he must return forthwith to Cadbury Castle and make the necessary arrangements, and hope and pray that no others had been lost since he left there.

As he was leaving he remarked to Igraine that he had found an old man, drunk as a lord, guarding a barrel of wine that he said he had brought from Tintagel and nobody was to touch it as it was for the King, but he had obviously helped himself to a considerable amount of it. Igraine smiled and said that sounded like Grimald the wine keeper who always insisted that he should test wine regularly to make sure it hadn't gone off. Uther liked the wine that much when he stayed that time that he demanded that Gorlois send him a barrel as a gift if he ever got married, Grimald remembered and brought it to her attention saying it was common knowledge at the fort, so she sent him with it for the wedding feast. *Now we know why it was at the castle,* thought Merlin, *but not who tampered with it and introduced the poison, and if it was common knowledge then it could have been anybody not just Gorlois himself who was the perpetrator. We will probably never know for sure but I wouldn't be surprised if it was the wily old Duke getting his revenge from the grave.*

Merlin made good time on the return to Cadbury and immediately sought out Taliesin and inquired how the patients were and whether they had lost any others. On hearing that everything was okay except that some of the survivors that had lost kin were still in a distraught state and there were mutterings of discontent beginning to surface, Merlin brought him up to date on the visit to the bishop and Igraine.

"We will need to speak to all these guests later and give them some idea of what happened, but I think it wise not to say where the wine came from as that would focus attention towards Igraine, she has had enough suffering to contend with and it would possibly expose Arthur to unnecessary danger. First I have a short errand to do before others think of it," and with that cryptic comment he headed towards the King's living quarters, returning a short while later with a smile of success on his face. "I needed to recover the King's sword and scabbard as it is the one that belonged to Maximus and it rightly belongs to the High King of Britain, when he is chosen, and not some unscrupulous lord or king to use for his own ends. It is now in a safe place until such time as it is needed."

Later that day Merlin gathered all the guests together and explained that the mayhem of the previous day had been caused by the wine being poisoned but it had not been possible to discover who had performed the atrocious act, or even when it might have happened.

"Although we have lost many good men and friends the situation could have been far worse if Taliesin and I had not been here, as it was we were able to save many of you from the same fate. I have arranged all the burials to take place here in four days time unless any of you wish to take your kin home and the Bishop of Glastonbury will attend together with the Lady Igraine, if she so wishes."

Many muttered that it was a sorry affair and wanted to know why it had happened and who would want to do such a thing when its affects were so random. Merlin replied that despite all his enquiries he was at a loss for an explanation of why or by whom and that they would probably never know.

The burials took place in the meadow below Cadbury Castle as the ground within the castle walls was too hard and stony for such a large scale laying to rest. The graves were laid out in a line according to rank with Uther at the head followed by the kings, lords, ladies, soldiers and servants and all were buried facing the castle. The Bishop of Glastonbury conducted the solemn proceedings and read the names of all the departed and cursed the perpetrator of the crime to eternal damnation for taking the lives of so many good and trusted people on what was supposed to be a happy and joyous occasion. He gave prayers for the deliverance of so many of the other souls present and praised the skills of Taliesin and Merlin in the quick action that helped save many lives and he asked that they all send out their thoughts to the Lady Igraine who had cruelly lost her husband to be. Now was the time to stand firm and together so that the gains that the King had made were not lost and this country remained united in those terrible times until a new High King could deliver them from the scourge of the foreign invaders.

"Let peace prevail between you all and we will stand a good chance, squabble amongst yourselves and we shall be lost, the choice is yours. On the first day of September we will gather at Silchester Abbey for the purpose of choosing a new High King as Uther left no heir to the kingdom, as far as we are aware."

As the bishop said this Igraine awoke from her grief as her thoughts turned to her son, and Uther's heir, and was on the point of saying something when she realised that Merlin was looking at her intently and gently shaking his head. Of course, he was not of age and to say anything could put his life in jeopardy, wherever he was, but she must ask Merlin about him all the same. The bishop brought them all together with a final prayer and then went to each grave in turn saying a few words at each and consoling the surviving kin, then stopping and surveying the saddening scene one last time, made the sign of the cross and slowly made his way back to the castle.

The guests slowly started to drift away and begin their various journeys home, still subdued and in the aftermath of shock. Several of the kings and lords approach Merlin and Taliesin and thanked them for what they had done and Merlin said that he would leave Greyfus in charge of the castle until a new High King was selected and it would be in good hands. Igraine managed to see Merlin before she left and he entrusted Uther's sword to her, saying that it rightfully belonged to the High King of Britain and asked her to bring it to Silchester in September, but not to tell anyone that she had it because others might want it. She agreed and asked how her son was getting on and yes she had been on the point of saying something when the bishop was making his address, but realised that it was not the time. Merlin said that he was doing fine but unfortunately it needed to be kept secret until he became of age and could claim his inheritance. The way the lords squabbled amongst themselves he couldn't see them agreeing on who should be the High King and none were strong enough at the moment to force the issue.

"We must wait and bide our time and hope that everything holds together in the meantime, that's all that we can do, and I will do my best along with the other Elders to keep the peace between them, although that is likely to be a difficult task."

Merlin said that he would call to see her when passing but could not say when as he would be very busy but he would be obliged if she would let Sir Ector know what had transpired here and ask him to pass the message on to those that he knew so they could all be on their guard. If there were major problems they should send word to Greyfus here who would do what he could to help, but that it would be limited as his role would be to protect Cadbury Castle from falling into the wrong hands. Igraine thanked him, giving him a hug, which took him by surprise, and joined her escort and the bishop for the homeward journey, still dazed from all that had happened in the last few days.

* * * * *

Merlin, Taliesin and the other Elders spent the next two months travelling the countryside informing all the minor kings and lords of the events at Cadbury and inviting them to Silchester on the first of September to agree on a new High King. As was their usual way the Elders had communicated telepathically and each was aware of what was happening and who was likely to attend and who didn't seem that bothered. This was often the case with the more northern kingdoms as they kept their own counsel and weren't concerned with what happened in the south. This north south divide had always posed problems for the High Kings of the past, even the Romans during their years of occupation experienced the subtle differences between the two, but they had the weight of numbers and a well trained fighting force to keep the peace throughout most of the kingdom. The Elders knew that the gathering at Silchester would not be an easy one and would no doubt be inconclusive in its outcome, but it had become tradition in an endeavour to forge a lasting peace across the country. Merlin understood very well the implications that would follow if agreement was not reached. As the next part of his vision did not bode well for the country, and was most likely to come to fruition with continuous infighting between kings, as they jostled for position and power, to take by force that which had not been granted them by common consent. Anarchy would raise its head again and all that had been gained so far would be lost. The foreign insurgents would take maximum advantage of the situation to further their influence and power base and carve up the land amongst themselves. Arthur was going to have a difficult time enforcing his Kingship when he eventually became of age, and that was still quite a few years away, and much could happen in that time. All the Elders could do in the meantime was to try and minimise the fallout by diplomacy and even subtle coercion in an endeavour to maintain a fragile peace between potential warring factions.

* * * * *

Silchester was teeming with people as many folk had gathered to see who would be the next High King, most were from the southern regions but several minor kings and lords from the middle kingdoms and a few from the northern lowland areas had surprisingly arrived, together with two from the islands. *A good turn out,* thought Merlin, *but with those here there was unlikely to be any common consensus on who should take Uther's place. Always a problem when there was no heir to succeed to the Kingship, even that did not guarantee universal acceptance and often led to conflict. No one king or lord here had the following or power base to sway the others. Uther had been clever in that respect, not let any become powerful enough to challenge his authority and that is a good position to be in at the moment, as if we can keep it that way it will be a little easier when Arthur comes of age. Although he will still be young to take on the role what he is being taught at the moment will put him in good stead in the difficult times that he will face, and with ongoing help and advice to guide him there is hope that peace will eventually prevail again.* Merlin noticed Igraine in conversation with several of the lords and was pleased that she had decided to attend and she had mentioned to him when she arrived that she had brought Uther's sword as requested, in case it was required. Although that seemed doubtful, at least all the contenders could witness that it was here. Although Uther and Igraine had not been formally married they had been betrothed to each other and as such she had certain rights, relating mainly to his possessions, the sword being one of them.

A warm close night heralded the dawning of the first day of September as the kings and lords gathered at last in the cool interior of the abbey just as the sun burst forth, cascading its golden rays across the landscape and penetrating the dark interiors of buildings. As the bishop commenced the proceedings with prayers for a successful and peaceful outcome the sun streamed through the window slits illuminating the cross and enveloping him and Merlin in a beautiful golden aura. The rest of those gathered remained in the half light as if it was an omen reflecting many dark thoughts running through their minds, as they sought ways to gain advantage over each other. Merlin opened the debate saying that they were all gathered there to agree on a successor to Uther and that they needed to reach a unanimous decision if possible, otherwise any new king would be in an untenable position. Each one could have their say and put themselves forward for consideration, and debate would continue until a decision was reached or until it was obvious that agreement would not be forthcoming. With that he sat down and allowed the wrangling to start.

Canaut was the first on his feet and declared that the High King should come from one of the larger southern kingdoms, such as his, able to support the war chest from his own funds, insisting that the freedom of Britain relied on the freedom of the High King to rule without hindrance to the war chest from lesser kings. Otherwise undue influence could be applied by them in withholding taxes unless granted greater favours. The High King needed to rule using his own wealth to guarantee autonomy. Others disagreed and stated that all should pay their dues into the war chest, depending on the size and wealth of their kingdom, therefore it was not necessary for the High King to be chosen from a large wealthy kingdom. The debate continued throughout the day on these two points alone without agreement being reached, as Merlin sat quietly in the background listening and observing, knowing that it was going to take a long time to resolve even such minor points. Igraine had slipped in quietly and unseen, even by Merlin, and stayed for awhile listening to the lords trying to outdo one another and gain an advantage that they could capitalise on and gather support to their camp, but many were too wily to fall into that trap, and the debate just went round in circles getting nowhere.

The following day was just a re-run of the first and all the while Merlin just sat quietly listening and smiling to himself at how pathetic they all looked and sounded, not one of them had the character and strength to carry the day and they couldn't even see it as they jostled for position. They were all blind to their own inflated egos and sought only for what they could gain personally for themselves if elected, they didn't give a damn about the country. *It was plain for all to see,* thought Merlin, *none of them would survive a month as High King. These people never learn, once the ego takes command they are doomed, yet they never see it. It requires a strong character to put country and people before their own desires and they have lived too long in their own materialistic shadow to ever be able to break free and change their ways. It will take an exceptional man to lead these people into new pastures and leave the old ways behind, building a lasting peace that will begin to change the face of this country for the better. A place of justice and tolerance, peace and goodwill that could permeate through to other lands. Maybe one day this will happen and all that we can hope for is that Arthur, when his time comes, can start this process off, that others can continue and build on over the aeons of time. Only time will tell as time is only a perception of the human race and does not exist outside of their realms of existence. What a lot they have to learn before they can move on and discover the real beauty of everything there is and the never ending possibilities of life beyond even their wildest imagination. It took my people along the same route before we saw the light and changed our ways and we have never looked back since. A long journey but worth the pain of learning along the way, and now some of us have returned to help these people through the same hurdles.*

Raised voices brought Merlin out of his reverie and back to the events at hand. Canaut was on his feet in heated debate with several of the lords opposite him but seeing opposition growing quickly against him waved his arms in a dismissive gesture and sat down again. The day rolled on to a close with fierce argument on all sides, and still nothing had been decided.

The third day passed and went in much the same way and all the while the arguments went backwards and forwards without a single point being agreed. The fourth day followed the same pattern with voices getting even more agitated as the tension built up and it was obvious to Merlin that it would not be long before violence erupted unless some agreement was reached shortly. Igraine had again crept in unseen several times, staying in the shadows at the rear and not staying too long on each visit, but enough to keep in touch with whatever progress was being made, finally she slipped out with a thoughtful look on her countenance. *Tomorrow would be an interesting day one way and another, make or break time was her conclusion, time to take a hand perhaps and show myself and force the issue, but without making Merlin aware of her intentions beforehand. He would probably try and stop her, but she had a right to be there being Uther's betrothed, besides she had the Sword of Kings that now belonged to her and she could do what she wished with it. Yes it would be an interesting day right enough,* and she smiled at the thought of the consternation of these egotistical minnows fighting over the pot of honey when she made her entrance.

Merlin spent a troubled night of tangled dreams and visions that gave him no clear answers to the problem at hand, but shortly before dawn they subsided and a peace and calm descended on him, such as he had not experienced for some while. *A sign of something totally unexpected that would happen to diffuse the situation,* he thought, *so be prepared to capitalise on it and turn it to good use and take them all by surprise before they could react to the contrary.* For the first time for days he was in a jovial mood as he made his way to the gathering, even smiling at his own thoughts.

As they all arrived you could feel the tension in the air rising, even before the debate had begun, today was certainly going to be different, the mood was dark and unyielding and groups had gathered in separate clusters, each with their own viewpoint. Whispering intently amongst themselves whipping up support for their own candidate, but there were too many groups and not one of them was large enough to hold the balance of power.

Merlin called them to attention and reminded them that today a decision must be made before the sun went down otherwise the council would be dissolved without a result and would not re-convene for another year, during which time the country would have no High King. No sooner had he finished than Canaut was on his feet as usual and the onslaught began, decrying the claims of all the others as he tried in vain to push himself forward as the natural choice. Other voices rose shouting him down, they had heard it everyday and were sick of the same tirade but he refused to budge and continued unabated.

Suddenly all the voices except Canaut were still, a hush had descended across the gathering, then he too realised that all had fallen quiet and thought for a moment that he had taken the day, until he looked around the gathering. Standing at the edge of the circle beautifully attired and wearing a long flowing black and gold cloak with a gold and jewelled clasp stood the Lady Igraine. Lord Canaut, taken by surprise, asked her what had brought her to the council and why hadn't she interrupted him, to which she replied that although it seemed that the only way to be heard was to shout abuse at all and sundry, she was a lady and had no wish to appear rude. Therefore she had waited until he had finished abusing everyone else and begun extolling his own virtues, as he did everyday. At his surprised look she indicated that yes she had been in attendance many times, but undetected in the shadows, as she listened to and observed the farce unfolding before her. As to why she was here it was because she had a right that she was exercising as Uther's betrothed, and looking directly at Merlin added that as he had no known heir all his possessions were rightly hers. Moving to the centre of the circle she turned to face them all and removed her hand from beneath her cloak and held aloft the Sword of Britain, including this my lords The gold and silver shimmered in the rays of sunlight creeping into the great hall and the jewelled hilt appeared as a sparkling ball of fire in her hand. This was why they were there, but listening to them one would be forgiven for thinking otherwise. There were gasps from the crowd, all had forgotten about the sword except Merlin, who had been sitting quietly watching the scene unfold, smiling gently to himself as he reflected that something different would happen today, and it certainly had. The tension had vanished as if blown away on the wind and was now replaced by uncertainty. What did this woman want and why tease them with the sword, what was she up to? They soon found out as Igraine reversed the sword and stuck it in the earthen floor in the centre of the circle.

"My Lords this is the Sword of Britain, held by each High King except one since Maximus the Great wielded it as the first High King of our land. It has now passed to me, a Lady of the realm, but I have no wish of it, nor could do it honour in serving our great country, except by seeing that whoever holds it does so with pride, virtue and honour, not for themselves, but for the greater good of this country. Persuade me if you can why it should be one of you as I come to you in turn. If you think you can humour me or take the sword by force because I am a Lady then beware, my father taught me the skills of the blade and the importance of its weight and balance, you would be dead before you knew it Lord Canaut so banish that thought from your mind."

Lord Canaut was so taken aback that she had read him like a book that he could only mumble an incoherent reply. Merlin smiled even more at the way the tables had been turned on the lords, this lady was no fool, no wonder she had been selected to be the mother of Arthur above all others. Igraine went to each lord in turn carrying the sword with her and many could not take their eyes off it as they tried to persuade her why they should be the High King and not one of the others. When she had heard enough from each she held up her hand and thanked them and moved on to the next, leaving Lord Canaut to last, but allowing him the same amount of time as the others. When she held up her hand to stop him he started to complain that he had not finished, she raised the sword slightly indicating that was the final word as she returned to the centre of the circle. Surveying them all she thanked them again and said that she was now going to pray for guidance and they were most welcome to join her in silent prayer if they wished, and gently sank to her knees, holding the sword hilt in both hands she rested her forehead on them. Whatever she actually prayed for no one knew but most of the lords feeling a little ashamed of their selfish behaviour over the days of the council bowed their heads and joined her. Merlin gave his own prayer of thanks for her timely intervention in what was developing into a hostile situation, but knew that it was not over yet by any means, and although she had guaranteed their attention they were now expecting her to deliver, well they might just be in for a further surprise.

Igraine slowly rose to her feet. "My Lords of Britain, my betrothed Uther Pendragon had many faults as most of us do but he loved his country and all his endeavours were focussed on uniting this island home of ours and bringing peace and prosperity to the people. His life was not made easy by the continuing petty squabbles that saw neighbour take up arms against neighbour, whilst our country was being infiltrated by foreign invaders. I have listened to you all and not one of you that has spoken has shown the vision, courage and determination that Uther possessed, you are only concerned with your own short sighted materialistic greed that would better your own position."

She was interrupted by many voices as they all took umbrage at her cutting words. Merlin smiled and thought they don't like this one bit, as Igraine held up her hand to continue.

"My Lords I tell it as I see it, as I have the same vision for this country as Uther, not one of you can even command the respect of the others and you would not last out a month as High King. This country needs a strong leader who is wise, bold and courageous and has the support of the people, not one of you comes anywhere near being able to fulfil those requirements. There is only one person in this hall capable of doing this, one who even exceeds the standards set by Uther, that person has not spoken for himself, even though I believe he is from an ancient and greater royal line than any here and everything he does is for the greater good of our country. Why then you may ask has he not put himself forward. The answer my lords is that in his long lifetime he has seen the futility of violence on a greater scale than we could imaging and now offers himself as an ambassador for peace and diplomacy in this world and would not accept the Kingship if it was offered to him. Therefore Lords of Britain this sword shall now pass to his hands for safe keeping until such time as one in this land shows that he is worthy of the Kingship." With that Igraine walked slowly towards Merlin and giving him a curtsey placed the sword in his hands. "I was given the words during my prayers and told what to do, but I had intended to give the sword to you anyway to keep for the right time," she murmured quietly so that the others could not hear.

Merlin was still in slight shock at how well she had handled the situation and had wondered where the words had come from as they were so unnervingly accurate on a personal level. The lords that had been struck dumb by Igraine's speech now found their vocal chords again and were bombarding Merlin with angry words, calling for an explanation. He strode into the centre of the circle carrying the sword and spoke.

"My Lords the Sword of Britain has been placed in my safe keeping until a true King comes forth, but mark my words it will be won by a leader of men, one who puts his country and others above himself, who will excel in courage, show mercy when needed, uphold justice and fight for right. He will treat others as equals whatever their station in life and command the respect of friend and foe alike, his men will share his glory and be raised by his enthusiasm. The land and animal kingdoms will be respected and nurtured to provide for his people on an enduring basis and his name will be sung in praise throughout all the lands of this world for many long years to come and others will seek to replicate his success. He will stand head and shoulders above all the rulers of the world in his valour, compassion and kindness and his light will shine brightly for all the world to see and marvel at, I Merlin the Wise, Emru of the Elders do prophesy this."

Complete silence reigned for a moment, then all the voices were raised at once echoing the one thought in their minds, like drowning men grabbing at anything to stay afloat as their ship sunk, how would they recognise this King, they needed a sign.

Merlin, realising he must finish this quickly and once and for all, rushed out of the hall into the courtyard brandishing the Sword of Britain above his head and headed for the great stone centre piece. Raising the sword above his head he plunged it down into the stone amidst cries of 'no stop him,' and to everyone's amazement it did not break but buried itself almost up to the hilt in a flash of light and burning stone.

"You asked for a sign," Merlin shouted, "well here it is. Whoever raises the sword from the stone is the true born High King of Britain, but until that day this land shall experience strife the like of which it has not experienced before and Britain shall have no High King."

A stunned silence followed as he walked away leaving the Sword of Britain firmly embedded in the stone, still vibrating gently and showering the area in dancing fireflies as the afternoon sun caught the jewelled hilt.

Chapter 6
A BAD SEED IS SOWN

MERLIN AND THE LADY IGRAINE left Silchester Abbey the following morning as a group of the lords, including Canaut, were gathered around the great stone, staring transfixed at the Sword of Britain sparkling in the morning dew, as if mocking them. There to behold, but refusing to budge to even the strongest arm or even arms as several tried their combined force to shift it, but to their intense and vocal frustration it did not even yield a fraction. Merlin smiled to himself, *no matter what they did it would never be released to the likes of them, and they still failed to comprehend why, even after all that they had been told by Igraine and himself. The sword would now wait for the arrival of Arthur to claim his inheritance and astound them all by the simplicity of its removal. Such a pity that more years would pass before that happened, some of them wouldn't even be around to see it. Life unfortunately was going to become very difficult for everyone now, chaos, strife and anarchy would blow across the land like a violent storm, refusing to abate, as clouds gathered in darker and tighter formations before attacking the foundations of society on all fronts. The petty squabbles of the lesser kings would pale into insignificance by comparison as the Germanic tribes increased their hold and influence throughout the land, as they would have many successes to build on. Thankfully they were just as disorganised as our own kings and would not operate as one large coherent force to push right through the land, but as small but growing raiding parties, out for what they could get. There is still time to prepare Arthur and lay the ground work for his arrival on the scene, but he will still be very young for such a responsibility when he his thrown in to the melting pot, although from what I have seen and heard he has the character and ability to succeed.*

His thoughts were interrupted by Igraine asking about her son and his progression, and how long must he be kept hidden from her and the world. Merlin replied he was doing exceedingly well but that he would have to remain unknown until he became of age and could legitimately claim the Kingship. He asked her how her son Cador was doing as he must be nearly of age and able to inherit his father's title, and what of her two daughters, Anna and Morgause, as he hadn't seen any of them for some while. She replied that indeed her son would become of age the following year and had been well trained in the ways of a knight and courtly behaviour by Sir Brastias, a trusted and long serving knight of her late husband Gorlois. Her two daughters were growing fast and were being educated in all manner of womanly duties by her ladies in waiting. Although Morgause, the eldest had a mind of her own and could be quite rebellious at times and needed a firm hand, whereas Anna was the quiet one who just absorbed what she was taught without question. Morgause was independent and got what she wanted, and she feared that she would be a thorn in any man's side that she became entangled with, especially if she did not get her own way.

They spent much of their journey discussing what was likely to happen during the time that there was no High King and the consequences for the country generally. Igraine jokingly said that she was a lady of substance now with a fort and a castle, but wasn't sure how she could manage both, Merlin told her not to worry he would sort out the care and keep of Cadbury, if she was happy with that. That would be most helpful she told him, as she was content at Tintagel, there was something about the place and the area that drew her back to it even when she was away. Merlin had a good idea why that was the case but kept his own counsel on the matter, part of her knew that there was something good there, but reason could not explain it and that was just as well in the circumstances.

In no time at all it seemed they arrived back at Cadbury to be welcomed by Taliesin who had volunteered to stay behind whilst they were at Silchester. As he and Merlin had already communicated telepathically there was little else to add but Igraine unaware of this recited all that had happened to an attentive Taliesin. Asking Merlin why he didn't say anything, he replied that he couldn't get a word in and she had done a good job of describing the events anyway. At this she blushed and apologised saying that she got carried away, Merlin laughed and replied that it was a good job that she did on occasions, remembering her speech to the lords.

Igraine left for Tintagel the following morning with an escort that Greyfus had arranged for her and reminded both Merlin and Taliesin to call on her as soon as they had the opportunity, to keep her up to date on what was happening in the country. They both promised to call but said it could be some while as they would most likely be very busy travelling the land in an endeavour to maintain some semblance of peace. *There goes a very astute lady, it's a pity in some respects that she is not a man, but then we wouldn't have Arthur, lets hope he has as much of her character as he does Uther's,* and Taliesin echoed his thoughts.

* * * * *

Sir Ector was having a busy time at Padstow, travelling regularly to Tintagel to liaise with Sir Brastias on the management of the fort whilst Igraine was away. Kay and Arthur always accompanied him and looked forward to those visits as they had developed a good friendship with the older Cador, Igraine's son, and it provided variety in their ongoing training and took the pressure off Sir Ector at the same time. Sir Ector, aware of the likely problems in the country following Uther's death thought the time was right to give the boys some wider experience and let them develop friendships and strengthen ties that could prove to be beneficial in the difficult times ahead. Sir Brastias, a steady reliable knight with a wealth of experience with much the same characteristics as Sir Ector, although slightly older, was delighted to have the boys visit as companionship for Cador, and a divergence to the normal routine. They were always keen to be active and doing something constructive and their happy disposition and infectious laughter when something went wrong was a pleasure to observe. Even Igraine's young daughters were seen on occasions to be watching their antics and shouting encouragement, although Morgause was the more vocal of the two and her comments sometimes most direct, and definitely not ladylike.

Cador, Kay and Arthur were allowed out of the fort on horseback provided that they did not stray too far and could return quickly if any trouble arose, but they had to take their weapons with them just in case. They looked forward to these excursions and were aware of the trust and responsibility given to them as part of their ongoing development and were mindful of not abusing it. However as often happens a situation arose that would test their resolve, but at the same time strengthen their character and give them a chance to prove their worth. They had decided to try a little hunting in the nearby woods and had taken with them spears as well as their swords, not that they had expected to find much game so close to the fort, but it was best to be prepared.

Most of the morning they scoured the woods, slowly penetrating deeper into them, but to no avail. Either they were making too much noise, which was unlikely as they moved quite silently, or there was no game in this part of the woods. The ground was beginning to slope down towards the shoreline when Cador called a halt and said that they should start to make their way back as they had gone far enough. At that moment distant voices came to their ears. Moving off the wide path into the trees and the cover of the bushes Cador motioned them to be quiet as he dismounted and crept back to look along the pathway in the direction of the voices. He quickly returned and whispered that there were four wild looking men approaching talking in a foreign tongue, but between them they were half dragging and half carrying two women roped together. It looked like the woodcutter's wife and daughter he stated but there was no sign of the woodcutter himself, which probably meant he was dead. They should rescue them said Arthur, otherwise who knew what would happen to them, and Kay agreed, but Cador was hesitant as he had responsibility for the two younger boys. They probably had a ship in the cove which meant that there might be more of them around and they hadn't got time to go for help. What was their formation? Arthur asked, two in front and two behind, to which Cador nodded an affirmative. Then they needed to surprise them, one of them to jump out and attack the leaders in front when they were close, and the other two to take them from behind with their spears. Cador thought for a moment and then agreed as that seemed their only alternative if they wished to rescue the women, He would take the front if they would take the rear. That agreed Cador moved quietly away from Arthur and Kay to take up position a little further along so that they could ensnare them like meat between two loaves of bread.

The voices grew closer and they seemed to be cursing the women for not moving quickly enough, their guttural voices not understood by the watchers, but the tone was self evident. Kay and Arthur were keeping their horses quiet as the group moved passed their hiding place, and then Cador sprung onto the pathway with a load roar that startled even them. The insurgents were taken totally by surprise and froze for an instant as Cador launched his spear at the leader taking him cleanly through the chest, killing him instantly. At the same moment Arthur and Kay broke out onto the path spears raised, as the rearguard hearing the noise behind them, turned as they drew their swords. Kay's spear ran true and took out the one on the left whilst Arthur had to wait a fraction of a second as one of the women was slightly blocking his aim and his spear pieced the man through the side, but he was still standing. Without thinking Arthur urged his horse forward and drawing his sword delivered a fatal blow to the insurgent's neck which almost took his head off. Meanwhile Cador had drawn his sword and attacked the only one left alive, who was still dazed from the speed of the surprise attack. He quickly fell dead under his withering onslaught.

Kay and Arthur had dismounted and were untying the women, who were both distraught and in shock. It was several minutes before they confirmed who they were and that the woodcutter had been slain by the barbarians as he tried to protect them. Cador had dragged the bodies into the undergrowth, after the gruesome task of removing the spears from the corpses, in case anyone came looking for them, and then asked the women if there were more of them around and if so how many. The mother said that there had been more of them but wasn't sure how many, but the rest had gone off in a different direction. Cador suggested that Arthur and Kay doubled up and take one of the women each on their horse, he would cover their flank in case they encountered any more trouble en-route. They had better ride back to the fort as quickly as possible, before they encountered any more of the raiders.

Their return journey was thankfully uneventful and each had cause to reflect on what had happened, with the realisation that all their training had paid off and they were unharmed, but that they had each taken a life. Not a pleasant thought, but entirely necessary at the time to rescue the women and uphold the code of chivalry expected of them, even when outnumbered, and they were happy with their actions. Word had been passed to Sir Ector and Sir Brastias well before they had entered the fort as the lookouts had seen the extra burdens on the horses, and they were there to greet them. Demanding to know what had happened as they took in the blood stained spears. Cador quickly related what had taken place and the action that they had taken, the women told of how they had been set upon and that if it had not been for the gallant lads they would not be there to talk about it now. Sir Brastias quickly sent word to gather thirty of his horsemen and bring his and Sir Ector's horse and set off to try and flush out any insurgents that were still roaming around and asked Cador to look after the women in the meantime.

The light was fading fast when the troop returned and by the odd wound that one or two of the men sported it was obvious that they had encountered the insurgents, but they appeared happy enough so it looked as if they had been successful. Sir Ector and Sir Brastias confirmed this once they had dismounted and their horses had been lead away. They had discovered a ship in the cove and set it adrift so cutting off escape for any that remained, then scoured the woods and surrounding area flushing out as many as they could, putting them to the sword. One group had put up a stiff resistance but were soon overcome, any that were left would have a long trek home unless they could find a boat, Sir Ector confirmed that they appeared to be mainly Saxons. He and Sir Brastias congratulated the boys on a splendid piece of work that was well thought out in the heat of the moment, and that they had put all their training to good use, but not to get carried away with their success because it would not always go to plan, things often never did.

Sir Ector was pleased with the boys progress and that their first real action had not gone to their heads, in fact it did not seem to affect them at all, they had just taken it in their stride. Taking them to Tintagel and introducing them to Cador had been a good move and he would continue with that even after Igraine had returned, which should be soon. Gwendolyn had been horrified when she first learned of Arthur's encounter from Sir Ector, but that was just normal motherly instinct that she had for him, even though she was not his real mother she had provided that necessary loving support. It would be hard when they eventually had to part, but she would be there whilst he needed her. Arthur and Kay continued their training in earnest before the days faded into winter again. Once a week they went to Tintagel and trained with Cador, but thankfully without any further incidents.

* * * * *

Merlin, Taliesin and the other Elders were busy in their areas trying to hold the peace together, and they were having a hard time of it with petty squabbles blowing up all over the place, but so far nothing major had occurred, even the Saxons were quiet and that was even more worrying. Perhaps they were biding their time and building up their forces, although no word had reached Merlin of any large scale influx from the continent. The Elders had convened a full council meeting which lasted three days and covered all aspects of the problems facing the country, from the external influences to the more important power manoeuvring that was taking place internally. All were aware that the fragile peace would not last, but there was no one strong enough to bind them together at the moment, so it was just a matter of time before anarchy reigned again, which would allow foreign usurpers to try and snatch power, or at least extend their influence.

* * * * *

Autumn passed quickly and winter arrived with a roar of violent winds, torrential rain and mountains of snow to grind the country to a standstill. Very little moved unless it was absolutely necessary, neither man nor beast forsook their shelter to venture out into the hostile world, and so peace prevailed a little longer across the land, and Merlin gave thanks for the small but welcome respite. The great mounds of snow slowly began to melt as spring nudged winter into forgotten history and the rivers swelled and overflowed onto the surrounding lands creating vast acres of lakes, transforming the landscape into new inland seas and drowning hamlets and ancient towns as if washing away bad memories. Nowhere in the country escaped natures revenge, it did not discriminate between Saxons or Britons, Picts or Celts, Jutes or Angles. It treated all with contempt as it scoured the land clean. Merlin viewed the whole catastrophe with mild humour, *no matter what mankind did Mother Nature would take her revenge, in her own time without warning, in a violent and unprecedented way causing much loss of life, yet always the animal kingdom would be aware beforehand and seek safety. The human race still had much to learn from the so called lesser intelligent species of this world, but would they, doubtful in the short term but possible eventually. At least the peace would last awhile yet as everyone from lord to serf would have too much to think about to salvage what they could, but then it would turn as each tried to recoup their loses. Another year closer to Arthur coming of age, and I am thankful of help from any quarter, however unexpected.*

* * * * *

The harvest was very poor that year as many of the fertile meadows had been swamped with so much water that they were unable to support the crops that would normally have been planted to provide winter food. Consequently the small amount that was gathered had to be fiercely protected by villages to ensure that they had something to help them through what could be a long and bitterly cold time, and attacks by marauding bands became a frequent occurrence. Village took up arms against village and neighbours attacked each other, even for the smallest amount of grain, and much blood was spilt as fear and greed spread like wildfire. The kings and lords of the regions were even worse as they had their armies to feed and sent their men out to seize and confiscate whatever they could find, irrespective of whose land it was, and soon they were fighting each other. Full scale campaigns were not possible as the scarcity of food would stretch them beyond their limits, so border raids became common place, before the weather made even those difficult. Hunting of game had to be done in force for protection from possible attack, but that was counter productive as the noise created by a large body of men soon frightened the animals into hiding. Many had moved their habitat before the flooding and were now more difficult to locate, especially for horsemen. Merlin's vision of anarchy and strife had begun, but this was only the tip of the iceberg, worse was to come as the weather tightened its grip on an already badly wounded country. Would it pull through and survive or would it fragment into thousands of tiny pieces and be at the mercy of the lurking vultures, waiting to pounce as the Island of Britain rolled over and died. Merlin and the Elders would do their best, but they were so few and without any real authority, they could only rely on their diplomacy and cunning.

* * * * *

The year passed into oblivion and with it many thousands of souls, either through hunger and cold or if they were lucky, quickly at the end of a sword or spear. Fear and unrest were spreading fast and violence thrust itself upon the land and endured throughout the year and into the following one, and now the Saxons were beginning to make inroads into new areas, either by force or coercion. Time was counting down to Arthur's coming of age, but would it be too little too late, was there just too much for one man to accomplish, especially at such a young age. Merlin hoped not, otherwise all their hard work would have been in vain, but he would need help and guidance to steer him on the right pathway and the Elders would do their best to provide that, until he was strong enough to stand on his own.

The southwest did not suffer as badly as the rest of the country as the atrocious weather had come down from the north and east and its intensity had lessened by the time it had reached the peninsular, but there was considerable flooding as the torrents of water flowed downstream. The supply of food was affected but not nearly as much as the rest of the country and there was an influx of game into the higher ground as the animals migrated to safer havens. Surprisingly there was little trouble from outsiders except on the more northerly and easterly borders, these were quickly repulsed as the population in this region tended to stick together and protect each other. Very little trouble occurred between neighbours, most being just minor squabbles that were soon resolved, as they were a different breed of people inhabiting these lands, they needed to be with the sea pounding them on both sides.

* * * * *

Cador became of age during this time and inherited his father's title of Duke of Cornwall and a great party was held at Tintagel in celebration and many attended from all parts of the region including the King of Cornwall. Naturally Kay and Arthur were there with Sir Ector and were introduced to so many prominent people that their heads buzzed with trying to remember all their names. Merlin had put in an appearance and so had Taliesin, it was too good an opportunity to miss to use their diplomacy and gauge the feeling and seek the thoughts of so many nobles. What they learned was promising and predictable, but this was only one small part of the country, concern was voiced for the well being and autonomy of their own region, but the nobles would consider working with the new High King when, and if, one was agreed upon. Until then they would fight for and defend their own territory against all comers, Saxon or Briton, and they were all strong in their resolve on this matter. Solidarity of one region at least was heartening news to both of them in these troubled times, and something they hoped to build on. The festivities lasted for three days during which time Merlin managed to speak with Igraine and discover how her two daughters were doing and Taliesin spent some time with Arthur and Kay recounting some of the many stories of his travels.

It was the talk of the villages for many weeks after and the boys spent many hours discussing who they had met and kept plying Sir Ector with questions on some of them that they thought were interesting characters. Even though Cador was now the Duke the visits to Tintagel continued as before, easing the burden on Sir Ector with the increased training schedule that the boys were undertaking. Learning more skills in the use of different weapons, horsemanship and care of their animals. Arthur was endeavouring to teach Kay and Cador how to see the aura created by the energy field around living creatures, by using their eyes differently, so that they could tell if an animal or human was suffering any ailment. They found this quite difficult at first but slowly started to have some success when Arthur emphasised that they should also go with their feelings and instincts and marry the two together. Later he encouraged them to try the same principal with flowers, trees and rocks as everything had this colourful haze around it, but was not as strong when there was little or no movement. Sir Cador and Kay were fascinated by this and spent many hours practising until they became proficient enough to be successful most times. Although as Arthur pointed out strong direct sunlight made it very difficult to see the haze and therefore was best done in subdued light. He also introduced them to the tell tale signs and sounds of the animals and birds and how to use them to their advantage as their acute senses would warn of danger long before they themselves were aware of it. Look and listen to their surroundings he instructed, as there was much useful information to be gleaned and it would heighten their senses and awareness and could save their life, even silence told them something and sharpened their instincts.

* * * * *

The year rolled on without any major incident in the region as the boys learned more and more of the ways of life and how they should conduct themselves. Visitors were frequent and they were gradually introduced to the finer points of etiquette expected of them in the social aspects of entertaining, both at home and when visiting other dignitaries. As usual they were quick learners and received many gracious compliments from their peers and it was particularly noted that they also showed respect to servants and those of lesser rank, and this found favour in many quarters. Igraine's eldest daughter Morgause became of age and a great party was held at Tintagel, which many attended. She seemed to have taken an obvious fancy to Arthur and spent some time in his company, which embarrassed him slightly, although he didn't understand why, as he was at ease with most people. Perhaps it was because she was a good looking woman in full bloom and those inner stirrings were awakening, as boy moved towards manhood, causing some confusion in his mind so that he wasn't sure how to react. Luckily Sir Ector intervened and saved him from further embarrassment by indicating that they really must go as he didn't wish to be on the road too late. Disappointed Morgause let him go, after extracting a promise that he would call on her on his next visit, which he agreed without thinking if it would be possible, as he felt entirely out of his depth for once.

A month later Kay became of age and Sir Ector hosted a party on his behalf and although on a smaller scale it was thoroughly enjoyed by everyone, and Arthur was half relieved to find that Morgause couldn't make it, as he hadn't seen her on the weekly visits to Tintagel, although Igraine attended as expected.

The year slipped quietly to a close with little chance of socialising after that. At least the weather had been kind of late and the harvest had eventually been fairly good and the troubles of the previous winter did not re-occur. Merlin and Taliesin were notable this time by their absence and it hadn't gone unnoticed by the boys or Sir Ector either, no doubt they had more pressing engagements. It was as well that they did not know the reasons as the south west regions were insulated from events in the rest of the country and went about their own business often ignorant of anything happening elsewhere.

* * * * *

Merlin was travelling the welsh kingdoms and was having a difficult job trying to keep the peace between the various kings fighting for position. His diplomacy was stretched to the limit and it was only because he was well respected there, as that was his homeland, that he was having any success at all. The biggest problem was keeping the northern kings from tearing out the throats of the southern kings, as there had always been great rivalry between the two, and at varying times a great deal of animosity. At the moment it was in the balance with just minor clashes but it was starting to look ugly, unless he could diffuse the situation.

Taliesin on the other hand was having just as much trouble with the kingdoms of southern Britain, but his problems were twofold, the infighting between kings and the Saxon encroachment into the lands. He was trying to convince them to stop fighting each other and join together against the slow Saxon advance, some were for and others against concerted action, especially if they were not directly affected. Taliesin politely pointed out that if they did nothing to help it would not be long before the Saxons would be at their door, and where would the help come from then. It was hard slow going trying to convince them and drum up enough enthusiasm to get a positive response, but he kept on, hoping to wear them down by his influence as he too was well respected in the area.

* * * * *

Winter meandered in to early spring and the Elders met for another full council and Merlin was reminded that Arthur would soon be of age, although Arthur had not yet asked anyone the date that he was born, it would only be a matter of time before he did. For once Merlin had forgotten the problems that this might cause if Arthur's correct date was used, as Igraine would possibly come to the conclusion that he might be her son, and ask awkward questions that could jeopardise the situation before he was ready. Merlin thought it best if it was closer to the annual King making council on the first of September and he would speak to Gwendolyn, Arthur's surrogate mother, and advise her of the need to move it for the lad's sake. Arthur needed to come to this ceremony as it was possible that it would be the time for the vision to be fulfilled. He would see to it that Sir Ector brought both Kay and Arthur, supposedly for the experience, let the cards be dealt and the hands played out, Merlin reflected. So it was agreed, and as the other matters concerning the state of the country and the Elders high profile diplomacy had been discussed, they dispersed and Merlin headed for Padstow and Tintagel.

* * * * *

On one of their frequent training visits to Tintagel Arthur had taken the opportunity, during a lull in their schedule, to take his horse out for a workout as it was a new animal that he was using now and he wished to bond with it and learn it's little quirks. His ride took him in the direction of the rock that he had mysteriously entered when a young lad and he thought it was time to pay another visit and maybe explore it a little more. To his consternation he noticed that tall thorn bushes had grown up around it, partially hiding its base and making it seem smaller than actually it was. Riding slowly around it he noticed several animal runs through the thorns and selecting one that was larger than the others he dismounted and laying on his stomach was able to crawl slowly through without getting ripped to shreds by the menacing spikes. There was just room to stand up close to the rock and edge carefully around it until he found the recess that he had used to enter it previously. Studying the rock he began to see the shimmering haze emanating a little way from the surface, and stretching out his hand to it he gently moved it backwards and forwards, allowing his energy to merge with that of the rock. Slowly he pushed his hand forward and just as before it appeared to disappear into the solid structure, and using a circular movement it widened the gap until first his shoulder then his body were through and he was standing in that cavern again. He sat down and allowed his eyes to adjust to the dim light that was coming from a multitude of places, not natural light but energy glowing faintly from ghostly objects scattered about the cave. A voice came into his head breaking the eerie silence and startling him, enquiring what had brought him back again. *What strange manner of things is this,* he thought, *am I dreaming, there is no one here,* to which the voice answered him saying that he, the guardian of the cave was here and reiterated his question. Arthur answered that he was intrigued by this place and how he had managed to enter it and now that he was older wished to see if he still could and maybe understand how it had happened.

"Then you have not come to steal the ancient treasures hidden here?" the voice replied.

"What treasures?" queried Arthur, "for I see nothing except dim lights glowing in the shadows," as he said this the light slowly increased, bringing into view a wondrous assortment of weapons and strange looking objects that he had never seen before.

"All this," the voice indicated, "that has been hidden here for many a long year under my guardianship, but no one has ever returned to lay claim to any of it, and that is a pity. You are one of the few," the voice continued, "that has the ability to enter here and therefore you must have some blood of the Elder race in you from somewhere in the past. I see great things for you Arthur in your life ahead, but fear that like so many your human side will let you down at some point and it will be your undoing."

"Who are you?" questioned Arthur, "that you know my name, but I do not know yours."

"In my time here I was known as Eudaf Hen, King of Ewyas and Lord of the Gewisse, also known as Octavius the Old in some quarters. Before that I had many names but none would be familiar to you as they were so long ago and go back to the time of the Elder race."

Arthur replied that he had heard many tales of his exploits and some said that he was the first real High King of Britain.

"That is an exaggeration," Eudaf replied, "as I was only the Overlord of the southern kingdoms. My son-in-law, Magnus Maximus, who succeeded me became the first High King of all Britain, and most of the High Kings since have descended from my blood line."

Arthur wanted to know more about what lay ahead of him in his life but the voice was not forthcoming as he said that he was not at liberty to go into detail but that there were two items in the cave that would be of use to him in the future, and that he would know the time to use them. They were made of material that would be unknown to him, Eudaf said, but would serve their purpose admirably although he would need to keep them covered and hidden until that time and should not mention to anyone where they came from.

"The secret of this cave and its location must remain hidden from all until such a time as you might have a need for it, but remember only one with blood of the Elder race in them can enter here. I will dim the light and you will find the items by your feet for it is time for you to leave, always follow your instincts and you will rarely go wrong, let your light shine forth, good luck and god speed on your journey."

Arthur thanked him as the light dimmed and he heard a gentle thud of something landing by his feet, gathering the items up he stood and turned, letting his eyes adjust and focus on the rock face to find his exit in the same way that he had entered. Once outside he surveyed what was in his arm that he had kept close to his body as he pushed himself through the opening. A covered shield in a different shape to what he was used to and a roll of some type of white material whose texture he did not know. Under the prickly thorns he crawled again to where his horse was grazing contentedly on the lush grass. Slinging the shield on his back and stuffing the roll of material in his tunic he unfolded his cape, that he had left on his saddle, and put it around himself to hide the shield from view. His return to Tintagel was uneventful and he found a safe place to hide the shield in the stable until they left for Padstow a little later.

Merlin arrived unexpectedly the following day whilst the boys were out training with Sir Ector and he took the opportunity to seek out Gwendolyn and speak to her in private. She was pleased to see him as the thought of Arthur's coming of age had been on her mind recently and she was not sure what to say if asked, knowing the secrecy surrounding his birth. Merlin gave her instructions, including the date that she was to quote, and he would speak to Sir Ector because much would be happening around that time and it would not be possible to have a party here. He also spoke to her in confidence about the role that she had played in Arthur's upbringing and thanked her for all her efforts and that on or shortly after his coming of age it was most likely that his birth mother's name would become common knowledge. She reminded him that she had accepted that at the very beginning of the relationship with Arthur and was prepared for it. But it was nice that he had given her forewarning of the likely hood of it occurring in the near future, so that she would not be taken by surprise when it happened. As they finished speaking the trio returned and catching sight of Merlin the boys gave a whoop of joy and rode over to him shouting that it was good to see him and not to leave before they had finished seeing to their horses.

"Don't worry," he laughed, "I shall still be here as I have much to speak to Sir Ector about, so do not rush your chores, otherwise you will be waiting around for some while before I am finished and can listen to your tales." They departed in a flurry and Sir Ector invited Merlin to come and join him in some refreshment, which he gratefully accepted, whilst he brought him up to date on events in the land.

They spent several hours in conversation and eventually the topic turned to Arthur's coming of age, Sir Ector had been waiting to speak to Merlin about this for some time as something had held him back from mentioning it to Gwendolyn or even Arthur. Merlin said that he was pleased that he had waited as it was a delicate situation after all, but it would have been alright to approach Gwendolyn about it as she had been expecting an inquiry, but never mind as that was hindsight. Merlin mentioned the King making council on the first of September and requested that Sir Ector should attend as he thought that this year they might get a result and that he should take Sir Kay and Arthur with him, for the experience. As it was only two days after Arthur's coming of age he thought an initial party should be held for him at Silchester, as he was inviting Igraine and Sir Cador to the event as well, followed by one later on their return here. Sir Ector thought about this for a moment then queried the need for them to go in the first place. Merlin had anticipated this and said that if the new King was chosen, then he would require all the show of support that he could get to make his position tenable, and that was what the country needed at the moment, a strong High King. Sir Ector saw the logic of this and agreed but thought that Arthur might not be too happy about celebrating his coming of age in a strange place. Well, said Merlin lets ask him as he saw the boys lurking in the shadows, waiting to join them, and he waved them over. Arthur jumped at the opportunity as he had never been that far a field and didn't really mind where it was, but asked that his mother could come as well to make it a proper family gathering. *Good lad,* thought Merlin, *that saves me the problem of persuading Sir Ector to take her along, without raising any suspicions.* They both agreed that in the circumstances she should accompany them, and the talk then turned to the boys exploits since they had last seen Merlin, but Arthur never mentioned the cave or what he had been given, as he always kept his word.

Merlin departed two days later and made for Tintagel to see Igraine and persuade her to attend the King making council. She thought it would be good experience for her son, the new Duke, to be seen by the other lords from around the country and she would leave her eldest daughter Morgause in charge of the fort jointly with the Duke's battle chief. That would keep her daughter in order and give her some sense of responsibility that sometimes she seemed to be lacking, but keep her reigned in to some extent as even she did not argue with Sir Brastias. So it was settled, she would travel with Sir Ector and his party as they would call en-route to collect them and whatever escort she felt that she required. Merlin was pleased as all the major players were being brought together at the same place and the same time and something should certainly happen, hopefully for the best, but only time would tell. The next part of his vision was getting stronger all the while, soon it would be time for Arthur to stake his claim and make his mark with all the dithering and self centred lords and kings. It promised to be a most interesting time, but Merlin needed to see that Arthur could generate the required support for one so young, so he must continue his travels, and shortly took his leave of Igraine.

* * * * *

Summer was upon them and this was the time of year that Arthur and Kay revelled in as although the training had become quite strenuous they had the light evenings to relax in and often these days Sir Cador visited them and joined in their merriment. Weekly visits were still being made to Tintagel to break the monotony of the same location, but Arthur had still not paid a call on Igraine's daughter Morgause as he had promised, mainly because they were always on the go, but also because he was unsure how to handle her. The situation was about to be taken out of his hands however, as a week before they were due to leave for Silchester and the King making council Arthur felt that his horse was not quite right whilst training at Tintagel and said to the others that he was going to take him back to the stables and give him a good going over to try and find out what the problem might be, and that he would rejoin them later.

Stripped to his waist he had washed his horse down and given him a good brushing and was studying his animal's aura to detect what area might be causing him a problem, when a voice startled him. Turning around he found Morgause starring at him with a mischievous sparkle in her eyes, commenting that this was where he hid out when he could be calling on her. He was lost for words again, not knowing what to say, and could only mutter an incoherent reply as she purposely stepped forward, sure in the knowledge that she had him where she wanted him and he would do her bidding without a murmur. She ran her hand seductively across his chest, whispering with a fiery passion that he had a beautiful manly body and it was a shame to waste it. Arthur was totally mesmerised and he appeared frozen to the spot as she brought her body into contact with his. Her thrusting breasts almost spilling out on to his bare chest as she pushed her groin against his, gyrating her hips slowly as she teased him, then gave him a long passionate kiss. She took his hand and placed it on her bosom gently rubbing herself with it. Arthur seemed transfixed as if in another world as all sorts of feelings rushed through his body, nice feelings and total confusion together, but all out of his control. Kissing him passionately again she slipped her hand between his legs and felt his passion rising and throbbing to her touch, sending a thrill of delight right through her body at the realisation of the monster she had released. This really was some man she thought with genuine surprise, as she gently pushed him to the ground and removed his breeches with a gasp of pure pleasure. She was hot for him and Arthur could do nothing, he was so totally mesmerised he seemed unable to move as she quickly removed her skirts, straddled him and impaled herself on his passion with a cry of ecstasy that reverberated right through her body. Morgause rode him like a stallion, hard and fast, until she could hold her passion in check no longer and as she exploded in a sea of immense pleasure again and again Arthur's thunderbolt hit her insides and she cried out in pure delight. She slowed, but was determined to make the most of the situation whilst Arthur had lost his senses and unhooked her bodice letting her heaving breasts spill out, little rivers of sweat running down the valley and gently on to his body. Taking Arthur's hands she rubbed herself with them until she felt his passion rise in her again, matching her own swelling desires, and rode him hard again until they both exploded together in pure sexual ecstasy.

Arthur by now had begun to regain control of himself and was thoroughly enjoying his induction to the pleasures of a sexual encounter, but was determined not to let this lady keep control of the situation, he must show her who was in command. As she slowed her gyrations Arthur took her by surprise and rolled her over and began to kiss her passionately and caress her breasts until she started to moan with pleasure, then he mounted her and coupled with her forcing her buttocks into the hard damp earth with each deep thrust of his passion. She moaned and groaned and exploded in pleasure time after time but Arthur still kept on until he could contain himself no longer and his passion exploded like an erupting volcano that caused her whole body to shake and an intense sigh escaped from her lips.

They both rested for a moment and Morgause managed to whisper asking him if he would stop if a lady asked him to and he replied, with a smile on his face that of course he would, and then started to kiss and caress her again and thrust deep into her as his passion returned again. He kept this up for another hour, happy that he had taken control of the situation at last (unbeknown to him, just what his father would have done) until Morgause could take no more and cried out for him to stop, and being a gentleman he did. She wanted to know why he had not stopped before, and his reply was that she only asked if, not a will you please, so he thought she was quite happy to carry on. Morgause realised that Arthur had turned the tables on her, but what a man, she was glad that she had ensnared him even though he had eventually taken control, no man had done that to her before, nor performed like he had, she would certainly remember this encounter for a long while. They dressed swiftly and Morgause determined to get the last word at least, told him that what he had just experienced was his coming of age present, to be seduced by a real woman. Arthur, smiling and not to be outdone told her that now she new what a real man was like, as he turned to his horse to continue looking for the problem that he was in the process of doing before he was so nicely interrupted. Morgause was fuming, knowing that even at the end Arthur had defeated her and she stormed off thinking that one day she would get her revenge and better Arthur, one way or another.

GORDON ETHERINGTON

Chapter 7

MERLIN'S PROPHECY FULFILLED

ALL THE ELDERS had been touring around their regions of responsibility trying to persuade as many of the kings and lords as they could to go to Silchester this year for the King making council, as it promised to be something different. When challenged on this, all they would say was that indications were that a new High King would be found, as Merlin had prophesised. This little bit of intrigue aroused the curiosity of many, but some were still not convinced, or if it be known, not bothered, as they had been left to their own devices the past few years and were more than happy with the situation as it was. Still, sow the seed and see what happened, was how the Elders viewed it, as curiosity often got the better of the human race and should ensure a good turn out. Merlin was concerned that even if Arthur should show his hand by some means or other, would he receive enough support or would he have to fight for the right to be King. One never knew in those situations, but his birthright would be there for all to see if he had the opportunity to remove the sword from the stone, he would make sure that circumstances arose that would give him the chance. Arthur's age would be the problem, but what he had seen and heard from Sir Ector indicated that he had been trained well enough to cope with that, and there wasn't much more that could be done anyway, time was too short.

The Elders had kept in touch with each other through their normal telepathic communications and it looked as if the turnout would be good, even if a little volatile, due to the recent disputes between several of the kingdoms. There was an unwritten law at these councils that no major conflict should be entertained in its vicinity or surrounding area, even if fatal clashes should occur between individuals whilst there, and this had always been adhered to by the British Nobility. The Britons nearly always stuck to the rules, written or otherwise, even when other nations didn't, and although a good principle to uphold was often their undoing unfortunately, but in that respect they stood apart from others and were proud of their heritage. This was one of the many reasons why the Elders had given so much of their time and effort over many generations to such a relatively small country. One that could one day change the destiny of the world if they persevered, and helped bring peace to all mankind in the process. There were still many centuries to go however before that had a possibility of occurring, the important thing in the meantime was to help the likes of Arthur move this nation into a period of peace and stability, and hopefully build on that for the future. Much would depend on his resolve and strength of character to bring that about, but Merlin and the Elders were quietly confident in his ability to succeed, even though the cards would be stacked against him in the beginning.

* * * * *

In the west final preparations were being made for the long trek to Silchester, Kay and Arthur had been detailed to check the horses and make sure that there were enough provisions for the journey for all that were going. They would travel fairly light, but well armed, with a troop of only fifty horsemen drawn from the area around Padstow and Tintagel, as neither Sir Ector nor the Lady Igraine wished to leave the region under defended, even though a concerted attack from outsiders was unlikely. Sir Brastias, Igraine's battle chief and senior knight, would act as constable for the area whilst her daughter Morgause would look after the social and domestic running of the fort. Morgause had ignored Arthur since their passionate encounter in the stables, which he found quite amusing as it showed the shallow aspect of her character and how she attempted to use people by bestowing sexual favours on them. *A woman to beware of unless you were strong enough to counter her advances and then she would probably find a way to ensnare you if you weren't on your guard,* he thought, *I will not have to worry about that for several weeks as she was staying behind, which she appeared none too happy about for some reason.* Kay's voice brought him back to reality, asking him if he was ready as they were moving out on their long journey to Silchester.

* * * * *

Across many parts of the country heavily armed groups were making their way slowly towards Silchester. Some had a great distance to travel and had already been on the road sometime, whilst others were just starting out, but all were glad of the legacy that the Romans had left behind of many good straight roads crisscrossing the land. The majority of the British nobility were on the move towards the King making council, some still determined to prove themselves as a contender for the High Kingship and others just out of idle curiosity, intrigued by the Elder's comment that this year might be special. Even the northern kings and some from the isles were making the long journey south, only some from the northern welsh kingdoms appeared to be missing, which had been expected. Surprisingly none encountered any hostilities on the way, everywhere seemed peaceful, or was it just an illusion, the lull before the storm as hostile forces made their preparations and plans for battle. None knew, but many were unsettled by the eerie calm and general feeling of foreboding that was in the air. It was too quiet and peaceful and that spelt trouble, somewhere and sometime in the not too distant future violence would raise its ugly head again.

* * * * *

Kay and Arthur were enjoying their travels, seeing new places, listening to stories recounted by their travelling companions and no training schedule to think about. This was the life they joked, total freedom and not a care in the world but still wise enough to know, even in their youth, that this was just a brief respite in what was likely to be a volatile existence fraught with danger and intrigue. They stopped at Glastonbury and were introduced to the bishop and were shown around the Abbey church, then took prayers with him, which Arthur found a moving experience. He asked many questions of the bishop in the short stop that they made and was given clear answers on the role of the church and how Joseph of Arimathea had arrived on those very shores and set up the first Christian church in Britain at Glastonbury. How that had begun to change people's thinking and was influencing, for the better, the way of life of many souls. The bishop suggested that during his life he should always be firm but fair, uphold justice and right, show mercy and compassion, help the poor and listen to other's points of view before making decisions and acting on them. He would not always be popular by following what he had advised, stated the bishop, but he would earn respect and trust and people would listen to his words of wisdom. Arthur thanked him as they departed and said he would give his words much thought and try and live by that sound advice in word and deed. The bishop replied that he would not regret it and as they moved off he had a thoughtful expression on his face as he watched Arthur disappear from view, an inner insight perhaps on a young man that was going to have an exceptional life and leave his mark on society. One that would be spoken of throughout many lands for his deeds and valour, a man of the people, for the people, renowned for the peace and prosperity that he brought to his country.

They made their way to Bratton Castle for the next overnight stop, then east to Sidbury the following day and finally to Beacon Hill, where it had been decided to rest for a day before the final leg of their journey to Silchester. They were in plenty of time as the King making council was still five days away, and from their vantage point on Beacon Hill they could see the settlement of Silchester not a dozen miles away shimmering gently in haze of the afternoon sun.

Many people were already gathering for the council and more arrived each day as kings from distant parts set up camp for their entourage in the surrounding area. Merlin and Taliesin were busy checking on the arrivals to see who was still missing of those that they expected to turn up. The major surprise was that King Lot of Lothian and Orcanie had shown up, as he was known to keep himself to himself and not meddle or be concerned with what other kingdoms were up to. Merlin welcomed him and expressed his surprise that Lot had ventured so far south when he was not known for travelling far afield. He laughingly replied that the comment that Ganieda the Elder had made intrigued him and aroused his curiosity. Merlin Emrys had indicated that this year's King making council might be different and his prophecy could be fulfilled, so here he was old man to see if he could deliver, and with that he wandered off still laughing to himself.

Taliesin meanwhile had discovered Sir Ector's and Lady Igraine's camp and was busy as usual answering questions from Arthur and Kay as to what he had been up to since they last saw him, which gave Merlin the opportunity to slip in unseen and speak to Igraine privately, before joining them. Merlin also had to recount the story of his travels, as soon as the two young men spotted him, and Sir Ector, Gwendolyn, Lady Igraine and Sir Cador joined them to hear to his story. Quite a crowd had gathered to listen to his colourful tales by the time that Merlin had paused saying that was enough for the moment, turning to Arthur he reminded him that the following day he would come of age and asked him if he had any plans for the future. Arthur looked surprised and glanced across at Gwendolyn for confirmation, who smiled and nodded in reply. He said he had forgotten all about it on their travels to Silchester, as for plans he had none other than to follow his heart along whatever pathway life directed him to take, and to take note of the bishop's advice that he had been given at Glastonbury.

"Whatever life has in store for me I will deal with to the best of my ability along the way and pray to God that I make the right choices for all concerned," he answered in a gentle voice uttered from the heart.

Merlin had been smiling to himself and nodding his head as if in agreement as Arthur made his little speech, then he broke the silence that had descended on them all by suggesting that they celebrate. Then tomorrow visit the other camps and meet some of the distinguished kings and lords whilst they were gathered in one place. Everyone agreed that it was the best idea that they had heard in a long time and the party began, lasting well into the night, with many attracted by the noise and wondering what was going on, coming over to their camp and joining in on hearing that it was Arthur's coming of age.

Needless to say there were quite a few sore heads in the morning and the camp was late to stir as a consequence. There was a hive of activity all around them, the numbers that had gathered had swelled during the night and early morning as more arrivals poured in looking for a space to set up camp. Merlin and Taliesin were not to be seen as they had risen early as usual and were doing their rounds, checking the newcomers and noting who was still missing from their expected list. A good turn out they agreed as there was still two days to go to the council meeting and all the main participants that they were sure would attend had arrived, plus some that they did not expect. Obviously the Elder's comment had sufficiently aroused the curiosity of even the most uninterested and distant kings. Merlin was asked several times at various encampments what magik he was going to conjure up to produce a new High King, to which he replied that he needed no magik as the true born king would reveal himself in the manner that he had prophesied, and all of the congregation would bear witness to his claim. When a prophecy was made, he added, it could not be changed or undone by anyone, it could only be fulfilled as decreed, and this year the time was right for that to happen. Everything that happened did so at its appointed time and they had reached that point, was his parting comment as he moved on scouring the masses for faces that he knew and wished to speak to.

Sir Ector, and the Lady Igraine spent the day renewing old acquaintances and being introduced to others, Arthur and Kay went along with them as they knew a few of the people, but so many names to remember in one go, it was a daunting experience. It was surprising how many people seemed to know Lady Igraine, even just by name, as few had met her and then often just in passing when visiting her husband Gorlois, before his untimely death. It was a man's world and the women tended to stay in the background most of the time, only being seen at social functions and tournaments. Surprisingly she got on well with King Lot when introduced to him, and invited him to Tintagel before he returned home after the council meeting. He seemed quite taken aback by this generosity and readily accepted, as most kept their distance from him due to his known unruly and sometimes hot headed temperament. Perhaps this reminded her of her late husband as their characters were very similar in that respect, although Lot was much younger than Gorlois.

The day drew on and even though many introductions had been made they hadn't covered the whole gathering and Arthur and Kay were feeling quite mentally exhausted at the end of it, as they were not used to such a long period of what they classed as inactivity. They much preferred physical exertion and being out and about on horse, as against saying the same thing over and over again to different groups of people. However they were both astute enough to know that at times it was necessary if they were to get to know others well. Merlin and Taliesin rejoined them at camp in the evening, indicating that their day had been interesting and that they were very pleased with the number of people that had gathered for the King making council. As Merlin emphasised it was always of great benefit to have the majority of interested parties at events such as this, as the more people that could physically see the result made it much easier to be accepted as genuine and not just engineered by a select few for their own benefit.

Arthur was interested in what would take place at the council meeting, so Merlin outlined the proceedings and added that they would all be there to see for themselves who removed the sword from the stone. It promised to be an interesting time and not all would be happy with the result, but such was the way of life, it was rare to get unanimous approval from all the kings, whatever was being proposed. They all had their own agendas and were not used to working together as one, each had their own power base of which they were fiercely protective, and they were not inclined to tolerate outside interference, as they saw it, in the running of their kingdoms. It was a short sighted view and many of those kingdoms changed hands frequently as they were continually warring with each other over minor matters. The Romans had used this to their advantage when they took over this land and the Saxons would do the same, unless the kingdoms stood together under one High Kingship and pushed them back into the sea from where they came. Time was running out my friends, therefore his prophecy would be fulfilled this year, one way or another and the new High King would reveal himself and lead this country into a time of peace and prosperity. Creating a new era of understanding that would change the way of thinking in the world.

Igraine asked him the question that was on everyone's mind, did he know who the new High King would be. Merlin smiled as he confirmed that all the Elders knew and had for many years, but it would only be revealed at the right time, by the High King himself, not by any of them in advance. Igraine was very thoughtful as she followed up her question by asking if the new High King already knew of his destiny. Merlin's reply was deliberately vague, indicating that it was possible but unlikely, and he had not sought to read his mind lately as some things were best left alone to avoid any undue influence taking a hand.

The group were fascinated by this revelation as they would see history being made right there in front of them, totally unaware of the reason behind Igraine's pointed questions, but that no doubt would become apparent to them later. Igraine expressed her thanks to Merlin that he had been so forthcoming in his answers and that she looked forward to the coming council meeting with renewed interest. Merlin bowed his head in acknowledgement, knowing that she had understood exactly what he had meant and pleased that she had raised the topic in open forum so all were aware that something out of the ordinary was likely to happen.

Arthur and Kay were totally enthralled by the conversation and it seemed to put in perspective for them all the wanderings of the day, meeting all those different people and that somewhere amongst them was the new High King, and he would soon be revealed to them. Their excitement grew and they understood now why a lot of those that they met during the day had been in a buoyant mood, the anticipation was growing as the day and time drew closer, and the fact that Merlin had promised a result this year. They too looked forward to the coming event with great interest and wished it was the following day, but alas no, there was still another day to go before history was made.

The final day seemed to drag, although they still had some other camps to visit, but Arthur and Kay managed to slip away in the late afternoon on their own to look at Silchester itself. Hoping to get a glimpse of the sword in the stone, but their way was barred by guards who turned them back.

"Never mind we will come back and get it tomorrow, if it isn't stolen whilst you sleep tonight," they jested as they rode off back into the town proper.

Back at the camp Merlin had found Sir Ector on his own and decided that he should make his friend aware of some of the things that were likely to happen the following day, so that everything did not come as a complete shock to him. He explained about Uther, Igraine and Arthur and what the Elders had decided as the best course of action to take to protect all those involved, and mentioned the healing sanctuary at Lydney and Gwendolyn's part in it all. He apologised for not being able to say anything beforehand, even to such a good and trusted friend as him but the Elders view was that total secrecy was needed to protect Arthur and those around him from any possible harm, and it still had to remain secret until the sword was removed from the stone. Sir Ector was taken totally by surprise at these revelations and was speechless for a moment as it all sunk in, the fact that he had been bringing up the future High King of Britain in total ignorance. Then he wanted to know why he himself had been chosen for this 'fostering' role and why so close to his birth mother anyway. Merlin responded that he had been chosen because he was the best knight to teach Arthur all that he needed to know, and that being so close to his mother was the last place anybody would think to look if wind of his existence had ever leaked out.

"You my friend," Merlin reinforced, "had the best credentials, and your part of the country was away from the main trouble areas allowing you to concentrate on teaching your son and Arthur what they needed to know, to prepare them for life in the best possible way. I am sorry that we could not let you into the secret before, Igraine knows I am sure, by her questions yesterday, that her son is here, but she has no idea who he is and she has waited all these years to be re-united with him after that difficult sacrifice she made long ago. It will also come as a shock to Arthur as he has only known Gwendolyn as his mother, and has not been told otherwise. She is aware and has accepted that his mother will be made known soon but she is not aware of Arthur's pedigree, that will come as a complete surprise to her even though she knows he is of noble birth outside of wedlock. There my friend, as you see there is much that will come to the surface tomorrow, and you will understand the necessity for total secrecy, thankfully that has been preserved over these long and difficult years."

"But he is so young for this responsibility," commented Sir Ector, "how will he be accepted, if at all?"

"We do not know the answer to that one," answered Merlin, "we can only hope and pray, but from what I have seen and heard from you he is capable enough for the difficult task at hand and with support from his friends he will make it work. The problem I have at the moment is how to get him to draw the sword from the stone and I might need your help in this matter, as although he is of age he is not a knight or a lord and therefore not on the official list of those entitled to try. Although that does not disqualify him as all are entitled to have a go. It would obviously be best if I were not seen to interfere in any way by influencing the choice of participants or use any method that others could class as devious, purely to fulfil my prophecy. When it is your turn to try the sword, make sure that Kay and Arthur accompany you, offer Kay the opportunity after you and then Arthur, that would be acceptable to all the others as it would be the normal family way through the male line of succession."

"Yes I see the problem," Sir Ector replied, "but as you say that is the normal way and would get round it nicely, and something the lads would look forward to irrespective of the outcome, and talking of them here they come by the sound of it."

Two horses flashed into camp neck and neck and pulled up sharply in front of the two men as two bodies flew in the air and landed on their feet in front of Merlin and Sir Ector.

"Well who won?" they asked together.

The men laughed and Merlin said, "no one as you even talk at the same time, its got to be a draw again, now when you have seen to the horses you can tell us what you have been up to."

Some while later they returned and related to the gathering what they had seen in the town and that they had tried to see the sword in the stone, but guards kept them away, so they jested with them and said they would come back tomorrow and collect it if it was still there. Sir Ector and Merlin exchanged glances at this totally innocent comment that held so much truth in it. Sir Ector informed them that they would get their chance to remove it from the stone when it was his turn.

"That's great," muttered Kay, "we can show it to the guards on the way out," and everyone burst out laughing and that set the scene for the evening, laughing and joking and listening to tales of old from Merlin and Taliesin.

Arthur requested that they hear some of the stories concerning Eudaf Hen and Magnus Maximus and they listened intently well into the night to the exploits of those two great leaders, as they gathered around their camp fire.

The day of the King making council dawned and there was soon a hive of activity all around the camp sites as people prepared themselves for the big event, which would start at noon in the great church hall. Merlin and Taliesin had left early as usual as they had much to do they said, they would see them all at the great hall later. Everyone sorted out their best attire to wear and made sure that their weapons were clean and shining for this was as much a social event as it was a serious council gathering, and everyone was keen to show their status and importance by the robes they wore.

Soon there was much movement across the area as small groups of nobles headed for the town and its church, others would follow later as they would have to take up position outside as dictated by their lower rank, whilst the main body of escorts would remain in camp. Sir Ector together with Sir Kay, Arthur, Gwendolyn, Lady Igraine and Sir Cador were amongst the first to arrive at the great hall, their stable lad who had accompanied them would look after the horses during the proceedings and see that they were watered and fed, as it promised to be a long day. Taliesin saw them enter and hurried over to welcome them and usher them towards Merlin, who was deep in conversation with the bishop. On seeing them said something to the bishop and waved indicating that they should join him. Merlin made the introductions to Bishop Dyfrig, also known as Dubricius in some quarters and said that if any disputes arose from the council gathering his word would be the law in settlement of the matter, as if laid before God himself.

The hall was beginning to fill up now so they took their leave and moved to one side as others approached the bishop for introduction by Merlin and Taliesin, and Arthur and Kay watched to see how many faces they could remember amongst the new arrivals, alas not many. Soon the gathering was complete and Merlin called for their attention to explain the procedure that would follow before handing over to Bishop Dyfrig to lead them in prayer. The Bishop blessed the congregation and prayed for a successful outcome to what was about to take place and reminded everyone of the benefits of supporting a new High King, whatever their personal feelings, if they wished to protect the country from usurpers. United they would prevail, divided they would crumble and disintegrate, one at a time, and this land would be lost forever. With those strong words he handed back to Merlin, who led them out into the large walled courtyard with its stone centrepiece from which protruded the hilt of the Sword of Britain, gently moving in the breeze, catching the sun's rays and sending darts of light all around the faces staring at it. Many had seen it before but for some this was their first glimpse of this famous sword and always produced gasps of awe from the newcomers, including Sir Kay, Arthur and Sir Cador. Although only partly visible it was still magnificent to behold, even Lady Igraine was moved when she saw it again, such was its majestic splendour.

Merlin spoke and said he would call them forward one at a time to try and remove the sword and each would be allowed the same amount of time as shown by his magik light stick. The crystal ball at its top would start as white when he rubbed it and gradually go through various colours until it got to red, then it would go out and time would be up. He stuck the staff firmly in the ground and called the first name, a minor lord from one of the welsh kingdoms, and when he was ready rubbed the crystal and started the light display. Arthur and Kay were fascinated as Merlin had never shown them this on his visits, they weren't watching the attempt at removing the sword, just fascinated by the crystal changing colour. Many tried and failed to remove the sword but Arthur and Kay couldn't say how many as they were so intent on watching the crystal. They were brought out of their mesmerised state by voices being raised complaining that it was taking so long and Merlin's reassuring voice saying that everyone would have their turn until someone removed the sword. Arthur and Kay started to take an interest in the various methods of trying to release the sword, from one handed to two handed and even a father and son trying at the same time until they were politely told that it was not allowed, only one person at a time as only one could be High King if successful.

The complaining voice at the back of the crowd had started again and was pushing himself to the front when Sir Ector was called forward, and motioning to Kay and Arthur they walked out into the centre. Just as Merlin was about to rub the crystal a giant of a man pushed himself to the front amidst great complaining, that subsided quickly when they saw his size. He strode purposely towards the sword, pushing Sir Ector and Kay to the ground as he muttered 'out of my way,' this needs a man. Sir Ector fell awkwardly on his shoulder and was obviously in pain. Kay jumped to his feet to help his father, trying to draw his sword at the same time to attack the giant.

Arthur moved forward and raised his hand towards Kay, "leave this to me Kay, see to your father as he appears to be hurt,"

Merlin was going to intervene and was just about to speak when he saw Arthur start to take a hand and stopped himself and decided to watch what developed. The giant was trying with all his strength to remove the sword when Arthur's voice cut into his exertions.

"Sir Knight are you always so rude and arrogant? You are a disgrace to your title."

The crowd gasped at this, a young lad throwing down a challenge to this giant who must have been a foot taller and very much broader, just plain madness they thought to throw his life away, even for the sake of honour and chivalry. The guards in the courtyard looked towards Merlin for advice but he shook his head for them to stay put, at which they breathed a sigh of relief.

The giant of a knight turned and surveyed the voice that had accosted him and laughed, "go home lad whilst you still can, or I'll run you through," and turned back to try and remove the sword again.

Arthur's voice cut through him again, "is that what you do Sir Knight, kill young lads and old men and women? If so you are not only a disgrace to your title and family, but you are also a barbarian."

The crowd groaned at this as they could see bloodshed very quickly happening, and the end of this lad.

Arthur's last comment was like a knife in the ribs to the giant and he turned and drew his sword and advanced towards him.

"Time has run out for you lad after that vicious comment, not that I will have pleasure in dispatching one so young, but with you I will make an exception."

Arthur stood his ground and drew his sword, and as the giant made his move he countered the blow and moved in to the attack, slicing into material but missing his body. This shook the giant and he realised that the lad knew what he was about and he better be wary. The clashing of blades, as attack and counter attack moved them around the courtyard, reverberated around the walls. The crowd became enthralled as Arthur held his own against this giant and at times forced him to back off, but now and then they had to get out of the way for fear of losing their own heads. The giant had begun to realise that he had certainly met his match with this lad, who showed no fear as he attacked or countered and he obviously had complete confidence in his own ability, and that was worrying. They had been fighting for some while when Arthur ducked from a particularly vicious swing and turning quickly caught the giant with a blow in the side, which drew blood. This infuriated him and he renewed his attack on Arthur with even greater force which was met with equal force, then luck turned against Arthur, as in one almighty clash his sword went spinning out of his hand to land at the giant's feet.

"Now my lad what are you going to do without your sword? Come and get it if you want so that I can slice your ears off."

"You have me at a disadvantage at the moment Sir Knight as you have both swords and I have none."

"If you need a sword lad then use the one behind you, if you are man enough to remove it," replied the giant with a great laugh, referring to the sword in the stone.

That's an idea, thought Arthur, *if I back towards the stone so that the giant moves forward then my sword will be behind him and if I vault the stone I might be able to run around and retrieve it before he realises what I am doing.* Slowly Arthur backed towards the stone until he came to rest against it and as expected the giant moved forward, wary in case he had another weapon. Arthur saw that his sword was a good distance behind the giant now and waited for a moment until he saw him relax slightly, then he turned quickly, saw the energy vibrating gently around the sword in the stone as he grasped it and vaulted agilely over the obstacle. Landing lightly on his feet the other side he shot around the rock to gather up his sword before the giant had time to react fully.

The giant was astounded as one minute Arthur was there then he was gone, realisation dawned on him as to what he was up to, at the same time that he noticed that the sword in the stone was missing. It can't be, he thought, that's impossible, and swung around as Arthur came haring round from behind the rock, sword in hand.

The giant dropped to one knee and pushing the point of his sword into the ground cried out in a loud voice, "I yield my lord."

Arthur stopped dead in his tracks, halfway to his sword, and saw the giant on one knee head bowed.

"I am no lord Sir Knight, just Arthur the squire."

"No sire, by the grace of our Lord you are Arthur, High King of Britain, you hold the Imperial Sword of Britain in your hand and I Sir Bors will not raise my sword against my King. I humbly beg forgiveness for the error of my ways sire, and place myself at your mercy"

Arthur had not realised that he had the sword in his hand, so intent was he on retrieving his own sword, but there it was for all to see. Nobody else had seen it either until that moment, as they were all engrossed in the enthralling fight and Arthur's dash for his sword.

"Arise Sir Bors, you are forgiven, you fight well but I must teach you some manners, and I will be a hard task master, otherwise who knows what trouble you will end up in." Arthur said laughingly.

The crowd had just begun to realise that Arthur indeed held the Imperial Sword of Britain in his hand when Merlin's loud voice cut across everyone.

"The prophecy of Merlin Emrys the Elder has been fulfilled, behold, King Arthur the first born son of Uther Pendragon and the true-born High King of all Britain"

Chapter 8
ARTHUR – HIGH KING OF BRITAIN

MERLIN'S WORDS BROUGHT A TOTAL SILENCE to the crowd as the full import of what he cried out sank in, then everyone started talking at once and wanted to know what happened as none had seen Arthur remove the sword from the stone, only that it had ended up in his hand somehow. A chant soon arose that questioned Arthur's success and wanted to see it done properly so that all could witness it, but Merlin said that it might not be possible as the prophecy had been fulfilled correctly the first time and therefore he could not repeat it.

Arthur was deep in thought, and had moved back towards the great stone and was studying the energy field around it, remembering how he had entered the cave and spoke with Eudaf Hen. The crowd were getting agitated and calling Merlin a false prophet and mystic when Arthur made his decision and called aloud to the gathering that it would be done. Whereupon he took the sword and pushed it gently back into the rock, right up to the hilt. The crowd gasped and Merlin was taken totally by surprise at how easily Arthur had done it, *this King has surprises in store for all of us,* he thought, *what will he do next.* Arthur asked Sir Bors to try and pull it out, but despite his strength it did not move a fraction. He then invited King Lot to check that it was still stuck firm and had not been loosened by Sir Bors, and although he tried all ways it would not move. Arthur asked all those in the arena if they were happy that it was immovable and received unanimous acceptance that it was, at which point he played with crowd and started to walk away. Merlin smiled at this, as a cry went up of 'where are you going, show us how you pulled it out.' Arthur stopped, turned and walked back towards the rock, studying the gently pulsating energy around the sword before grasping the hilt and withdrawing it effortlessly, holding it up so that all could see.

"Just like that," he said. "Are you satisfied now that only the true-born High King can fulfil the prophecy?"

Well done Arthur, thought Merlin, *you have just increased your standing amongst them and converted some of the waverers to your camp, although there is a long way to go yet before you enjoy total support.*

There was a subdued roar of approval, as some were still not convinced that Arthur had fulfilled the prophecy without some form of trickery. A voice from the back of the crowd asked how were they to know that he was indeed the son and heir of Uther Pendragon and others echoed the same thought, as they clutched at straws to explain away what they had just witnessed. Merlin held up his hand for quiet and replied that was what the prophecy said, only the true-born High King could accomplish the feat and that meant a son and heir of Uther. The same voice replied that he did not have any children, let alone a son, and again elements of the crowd agreed. Merlin could see the mood of the gathering beginning to swing away from accepting Arthur as High King as doubt crept in, when an angry female voice cut through their mutterings and the Lady Igraine stepped out into the centre and stood beside Arthur.

"My Lords, you are men of standing in this land and yet you act as if you are rebellious young children refusing to accept what your eyes have shown you and your hearts tell you. You all wanted the crown to satisfy your own ego and this young man has put you all to shame. He stood his ground against Sir Bors, despite his size, and gave a good account of himself to rectify an injustice against Sir Ector. He has removed the sword in the stone twice as proof of his birthright, when none of you could, and you still cast doubts on his lineage and right to be High King. You have had your chance over the years to challenge the prophecy, but none has, and now that it has been fulfilled some of you do not want to accept it because you cannot have the Kingship yourselves and you seek a way out. I stand before you all with pride and without shame when I say that Uther Pendragon seduced me in my slumber when I was worse for drink and was discovered by my maid, who suffered the humiliation of his attentions as well. The result of our union was a son, who was placed in safe care until he was of age, without me seeing him or knowing where or who he was. If Arthur is my son, and heir to Uther, he will be known by the sign of the cross on his right shoulder, which he was borne into this world bearing."

Arthur had been quietly listening to Igraine and absorbing her words, and they seemed to make sense and explained the feelings of an indefinable bond when in her company, that he had never really understood until now. He was not aware that he had a mark on his shoulder but removed his tunic so that all could see as he rotated his body and showed his back to the crowd. By their reaction he knew that he did indeed have the mark of the cross on his shoulder, exactly where Igraine had said.

Excellent, thought Merlin, *you have turned the tables on them nicely and are a brave woman to bare your soul to them over such a delicate and personal matter. My heart goes out to you and it will do your reputation no harm, as all were aware of Uther's lustfulness and his many conquests of the ladies.*

Igraine was speaking again. "My Lords, you have seen the final proof, now show that you are true leaders in this land, banish your inflated egos and own self importance and unite together for the good of our country and swear fealty to your new High King," and with those final words Lady Igraine knelt before her son Arthur, and taking his hand kissed it with tears of happiness in her eyes and swore, in a clear voice, her allegiance to him for all time.

Absolutely brilliant, mused Merlin, *now let them wriggle out of that.*

All this time Sir Kay had stood there totally mesmerised, trying to take in all the events that had happened since his father had been so rudely pushed to the ground by Sir Bors. His life long friend Arthur, the High King of Britain, it was unbelievable but true, as he had seen it all with his own eyes even though it was difficult to grasp all at once. His father had followed Igraine in swearing fealty to the King and Sir Ector said to Arthur that he had been unaware of his birthright until yesterday when Merlin had confided in him, knowing that something would happen today. Arthur told him that he was a trusted and knowledgeable knight and thanked him for all his help and teachings, without which he wouldn't be prepared for this day, the full import of which had not yet sunk in. Sir Kay followed his father but was at a loss for words, feeling strange kneeling before his friend, but full of pride and joy at being able to serve him and continuing their friendship into the future. Arthur commented that life was full of surprises, he had never dreamt of a situation like this but one had to take them in one's stride, there would be much to be done to bring people together again in peace and prosperity. They had an interesting time before them, that occasionally would be volatile and violent, but if they persevered they would succeed, and Sir Kay acknowledged that he was ready and willing to undertake whatever befell them. Igraine's other son, Sir Cador, approached Arthur next and with a smile said that he knew there was something different about him from the first time that they met, and now they knew what it was brother, and his sword was his.

There followed a steady stream after that led by Sir Bors, King Ban of Bennick, Custennin of Dumnonia, Cadell of Powys, Colgrevane, Peredur King of York, Urien of Gore, King Auguselus, King Caradog of Gwent, Baudwin and many more, but not all stepped forward. There were quite a few who stood firm as they were not happy with one so young taking the Kingship, Agwisance King of Ireland, King Yder of Cournovaille and Clariance of Northunberland included. King Lot of Orcanie had not moved either and Arthur, a little surprised, asked him the reason for this. Lot replied that he was neither for nor against, but that Arthur was young for the responsibility and although he had shown his capabilities against Sir Bors, a King earned his respect by the deeds that he accomplished. He would keep his own counsel for the moment and watch Arthur's progress, and if Lot was happy he would then pledge his fealty and sword. Arthur thanked him for such an honest answer, which was like a breath of fresh air, and he would do his best to prove his worth as High King by word and deed. Lot smiled, he was glad that they understood one another and was sure that he would deliver.

Finally Merlin approached Arthur, who commented that even as High King he should go on one knee and pay homage to Merlin the Elder as he belonged to a time and race far greater than any that currently lived, and as such served no living man. Merlin's destiny was for the greater good of all, accountable only to his Lord. *This young lad either knows or senses much more than we would expect of him,* thought Merlin as he held up his hand indicating that it would not be necessary or indeed advisable in the circumstances. Merlin faced the crowd and said that as the majority had sworn fealty to their new King, he would be crowned in the great hall of Silchester church at noon the following day and Bishop Dyfrig would lead the service.

As the crowd began to slowly disperse Arthur surveyed his friends searching for one missing face and Merlin seeing this and understanding spoke quietly to Sir Ector and then took Arthur's arm and said that Igraine had sought out Gwendolyn and both the women had gone into the church for the peace and to get to know each other better. It was best to leave them alone at the moment as although they were both prepared for today it would have been an emotional and traumatic time for them.

"I have asked Sir Ector to take the party back to camp and we will wait and escort the women when they are ready."

"Thank you," murmured Arthur. "It must have been a shock for both of them as it certainly was for me."

The others took their leave and headed back to camp, whilst Merlin and Arthur waited for the women to emerge. Arthur asked him what his father was like and why all the secrecy surrounding his birth and whereabouts after. Merlin explained that the Elders felt it best for the safety of all concerned that nothing should be known until the time was right, as there were some who would have sought him out and killed him, as he might have posed a threat to them. Fortunately nearly all those had since met their own death in their incessant greed for more power, but it was still felt secrecy should be maintained until he became of age, which Merlin admitted had been changed for obvious reasons. He was actually born on the first of May not at the end of August as they had made out, but that was necessary as his birth mother Lady Igraine, being a very astute woman, would no doubt have realised the connection. It would have been too obvious, even though he enlisted Taliesin's help in taking him and Gwendolyn to Sir Ector, if it was known in certain quarters that he was involved. Arthur laughed, to think that he was one of those lucky souls who had two mothers. Yes, agreed Merlin, and it was lucky for them and the women at the healing sanctuary that Gwendolyn became available just at the right time, having recently lost her own child and the father. Lucky, Arthur smiled, or divine providence, sometimes Merlin did not tell the whole story, only what was necessary. Now it was Merlin's turn to smile at Arthur's uncanny insight into his character, as he replied that it was often the best and wisest way, tell the truth, but not necessarily all of it, sometimes some things were best left unsaid to avoid confusion or hurt.

Their conversation continued for another hour before the women came out of the church, full of smiles and laughing. Merlin realised that this was one of only a few occasions that he had managed to talk to Arthur alone and at such length and was pleasantly surprised at the depth of knowledge and understanding this young King had, which bode nothing but good for the country. As they approached Merlin melted discreetly into the shadows to allow them time together, as Arthur put his arms around them and drew them close, both of equal standing in his eyes, two mothers, how lucky he was when some had none to hold.

On their return to camp they found a party in full swing with many visitors from around the neighbouring camp sites joining in the celebrations in his honour. As they approached a cheer went up, followed by the usual jests. Someone made the comment that he had probably put the sword back in the stone and then couldn't get it out again, which initiated peels of laughter, and even more when Arthur asked for volunteers to go back with him and try and remove it. That set the mood for the rest of the night and the festivities continued into the early hours, with many people coming and going with fresh supplies of food and drink as they relaxed and enjoyed themselves to the full.

The crowning of Arthur the next day was a sombre affair by comparison as Bishop Dyfrig lead the service and reminded all those present that the future of the country was in their own hands and that by working together under the new High King success would prevail. It would not be easy he reminded them and many battles would need to be fought before a lasting peace descended over the land, but to trust in the Lord and their High King and forego their own egos. That way they would succeed he concluded as he blessed Arthur and all those present. Arthur, High King of Britain arose, sword in one hand and the cross in the other he lead the procession out of the church into the courtyard, then out into the open for all those to bear witness that could not be accommodated in the church. As he moved into the open a huge cheer arose from the large throng of people that had gathered to see this rare event, and he raised the sword and cross into the air in acknowledgement of them. He had been advised by Merlin beforehand that it would not be safe at the moment to wander into the crowd, but just to stand and be seen. After awhile Arthur returned inside and spent some moments in discussion with the bishop before gathering his party and returning to camp where they had decided to spend the night, before starting their return journey.

Arthur would remain at Cadbury Castle, which would be his base initially, as he came to terms with his new role and learnt more of what was expected of him. The others would be at liberty to return to their own areas as and when they felt ready, that was the part that he would find difficult, saying goodbye to his friends for the time being, but that was the way of life. Nothing stood still, everything had to move forward in life otherwise it ground to a halt and passed you by, leaving you wondering what opportunities you had missed in the process. Time was continuous and waited for no man, so the only way forward was to go with his instincts and that is what Arthur intended to do, and to do everything to the best of his ability. No doubt he would make mistakes, but no one was infallible, not even Merlin, as long as you learned from your errors and moved forward then you could get back on the correct pathway in life and everything would turn out as it should, in the long run.

Sir Bors had decided to accompany them, with his small retinue, on the journey to Cadbury Castle whilst King Lot had indicated to Lady Igraine that he would make his own way to Tintagel as there was some other business he had to deal with first. Arthur requested they take a different route back, to enable him to see more of the country and Taliesin suggested that they head south towards Winchester and shortly before reaching there head due west to Tisbury, then a final days ride to Cadbury. It was agreed, as it would not add any extra time to their journey and there were more villages and hamlets further south should they wish to tarry awhile en-route. When all were ready to move out Merlin approached Arthur and gave him a rolled up pennon and said that now he was High King he could fly his father's banner to proclaim who he was. Unrolling it Arthur saw that it was the Pendragon emblem, and looking at Merlin in surprise, thanked him and promptly tied it to his spear to flutter in the breeze for all to see.

The party moved off, nearly seventy of them in total now, with Arthur in the lead and Merlin and Taliesin beside him, as the Elders knew the easiest route. Other groups were on the move too, dispersing back to their own areas of the country, some were in a joyful mood whilst a few harboured dark thoughts concerning Arthur and others appeared unconcerned with the outcome of the council, as they were from distant lands. The overall mood was encouraging considering Arthur's young age, but it only needed one rotten apple to contaminate the rest, unless the King showed a strong hand in dealing with trouble amongst his kingdoms. There was much to be done to bring everyone together, fighting the same cause and not each other. Arthur had done well so far, but much more was expected of him and the destiny of the country, as well as his own, lay in his own hands, and as King Lot had rightly said, now he had to deliver.

The day wore on as the sun moved across the meridian in a blue and cloudless sky, bathing the land in a gentle warmth, as the group followed the low ground of a slow meandering river passed several small hamlets. The few people about stopped and stared as the procession went by and relaxed as they realised that it was not a Saxon war band, and continued about their business, some braver souls with a wave of acknowledgement. *You can sense the unease and anxiety,* thought Arthur as he returned their wave, *these people do not know what to expect next and obviously live in fear of what each day might bring. It is going to be a long hard road to put this country back on its feet again and give the people back the freedom to enjoy life without fear. We have been lucky in the southwest, detached from much of the upheaval and fighting going on in the rest of the country, either between kingdoms or against the invaders from across the water. I have much to do and a lot to learn in a short time, if I am to succeed in bringing about peace and prosperity.* Arthur was jolted from his thoughts by the sight and sound of one of the forward scouts descending from the higher ground on their left and rapidly approaching them. The party came to a halt as the scout reigned in his horse in front of Arthur with news of what he had seen ahead.

"My Lord there is a large hamlet not two miles ahead nestling close to the river and to the south of it there is a large wooded area stretching about half a mile and approaching the far side of this is a large body of foot soldiers that are moving fast and are not dressed as we are."

"That will be Stocksford ahead, thirty or more huts spread like a half moon where the river can be forded," volunteered Taliesin, and the scout nodded in agreement at this observation. "Looks like we have encountered a Saxon raiding party about to attack the hamlet, and they will not be seen until they emerge from the pathway through the wood, just four hundred paces from the settlement."

Arthur had been listening to all this and deciding on the action needed to counter this probable attack, then he gave his orders in a clear and unhurried way as if he had been in this situation many times before.

"Sir Cador take five men and ride fast to the hamlet and raise the alarm, then await our arrival." Turning to the scout as Sir Cador departed he enquired if the trees surrounded the hamlet and was told no, only about half way as the land rose fairly steeply and had obviously been cleared except for a few lone ones. The main area of the wood was to the south as the low ground was much wider there. Arthur turning to Sir Ector, continued, "your shoulder is still causing you pain, I want you to select ten men and stay here with the ladies and our supply horses in case any of the raiders break through and head this way and Sir Kay, remain with your father and give him support, Sir Bors, take half the men and when we get close to the settlement swing away to the trees and conceal yourself there if possible, until you see me lead the rest of the troop out of the hamlet and challenge the raiding party once they are out in the open." Sir Ector was about to protest, but Arthur had already moved on. "Merlin, Taliesin, I would prefer that both of you remained here as your healing talents will be needed later. Any comments?" Receiving none, as both were recovering from the speed and decisiveness of Arthur's commands he lead the troop off at a gallop, his pennon flying proudly in the breeze.

Merlin echoed the thoughts of the remaining group as he muttered, with a smile, "that boy still surprises me at times. No wonder he was born to be High King, calm and confident in his own abilities and not afraid to take action to defend others. He will do well for his country, mark my words"

As Arthur and his men approached within half a mile of the hamlet they heard the loud banging of metal upon metal as the alarm was sounded, and no doubt the raiding party had heard it too and it would urge them on faster. Sir Bors and his men veered off and headed towards the few trees at the perimeter of the wood and sought out a more populated area for concealment, whilst Arthur with his pennon flapping wildly in the wind galloped straight into the hamlet before slowing down on seeing Sir Cador waiting for him. At least they had made it in time before the raiding party had emerged from the wood. Villagers were still hurrying to the relative safety of their huts and some stopped and stared briefly, recognising the Pendragon Standard, before continuing on their way.

Arthur motioned for his men to conceal themselves as best as possible amongst the dwellings as he took up position so that he could see the track leading to the wood. He did not have long to wait before a steady stream of sword wielding Saxons burst out of the wood and into the open as they ran towards the hamlet, nigh on a hundred of them. Arthur drew his sword and waiting until they were right out in the middle of the open ground before shouting 'Saxons' and urged his horse into a gallop as the rest of his men broke cover and joined him. The raiding party was taken totally by surprise for a moment as twenty five well armed horsemen bore down on them from out of nowhere, then realising they had greater numbers they pushed forward again. Too late they realised their error as Sir Bors and his men descended on them from the flank riding them down with skilful use of spear and sword. Arthur was amongst the Saxons, with Sir Cador by his side, thrusting and cutting with such ferocity that all fell before them. Although Arthur and his men were outnumbered the speed and surprise of the attack soon had the Saxons in total disarray as the horsemen galloped through their ranks cutting them down left and right. Some tried to escape back to the wood but were headed off by Sir Bors and quickly despatched to the hereafter, whatever their beliefs.

It was soon over and only two Saxons were left alive out of the hundred or more in the raiding party, both were wounded and unable to defend themselves and stood together expecting certain death, but it was not to be so. They were denied that choice as Arthur instructed his men not to harm them, and in surprise they were lead away, having first been searched for any hidden weapons.

Arthur surveyed the carnage, *such a waste,* he thought, *but there will be a lot more of this yet before we can bring peace to this country. Many battles in which good men will be lost on both sides, for what, to satisfy someone's greed and personal ego by trying to impose their will on others. Merlin's experienced all this many times before, you can see it in his eyes and it pains him greatly, but he continues to help as if he knows that one day we will move forward as a people and live in peace.* He took a last look around before sending one of his men to fetch Sir Kay and the ladies now that it was safe. Merlin and Taliesin would be needed for their healing skills as several of his men had been wounded, although he had lost very few in the skirmish as surprise had been on their side. The wounded, including the guarded Saxons were helped to the hamlet where the others had just arrived and Lady Igraine and Gwendolyn insisted on helping Merlin and Taliesin in administering aid and healing.

When they had done all that they could Merlin asked Arthur what he was going to do with the two Saxons, to which he replied that he would send them on their way to take a warning to their leaders not to interfere with the people of Britain, if they managed to survived the journey without any weapons.

"You realise," Merlin replied, "that what you want them to deliver sounds very much like a challenge."

"Yes it does, and it is," Arthur answered, "but it might make them think a little, or bring them out into the open where it will be easier to deal with them compared to these minor skirmishes. To bring lasting peace it is necessary sometimes to force the issue, even though I am not yet ready to take them on in force, they do not know that, so it will unsettle them a little and make them wary, and hopefully give me time to prepare. Do you think I am wrong in my thinking?"

"On the contrary," Merlin answered, "I think your wisdom far exceeds what even I thought it would be at this moment, you have only just claimed the Kingship and yet you talk and act as one would who has many more years of life's experiences behind him."

"I take that as a compliment and thank you for your honesty," returned Arthur, "I just have this inner feeling when I do or say things that they are the right thing to do. I cannot explain it, it just feels right. If you understand what I mean?"

Merlin replied thoughtfully that he understood exactly what he meant and some day he would try and explain it to him, when he felt the time was right, but for now to carry on following his instincts and inner feelings as they would seldom let him down. Arthur asked him if he understood the Saxon tongue and Merlin indicated that he understood enough to converse in a limited way and did he want him to convey the message to them. Arthur nodded and said that when their wounds had been tended to they were free to go and return to their own people, but that he would not be so merciful if they met again on the battle field. Merlin said that he would go and speak to them now and Arthur agreed the sooner it was done the better, and that the Saxons should be taken to the wood and sent on their way as soon as it was possible, before the villagers became aware. He was going to see how the wounded men were and praise them for their splendid efforts and then speak to Sir Bors and congratulate him on the perfect timing of his attack.

The villagers came out of hiding and the local elders approached Arthur and thanked him for his timely arrival, which had prevented a massacre of them all, and although they had little to spare extended the hospitality of the hamlet to him and his men. Arthur acknowledged their gratitude and replied that it was only by chance that they had decided to come this way en-route to Cadbury Castle and as for food he would see what his men could find in the wood that would make a good meal. There were deer and boar he was told, if they were quick enough to catch one, mainly in the east of the wood on the lower slopes. Arthur told the village elders to send men out to collect all the Saxon weapons and keep them safe, in case they were needed in the future, and to remove the bodies from the meadow and arrange for their burial or burning to stop the risk of disease spreading amongst the inhabitants. He had lost three men in the fight and needed graves dug for them so that they could pay their last respects in the proper way. The elders agreed that they would see to it but before leaving asked Arthur about his pennon as they recognised it from the time that Uther Pendragon has passed through their hamlet. He replied that it was indeed the same pennon and that he was Uther's son and heir, Arthur, the new High King of Britain.

"Indeed we are honoured sire," they replied, "and we redouble our thanks for your timely arrival in our humble hamlet that spared us from certain slaughter."

Arthur asked them if they had been troubled by raids before and was told that it was many years since raiders had come this far inland. *A certain sign,* thought Arthur, *that the Saxons are becoming bolder and striking further into our land, but maybe this skirmish will deter them for awhile as it went so decisively against them. I hope my message reaches their leaders and makes them wary and contains them until I am ready to face them in strength.*

The meadow had been cleared and Arthur had presided over a short ceremony as they buried their dead and Merlin contributed a few words of wisdom and encouragement to all who had survived, extolling the virtues of Arthur's command and the quick and decisive outcome of the conflict. Several of the men had gone hunting and returned laden with two small boar and a good sized deer which were soon prepared and were roasting nicely on the open fires. Arthur invited all the inhabitants of the hamlet to join him in celebration, not just of their victory but of the success of the hunt as well, and soon a relaxed and joyful atmosphere developed, especially as the villagers had brought a good supply of mead for all to partake.

Arthur sat on the ground with his two mothers proudly next to him, one on either side, with Merlin and the others in a small half circle around him as they watched everyone else laughing and singing, totally at ease with life for a change. *If only life were like this most of the time what happy people they would be, relaxing after a hard days productive toil, without the worry of where the next conflict would come from,* thought Arthur and Merlin in unison, as they looked across at each other as if reading the other's thoughts, and perhaps they were. Several of the young children, drawn by curiosity, came close to the fire staring at Arthur and he motioned for them to approach and to come and sit by him. Gwendolyn stood up and went and took their hands and brought them in closer, telling them not to be afraid as he was a good king and wouldn't do anything bad to them. One of them, a little bolder than the rest said that he didn't look or dress like the King and Arthur replied in a gentle voice that it did not matter what anyone looked like or how they dressed it was what they were like inside that mattered.

"Come all of you and sit by me and tell me what you do or ask me questions if you so desire and I will do my best to answer them."

The bold lad wanted to know why the Saxons had come and would they have been killed if the King had not arrived when he did and Arthur replied honestly that it was most likely. "There are some people unfortunately that are not satisfied with what they have, and instead of working to make things better they are greedy and try to take from others, even if they have to kill to do it."

"Why are people like that?" the lad wanted to know.

Arthur responded that it was the current way of life for some and that he was going to do his best to try and change that but it would take a long time. "You should ask Merlin here if you want to know more as he has a greater experience of life than I do."

The lad had heard many stories about Merlin and his mysterious and magical powers and exclaimed, "I meet the King and a Wizard in one day, that is more than I could ever hope for in a lifetime, the other lads in the village wont believe that."

"Then perhaps you should go and tell them now," answered Arthur, "and say that I have invited them to my fire, whilst they have the chance as tomorrow we shall be on our way."

The lad jumped up, "thank you sir I will go and fetch them," and with that he was off running towards the other fires.

"You continue to surprise me," Merlin said, "you have the foresight to give time to the young."

"They are the next generation and as such this is the time to influence and educate them and lay good foundations for the future, they are tomorrows administrators, magistrates, knights and worldly influencers" replied Arthur, "the country will need the right people to be able to move forward and I will need support from all age groups to be successful in my endeavours."

"You speak like a sage who has already lived a long life, no wonder you were chosen to lead the people forward, against all odds. Your divine mission becomes clearer the more I see and hear," stated Merlin.

Their conversation was interrupted by ten to fifteen boys nervously approaching Arthur's group, led by the bold lad who was making the most of the situation.

"There I told you it was the High King and Merlin the Wizard and we've been invited to join them," he exclaimed.

"Come forward lads and sit here with the others," said Arthur as he pointed to the children already seated, "and we have two wizards not one as Taliesin is with us also, and I am sure that they will tell you some good stories if you ask them."

The boys were kept enthralled for the next couple of hours as first Merlin, then Taliesin recounted stories of old concerning mystical creatures and bold men and their fight for justice and right and how they succeeded even against overwhelming odds. Each story had a moral to it where right prevailed in the end due to the hero persevering against evil through strength of will and determination, even if they lost their own life in the end. Some of the villagers had also gathered around listening to the stories when they had come to retrieve their offspring. Arthur eventually had to interrupt the lads asking for more stories, indicating that it was getting late and it was time for rest, they had met the King and two wizards today and that would give them much to talk about in the coming weeks and something in later years to tell their children. He bade them good night and said that they would be leaving in the morning but if passing this way in the future would stop by, maybe with more stories. The bold lad expressed his thanks to Arthur and his wizards, which were echoed by the others and they went off merrily chatting about the stories that they had heard.

Arthur and his party left early next morning shortly after sunrise, to a chorus of thanks from the villagers who had turned out in force to see them off as they left the hamlet behind and headed across the ford for the next part of their journey to Tisbury. The day rolled on quietly compared to the previous one as they passed by many small hamlets with occasional stares and waves from the few souls that they saw and soon after midday they saw the derelict fort at Old Sarum not far off to the left. Less than two hours later they pitched their camp on the outskirts of Tisbury and Taliesin said that he would go and see what news they had to tell as he was acquainted with one or two of the village elders there. Within two hours he had returned with nothing to report as he had been told it had been unusually quiet in the last few months with very little movement of anyone in the area, which wasn't necessarily a good sign.

They broke camp early the next day as the wind had got up and it looked as though there might be rain later, so they wished to be on the move early as they only had just over twenty miles to go to complete their journey. The rain held off and early afternoon brought them in sight of Cadbury Castle, looking slightly menacing in the light hill mist that was wafting around it, as if it was deserted. Merlin was a little worried by its appearance as he had left Greyfus in charge and it did look lifeless from here, perhaps just a trick of the mist. As they approached closer there was still no signs of activity and the main gate appeared closed, which in itself was unusual during daylight, unless trouble was expected. Arthur had noticed it as well and said as such to Merlin and that all did not look well and that they should proceed cautiously.

Arthur stopped the troop two hundred paces from the gate, which indeed was closed, and there was still no sign of life visible.

Arthur turned to the company, "Sir Bors, Sir Ector, Sir Kay and the first ten men, we are going to approach the gate and see if we can enter. Sir Cador stay here with the rest for the moment but be prepared for anything, especially if we return at the gallop, act on your own judgement, but see that the ladies are protected. Draw your weapons," he said to his group, "and let us proceed and solve this mystery," and he urged his horse forward at a steady walk, watching and listening hoping to detect any sign of life.

On reaching the entrance still nothing had stirred so Arthur reversed his spear and pushed gently at the gate, and surprisingly it moved, opening slightly. He edged his horse forward and pushed and the big gate started to swing open, and still no sound from within. Moving forward slowly he turned to Sir Bors and told him in a quiet voice to stay by the gate and hold it if necessary so that the rest of them could escape if it was a trap. Sir Bors nodded and took up his position as the rest of the troop entered the gateway, Arthur turned to the rest and said for them to stay on their horses and take up position in a half circle, with him at the head, and wait for his command either to dismount or leave in a hurry. Still there was no sign of life as they moved further inside and Arthur brought them to a halt, looking around carefully to detect any sign of movement or noise that might indicate hidden enemies.

A slight noise came to his ears and as he listened intently, he recognised the footfall of a horse, quickly turning to his men he told them to be vigilant as the castle was not empty. Sure enough he heard the noise again but more than one horse, although not many, and then out of nowhere sprang a dozen horsemen shouting loudly as they raced towards Arthur and his men and another dozen appeared from a different direction bearing down on them. Arthur and his men stood their ground as the horsemen reigned in their mounts and stopped close in front of them.

"Welcome King Arthur I do believe we have you outnumbered."

"On the contrary King Lot most of my men wait just outside the gate ready to move in if necessary," Arthur replied with a smile.

"That is good," said Lot, "a man needs to be cautious, you have gone up in my esteem already as I thought that you might fall for this simple trick of luring you into a trap."

"I am wiser than you give me credence for," replied Arthur, "and it is not advisable to underestimate a potential rival, that could be fatal."

"Well said," conceded Lot, "perhaps I have not considered you in the correct light, my apologies for that, it could be that my first impression of your youth was a little misguided, but you are an unusually bright young man, that is becoming obvious now, so let me welcome you to your castle and pardon me for my little bit of fun to see how you reacted." He waved his hand and many more people appeared and gave a cheer for their new High King.

Chapter 9

ARTHUR ENCOUNTERS THE SARMATIANS

ARTHUR AND HIS MEN RELAXED as it became obvious that King Lot was having a little fun and testing the new King out, such was his character, and Sir Bors waved forward the rearguard party waiting outside the castle. As the rest of Arthur's party arrived the Lady Igraine was surprised to see King Lot, as he had previously indicated that he had some business to deal with before he made his way to Tintagel and she challenged him on this.

"My apologies my lady, but this was the business that I had in mind, to test our new King and see how he reacted, and he has passed the test and gone up in my estimation and if he carries on in the same way I will have no hesitation in supporting him, but it is early days yet."

Merlin enquired as to the whereabouts of Greyfus, the guardian of the castle, and Lot answered that unfortunately he had been rather difficult with regard to the surprise that he had planned and refused to allow it.

"What have you done with him?" asked Merlin.

"He refused to join us or give up his sword, he is safe but no doubt not very happy with me," replied Lot. "He kept my men at bay, but we cornered him and locked him in a store hut with a guard on the door, it might be best if you went with one of my men to release him as he is likely to come out fighting, and I wish him no harm, I like his fighting spirit, he is a good man to have around."

Merlin went off to release Greyfus and explain the situation to him, that all was well and no harm was meant, he was a wise and steadfast knight and would not bear any grudge or malice towards King Lot, which was why he had been left as guardian of the castle all this time.

King Lot showed the newcomers the stables and by the time the horses and pack animals had been seen to Merlin and Greyfus joined them and they all moved into the great hall to have some well earned refreshment. Greyfus was introduced to Arthur, surprised by his apparent youth, but as their conversation progressed realised that he was talking to an old soul and that his knowledge and understanding of many things belied his age and that here indeed was a man worthy of the Kingship. Sharp like his father but with a greater understanding of the needs of the people and the country. He explained to Arthur the layout of the castle, the boundary of his lands for collecting taxes, who the local lords and elders were, the number of men that he had at his disposal and how many of them resided in the castle grounds. The state of the finances, which were quite healthy as Uther had been prudent and fair with his taxes. King Lot was in conversation with Lady Igraine and Merlin and Taliesin were deep in conversation in a quiet corner of the hall away from the others.

Some while later Merlin and Taliesin joined Arthur and Greyfus and stated that they would soon be off on their travels as there was still much to be done in gauging the mood of the country and whether having a new High King was creating any changes in attitude, even though it had only recently happened. The Saxons and other foreign usurpers would undoubtedly soon know of Arthur, even if they didn't already, and how would they react to this news. Merlin indicated that trouble would probably come initially from the south and south east as that was a Saxon concentration but there was likely to be trouble between British kingdoms at times, as not all were for Arthur and his intervention would be needed and possibly requested by his supporters. That was more likely to be in the west and north predominantly but to be prepared for trouble from any direction as there were still many lords that were not happy with the fact that Arthur had legitimately claimed the Kingship. They were still power hungry and would possibly throw down a challenge.

"You do not have many men locally at the moment so you need to increase the numbers available to you, should the occasion arise that you need them and undoubtedly you will, as you might require some tough bargaining power. As Taliesin and I travel around we will act as your ambassadors as well, if you are happy with that, to illicit mutual help and support when needed. This way we can cover a large area of the country quickly and allow you time to build up your fighting strength here. There will unfortunately be times when to fight for your kingdom is necessary, but hopefully over time you will help bring peace to this country and it will all have been worthwhile."

Arthur agreed that it would be good for them both to be his ambassadors and help in uniting the country, besides they seemed to be able to cover great distances very quickly, and that had always puzzled him, but he would ask no more of that at present. Merlin and Taliesin smiled but said nothing, it was agreed that they would leave the next morning and return on completion of their travels, which could take some months.

Now it was time for some merriment and laughter voiced Taliesin and to everyone's surprise began to sing in an unknown tongue. An old ballad of love and romance, in a soft lilting voice that seemed to carry gently to all the corners of the great hall so that everyone stopped talking and listened in wonder at such beautiful sounds. The great hall remained quiet except for Taliesin's singing, as all were enthralled by such music as they had never heard before. Surprise increased even more as Merlin joined in and harmonised with him at certain points, two voices as one producing wonderfully moving feelings as their gentle melody reached the heart and soul of all those present. All too soon for those listening they came to the end of the ballad with cries of 'more of the same please,' and to oblige they sang one more, even more moving than the first. That set the scene for more brave souls taking up the challenge and breaking into song, and so the day passed into night as all relaxed and enjoyed the festivities.

The next morning was a sad one for all, as those whose destiny or need to depart were leaving to go their separate ways. Sir Ector, Lady Igraine and Sir Cador were leaving for Tintagel accompanied by King Lot and his men. Gwendolyn was returning to the healing sanctuary at Lydney escorted by Merlin, and Taliesin was heading south and east to begin his travels. Sirs Bors had declared that he and his few men would remain with Arthur, and Sir Kay after much discussion with his father, had opted to stay also and serve his friend and King at Cadbury. Merlin had spent a little time with Arthur on his own, going through the final details of what needed to be done to ensure that he was prepared for any eventuality, and to seek advice from Greyfus if needed, as there was a wealth of experience and wisdom in him and he was totally trustworthy and discreet.

Arthur had spent much of his time with both his mothers, with promises to see them as often as it was possible, telling them that they would always be in his thoughts, wherever he was in the country. He gave them both a hug and kiss and wished them well on their journeys. He thanked Sir Ector for all that he had done to help him get to where he was now and promised to look after Sir Kay. King Lot approached him and wished him luck and that if he continued to prove himself then his sword would be there for him at some point, but it would never be against him. Arthur thanked him and said that he would do his best, and Lot replied that was all he asked as he mounted his horse and joined the others as they moved off, with the women looking back and waving as they passed through the gate.

Now I must start my new life, thought Arthur as he watched them depart, *and deliver my vision of a stable and peaceful country, although there will be much pain to go through on the way I know that I can achieve it with help and guidance of that greater power within me. If I trust in those inner instincts and do not waver from my task, then I will be successful, to fail is not an option that I care to think of. I must be strong and fair in word and deed and lead by example and look to the needs of the people before my own, though my own are important as well, to help me deliver that which I feel is right and just.*

Turning to Sir Bors, Sir Kay and Greyfus he said, "my friends we have much to do, the sooner we start the better. It is time to discuss our future and the way forward, let us adjourn to the great hall and begin the process, lest we waste the day in thoughts of our departing friends, there will be time for that later in the peace and quiet of the night."

They all nodded in agreement and made for the great hall to start to plan the way forward and what needed to be done and when.

It was a long day but much was accomplished and agreed upon, the priority was to train the men in the castle and get them fighting fit again after such a long period of inactivity. Sir Bors and his men would test skills with weapons whilst Sir Kay would review their riding skills, with Greyfus in overall charge of the training, as he had the experience to co-ordinate the whole thing and was respected by all who knew him. Arthur wished to get a feel for the surrounding countryside and asked Greyfus if he had anyone that would be suitable, with a good knowledge of the land and people and who was known and respected locally. Greyfus had just the man, Andulus, reputed to be of Roman origin through his family line, very knowledgeable about the area and its history and well known and liked by the local people for his friendly disposition.

"That's good," commented Arthur, "because I need to be seen and for people to know that I am approachable. When you feel the men are ready Greyfus I intend to carry out small sorties further afield to show my presence, so that the people, local lords and land owners know who they are dealing with, and possibly recruit some extra fighting men, for we shall surely need them at some point. I want to make sure that we are fully prepared and able to respond quickly to any situation that might develop, we have the space here to accommodate more men and thanks to my father we have a good war chest. Tomorrow we need to gather everyone together so that they know who I am and to explain what is going to take place, if I can leave that for you to arrange Greyfus. Those are my thoughts on the immediate future, now I will explain my long term vision to you and what I would like to see for the people and the country. It is not something that will happen quickly but I am determined that we shall be successful and your thoughts and suggestions will be most welcome. If you feel that I have got something wrong, please say so, I cannot be right all the time and your advice will be invaluable in making my decisions, as those are what I will be judged on as poor judgement is remembered more than the good."

The hours passed and the light was beginning to fade when Greyfus excused himself to go and make the arrangements for the following morning, before it became too late. Sir Bors stretched and said that he too should go and see to the welfare of his men and shaking his head he said laughingly, "and to think I wanted to run you through with my sword my lord when we first met, because I thought you were a cheeky lad acting above his station. Life is certainly strange at times with what it throws at us to see how we respond, thankfully no damage was done, except to my pride, and that was obviously a lesson that I had to learn."

Still laughing he departed, leaving Kay and Arthur to reflect on how life had changed for both of them in such a short space of time, and the surprises that they had both experienced. They spent the next couple of hours talking about their childhood together, the things they had done and the fun and laughter that they had on the way, both agreed that they wouldn't experience much of that going forward, but at least they had their memories of those happy times.

The following day saw all the inhabitants of the castle gathered in the great hall to welcome their new King, introduced by Greyfus, and seeing the look of surprise on some of the faces, he added that they should not be put off by his youthful appearance as on his shoulders was a wise old head. "I know," he continued, "as I had spent most of yesterday in his company and his foresight and vision for the people and our country exceeds even the wisdom of my years, I know his words are not empty words but a passion and resolve within him that will see him successful and I have no hesitation in pledging my loyalty to him. Like his father Uther Pendragon in many ways, but even more of a peoples' King, with a greater wisdom and understanding of what we all seek, whatever our rank in life, he will lead us to that peace. He is the peoples' King, Arthur High King of Britain.

Arthur thanked him for his loyalty and compliments and said he would do his best to make his vision come about and returned the compliment by praising Greyfus on his excellent stewardship of the castle over the intervening years. He then explained to the gathering his vision and that it would not be an easy task and there would be bloodshed along the way as others fought to resist the change, but he was determined to be successful and carry on what his father had started, but in an even better way for the people of this country. Arthur finished by saying that he hoped that they were all behind him as that would make his task that much easier, thanking them all for attending and should any of them have a problem with any aspect of life he was there to help and they should make themselves and their problem known to him.

"Greyfus will be the point of contact should you wish to speak to me as he will be aware of my itinerary. I will see you as soon as possible and you do not have to declare your reason beforehand if it is of a delicate nature, your confidence will be respected. All those of you who pertain to be fighting men please stay behind and I will explain what we are going to do to get you in shape and improve your skills, which will help you all attain a good age like Greyfus here, and not throw your life away needlessly because you weren't trained properly."

Nearly two hundred remained and looking around at some of the faces Arthur surmised that not all had fought before, going by their apparent ages, but he started young and that was no barrier and he would not discourage them. Today's young were tomorrows fighting men and potential knights, good luck to them. Greyfus soon sorted them into groups, the seasoned fighters, those that had some experience with weapons and those with only a little or none. Those that had weapons he sent to fetch them and for the rest he said that they would be provided with them a little later as they had a good store of a variety of swords, spears and other paraphernalia that they could use. Not wishing to lose any time Greyfus soon had them organised into smaller groups so that the senior and skilled could check on their abilities and divide them into appropriate groups for training. Wishing them well Arthur motioned to Andulus to follow him, leaving Greyfus to carry on, indicating that he wished to ride out and survey the area.

For the next few days Arthur and Andulus travelled the surrounding land, talking to all those that they met en-route with Arthur asking many questions about the landscape, history and locations of the surrounding hamlets. Andulus was pleasantly surprised by his thirst for knowledge and his capacity for taking it all in very quickly. Even the local people that they met were impressed that the King had taken time to speak to them and engage in conversation as if they were equals.

Those first days greatly enhanced the King's growing reputation as a man of the people, which was just the affect that Arthur hoped for, to build up trust and respect as well as to show that although he was young in years he had a wise and knowledgeable head on his shoulders that would serve him and the people well.

In the meantime Greyfus with the help of Sir Bors and his men, and Sir Kay, were busy with the rigorous training programme to improve the skills of those that wished to serve their King as a soldier when needed. Such was the skill and perseverance of the instructors that progress was good and the cohesion into a fighting troop began to take shape, although there was still much work to be done before they would be good enough to do battle with an enemy. Time might not be on their side so the momentum had to be maintained and each day brought improvement to their knowledge and skills that would serve them well in battle.

Arthur decided that he wished to travel further afield and discover the lie of the land, meet more of the local people and dignitaries and make himself known to them, so he called Greyfus, Andulus, Sir Bors and Sir Kay together one evening to outline his plans. Andulus suggested that they travel a day or two's ride south towards Cerne Giant and Dorchester, as very little contact had been made for some while with the peoples in that region. Then west towards Pilsdon Pen, finally turning north to Hams Hill, then north east back to Cadbury. Should take no longer than a week if all went well he indicated. Arthur agreed that the route sounded ideal and said that along with Andulus as guide he wished Sir Bors and Sir Kay to accompany him together with eight of the more advanced recruits as a well earned break from their training. He asked Greyfus if he could manage the training for a week with just Sir Bors' men to help, and received an affirmative. In that case let the trainees know that the eight who showed the best improvement over the next couple of days would be travelling with him, and he would leave the selection of them to him. Turning to Sir Kay he asked him to arrange for the necessary provisions and a couple of pack horses, as they would be travelling fairly light, although they needed to be prepared for any hostile reception that might be encountered.

* * * * *

Three days later the small party of twelve left the sanctuary of Cadbury Castle and headed south, into what was unknown territory for all except Andulus, who had travelled the region extensively in the past. At each village and hamlet they came across Andulus told Arthur its name and introduced him to the elders, if he knew them, or let Arthur introduce himself on the occasions when he did not. They stopped nearly an hour at each one and Arthur learnt much about the local inhabitants and their thoughts and feelings as to what was happening in the country in general and he explained what he had set out to do to help bring peace and stability for all. He did not hide the problems that they all faced but stated that if they all pulled together then peace would prevail. That if any of the young men wished to serve their King and country, then they should make their way to Cadbury Castle where they would be well provided for and given proper training. As the hamlets were some distance apart and they were travelling more or less due south all the time there were not too many stops made and the second day saw them approaching the larger village of Cerne Giant where they set up camp for the night. Riding into the village they found their way blocked by twenty or so men bearing cudgels and staves and were challenged as to who they were and what was the nature of their business.

"Gentlemen," replied Arthur, "we come in peace and wish to speak to your elders and enjoy the hospitality of your village for the evening."

"Who are you and from whence do you come?" was the challenge uttered again.

"Arthur, High King of Britain and his small entourage," Arthur replied.

"We wasn't born yesterday lad," their leader laughed, "away with you before we set about you."

Arthur unfurled the pennon on his spear and asked him if he recognised that?

"It's the Pendragon," said a voice from the back of the throng, pushing his way forward. "Is that you I see there Andulus?" asked the old man, emerging at the front.

"Yes Severus it is I," replied Andulus recognising the aged elder, "and this is your King. What is all this hostility about?"

The elder addressed Arthur apologising for the reception but there were strange goings on lately and they had to be careful when encountering a small band of armed men, "follow me and we shall sit around the fire whilst I tell you about the stories being told."

The reception committee melted into the shadows of early evening as Arthur and his troop followed Severus to a large fire, situated in the village centre and around which were seated several people. They tethered their horses and joined the fireside gathering as curious faces looked at them as Severus indicated the company that they were honoured with.

"It all began nearly two years ago when we started to hear stories of a band of rogues looting and killing over towards Pilsdon Pen way, then it quietened down for awhile but now stories are coming in regularly as travellers pass through, in a hurry to leave the area."

"What has Sir Peredrue done about?" it queried Andulus. "Surely he would have hunted them down?"

"That's the point, nobody has seen or heard from him since it started," replied Severus, "and he was getting long in the tooth and rather forgetful in recent years, and no one has seen his son either, some say they were killed by these rogues, but we have no proof."

"Who leads these rogues and how many of them are there?" asked Arthur, curious as to why Taliesin or Merlin had not heard the stories on their travels, but then they had been rather busy in the previous years in many parts of the country. This was obviously a small localised problem compared to what the two of them were involved with and had not spread wider afield to come to their notice, they had been interested in bigger and more far reaching problems.

"The story goes that there are about twelve of them, supposedly lead by Llewellyn, a surly and ignorant man who was once on a retainer to Sir Peredrue but was dispensed with a few years ago because of his nasty temper. Perhaps he heard that Sir Peredrue's mind had begun to falter and saw the chance to cash in, hoping that his failing memory would not recognise him from previously."

When asked who collected the taxes and appointed the magistrates Severus replied that from what he had heard Llewellyn and his rogues did and they seemed to be spreading out to more villages recently, hence the reception committee tonight.

"Well," commented Arthur, "we shall be paying them a visit tomorrow as Pilsdon Pen is on our itinerary and instinct tells me that we should get there with all speed in the morning, as I feel an ill wind there tomorrow, but for now we have other things to discuss."

Arthur proceeded to outline his views and vision like he had done at all the other hamlets that they had paused at briefly. There followed a lively discussion with many questions being thrown at Arthur, all of which he answered to the best of his ability as to what might happen in certain situations, and the crowd that had gathered appreciated his open and honest replies.

The sun was only just beginning to show itself in the morning as Arthur and his men set out for Pilsdon Pen, some instinct was urging him to get there before midday. Although only fifteen miles away the ground was undulating according to Andulus, with several places where a slight detour was needed to miss the higher ground and woods, and follow the meadows. They varied the pace of the horses to conserve their strength, allowing them to walk for awhile, then canter, then walk again, as Arthur wished to get there without any major stops. Just a little water occasionally when they came to a clear pool or stream, enough to keep them going but not too much that it would slow them down.

The morning moved slowly on as the blood red sun climbed gracefully higher into the sky, just hanging there. Almost as if it was waiting for Arthur to reach his destination with time to spare, and the colour perhaps indicating what was likely to transpire. They passed by several small hamlets without time to pause. Eventually Andulus mentioned that it was not far to go but it would be quicker if they actually passed through the next hamlet and not made a detour around it, as it nestled in the valley and would shorten their journey by a couple of miles. Arthur agreed and slowed them down to a walk as they approached the few dwellings grouped around the shallow stream running through the middle. A few people were about and they glanced curiously at the horsemen as they approached before disappearing into their huts, all except one ancient gent sitting outside one of them who spat on the ground and spoke as they came close.

"Going to watch them burn that poor young wench because she healed the sick?" and he spat again. "You're the ones that ought to be burned, look at you all, most of you are younger than she is," and this time he spat directly in front of Arthur's horse.

"Sir," exclaimed Arthur, "we have not come to watch any burning, explain quickly as it appears that there is not much time before this is supposed to happen."

The ancient gent was taken by surprise. "Then who are you and what do you seek if you are not here to glorify such a wicked act?"

"I am Arthur Pendragon, High King of Britain and I have come to take Llewellyn, if that is his name, and his ruffians to task for their thieving and killing, to find out what has happened to Sir Peredrue, whether he is dead or alive."

"Bound to be dead with that lot," was the reply, "but you had better hurry as they are going to burn her at midday in the village square. Good luck to you Pendragon if that is who you are, now get yourself moving before I spit again, you've still got two miles to go."

He made the motions to spit as Arthur and the troop urged their horses forward at a canter. What was the layout of the village? Arthur asked Andulus, who replied that the track went straight through the square if they stayed on it.

"How easy is it to pass around and come in the other end?" inquired Arthur.

"Very easy, just follow the line of the huts either side, a couple of minutes only by horse," replied Andulus.

" Good," answered Arthur, "you stay with me and Sir Kay and the first two men behind us. Sir Bors take the rest of the men around the hamlet and come in the other end, if any armed men try to escape, stop them but try and take one alive, we might need some answers."

As he finished speaking the hamlet came into view and they could all see the thin wisp of smoke rising steadily into the air from the centre. Lets hope they were in time to stop this travesty of justice, Arthur murmured as he spurred his horse into a gallop. Sir Bors and his detachment broke away to circle around as Arthur slowed his horse to a canter as he entered the hamlet, then slowed to a walk as he could see the crowd in front of him.

There was much shouting and jostling going on and the mood of the crowd appeared ugly. Arthur could see that they were being kept back by a fair sized group of armed men and he turned to his men and warned them to be prepared and keep their weapons handy as they would no doubt be needed. In the centre of the circle he could see a young woman tied to a stake, her hair dishevelled and tears gently running down her face, but her head held high. The fire built around her was struggling to ignite, as if waiting for Arthur to arrive. One of the armed men was trying to get some life into it but apparently without much success and was voicing his frustration in a vitriolic fashion. Whilst the apparent leader was waving his sword towards the crowd with threats to keep back or he would have their heads. Arthur and his small troop approached quietly, unseen and unheard amongst all the commotion until they reached the gathering, when those at the back became aware of the horsemen and moved aside. Surprised and uncertain of the motive of these new visitors, and a hush descended on the crowd. The leader of the ruffians did not notice the arrival of Arthur until he and his men emerged from the crowd, thinking that his threats had subdued the crowd. Arthur challenged him asking what was going on and why the lady was tied to the stake, noticing that the fire had still not taken hold.

"My lord you are just it time to witness the burning of a witch," replied the surly leader.

"Who says she is a witch and under whose authority are you doing this?" Arthur queried.

"I say she is a witch by what she has done with her black magik, it is under my authority that she be burnt for her crimes, and that is therefore no concern of yours as this is my domain and I am the law here. Who are you anyway to question my authority?"

"I ask the questions, not you. Who are you and under what capacity are you acting? for this land comes under the jurisdiction of Sir Peredrue not you. Where is he?" replied Arthur in a cold authoritative voice.

The crowd were becoming aware that something was likely to happen here, whoever this young man was he was pushing his luck with the likes of this lot, who thought nothing of killing to further their ends and these young men were out numbered twelve to five.

"Who I am is no concern of yours, so either stay and watch the law be carried out or be on your way," was the terse reply. "We do not have time to dally," and turning to the one trying to get the fire into life told him to pour oil on it and that would bring it to life quickly. There were shouts of 'no' from the crowd, 'she's innocent let her go,' but their cries went unheeded.

"LLEWELLYN," Arthur's voice thundered out. "Release her in the name of the King, - now," and unfurled his pennon midway up his spear letting the wind catch it and display it for all to see.

There were gasps from the crowd as many recognised the Pendragon and what it signified, surely this young lad couldn't be the King, especially travelling with so few men. Llewellyn momentarily stopped in his tracks surprised on hearing his name and turned, catching sight of the pennon, causing his heart to miss a beat, then smiling as he realised that there were only five of them and his men could easily deal with them. That was when he made his fatal error and turning again to the man with the oil told him to pour it on the fire. As he turned to carry out Llewellyn's command Arthur changed his grip on the spear. So quick was Arthur's move that everyone was taken by surprise as the spear flew through the air, taking the man through the side. The earthenware jug crashed to the ground spilling it's contents on the earth and running towards the fire igniting the wood and bursting into flame. Arthur saw all this as he drew his sword and pushed his horse forward towards Llewellyn, shouting to Sir Kay to get the girl and the rest to protect him from attack. Arthur's men responded quickly and attacked the ruffians, who were taken by surprise, such was the speed of the mounted assault, falling back in disarray. Arthur raised his voice and shouted for Sir Bors to join them as he jumped from his horse and engaged Llewellyn in combat. Sir Bors and his men arrived in an instant and the ruffians were caught between two factions as the villagers scuttled for safety, leaving them in the open with no way of escape.

The fight was over very quickly and all the ruffians were either dead or dying. Sir Kay had released the young woman just in time and carried her to safety. Although Llewellyn was good with the sword he was no match for Arthur and was bleeding profusely from several wounds before he was kindly put out of his misery by a thrust through his body. Sir Bors came up to Arthur and apologised for not being able to take one alive as they had fought like condemned madmen but he had managed to get some sense out of one of them before he died that he believed that Sir Peredrue and his son were dead, killed by Llewellyn before the rest of them had arrived. Arthur retrieved his spear and asked if there were any casualties amongst the men and was told there were a few wounds but nothing too serious. Sir Kay and the young woman were tending to them in what served as the village chapel, pointing to a slightly larger hut that they were walking towards.

Andulus was helping with the wounded as Arthur thanked them all for a quick and decisive conclusion to the trouble and that they had done well, and he asked the young woman if she was alright after her ordeal. She replied that she was and knew that help would arrive in time but did not expect it to be the King. Arthur confided in her that he knew that he had to be here by midday, but did not know why at the time. Asking where the village elders were she told him that they had been poisoned by Llewellyn with a so called gift of wine. He had discovered that they were thinking of sending for help to find out what had happened to Sir Peredrue, but she had managed to save them with her potions. That was why he had wanted her burnt as a witch, because she had thwarted his plans and he wanted to show the village what would happen if anyone got out of line. Arthur wanted to know if he could see them later and she indicated that she would arrange it if they were well enough, but needed to see to the wounded first. Arthur took this as a polite dismissal and left her to carry on whilst he let Sir Kay know that he was going to take Sir Bors and Andulus and go to Sir Peredrue's place which he understood was nearby.

Andulus led them to a small hill fort overlooking the village nestling in the valley below. All seemed deserted as they approached, but they took no chances and drew their swords. The place was run down and empty but showed signs of recent habitation, no doubt Llewellyn and his men had operated from here some of the time, as there were fresh horse droppings in the stable and wine and food in the cellars. Possibly some of their ill gotten gains were hidden there too, but that would have to wait for another time. Arthur was in a thoughtful mood as they made their way back to the village. Sir Peredrue and his son were certainly dead, and it was doubtful that there were any heirs from what Andulus had told him, but it needed someone to look after and run this region which covered a reasonable area. He made his decision and would mention it later when he saw the elders.

They arrived back to find the whole village gathered around the large fire, now burning freely without a problem, discussing the events of earlier in the day in a merry and jovial mood that they hadn't obviously experienced for a long time. Sir Kay stood up as the three of them approached and turning to the elders, who the young woman had decided were well enough to join the celebrations for awhile, carried out the proper introductions. The elders went to rise and Arthur bade them stay seated as they offered their thanks for his timely intervention. On being asked they explained to the King what had been going on in the area for some time, that they were not the only village affected. Initially some people had rebelled against what Llewellyn had demanded, but they just disappeared never to be seen again, so most people fell in line as they feared for their lives.

The elders had decided to send for help but somehow Llewellyn got to hear of it, without them knowing, and had turned up with a barrel of wine for them as a gesture of good will. He and his men declined to join them in a drink on the pretext that they had other barrels to deliver around the villages but to enjoy the wine as it was a good one recovered from a wrecked ship. The elders were wary of the reasons behind this totally out of character gesture but discovered that the wine indeed was good and over indulged themselves. Feeling a little poorly next morning they put it down to too much wine but they all became steadily worse throughout the day and Isabel was sent for to bring some of her potions to put them right. Nothing seemed to work, so as there was a little wine left she took some away to, as she put it 'to do things with,' and came back much later with different potions to treat them with saying that the wine was poisoned.

When Llewellyn discovered that the elders were still alive he wanted to know how and found out that Isabel had treated them and saved their lives, so he branded her a witch and sentenced her to death by burning at the stake. Arthur had arrived just in time to prevent that happening to Isabel who had provided her herbal potions for many ailments that people in the village had suffered from. Although some people might call her a witch they knew that it was not true as she did not perform black rituals to harm people, all her remedies came from nature with knowledge she had learnt from her dear departed mother. They were powerless to stop them as they had no weapons and there was great fear upon them should they try and fail, many in the village would have been slaughtered.

Arthur had listened intently and agreed that their choice was indeed a difficult one against armed and dangerous men, and to act differently could have been disastrous for all, then went on to ask about the taxes that Llewellyn was undoubted extracting from them, and was told how he was forever demanding more. Such was the extent in some cases that people did not have enough for themselves or their families. Arthur considered this and saw a fair way to help their situation and strengthen his standing and influence in the region at the same time.

The elders saw that he was in thought and paused waiting for the King to speak. Arthur looked around at their faces and saw the strain there beneath their current merriment. That continual fight for survival, not just against the quirks of nature but their fellow man as well, then he spoke. He explained that for the country to seek peace and prosperity it had to pull together. That meant establishing law and order and justice for all, irrespective of their rank in life, proper administration of all the regions and the capability to defend against hostile intent.

"All these things require the finances to support them and in that respect taxes are necessary, but they should be fair and payable in different ways according to a persons means, such that they are left with sufficient for themselves and their families, with some left over for the bad harvest that can occur. You have been bled dry by a band of thieves and have suffered badly as a consequence. As your King my duty is twofold, one is to see that you are treated fairly as people and the other is that the country as a whole prospers and grows for the benefit of all. We need to work together to achieve this, Sir Peredrue's fort is run down through neglect and needs work doing to it to make it defendable and habitable. This will be your way of paying taxes as a village, your time and effort, nothing else until the next harvest, by which time I hope to have in place a fair system of contribution for each person. Those that work directly for the local lord will not pay taxes but be paid according to their skills and receive food and lodging in some cases, depending on the work that they do."

He looked at the elders and the villagers gathered around, seeing genuine surprise at his words, and asked if they had any questions.

"One sire," said one of the elders, "we do not have a lord with Sir Peredrue having been killed by those ruffians."

"A good point, and one that I was coming to," replied Arthur, and turning to his left looking at Sir Bors carried on, "this is your new lord, Sir Bors, he will serve you and me as I serve you all and you serve your lord, King and country."

Sir Bors was completely taken by surprise and spluttered his thanks to Arthur with an embarrassed smile and genuine appreciation, as although a lord he did not have a proper title until now, he had been a wandering knight with no land to his name. As there were no further questions at that point Arthur indicated that he and Sir Bors would stretch their legs and discuss the finer points of his new role.

Arthur and his party left the following morning to return to Cadbury Castle and they had decided just to stop briefly at Ham Hill on the way. Sir Bors and two of the young men were staying on for a few days to talk more with the elders and have a longer look at the old fort and to take the twelve horses that had belonged to Llewellyn to the stables there where they would be better housed, as the village had very little room for that number.

The return journey was uneventful, they made a brief stop as planned at Ham Hill and Arthur spoke to the villagers there who pledged their support and it was a weary troop that finally came in sight of Cadbury just as the sun had started to go down. It had been a long ride to do in a day, even with the short break, the horses as well as the men were beginning to feel the strain. Word of their arrival had reached Greyfus and he was there to meet them on arrival. Noticing the dressed wounds on some of the men and that they were three short asked what had happened and where were Sir Bors and two of the lads.

"Never fear," Arthur told him, "they are alive and kicking, we had a little spot of bother to deal with but that was taken care of and these lads did well thanks to your good training. Sir Bors and the others will be back in a few days, but I expect that they will want to get off again shortly after they return as they have much to do."

Some of the other trainee soldiers had come out and seeing the wounds on some of the returning group wanted to know what happened. Arthur, Sir Kay and Andulus dismounted and gave their mounts to the stable lads and followed Greyfus into the great hall to fill him in on the events of the last few days and to find out what had been going on there, if anything.

* * * * *

Sir Bors and the two lads returned a week later full of smiles that they had accomplished so much in a short space of time, and they had brought one of the spare horses with them laden down with bundles. They carried the bundles into the great hall and unwrapped them. Llewellyn's loot that they had found in one of the cellars hidden in a large barrel stored with the wine, indicated Sir Bors. There were all sorts, jewellery, gold and silver goblets, crosses and items obviously taken from churches, daggers and weapons and two quite large bags of coins. *All this and they still wanted more,* thought Arthur, *how greedy people become, more leads to wanting more and there is no end to it as they squeeze people dry or steal it, for what, to hide it in a cellar where it is no good to anyone. It's the power that these people really crave for, the power over others to subjugate them until they break or retaliate and then they dispose of them as being of no further use or because they are causing trouble. How sad and selfish the human race can become when they want to further their own ends instead of working together for the benefit of all, and sharing their good fortune with others. What I have taken on is going to be a long hard struggle but if I persevere hopefully it will make a difference in the long run and change people's attitude, if not we are all doomed.*

"This needs to go to the book keeper to be made a note of," Arthur indicated to Greyfus, "not that we stand much chance of returning any of these items to their owners except maybe the church items, but it will help to top up the war chest if needed."

* * * * *

The days of autumn rolled on, training the soldiers continued to go well but then Sir Bors decided that he should return to Pilsdon Pen and see how things were going and would take his men with him this time and get organised before winter set in. This caused a rethink in the training programme but had been expected to happen at some point. Sirs Bors and his party set off early one morning whilst the mist was still hanging loosely across the meadows with cries of good luck ringing in their ears.

An hour later a sentry reported to Sir Kay, who happened to be in the main square at the time, that Sir Bors and his party were returning at a fast gallop and it didn't look good. Sir Kay sought out Arthur and gave him the news and was told to go and get Greyfus and alert the men that there might be trouble coming, as he ran towards the gate to wait for Sir Bors and his troop. Moments later they came riding fast through the gate and seeing Arthur came to a halt and explained that they had spotted a very large group of horsemen headed this way, upwards of three hundred was the guess and they were dressed in strange attire, long cloaks and strange conical helms.

"I hope they are not who I think they are," stated Greyfus who had just joined the group, "unless they come in peace."

Arthur did not get a chance to ask what he meant as just then a sentry shouted that they were drawing close and had come to a halt, there were hundreds of them, but a small group were approaching on their horses at a walk. Sir Kay had brought horses for Arthur and Greyfus and they mounted and went out to meet them with instructions to Sir Bors to be ready to close the gates if they were hostile.

"Who do you think they are Greyfus?" asked Arthur seeing the strangely glad horsemen with their colourful robes and pointed helms approaching them.

"The fiercest warriors on horse, both men and women and regarded by the Romans as the finest cavalry - the Sarmatians," replied Greyfus, "they destroyed our forces when the Romans imported them many years ago, I thought they would have returned home to their own country by now. I wonder what they want?"

Chapter 10
DISTURBING NEWS FROM TALIESIN

ARTHUR WITH SIR KAY AND GREYFUS on either side brought their horses to a stop and waited for the small group to approach them.

"Welcome to Cadbury Castle, how may I be of service?" Arthur said smiling.

"Thank you my Lord, my name is Legionus and we seek Arthur, High King of Britain to offer our service. We have travelled many days from the City of Legion, it has been further than we thought and we are a little weary of the saddle." There was a hint of a foreign tongue, although the common language was well spoken.

"Then my friend your journey is at and end, I am Arthur whom you seek, come let you and your company enjoy some rest and hospitality and you can tell me what brought you all this way south to seek me out. There is room for you to make camp within the castle grounds, as our numbers are not great at the moment."

Legionus turned and waved his company forward and as they all moved towards the gate Arthur asked Greyfus to show them where to camp, then to bring the guests to join them in the great hall for some welcome refreshment. People stopped and stared as the strangely attired procession made their way through the gate into the castle grounds, as if there was no end to the number of them, nigh on three hundred with four large carts bringing up the rear. Speculation mounted as to who they were and what they wanted. Sir Bors seeing that all was well indicated to Arthur that he and his men would continue on their way unless there was a need for him to stay, there wasn't, so they departed once again.

Some while later Greyfus, accompanied by Legionus and a dozen of his party, arrived in the great hall and introductions were made all round, Arthur noted that three of them were indeed women. Legionus indicated that the rest were setting up camp and as they had sufficient supplies would not be joining them this evening. They all sat at Arthur's table and enjoyed the food and drink that the kitchen had hastily put together, just indulging in small talk about their journey south, before Arthur turned the conversation to the topic of what had brought them here.

Legionus took up the story and said that he had been approached by his commander, who had informed him that there was a new High King of Britain who was determined to bring peace to the country, but would need help to prevent warring between different factions, and to keep the Saxons under control. The commander had been approached by the King's ambassador for help in this matter, and as he knew this wise old man personally gave some thought to this request. The outcome of which was that he asked for volunteers to serve the King directly and were prepared to move south. *Merlin has been busy acting as his ambassador,* thought Arthur as Legionus continued.

"The Sarmatians are a warrior people, such has been our history, and life has become too quiet for some who want to fight and prove themselves. Others have settled into a different way of life and taken local wives and are happy with the situation as it is. Nobody makes trouble for the City of Legion as there are many Sarmatians and our reputation is well known, therefore those that have joined me are the younger ones who seek to prove themselves and are eager to travel anywhere to accomplish this. You have probably noticed that some of our warriors are women, that has always been the way of our people, they fight as well as any man amongst us, often more so, and they are treated no differently. They all know why they are here as they volunteered and are happy to be of service, all of them understand your language and speak it. At the moment they are not used to taking orders from others of a different race or culture, as they have not been exposed to that before, but we can change that. As a race we respect bravery and good leadership and we have much knowledge of tactics in using horsemen in battle, which we are willing to share with you should you so desire, we live and die by the horse, he is our best companion."

Arthur listened intently to all that Legionus said and realised that these people were just what he needed, skilled horsemen and born fighters, doubling his available fighting force in one go, before calling for assistance from others should the occasion arise. Merlin had certainly been busy and as good as his word in acting as the King's ambassador. Arthur was painfully aware that his fighting force was small at present but he looked to increase it over time. It was just like Merlin to look ahead and perhaps he saw, or was aware that trouble was lurking on the horizon, as he didn't do things without good reason. Arthur must be on his guard and look on it as a subtle warning, perhaps he didn't have much time to prepare. The conversation continued with Legionus giving an explanation of the clothing and protection that they wore, their favoured weapons in battle and how they used them. Arthur explained his thoughts and vision for the country and the training that they were carrying out to improve the skills of the fighting men. Legionus offered their assistance in this and Arthur gratefully accepted as it would take the burden off Greyfus and Sir Kay, now that Sir Bors and his men weren't there. The talk gradually turned to where it was thought trouble might likely start and from whom, disgruntled lords or the Saxons. It was difficult to tell as any small event could start a major conflict, they just needed to be prepared. With this the gathering broke up, the talking had gone on for a long while as the day had passed and dusk was upon them.

* * * * *

The days and weeks passed and as autumn began to wane Sir Bors returned with his men, with reports that all was going well and the villagers were responding with all kinds of help, there was an air of hope and joviality amongst them that was not there before. The Sarmatians had settled in and were helping with the training, showing their prowess on horseback and teaching riding skills, which took the pressure off Sir Kay. Regular hunts were organised to seek out game to help feed the increased numbers through the coming winter months and extra corn and flour was sourced from a wide area. Word soon spread far afield that Arthur was building an army and a steady stream of individuals arrived offering their services. Mainly country lads on foot but occasionally an aspiring knight on horseback, some possibly just seeking quarters to see the winter through. All were made welcome and assessed for their skills before being allocated a role in the castle, those not suitable as fighting men were needed elsewhere, in the kitchens, the stables and many other places, to service the steadily growing numbers.

Although Arthur was kept busy he still found time to regularly take small parties out around the nearby hamlets, to keep in contact with the people and listen to their problems and grievances. Nothing had been seen or heard of Merlin or Taliesin other than the unexpected arrival of the Sarmatians, who had settled in well. Arthur was developing a good rapport with Legionus and his subordinates, including the women, one of whom appeared to have taken a fancy to him by the glint in her eyes when she looked at him.

Winter brought strong winds and driving rain for several weeks, then the weather eased and a calm prevailed before the snow came and covered the whole area in a deep white carpet that hung in the trees in beautiful patterns. The bitterly cold air freezing them during the night, the weak watery sun melting them slowly during the day, only to freeze again later into new shapes as night fell. Very little stirred in the countryside and life in the castle was restricted to essential activities only and the great hall became a haven to those seeking a little warmth and company, not just during the day but at night as well, with singing and storytelling being the main activities.

* * * * *

Time passed slowly, but there was an air of calm and peace within the castle, a time for reflection and planning the way forward to bring unity to the country. Arthur spent much time in dialogue with the others as he expanded on his thoughts and vision, listening to their wisdom and digesting their thoughts and concerns also. Legionus and his commanders were impressed by Arthur's willingness to learn from others, no matter who they were or what rank they were, and shared their insight into the way of different peoples. Battle tactics were frequently discussed and Arthur learnt much on how to deploy cavalry to the best advantage in different situations and in a variety of terrains. The women fighters amongst the Sarmatians commented that they often caused confusion and hesitation with an enemy due to their sex which they capitalised on very effectively. The one called Gelda, who frequently looked at Arthur with a glint in her eye as if stalking her man, stood up and let her long hair swirl around her as she pushed out her ample chest saying that a man soon became confused. Everyone laughed and Arthur smiled at this display as he felt himself become hot and his body started to react, understanding exactly what she meant, and she was not unaware of the affect that she had on him either. The talking continued for some while and then the Sarmatians excused themselves, leaving Arthur, Sir Bors, Sir Kay, Greyfus and Andulus mulling over recent events and how well everything was progressing in such a short time. Sir Kay voiced what was in all their thoughts at the lack of news from Merlin and Taliesin, but Arthur reminded them that they had great distances to travel and that they would hear soon enough if there was major trouble brewing, that was their way. No news was good news and he did not expect to see them until spring eased the grip of winter on the land, enjoy the peace whilst they could he told them as it would not last, but at least they would be prepared. With that the group broke up as night was upon them and each sought some well earned rest before the start of a new day dawned.

Arthur made his way to his quarters deep in thought, *how fast everything had moved since he had removed the sword from the stone and been proclaimed High King of Britain. Many supported him thanks to Merlin's good work, but some didn't and others like King Lot would wait and see before deciding. Would trouble initially come from some of these kings and lords or would the Saxons make a move before his support became too strong. He favoured the Saxons but there were other tribes as well that had caused the country problems, these could unite and there was no saying where they would strike first or how, but he was certain it would happen. Any new King is there to be challenged by those that seek power and they would do it before he became strong enough to counter it. From what Legionus had said, nobody other than the Sarmatians themselves and Merlin were aware that this detachment had come to join him, so hopefully word had not spread very far yet and would be a surprise to any that caused trouble. They had not sought directions en-route as Merlin had provided sufficient information that had also guided them around large settlements that would otherwise cause comment and speculation as to the nature of their business. The two skirmishes that had occurred indicated that he was developing a cohesive fighting force and the training had progressed well, but he* must not be complacent. There was a long way to go yet and much still to do in bringing peace and stability to the country and instigating the same law and justice for everyone. Not an easy task but one that he knew that he had been entrusted with to carry out to the best of his ability. He was human and would make mistakes and errors of judgement, but as long as he learned from them and continued to move forward the right way, then he was confident that in the long run he would succeed and establish a new and better way of life for the people of this country. Maybe his ideas would help to promote peace throughout all the countries of the world, even if his small effort just paved the way for future generations to build on, that would indeed be something. Sow the seed so that others could eventually reap the harvest, from a little acorn the mighty oak grows, this country could show the way for others to follow.

He had entered his quarters and sensed that he was not alone, he heard a gentle breathing in the direction of his sleep area but not having thought to bring a lamp could not see who it was, but it sounded as if they slept. *I wonder what the meaning of this is and who it might be,* he thought as he moved closer towards the slow rhythmic breathing, reaching out his hand to touch whoever was sleeping in his quarters. Slowly he moved until he felt resistance and traced the outline of a body hidden beneath the animal skins that served to keep him warm at night, being careful so that he did not disturb the sleeping incumbent and startle them. As his hand found bare flesh and long flowing hair the breathing altered its rhythm and he heard a gentle sigh and a soft voice saying how lovely his touch was and was worth waiting for.

Arthur instantly recognised the voice of Gelda and asked gently, "what are you doing here in my quarters and sleeping so peacefully too beneath the skins?"

She replied, "I am waiting for you to join me, it is warmer and more private here, away from the eyes in my camp, my lord." She paused and then continued, "my father is of high rank back home in my land, a King like you, but I chose to fight with my people and made my way to your country to join them. I know that my life is likely to be short as a warrior, more so because I am a woman and my strength will weaken quicker than a man's, that I accept as service to my people. I am 22 and there is one thing that I wish before it is too late and that is to be made a complete woman, I have never lain with a man before but I wish to now. Grant me my wish as a lady of high birth my lord, take me and make me that complete woman before my life may end on a battlefield somewhere."

Arthur, being human and a virile young man, needed no second bidding to honour the request of this good looking young lady and quickly dispensed with his clothing and slipped under the covers to join her. Their desire soon took hold of them as they caressed each other, their passion taking them both to new heights of ecstasy neither had experienced before, as their thrusting writhing bodies exploded in unison time and time again during the next few hours. Until exhausted they fell asleep, entwined in each others arms. When Arthur awoke the sun was already up and Gelda had gone, just the lingering smell of her and their passion remained to remind him of the unexpected but very pleasurable encounter of the night.

·   * * * * *

The winter solstice came and went with much celebration as that was the turning point that brought the onset of spring closer by the day. Although the winter weather was bitterly cold with the snow lying deep and treacherous in places, restricting activities to the minimum, people were humming and smiling and an air of quiet expectation was about the castle. There was still officially a good ten weeks of winter to get through, but once the solstice had passed it meant that better weather was drawing ever closer and now with the new year dawning there was hope in the air for a better year, such was the way of human nature at its best. *Positive thinking that heralds the new era, but unfortunately so susceptible to being set back by even the slightest knock, that it never lasts very long and negativity returns again, and with it the problems that manifest themselves,* thought Arthur as he glanced around the castle grounds. *How can I instil confidence and maintain it so that everyone can feel positive about tomorrow and break this never ending cycle that revolves around gloom and doom. I must set the example and be positive in my leadership and trust to my instincts, listen to the people and encourage them to think of the good things in life and act on them,* he concluded.

* * * * *

The weeks passed, Arthur saw very little of Gelda, the snow melted and the chill in the air decreased but little moved outside of the castle grounds, people were still in hibernation. Then one morning a guard at the gate reported a lone rider approaching and word was sent to Greyfus and Arthur. The first visitor since winter gripped the country, what news would they bring. It was Taliesin, looking weary and worried but smiling when he saw Arthur, noticing a difference and how he appeared to have grown in stature since he last saw him. No longer the boy King that he saw last summer, now looking like every inch a man in his own right, that would make it easier with the disturbing news that he brought.

Arthur welcomed him and bade him join them in the great hall to indulge in some refreshment and warmth, as it looked as if he had travelled a long way. What news did he have? Arthur enquired after he had introduced Legionus and the Sarmatian commanders and Sir Kay and Sir Bors had joined the gathering. Taliesin looked around at their faces and said that trouble was brewing with the Saxons in the southeast, bad trouble by the sound of it and soon.

"They are moving small forces, almost on a daily basis, towards the boundary marked by the Rivers Glynde and Mid-wynd, the south and east of which has long been recognised as their domain. There has been very little trouble there in recent years, except the odd skirmish from trouble makers and looters. Saxons and Britons along with the Jutish settlers have co-existed in relative peace with just the river separating them. All this is changing now, as it appears that Aelle is seeking more land to expand his kingdom by pushing westwards and consequently there is much unease in the area."

Arthur asked him if he had travelled the Saxon side of the river and seen these things or had it come to him from other sources. Taliesin replied that he had seen the build up of forces with his own eyes but had also gathered some information from influential contacts. Not everyone on the Saxon side was happy with the current events but there was little they could do about it as the power of their leaders was ever increasing and to speak against them was ill advised. Arthur digested this information and asked Taliesin if he had any idea of how long they had before the Saxons would be in a position to push across the river with enough men to take and hold the west bank and secure a strong foothold, enabling them to expand at will. Not long he answered, a couple of weeks at the most, they still needed to bring in more men and Esla of Y Went [the Celtic name that comprised of parts of what is now Hampshire, Wiltshire and Somerset - sometimes known as Gwent] was aware of what was happening and had moved men to the area to counter it. But they were not many in number, as they needed to watch the coastal areas too as the Saxons were known to use their keels to attack from the sea. King Esla was one of those that had supported his crowning and sent an urgent request for help, he was not sure if he could hold them back if they crossed the river and landed along the coast as well. Esla would have his support confirmed Arthur but wanted to know more of the likely numbers that would oppose them and who they might gather support from on the way.

The discussions went on for some time as they worked out the supplies necessary to support them on what might be a prolonged campaign, together with the fact that they wanted to travel light and fast. Greyfus would remain behind with a small fighting force, the rest of Arthur's men would set out in two days time. Meanwhile Taliesin would return to Esla and advise him that Arthur was on his way with as large a force as he could muster in a short time, and on his journey back attempt to enlist help from others that he was acquainted with.

Taliesin set off the following morning and Arthur with nigh on six hundred horsemen followed the following day with Andulus again acting as guide. He had travelled much of the southern region in his youth and was familiar with the countryside, the direction that they needed to go and the large and small hamlets that they would pass on the way. They were making for Winton [Winchester] initially, some two and a half days ride, stopping at Old Sarum [Salisbury] briefly, as this was roughly mid way on their journey and one of the places that Taliesin hoped to enlist aid for Arthur to strengthen his force. Good to his word Taliesin had secured the help of the local lord, Marcus Tryfig, who together with fifty horsemen joined with Arthur, not many, but every extra man counted. Even better news on arrival at Winton as even more had arrived there to swell the ranks of King Esla as he joined with Arthur as they set off on the ride to Hlew [Lewes in Sussex] some three days away.

Many people turned out to see the High King, his pennon proudly blowing in the wind and their King Esla riding by his side, as the mounted army set forth to do battle with the Saxons. It had been many years since such a large body of cavalry had been seen, even though it was small compared to the likely numbers they would encounter. The Saxons were mainly foot soldiers with only a few horsemen amongst them, their nobility, and they would be at a disadvantage against the speed of attack from a well trained mounted army.

Hlew was on a steep sided hill that overlooked the River Mid-wynd as it passed through the narrow valley below and was an excellent observation post, but there were a few areas above and below this stronghold that the Saxons could cross the river easily at low water, when the depth was shallow. King Esla had mounted troops strategically placed so that any crossing of the river would be seen and a stronger force could quickly be despatched where needed.

The build up had been continuing according to Taliesin, who had been waiting for them, but the Saxons had not yet attempted to cross the river and with luck would not be aware of Arthur's arrival. He traced the river in the dirt indicating where the Saxons had camped, where the crossing places were on the two rivers and where they themselves were in relation to all those. Taliesin looked at Arthur and said that according to his contacts Aelle was nearly ready to move but would try a probing raid first at two crossing points south of them to draw forces to them, but the main thrust looked as if it would come from the north. The River Glynde flowed into the Mid-wynd here, tracing another line in the dirt, and the best place for a large body of men to cross quickly was at Glynde Reach, marking it with a cross, enabling them to circle round behind and take them by surprise. With luck they did not know that they were there in force, commented Arthur, therefore the surprise was likely to be theirs, so they would prepare that for them. He asked what forces Esla already had in place along the river and where they were located, and having them pointed out looked at Sir Bors and Sir Kay and told them to select a hundred horsemen each and cover the crossing points. But to stay out of sight until the Saxons made their move. Turning to

King Esla he stated that it would be good to ride together into battle but felt it necessary that he was seen leading his men in the south, to mislead the Saxons into thinking that this was his main force and that the area to the north around Glynde Reach would be less well guarded.

"Sir Bors and Sir Kay will serve you well. When you have dealt with the invaders leave some men to guard the river and bring the rest to join me as we teach the Saxons a hard lesson." He addressed Legionus, "I would like you and the Sarmatians to join me in the main force, as that will be quite an unpleasant surprise for these Saxon foot soldiers. I doubt that they have encountered your people before, even if they have heard stories told of your exploits, which I hope they have as that will unnerve them even more."

Legionus and his commanders smiled at this as Arthur asked if there were any questions, or suggestions if they felt that he had read the situation wrong. No one commented as Arthur asked Andulus to join his party, due to the fact that he would be the only one with them that knew the area. Taliesin would not be required to accompany them as his place was to remain behind, not being a fighting man but an ambassador for the King, it was not his place to be directly involved.

Preparations were made and all left the following morning to take up their stations and wait for the Saxons to make a move. Arthur under Andulus' guidance keeping well away from the river until close to their destination, where they secreted themselves in a hollow screened from the river by a narrow belt of trees.

King Esla on the other hand was met on the way by one of his river guards from the first crossing point, with the news that the Saxons had crossed the river and battle was in progress. They were losing ground to them as they were greatly outnumbered and would not be able to hold them for much longer. Esla turned to Sir Bors and told him to take his men and follow the guard to the crossing and take control there, repel the Saxons and secure the crossing was his command. Turning to Sir Kay he indicated that they still had two miles to go to the next crossing and speed was now essential, as Taliesin had indicated that the Saxons would cross at two places at the same time, to split his forces. Sure enough that was what they had done and Esla found his foot soldiers hard pressed trying to contain the hordes crossing the river, having to give ground as they were greatly outnumbered. Take the right flank he shouted to Sir Kay and he would take the left, as with his pennon flying he broke to the left to engage the enemy. On the far bank a lone horseman watched the arrival of the king with interest, just as anticipated, and with a smile on his face turned and rode away from the river to take this news to Aelle.

In the hollow at Glynde Reach Arthur had outlined his plan of attack to Legionus and his commanders, he would take two hundred horsemen and wait hidden until half of the Saxons had crossed the river and the rest were either fording it or waiting to cross. He would then attack in arrow head formation, aiming for the rough centre body of men, with the intention of driving a wedge through them and splitting their forces in two. Once he had engaged them and had their attention two Sarmatian commanders would lead their troops out from either end of the hollow depression and attack the Saxon flanks. Legionus and another troop would stay hidden in reserve to deal with any of the enemy that broke through and to reinforce the centre or flanks as the need arose, it was his judgement as and when to intervene. Legionus congratulated him on his sound tactics, he had listened and learnt well on deploying cavalry to best advantage, especially against what would be mainly foot soldiers. Arthur thanked him and reiterated what was already widely known, that he was always ready and willing to listen to those with greater experience and utilise that knowledge gained.

They were interrupted by a lookout arriving with the news that hordes of Saxons had arrived on the far bank and had started to cross the river shallows, thousands of them in fact. Arthur climbed up out of the hollow and into the thin belt of trees to assess the situation himself and the lookout was right there were many of them, but so far all on foot, the advantage would be his. He watched them for a few minutes before deciding that it was time to introduce the Sarmatians to them, and sliding down the bank he mounted his horse and looking around at the men said that it was time to give the Saxons a surprise and unfurled his pennon as he led his troop out of the hollow.

Surprise was perhaps an understatement, as the Saxons had been led to believe that there would be little or no resistance there, as the king's forces had been drawn south to the other crossing points. Yet here was either a lord or king descending on them out of nowhere with a force of strangely attired cavalry, not that many but enough to cause havoc amongst the foot soldiers. Arthur headed the arrow formation as they ploughed and hacked their way through the centre of the Saxons, turning and driving a wedge to split the force in two, swords flashing in the early morning sunlight amidst the clash of steel.

The Sarmatian commanders had appeared and were attacking from the flanks, pushing the Saxons back towards the river, but the way was barred as others still in the river were in the way, trying to push forward. The battle was fierce and there were bodies everywhere as the Saxons tried to fall back from the onslaught, but having nowhere really to go. Arthur was like a demon possessed as he relentlessly drove through them cutting them down in droves and Legionus seeing him push forward so quickly and the danger that he was getting into, brought his reserve troop out of hiding to protect his King from being cut off and surrounded.

These additional horsemen created even greater mayhem for the Saxons and those still crossing the shallow water stopped pushing forward and began to retreat to the far bank realising how vulnerable they were, caught in open water by such ferocious cavalry. The river turned red as Legionus and his troop showed them no mercy and cut them down as they tried to flee from the onslaught, leaving limbs, heads and bodies barely floating in the shallow water.

Arthur was nearly at the waters edge when he was suddenly confronted by a giant of a man wielding an axe and about to strike with it, instinctively raising his sword in protection. Sword and axe clashed, enough to deflect the blow, but the force of it knocked Arthur from his horse and he went crashing to the ground, stunned and with his sword shattered in two by the impact of the axe. The giant pounced and raised the axe again to finish him off, when a horse thundered up and a sword flashed, the axe and the giants severed arm tumbled to the ground amidst a roar of pain and anguish. Arthur heard what seemed a distant female voice say 'that's for my King; and this is for me.' There was a thud and Arthur was covered in a spurt of blood as Gelda swung her sword again with tremendous force, the giants head hit the ground, eyes staring up in surprise and shock in that last split second of life.

"What would you men do without a woman to look after you my lord?" muttered Gelda as she helped Arthur to his feet and onto his horse, "lets get you to a place of safety to recover from your fall."

The Sarmatians pushed the Saxons across the river mercilessly, few reached the other side and those that did soon fell as they were pursued and hunted down until Legionus recalled his cavalry, leaving the few remaining survivors to escape and take word back to their leaders of their defeat and massacre.

Several thousand bodies lay on the river banks and in the water, either dead or in the last throes of dying, together with a few horses, not all were Saxons. Gelda was watching him as Arthur surveyed the scene and she asked him what he was thinking, seeing the pained look in his eyes.

"If it hadn't been for you I would have been one of those bodies laying there, unable to accomplish what I have set out to do, I thank providence that you arrived in time," he replied looking her in the eyes.

"It wasn't your time to go sire, not for a long while yet, you will outlive me that I know, we are here to help each other in many different ways, even like you did in granting a lady her most desired wish. When its time we will know that we have fulfilled our task here and it is time to move on to another place and prepare for our next mission in our evolution, it doesn't matter how long or short that time is, we would have done what we set out to achieve."

He looked at her saying that she had much wisdom and understanding, and if more people thought that way they wouldn't have all this needless slaughter, waving his hand towards the battle field, people could live in peace and harmony with each other,

"How long is it going to take the likes of us to help bring that about?" queried Arthur.

To which she answered, "way beyond our lifetimes I fear my lord, but we can at least start that process and hope that others carry it on."

They were interrupted in their conversation by Andulus shouting out that the other troops from the south were approaching, but he couldn't see King Esla, Sir Bors or Sir Kay amongst them, and there were only about half the number that had gone to the crossings. *That is not good,* thought Arthur, *I wonder what has befallen them that they are missing, and only half the number have made it here, was Taliesin's information wrong or did I read the situation incorrectly.* He did not have long to wait to find out as the horsemen rode up to him.

Chapter 11

EXCALIBUR AND THE
LADY OF THE LAKE

"YOU HAVE BEEN BUSY MY LORD," commented the lead horseman, surveying the carnage as he stopped in front of Arthur.

"What news Flindel?" recognising one of Sir Bors' men. "Where are the
others, your numbers are not as great as I had expected?"

"We experienced a heavy concentration of Saxons at the southernmost
crossing," explained Flindel, "and suffered some casualties, including King
Esla and Sir Kay, but fear not my lord they still live and Sir Bors has escorted them to Hlew with fifty men to receive attention to their wounds."

"That is better than I hoped when I first saw that they were missing,"
replied Arthur, "and at least Taliesin is there to see to them."

Arthur remembered that his sword had been broken by the giant and
enlisted Gelda's aid to find the broken piece, being the Sword of Kings that
had been handed down over the years, with the hope that Merlin with all
his knowledge knew of a way to repair it. Having successfully accomplished
that, as Gelda knew exactly where to locate it, Arthur gathered his men
and congratulated them on their success. Remarking to Legionus that he
had learnt something new that day, and that was not to get carried away in
battle but keep his wits about him as Gelda might not be there to rescue
him next time. Legionus smiled and said that it would be a good idea otherwise she might get mad at him, and she was not a woman to tangle with,
as he saw.

They made their way back to Hlew without incident and Arthur immediately sought out Taliesin to discover how King Esla and Sir Kay were. Being
greatly relieved to discover that their wounds were not life threatening, but
several days rest would be needed as they had lost a fair amount of blood.
Arthur found them resting and asked what had happened, then recounted
the events at Glynde Reach and the benefits of well trained cavalry, especially against foot soldiers and overwhelming numbers.

"We lost very few men in total compared to the Saxon loses," Arthur
observed, "that should make them think very seriously for some while before considering mounting another attack in this area. I suspect that it has
depleted their forces somewhat with the massacre that they suffered today.
They will certainly know that I mean business now even if they ignored the
message that I sent to them before, when we intercepted their attack on

Stocksford and virtually wiped them out then. One of the sad events of to-day however was the damage inflicted on the Sword of Britain, even though in the process it saved my life, it is now in two pieces and I only hope that Merlin and his knowledge can somehow repair it, although it will only be of use as a ceremonial symbol and not as a weapon. It has served me well and I am disheartened to see it in such a state but I feel that it must be preserved as a mark of the High King of Britain to hand down through the generations."

King Esla thanked Arthur for his timely response for help in repelling the Saxon attacks without which they would have been hard pressed to contain. Arthur responded by saying that was why they should all pull together in the fight to bring peace and stability to the country, and it was what he would endeavour to do, but it would take some time to accomplish. They discussed how the battles had gone and what could be leant from them that would be of use in future conflicts, until Taliesin said that there had been enough talking and now his patients needed rest if they were to make a speedy recovery.

Arthur and Sir Bors wandered off in search of Legionus and Andulus, as they would remain in the area for a few days at least. Arthur's thoughts wandered, *it was a good opportunity to show his face around the villages and hamlets and get to know the people in this part of the country and give them the chance to meet their High King. He did not want to be a nameless and faceless King to his subjects, but wished to connect with them and be seen and known, to understand their problems and to explain his vision for the country. What better way was there than moving amongst them and giving them his time, creating a bond that would eventually bear fruit and bringing them altogether as one, with one vision and one direction. Showing them that he cared for their welfare, understood their concerns and would strive to bring peace, justice and right for all, irrespective of their station in life. No man should be looked on as better than another, all were important and entitled to a voice and he Arthur, High King of Britain, would listen and respond. It was time to change the way of thinking of the people to get them involved in their own destiny and to be proud of it. A heaven sent opportunity to lay the foundations of a different and better way of life, that future generations could reap the benefits of and look back and see how far they had progressed. It can be done, and I will do it, even if I do not live to see all of the benefits, it is still worth the pain and effort to bring it about, that hopefully others who follow would continue to build on. Merlin has seen it all before I suspect, but he is still here helping and has faith in us that at some point we will get it right, otherwise why would he bother and care so much. His vision for our future is good, but at the end of the day it is down to all of us to make it happen, even if at times we fall by the wayside we must still push forward and overcome these obstacles. Life will only return to us that which we put into it, so we must be positive in our outlook and push forward, removing those barriers that hold us back, slowly yes, but ever forward until we make that transition. Many generations will pass, as there are many ancient principles that we have forgotten and need to relearn before we can really progress and leave this power and possessive culture behind us and attain that true freedom of life that we all seek. There is a difficult time ahead, but I have made my choice and will follow it through to the end, whenever and however that might be, it is the right choice.*

* * * * *

The days extended into a week before Sir Kay was fit enough to make the return journey to Cadbury and Arthur had made the most of the time visiting many places with Andulus, in his usual role as guide. The reception that they received at all their stops was one of pleasure, if tinged with a little surprise, that the High King had taken time to stop by. It enhanced Arthur's reputation considerably as he listened to and spoke with the people. Legionus and some of the Sarmatians accompanied him on these trips and Arthur went up even more in their estimation as a good leader, not just in battle, but in his rapport with the people and his concern for their wellbeing.

They finally took their leave of King Esla, who was remaining at Hlew for awhile longer, Taliesin was staying in the area too so that he could carry on his work as the King's ambassador, and keep an eye on the Saxons at the same time. Arthur had asked Andulus to take them on a different route back so that he could see more of his domain, therefore they were following the coastal path to Portus Adurni [at Portchester]. Before swinging inland to the large estate at the old Roman Villa at Rockbourne, near to the village of Forde [now Fordingbridge]. This was a vast agricultural region that produced food for a wide area and had a thriving market, Arthur realised that he would need extra supplies for the increasing numbers at Cadbury and this visit would be a good opportunity to make those arrangements.

There had been sufficient stocks for the winter, but they were becoming rapidly depleted and would soon need replenishing to sustain his growing army. Greyfus had done a good job in seeing that enough food had been sourced prior to winter arriving, through the normal taxes and levies, but additional supplies would be needed now with the burden spread more evenly throughout the region. He would negotiate that on his arrival at Rockbourne, after discovering what taxes were being paid and to whom and decide if the distribution was fair, which he doubted, and reorganise them accordingly. His understanding was that this was a large estate with many tenant farmers, who were often squeezed hard by the local lord and left with very little for themselves. That was something that he intended to change, even if it made him unpopular in certain quarters, the taxes and levies must be fair to all concerned and the people must be left with sufficient for their needs, with some left over to be put by for a bad harvest, or to sell at the markets.

He did not know who the local lord was, Andulus for once did not know either, so it would certainly be an interesting discussion, but that was some days away yet, in the meantime they would journey towards Portus Adurni and learn about the people on the way.

Their first stopover was at Old Bury [Cissbury Ring], a magnificent major fortified position with commanding views for miles around, an ideal defensive position from attack by land or sea and one used by the Romans until abandoned a long while ago, and now utilised by the local populace as a safe haven from attack. News of the events at Glynde Reach had already reached them there and a warm welcome was extended to Arthur and his men with many requests to tell the story of the battle, which was done with the usual exaggeration of how many of the enemy there were. Such was the way of stories, it was not the facts that counted but how good the storyteller was in keeping the suspense going.

Arthur spoke to many people, listening to their views and how life was generally, being close to the coast and therefore exposed to many foreign raiding parties. Most accepted it as the way of life, something that would always happen and they saw no end to it, so they had people watch the sea for signs of trouble, to give them time to seek refuge within the fort. Arthur always learnt much just by listening, including the fact that the local lord lived some way inland and was rarely seen, only his tax collectors came there, nobody could remember seeing him or remember what his name was. Typical thought Arthur, living off the toils of the people but not concerned about them at all as long as they paid their taxes, so that he could live his good life of leisure.

The following day saw them on the way to the small hamlet of Fiseborne [Fishbourne], so called because the stream that ran through the middle of it contained an abundance of fish, more than was normally seen in a small stream. It was local knowledge that this was a breeding ground for several varieties and provided a good source of food. Arthur was greeted with suspicion at first, arriving with so many men, strangely clad Sarmatians that hadn't been seen before didn't help, but he was flying his pennon which was recognised by some. A feeling of ease was noticeable after he had introduced himself and the Sarmatians, then being made welcome, he spent a pleasant overnight stay, and was encouraged to try some of the local fish, which was a pleasant change to the normal dried food when travelling.

The next morning saw then on their way, following the lowland path towards Portus Adurni, winding through the multitude of colourful meadows and crossing many small streams. Few people were around and those that they saw watched them nervously until they had passed by, no doubt the only large body of men they normally saw were raiding parties, Arthur could sense there was a feeling of tension and unease about them. He asked Andulus about this and was told that attacks were fairly frequent along the coast, as there were so many little bays and inlets that boats could easily approach the shore and land men. The raiders would be small parties on foot though, to plunder and escape as quickly as possible, so seeing so many horsemen must be even more worrying for them. *This is our weak spot,* thought Arthur, *the Saxons and others could land in force anywhere along here and establish a strong footing before we could muster enough men to counter them and push them back into the sea, They could so easily get around behind us too by landing in several places at once and that could be disastrous, even though we would have the benefit of cavalry against foot soldiers, its bad tactics to allow yourself and your men to be surrounded and have to fight on all fronts at once. I will need to give this some consideration and speak to Legionus on the best way to deploy the men should we encounter trouble at some point, which I'm sure we will, as the Saxons are known for using their keels to make surprise attacks. After their recent defeat they will probably attempt something different and we do not have the men to permanently guard the landing places that would be easy for them to use, there are too many. I need a way of receiving warning without having to rely on Taliesin or Merlin to give me indication of trouble, as they will often be on their travels and delay could be devastating. They have their own way of communicating, and I believe even travelling in a mysterious way, but at the moment I do not share their knowledge or skills and need to make other arrangements to safeguard the people and the country.*

Their brief stay at Portus Adurni was interesting and beneficial to Arthur as he spoke to many of the people, as was his way, learning more of the different problems that these people had, being so close to the sea and subjected to unexpected raids. The fort had commanding views over the bay and surrounding area and was in a good defensive position, it was obvious why the Romans had built it there many years ago and it continued to thrive after they left.

They struck inland to circumvent the many waterways before heading west again, making camp on heath land at the edge of a vast forested area that was unsuitable for farming but rich in wild life, Several groups went hunting, returning with deer and boar, which provided a grand feast for the evening around roaring campfires, with plenty of singing and story telling as the men relaxed. Arthur took the opportunity to discuss with his commanders what had taken place recently, what their thoughts were on what they had seen and heard and their views on what they thought the Saxons might attempt next. Mentioning how difficult the coastal area was to defend fully with so many possible landing places. Sir Bors and Sir Kay could see what Arthur was driving at but Legionus reminded them that if they landed in force from many keels then they would be foot soldiers that could easily be dealt with by the mounted troops. Arthur agreed to a point, but indicated that if they landed in different places at the same time they could find themselves fighting on many fronts, which could split their forces. It would be better to let them come inland and join up with each other before attacking them, as the tables would then be turned to their advantage and they could attack them from different directions, cutting off their escape to the sea. It would be necessary to hit them hard to dissuade them from attempting other landings in the future, otherwise the Saxons would keep on probing their defences. They tried on land and failed so he expected them to attempt an attack from the sea, perhaps hoping to catch them unawares and get around behind them unsuspected, by landing in different places at the same time. They needed to have many coastal lookouts and a way of sending that information to them of any trouble as soon as possible, so that they could counter any attack, as it was a good three days hard ride from Cadbury after they had received the news. Andulus suggested that the old system of signal fires be brought into use again to send word of trouble and summon help, they hadn't been used for some years but had been very effective in the past. All agreed that using them again would certainly spread the word quickly and effectively and when Taliesin next appeared Arthur would seek his advice, but if that did not happen for some while then they would have to make arrangements themselves.

The following morning saw them on the way to their last stop at the hamlet of Forde and the nearby large farming estate, of which the immense and impressive old Roman villa was the focal point. According to Andulus the local lord had been Galbrane when last he travelled that way, and it was his residence. A wily old knight that lived in style, but not very popular with the local people as he squeezed them dry with the taxes and levies that he imposed on them, so that they barely managed to survive. Much of the grain produced was sent to the coast and sold or bartered for fine linen, silks and wine, to the merchants that dealt with the many ships that plied their trade along the coast. He had many tenant farmers that worked the land and was renowned for replacing them without regard to their circumstances if they failed to produce sufficient harvest, or complained in any manner. His rule was enforced by an unknown number of overseers so that he was never personally involved, thereby keeping himself at a distance from the peasants, whom he looked down upon and regarded as expendable. Arthur commented that it looked as if it would be an interesting meeting with him and doubted that their intrusion would be very welcome, especially when he heard what Arthur had to say about taxes and dues to the King.

Shortly before noon they came in sight of their destination in the distance, and set their camp some way from the outskirts of Forde, as it was far too small for them all to approach at once and such a large body of men would cause anxiety and panic amongst the inhabitants. Arthur, Sir Bors, Andulus, Legionus and six of his commanders approach the hamlet leaving Sir Kay to rest up at camp, as his wound, although healing well still gave him some slight discomfort. They inquired of the first person they saw who the elder of the hamlet was and where he could be found, and were pointed towards a hut near the centre of the main group. Elfinius came out of his hut on hearing several horses approach and seeing what were obviously noble lords, although some wore strange garments, welcomed them to the small hamlet of Forde and asked if he could be of service.

"We seek the village elder and wish to have dialogue with him," Arthur stated, without disclosing who they were or the nature of their business.

"Then you have found him," replied Elfinius, "alight my lords and join me inside and take some refreshment, although it might be a little cramped to what you are used to it will be private, there are too many ears around that like to cause trouble I'm afraid."

They dismounted and followed him into his hut, except two of the Sarmatians that remained outside keeping an eye on the horses and to see that they were not disturbed. Arthur said that they were going to call on Lord Galbrane and wished to know as much about him as possible beforehand, as the stories about him were not very flattering, and they were not sure of the reception that they would receive. Arthur noted that Elfinius became apprehensive and wary at this request, saying that it was not his position to judge others or give opinion, especially about their own lord, and certainly not with total strangers. Arthur acknowledged that was the answer that he had expected, especially from a wise one, so he had better introduce himself and the others and explain the reason for the request. Elfinius was totally surprised to find himself talking to the High King and was a bit sceptical that this was the truth, as he looked too young, until Arthur unfurled his pennon and clarified the point, as it had been well known in the area in the time of Uther Pendragon. Arthur explained what they were doing in the area and why, relating the events of Glynde Reach and how the Saxons were still a major threat to peace, and what he intended to do about it and his vision for the country. Peace and prosperity with all people treated the same, whatever their station, subject to the same justice and taxation, this was for the benefit of all in helping to protect the country from foreign usurpers as well as internal strife.

"A tall order my lord and I wish you well in your endeavours but to get the people on your side you will have to sort out the problems within the country caused by a few, like our own lord, who rape the land and people just for their own benefit."

"That is why I asked you those questions Elfinius, I intend to start with Lord Galbrane, show him the error of his ways and tell him what he must do from now on, or suffer the consequences of a refusal, I will not be trifled with and deceit will be dealt with very severely."

The discussion continued for some while and Elfinius told Arthur much of what he needed to know to deal with the situation, the problems he would encounter, especially from Lord Galbrane's overseers and the obstinacy and trickery of the lord himself. Not to be taken in by a welcoming smile, as he was at his most dangerous then for his brain would be hatching a plot to take advantage of the situation and him, no matter what severe measures might be called for, the life of another meant nothing to him. Arthur thanked him for his advice and information and it would be best at the moment if his identity was not revealed, they were just a group of lords seeking their fortune westwards, needing some refreshment and directions.

Arthur's group returned to camp, on the way he gave much thought to the forthcoming encounter with Lord Galbrane and the trickery that was likely to take place, during or after the meeting, for which they needed to be prepared. He discussed it with his commanders as they sat around the fire, feasting on the remains of the deer and boar slaughtered the previous day. Deciding on a plan that would involve several small groups strategically placed should trouble occur, whilst the main body of the army would keep out of sight some distance away, as they were unlikely to be needed. Arthur, Sir Bors, Legionus, Gelda and three others would be the main party, whilst Andulus who might be recognised by Lord Galbrane, would lead the other three groups to their given locations and wait in case they were needed. Sir Kay would keep the main army there in reserve and use his judgement should any be needed.

With that agreed they all took to their rest and Arthur lay for a long while in the clear warm night, staring at the abundance of stars in the sky, wondering what it was all about at the end of the day. *What was the real purpose of life, why were we here? Was it as Merlin had said once,'so that we could learn the real meaning of life and move forward in our evolution to a higher and better way of living.' Leaving behind our incessant struggle for power over others, our need for material things that just generated greed and our egotistical thoughts and behaviour that falsely convince us that we are better than others. Merlin had always said that the Ancient Civilisations knew the correct way to live and connect with everything around them but over time even they lost that knowledge and wisdom and descended to the depths that haunt us all now. Was this the start of a new beginning as people like me tried to re-lay the foundations that had crumbled, and sought to re-build them and gradually bring the peoples of this world back to the true way of life, however long it took? The wise ancients like Merlin and Taliesin had come back to help this happen. Why now? Was it to build on the teachings of the wise master known as Jesus, before man twisted those words of wisdom to suit himself and maintain mastery over others again? Holding us all back once more from achieving true freedom and peace that we all really strive for inside. I must speak more on these matters to Merlin when we next meet and learn more of his wisdom and understanding, that it might help me to see the way forward more clearly. I wonder what part of the country he is in now and what business he is about?* Arthur fell asleep as his mind sought the answers.

* * * * *

Merlin had spent his time travelling to many parts of the country as he usually did but at the precise moment that Arthur was pondering on his whereabouts he was with Nimue, the Lady of the Lake and the conversation was about Arthur. They were discussing how well he had progressed in a short space of time, the transition from young lad enjoying life to High King of Britain had been remarkable and taken in his stride, definitely the sign of noble birth. Learning quickly, with his willingness to listen to the wisdom of others and seek their views was admirable, yet still able to make decisions quickly and correctly when needed, although he nearly overdid things at Glynde Reach by pushing too far forward on his own. They discussed the breaking of the Sword of Britain in the battle and that it could be made as new again, but Nimue said she felt it was time to let him have his inheritance, Merlin was not so sure, but Nimue said he needed some stronger protection otherwise they might lose him too soon. Merlin agreed that would not be ideal if that happened and bowed to her judgement, asking where and when she would like it to be done. He would be back in Cadbury in a few days so they would do it there, and for once she would make an appearance before the people and they would know that she was not a myth or legend, they would see the power of wisdom and light and they would never forget. It would increase the air of mystery about her, but they would know that she was real and not just a story, for they would see for themselves. Merlin wasn't too happy about the idea of her showing herself to the people, but knew it was pointless to argue with her as she felt so strongly about it, so reluctantly agreed.

Arthur might have been a little concerned had he known that they then discussed his concern for the poorly defended coastal regions, because they could read his thoughts on occasion when he was concentrating on a problem or idea. They both agreed that Arthur was correct in his assumptions that the Saxons were most likely to try this next and they would endeavour to indicate when a number of keels left the Saxon enclave in the south east and moved along the coast westwards. Discussions moved on to higher topics and carried on into the night, as they usually did when they had the time and chance for face to face talking.

* * * * *

Arthur's party approached the Roman Villa of Lord Galbrane, the other small parties had been put into position by Andulus, now all depended on the welcome and reaction that they received; they were soon to find out. As they approached the villa gate an armed man appeared outside and seeing them turned his head and appeared to call to others inside and six more armed men appeared and joined him. It looked like they might have been half expected Arthur muttered quietly to his men, or was their normal 'friendly welcome.'

"Who are you and what do you want?" was the curt challenge.

"A party of knights to see Lord Galbrane," replied Arthur smiling and in a friendly tone of voice.

"What about?" was the sharp retort.

"We have come to see your master not talk to the hired help," replied Arthur, this time in an icy tone, "so be so good and go and announce us."

More menacing looking men had joined the others at the gate now and that bolstered their leader's confidence as he replied, "no one comes in without our say so, if our lord wasn't expecting them, no matter who they are. His lordship does not like visitors disturbing his peace, so turn around and ride away."

"Sorry we cannot do that, we have come to see Lord Galbrane and that is what we intend to do and any of you that tries to stop us will be cut down, so move aside," with that Arthur urged his horse forward.

Next minute there were ten more men that had suddenly appeared from within the gate house, each with a sword drawn, blocking the way. Gelda, who was at the back of Arthur's group turned and waved to summon the reserve group concealed in a small copse a short distance away, as she drew her sword and joined the melee. Arthur had taken the first man with his spear at the same time that he remembered he only had a broken sword, he hadn't acquired another yet. Luckily Gelda realised at the same time as he did and spurred her horse alongside his to protect his right side, allowing him to use his spear to the left. Within moments the reserve troop was on the scene and the skirmish was soon over, twenty of the lord's men were either dead or badly wounded and two had run off. Two of Arthur's men had slight wounds and one of the horses had a nasty cut on his rump.

"Time to visit Lord Galbrane I think," said Arthur, "and see what he has to say for himself," as they made their way up the long straight paved road to the villa.

No one was in sight when they arrived and a search of the villa yielded nothing either but there were signs that someone had been there only a short time ago and apparently left in a hurry. That's not possible thought Arthur, we would have seen them, they must be in hiding there still, so he sent the men to do a thorough search of all rooms and buildings, but told them to be wary of trickery as he was sure that someone was there somewhere.

He wandered around the large spacious rooms searching and looking, he noticed some female clothing in the bedchamber, and sitting on the bed as he cast his eyes around, realised it still felt warm. A slight noise made him shift his eyes at the same time as he jumped sideways off the bed, as a sword cut into where he had just been sitting. Standing there cursing was a tall scantily dressed old man about to wield the sword again and strike Arthur down. He had no choice as he drew the broken Sword of Britain, ducked under the old mans swing and drove it into his body.

Lord Galbrane collapsed with blood spurting from the wound. "Who are you?" he croaked.

"Arthur High King of Britain," was the cold reply, "all your wealth didn't save you in the end did it, now you wont get chance to enjoy it anymore my lord. Where is the girl?"

A hand waved weakly in the direction of the back of the bed as with a horrendous gurgle he took his last breath. There was a drape covering the wall, behind which was concealed a small chamber and crouching in the corner Arthur could dimly see a young girl totally naked and crying gently. Arthur spoke to her quietly saying that it was okay now and to wait there whilst he fetched someone to see to her needs, and went in search of Gelda. She was not far away, and he told her of his find and asked her to see to the young girl who was probably greatly traumatised.

Arthur gathered his men together and returned to their camp on the outskirts of Forde, with the young girl doubling up with Gelda on her horse. Summoning his commanders he reviewed the situation and stated that as there was now a void left by the demise of Lord Galbrane it was necessary to leave a small body of men at the villa as protection for the property, as no one was sure how many of his overseers might still be at large. It also needed a thorough search to find out, if possible, what he had been doing with the taxes and levies that were collected, all of which he appeared to have retained for his own use. He gave the task to Sir Kay and asked Andulus to stay and help him with thirty of the men, so that the estate continued to function as normally as possible. He asked Gelda if the young girl was less traumatised now and what information she had gleaned from her on the ride back. It appeared that she was the daughter of one of the tenant farmers who had been coerced to go and work at the villa but the lord only wanted her to satisfy his desires and threatened to throw out her family if she didn't agree to his requests. Nobody else worked there, she was expected to do all the cleaning and cooking as well as give herself to him, if she didn't perform well then she had a beating and was abused even more. She was confused and didn't know what would happen to her now as her parents didn't want her to go to the lord in the first place and doubted that they would let her go back home now, a fallen woman. Arthur said he and Sir Kay would speak to her to see if she was willing to stay on at the villa, strictly as a maid to help run the place. Perhaps she had some idea of where Lord Galbrane kept his personal records, after that he would return to Elfinius and advise him of the death of his lord and introduce Sir Kay to him. Tomorrow they would break camp and return to Cadbury, enjoy a good feast and much merriment and give their bodies a well earned rest from the saddle.

Arthur and his army started on the last leg of their journey as the sun rose on another glorious day. He was unaware that Merlin and two companions were also heading for Cadbury completely unnoticed by any living soul, such was their method of travel. It was a days ride, but spirits were high and often groups would break into song as the tension of the last couple of weeks eased from their bodies as they relaxed.

Arthur had taken Sir Kay to meet Elfinius the night before and had spent several hours with him, leaving him a much happier man than when they first met, knowing that life looked a lot brighter now for all the farmers in the area. The young girl had been very relieved that her ordeal was over and that she could stay on, if she so wished, as a servant and have extra help if she needed it. She thought that she might be able to help in locating Lord Galbrane's personal accounts if she was told what they looked like as he had many secret hiding places. *A good outcome,* thought Arthur, *bringing peace and justice to the area and letting the farmers have more freedom to do what they did best, after years of being squeezed dry by an unscrupulous lord. It would help raise his standing with the people when the news got about and that would spread to other areas, at last they had a King that looked to the people and was fair and just. Only good would come of it, even if other land owners rebelled against him, they would know what to expect in return, swift justice as he would not be trifled with. It wasn't just the soldiers he needed to bring the peace, he needed the people behind him as well, to keep everything else running smoothly, they were just as important, if not more so. Some of them would be the future leaders of their communities and help lead the country forward.*

Time had passed quickly and before they knew it the welcome sight of Cadbury was there in front of them, bringing his army to a halt he turned and raised his voice so all could hear as he praised them for all their recent endeavours and invited them all to the great hall later for some much needed refreshment, good food and merriment. A great cheer was raised in reply as he led them through the main gate and let them disperse and relax a little before the festivities began.

The great hall hadn't seen so many people since the fateful night when Uther Pendragon and many others had been poisoned. Minor lords and ladies from the surrounding area were in attendance as Arthur had sent riders ahead with invitations and also to warn Greyfus, there were also a few knights that had stopped by to offer their services to the king and had awaited his return. The only ones of note missing were Sir Kay and Andulus, who had remained at the villa near Forde, Taliesin and Merlin, wherever they might be, but in one respect Arthur was shortly to be in for a surprise and find out.

A horn was blown, its sound echoing around the walls of the great hall, a sound with such a gentle musical pitch, that had never been heard by any there before, yet powerful and mystical in its affect that everyone turned to seek the source. Merlin had entered accompanied by a lady wearing a full length purple and gold cloak, with her head and face hidden by the attached hood. Following them was a tall young man with long blond hair bearing a long object completely covered by a beautiful gold and silver cloth. People moved aside, curious as to who these people were with Merlin, as they approached the King at the end of the great hall.

"Arthur, High King of Britain," began Merlin in a voice that carried, "may I present to you Nimue, Lady of the Lake and fairest in the land."

There were gasps from the gathering as most thought that she was a myth, just ancient folklore.

The King arose astonished and addressed her, "My Lady it gives me the greatest pleasure in welcoming you to this court, but forgive me but I do like to see whom I am addressing so that I might recognise them in future and pay my respects properly."

"My apologies my lord but I am not used to such a gathering and am rarely seen in the company of others," whereupon she unclasped the cloak and hood and let them fall to the ground.

Gasps of amazement and wonder echoed around the great hall and the King sank to his knees before her.

"It is I who should apologise my lady, for I have never seen so much beauty, or felt the power of love emanating from anyone before, to such an extent that it overwhelms me and fills my whole body with so much joy and love in return, beyond what I thought was possible. Truly you are descended from the ancient high order of elves that are said to have inhabited this land in the distant past, with your long golden hair, angelic and beautiful face and the light and love that shines forth so dazzling and moving."

"My Lord," the Lady of the Lake replied, "you should not be on your knees before me, for what you see is but a reflection of yourself and how you are perceived by others."

Arthur arising replied, "thank you my Lady, you are so modest and kind but I couldn't match you in beauty or love, it radiates so strongly from you that it captures all our hearts."

"But my Lord, you have and you do, but you do not look into yourself enough to see it, that is why I have come," Nimue replied in her soft lilting voice, "You have portrayed yourself as a good and wise King that strives to do his best for his people and it is time to assist you in fulfilling your vision. Your sword has been broken in battle and if I may my Lord I would like to take it away with me and have it re-forged by a master elf smith and in its place I bring you this." She turned to the young man that had accompanied her and rolled back the gold and silver cloth in his arms to reveal a magnificent sword in a beautiful scabbard. Turning back to Arthur held it out to him. "My Lord I give you Excalibur, the Sword of Wisdom and Light, te anu (for you, in the ancient tongue)."

The King still overawed by the beauty of the Lady could barely mutter his appreciation as he took in the sight of the magnificent sword in his hands. As he withdrew it from its scabbard it began to glow with a soft light and when he held it aloft and muttered the name Excalibur in appreciation of such a beautiful sword, a brilliant golden light burst forth from it, far greater than thirty burning torches. The red eyes of the serpents that formed the handle and hilt glowed intensely and streams of red light, like fire, emerged from their open mouths, joining with the rest of the light and filling the great hall with the splendour of its brilliant rays. Gasps of amazement turned to cheering and echoed around the walls until Arthur, after what seemed a lifetime, returned Excalibur to its scabbard and extinguished the light.

Absolute silence reigned for a moment as everyone took in what they had just witnessed, then everywhere voices were raised as all present began talking at once and it is doubtful if any, except Merlin, were aware of the words the Lady spoke to the King.

"My Lord the sword will not fail your hand and will stay there until it is returned to its scabbard, only you or a guardian can unsheathe it, the sword will protect you if used for the greater good but should you break this covenant and use it in anger, or for your own reward, you will no longer be the appointed bearer of the sword. Its protection will immediately be withdrawn and the consequences could be dire and the sword will be returned to me as one of the guardians. With Excalibur I also leave with you my loyal companion Berius, the other guardian, who will be your keeper of the sword whilst you do not have need of it, and will look after it and protect it. Should it ever need to be returned to me he will see to it. You may have absolute faith in him as he is also of our lineage and of high birth, it is sad to part with him as we have been together a very long time, but it is for the greater good and at some point we will be reunited. Take care to use Excalibur wisely my Lord, it will serve you well and contains much of our knowledge and wisdom that it will let you have access to in times of need, just ask it whilst it is in the scabbard and see what answers come into your mind. It is time for Merlin and I to slip quietly away now as everyone is still engaged in talking about what they have witnessed. We will not meet again unless there is a need to, my love and faith go with you, beware anger and the covenant, I bid you good evening my Lord."

"I am at a loss for words my Lady and do not know how to respond, except to extend my thanks and undying love, and I will do my best to honour the covenant of the sword. Your radiance and beauty will stay with me 'til the end, safe journey my Lady, my love goes with you."

With that Merlin looked Arthur in the eye and told him to get the signal beacons working again as he would soon need them, and with the Lady of the Lake holding the Sword of Britain, slipped quietly out through a side entrance, without any noticing that they had gone. Arthur stared after them in puzzlement wondering how Merlin knew that he had been thinking of bringing the beacons back into use, then smiled to himself, he always seemed to know what was going on and was usually right about the outcome.

Much later the conversation died down and people began to realised that the Lady had gone, but each kept with them the vision of that evening, and it was talked about for many years hence.

Arthur felt that he was living a dream and would wake up, except for the fact that Berius was standing quietly by his side.

Chapter 12
THE SAXONS SEEK REVENGE

ARTHUR SURVEYED THE GATHERING, he could still feel the excitement in the air as everyone discussed what they had witnessed, all had a different story about that special something that they had noticed that others hadn't. It was surprising that consumption of mead and wine had increased at the same pace as the conversation, how they managed it he was not sure but the servants were topping up goblets as fast as they could. Arthur turned to Berius and suggested that they excused themselves and sought the cool night air, where they could talk without having to raise their voices. Again nobody noticed them leave, they were too busy with their vivid descriptions of the earlier events, the one time when the King was not the centre of attraction, and he found it a pleasant relief.

Arthur indicated that he would like to know more about the Lady, Excalibur and the role that Berius had as a guardian of the sword, he was interested to know why he had been chosen to be the bearer at this time. Berius explained that he was not at liberty to disclose much as it was a decision that rested with the Council of Elders. They might at some point in the future decide that the King was worthy of a fuller explanation of their role, and that of the sword Excalibur. The world was changing and the Elders were here to help with that transition, and had been for many years, the sword was part of that, as it contained much ancient wisdom and the light was to show the way forward, but only if used for the greater good. It would help the King make wise decisions, if asked, and its light would put fear into the hearts of enemies, so that they would become confused and falter. Only the bearer could wield the sword, no others could even unsheathe it, not even Merlin or the other Elders, except for the Lady and himself as guardians and keepers of the sword. Such was the power that was blended into it when it was originally forged in ancient times. The Elders themselves were guided as to who, if any, was worthy of being the bearer and many generations had passed on occasions before one was found, and that could be anywhere in this world of his, not just in this land. He had been chosen because it was foretold, he had already proven himself, even from a very young age, and had been guided and instructed along the way, he had learnt well. There was much work for him to accomplish to help move this world of his forward again, in peace and prosperity. The Elders had faith in him, he had continued to surprise them with his wisdom and actions for one still young in years that they did not feel the need to intervene, but would always be there to guide him, if he so requested. Arthur inquired how many Elders there were in this land, to which Berius answered that there were only seven. Five that looked to the needs of the people, the Lady who was the guardian of water creatures, lakes and rivers whilst he was responsible for the land, trees and animals. He explained that the Elders were here to help all living creatures in their quest for survival and to evolve to a greater and richer life, not in a material way, but to experience the joy of living together in harmony and peace, where the needs of all were catered for.

"My apologies sire, but that is all that I am at liberty to tell you at this time, other things you will discover for yourself along the way. I am here to guide you, if I am able, and so are the other Elders, ask in your mind and you will often hear the answer, you are connected to all of us. I am not here just as the keeper and guardian of the sword my lord, but as a trusted counsellor as well." Berius said as he concluded his explanation.

Arthur thanked him for his honesty and openness then asked him what his views were on the Saxons intent and where he felt trouble would arise next. Berius replied that Arthur already had the answer to that and should waste no time in arranging for the signal beacons to be brought back into use, they would soon be needed. They talked for some while about how Berius helped the animals and how the Lady took care of the water creatures, during which Arthur related his encounter with the bears and the raven that he nursed back to health. Berius surprised him by saying that he had heard the tales told in the animal kingdom and for a mere human they had a lot of respect for the King, and if the chance arose they would help him in return.

"Animals know instinctively who is good and who to beware of, much the same as young children do, and they remember the ones worthy of help, even down through their generations, something the human population has long forgotten. Humans seek what is best for themselves whereas the animals and birds look to the well being of the herd or flock, first and foremost. It has always been their way, just like the ancient peoples of your world before they lost their direction in life and sought possessions and power over others. Now it is time to change that and remind people of their ancient heritage by helping them re-connect with the old wisdoms and way of life that brought peace, togetherness and abundance. That is the task before you my lord, not easy but certainly possible, that is why the Elders are here, to help make it possible. We needed a strong leader and in you my lord we have one, we cannot do it without you, we are not able to assume that role ourselves as we are not of your people. We have the power, but we are not allowed to use it, this is your world and you have to put it right yourselves and learn the lessons along the way. The Elders can only advise and guide, hoping that at some point in the distant future you reach that everlasting peace and prosperity that awaits you."

Arthur was very thoughtful as he listened to Berius, he had felt this in his heart from a very early age but never fully understood the implications, or the enormity of the task that faced him now. He was here to start the process off and take it as far as he could in his lifetime. Hopefully others would then carry it on through the years into the future, until that point of transition was reached, when life was rich and rewarding in the true sense. No wonder his instincts and inner wisdom belied his young age, this was the mission in life that he had been prepared for and he could not have had any better teachers along the way than all those that had been involved in his education. Now it was up to him, but he was not alone in his task, the decisions were his, but help and good advice were still all around him whenever he needed it, and he sent out his silent thanks for that support.

They returned to the great hall and mingled with the guests until the early hours, during which Berius was plied with many questions about the Lady of the Lake and the King's new sword. His replies were deliberately vague, saying a lot, but on reflection not saying very much, yet instilling an air of mystery surrounding them that satisfied most. Tell the people a little and let them add their own conclusions, stories that would keep them speculating and talking for a long while, so that in the end the truth would be immersed and lost in fantasy and myth, but they would be happy.

Next day Arthur despatched riders south towards the coast to arrange the setting up of signal beacons and Sir Bors and his men went with them as the King's emissary, on a long circular route back to their residence at Pilsdon Pen. They were to see that the beacons were set up all the way from Harrow Hill westward along the coast to Blackberry Castle, so that each would be visible to the next in line and there was to be one inland at Cerne Giant that was visible from Cadbury Castle. This was Arthur's link to all the rest and would be the first place that his army would make for, as it was only half a days ride south and there he would learn the direction of the trouble. Sir Bors would call in on Sir Kay and advise him of the signal beacons and what action to take if one was seen.

That taken care of Arthur took Berius on a tour of the Castle and introduced him properly to Greyfus, then sought out Legionus and his Sarmatian commanders. They were in a group watching a couple of the men trying to control a horse that had been roped as he had gone berserk, and was bucking and kicking at anything and anyone that got near him. When Arthur and Berius arrived the Sarmatians were discussing the fact that they would have to put him down if he didn't calm down soon, as he was too dangerous to let loose, obviously suffering from some problem that was not apparent.

Berius surveyed the scene and asked the King what he would do, reminding him of the time he helped the bears. The horse obviously had a problem, but being an animal could not tell a human what it was, but it was always possible that he could show them if they could get his trust. Arthur smiled and agreed that they should give it a try, but Legionus warned that it was a dangerous and foolish thing to do with the horse that violent, but the King was determined that it was worth a try, so he and Berius slowly approached the animal. Arthur was talking very gently to the horse as he approached, in an effort to calm him down whilst Berius, unknown to Arthur, was sending his thoughts to the animal in a way that it would understand, to allay its fears and soothe its nerves.

To the onlookers surprise the horse began to respond, its bucking and kicking slowly subsided until it stood still, its whole body quivering slightly, with Arthur and Berius within touching distance, the King still talking gently. Arthur slowly extended his hand until he touched the horse's head and began to softly caress its face sending out feelings of affection and help with his thoughts and relaxing the quivering animal. Berius was running his hands over the horse's body towards its hind legs as his thoughts connected with the animal to locate the source of the trouble. As his hand neared the affected area he felt the nerves begin to tremble beneath his fingers. There it was, a small puncture mark on the leg that had been infected but was now healing, although there was something still in the wound. Berius took the dagger from his belt and whilst gently rubbing the skin a little way from the problem area made a small incision and removed the wriggling insect that had obviously been pressing against a nerve in the horse's leg in its endeavour to get out. The horse whinnied and stamped his leg as his head bobbed up and down in apparent approval as the pain had gone, Berius stepped back and Arthur rubbed its neck and whispered a last few words to the animal as the handlers lead it to the stables.

Legionus was amazed and admitted that if he hadn't seen it with his own eyes he wouldn't have believed it possible, and that was from someone who knew a lot about horses, he asked what had caused the problem. Berius said that the horse had received a small wound recently that had gone bad but an insect had found its way in and cleaned it up by devouring the poisonous area, then laid an egg before departing. That egg became a chrysalis that lay dormant for awhile before hatching, but the tiny creature couldn't get out because the wound had almost healed over. It began to move around seeking a way out but kept pressing against a nerve in the horse's leg, which became painful, causing it to kick and buck to try and get rid of it. Making a small nick in the horse's skin enabled the little creature to wriggle out and the pain ceased straight away. The horse was normal again with only a tiny scratch to show for it. Legionus and his commanders were clearly impressed, especially how Arthur and Berius had worked as a team to solve the problem in a calm and methodical way, despite the potential dangers of being badly injured or even killed by the horse in its frenzy.

That bit of excitement over Arthur properly introduced the Sarmatian commanders to Berius and indicating that Gelda was the one that saved his life when he broke the Sword of Britain. They wanted to know how Berius was so good with animals and he replied casually that he understood them as he had lived amongst them for many years when he was younger, but would not say more than that.

* * * * *

Several weeks passed before all the riders returned that had left with Sir Bors to arrange for the signal beacons to be set up. Each reported that it had been done and instructions understood, now it was just a waiting game. Life was relaxed, which was a pleasant change, with much coming and going at Cadbury and regular social events taking place. Even Merlin and Taliesin had managed to stop by in passing without being bearers of bad news, although they both warned that the calm would not last and to continue to be vigilant. As usual they were right and sooner than Arthur expected.

Not a week had gone by since their visit when a lookout sent for Greyfus as he could see what looked like smoke in the distance, but wasn't totally sure as it was a bright sunny day and it could have been the haze playing tricks. Greyfus couldn't be sure either but went in search of Arthur to check whether his young eyes could see any clearer and decide if it was smoke or not. Arthur and Berius quickly arrived at the lookout tower searching the area south towards Cerne Giant. To the King it looked like smoke in the distance and Berius confirmed that it was, also pointing out that there was another plume of smoke to the east of that one. Greyfus commented that the second one could be Hod Hill except they didn't have a signal beacon there, Arthur could only just vaguely make it out, if that was a beacon as well it looked like they were needed in a hurry. Time to get moving. It still took two hours to gather the army and provisions for the journey. An army does not fight well on an empty stomach so although they would be travelling light, as speed was of the essence, it was essential for each man to take a supply of food to last several days. Greyfus as normal would remain at Cadbury, but this time with only a handful of men as Arthur felt that he would need all the men he could gather.

They made good time, arriving at Cerne Giant in less than four hours to discover that Sir Bors with a large body of men had passed that way some two hours before, heading for the next beacon. This was not in fact Hod Hill that Arthur and Berius had seen in the distance but the one at Bradbury Rings which was in the same line of sight but ten miles further away. That was where Sir Bors was heading, so after resting and watering the horses for a short while Arthur lead his army in the same direction, at a slightly slower pace to conserve the strength of the horses.

Arriving there late afternoon only to find that Sir Bors had pushed on to Rockbourne, where Sir Kay and Andulus were, as that beacon was also sending out a smoke signal. If we could only have seen that one from Cadbury we could have gone straight there, thought Arthur, instead of this roundabout route. Although the horses were now quite tired Arthur decided that he could not leave his friends exposed to whatever danger lay ahead, deciding that they must push on and would just make it before darkness closed in on them in a few hours time.

The light was fading as they arrived at the gates of the villa near the village of Forde to find them securely closed. Arthur hailed the guards and requested the gates be opened in the name of the King and his army. The welcoming answer indicated that they were certainly glad to see him arrive so quickly, as all the others were up at the villa and awaited his arrival. Arthur asked who was there and was told that Sir Kay was in residence, King Esla, Sir Bors and Lord Tryfig had already arrived with a good number of men and also two new knights, by all reports they would all be needed. The King conveyed his thanks and led his army up the paved road to the villa to join the others, giving his orders to set up camp near the villa and get plenty of rest as the following morning they would need to be ready to move out again. Arthur and his commanders dismounted and made their way into the villa to greet their friends and find out the extent of the trouble, which the King was sure was a major Saxon seaborne attack, just as predicted.

They were welcomed with a sense of relief by the others as the news was not good. The Saxons had indeed landed a large force, they had been spotted off the coast at Portus Adurni late in the day then lost sight of as the light faded. They appeared to have gone around the Isle of Vectis then doubled back towards the estuary leading to the old Roman town of Clausentum (Southampton), with some keels heading up the inlet at Bucklers Hard. When this was discovered the signal beacons were lit and more men were sent out to try and locate the Saxons who appeared to have landed and disappeared into the forest. None had been seen yet but their forces were probably divided with several hundred in each group as twenty keels had been counted when first spotted, each containing at least fifty men, and they didn't all land in the same place.

"So at the moment," Sir Kay concluded, "we know the area that they are in but not the exact location of the groups, but hopefully we will have more news before morning."

Arthur considered this, it was worrying and posed a problem, they could be as close as ten miles away but as distant as thirty and split into several groups. They had changed their tactics but he felt sure that they would all join together at some point for a combined assault on their target, but what was it, he needed to think this through carefully.

Whilst he was deliberating a thought came in his head to consult his sword Excalibur, as the Lady of the Lake and Berius had indicated that it would give him guidance in time of need. He placed his hands on the hilt as they had instructed and quietly let the thoughts run through his head on the problem he faced. Sure enough he saw what the Saxons were up to, where they were headed and why. A smile passed across his face as he understood their intentions, sending a silent thank you for the guidance.

Everyone was watching him as he turned to face them and explained that the Saxons wanted to secure a foothold at Clausentum [Southampton] so that they could safely land a larger force later without fear of attack. This would also isolate Port Adurni by cutting it off inland, making it ineffective, even if not taken by them. He expected them to come out of the forest to the north, unless they lost their way, then join up before they moved on the old town. Arthur said that they would wait until morning before he decided how to split his forces, in case they had new information from those searching for the Saxons, in the meantime he suggested that they got some much needed rest.

Before they dispersed Sir Kay introduced Arthur to the two knights that had arrived with Sir Bors, Sir Drustanus from Lyonesse and his companion Sir Sagremor. The King bade them welcome and hoped they were prepared for a good fight, if they required anything just to ask and with that he excused himself, going outside to take the cool night air, letting his thoughts come together on what had to be done the next morning.

The camp was alive with activity before dawn broke through the misty start to the day and the blood red sun began to climb reluctantly into the sky. Even the birds were subdued reflected Arthur, as he waited for his commanders to join him, it was going to be a difficult day. Finally they were all gathered and Arthur had Andulus mark out a map of the area on the dusty floor of the villa so that he could explain his thoughts and plan of action. Messengers had arrived during the night with information on the Saxons whereabouts, which unfortunately was very little, two had failed to return and the worst was expected, either they had been captured or killed. Arthur explained his theory that the Saxons having landed at various points along the coast had then moved into the safety of the forest to conceal their intended direction of attack. He believed that they would move northward in several groups, joining up when they left the main forest somewhere between the villages of Lyndhurst and Netley, then swinging around the estuary to attack Clausentum from inland, taking the town by surprise. Arthur proposed that they head for the former and search the area, as they moved towards Netley. They would travel in three groups with a mile between each to maintain contact with each other. He would lead the first group with King Esla, Legionus the second, with Sir Bors bringing up the rear with the third. Andulus, as he knew the area well, was given the task of taking fifty men and scouring the coastal area and inlets to find the Saxon keels and destroy them and those that guarded them. That would probably take him several days but if successful would cut off the means of escape for any Saxons that fled into the forest. Sir Drustanus volunteered to be Arthur's guide for the main army as he had travelled much of the area and was familiar with the landscape, Sir Sagremor, equally knowledgeable would join with Legionus whilst Sir Kay had gained some local knowledge and would accompany Sir Bors. A token force of ten men would be left at the villa in case some of the Saxons penetrated this far, which was unlikely, not so much to defend it but to send word if it occurred. That concluded Arthur's plan. Asking for any comments and receiving none he gave the command to gather the troops and prepare to move out to search out the Saxons and destroy them.

Not for many years had such a large army of Britons been seen in that area and those that they passed on the way stared in apprehension and wonder at such a sight. There was a feeling of tension in the air that seemed to permeate throughout the landscape, the birds and animals were still subdued and the atmosphere was heavy with anticipation under the hot red sun. The only sound being the horses hooves pounding the solid ground as the army moved at a fair pace towards its initial destination not twelve miles away, constantly on the alert for any sign of Saxon activity.

Nearing Lyndhurst Arthur sent two men ahead to scout the country, with instructions to keep going towards Netley if they didn't find anything, but to stay within sight where possible and return forthwith should they spot any activity. He knew that the Saxons would not want to delay by burning and killing until they got close to Clausentum. The element of surprise would be lost as their aim was to secure a strong foothold that could be reinforced with more keels of men quickly, making it very difficult to contain them and push them back into the sea. This was a new tactic of theirs but one that he had foreseen, recognising the dangers of allowing this to happen. Today was going to be a bloody day, he thought, there was much at stake here, he needed to destroy them quickly and completely to deter them from similar actions.

They passed by Lyndhurst without incident, or any sign of the intruders and continued towards Netley, with Arthur wondering if he had read the situation correctly, as each moment that passed without contact increased the worry of being too late or in the wrong place. As these thoughts filtered through his mind he became aware that he could only see one of the scouts ahead and he appeared stationary, the other had disappeared from sight. Arthur despatched one of the men close to him to find out from the scout what was happening ahead. The man quickly returned with the news that the other scout thought he had seen movement in the distance to the south of Netley and gone on for a closer look but hadn't yet returned and was not in view of the stationary one. Arthur spurred his troop on at a faster pace to quickly arrive at where the scout waited, who indicated the direction that the other had taken, suddenly disappearing from sight. Arthur turned to Berius and asked him if he could see or sense anything in that direction.

After a few moments studying the landscape Berius indicated that the birds and animals were disturbed and troubled. Arthur noticed that Berius was looking up into the sky at a flock of birds that were circling high up over the area and he seemed transfixed by them, as if in communication some way. Berius lowered his gaze and looked at Arthur informing him that there was a very large body of men on the move in that direction and they had disturbed the birds, no doubt the Saxons we were looking for he concluded. Arthur looked thoughtfully at Berius and asked him how many was very large according to the birds. Berius smiled at this, realising that Arthur was very astute indeed to realise what he was doing, and told him the count was well over a thousand, although it could be much higher as not all were in view. There must have been more keels than were spotted, thought Arthur, or they were larger and carried more men than usual, this is certainly going to be an interesting confrontation.

He summoned two of his men and sent them to the other troops to request that his commanders come ahead and join him and turning to Sir Drustanus asked him how the land lay in that direction.

"Mainly flat and undulating," was the reply, "with some trees to the south as the forest comes to an end, the east is flanked by the water and northward two rivers join the estuary and there is Netley Marsh which it is necessary to navigate around to head towards Clausentum. The ground is higher here and extends about eight miles northward and back the way we have come, so we will catch them in the open with the water and marsh behind them and us in front of them, forcing them to go north or back south if they run."

Legionus, Gelda and another Sarmatian commanded arrived, shortly followed by Sir Bors and Sir Kay. Arthur quickly explained the situation and his plan of action. He and King Esla would mount the attack, with Legionus coming in shortly after, while Sir Bors and his troop were to swing around and come at the Saxons from the south so that they could not escape back into the forest. But to beware their backs as they might not all be together yet. With that Arthur wished them luck and said it was time to teach the Saxons another painful lesson they would not forget.

Arthur waited for his commanders to rejoin their troops then led his army forward at a brisk pace to seek out and engage the enemy, not two miles distant. Following the undulating landscape they topped a small rise and there before them were the Saxons, moving swiftly on foot across the plain, much closer than he had anticipated and many more than a thousand. The Saxons were equally surprised at the sudden appearance of Arthur and his men and they faltered for a moment before continuing forward at a greater speed, as they were far superior in number. Arthur drew Excalibur and rode into the moving mass, his pennon fluttering in the gentle breeze that had sprung up, cutting and thrusting as he and his men bore down on the Saxon horde. They were closely grouped and this inhibited Arthur's men and slowed them down as many got trampled on and the horses had to pick their footing carefully.

Some groups had stopped to engage Arthur's army but others had kept on the move, so the Saxon force began to split into several factions, obviously determined to continue towards their destination. The Sarmatians had joined the battle and were encountering the same problems with mass of numbers. The Saxons had learnt some new tactics when dealing with mounted horsemen and they were bearing fruit. Finally Sir Bors and his troop arrived from the south and had more success coming at the Saxons from behind and catching them unawares.

The battle was continually moving northwards as the Saxons were not standing their ground, but fighting on the move with many not engaged in combat at all. Many Saxons were falling under the onslaught but Arthur was also losing men, although nowhere near as many, perhaps one to their ten, such was the advantage of cavalry against foot soldiers. Several Saxons fell foul of the Netley Marsh so the main body changed direction heading towards the village of Charford, and away from their destination of Clausentum. Arthur and King Esla fought side by side and many fell before them as their swords flashed relentlessly with Excalibur gleaming in the sunlight as the Saxons were forced towards the River Afon and across Cerdicesford, their numbers rapidly decreasing.

They were moving steadily towards the villa from whence they had started their journey and it was more densely populated there so Arthur decided it was time to change tactics and stop the Saxons and contain them. He shouted to King Esla that they should withdraw some men and get in front of the Saxons and bring them to a halt and wheeling around cut his way through the melee, gathering those men that he could on the way, and raced ahead of the moving armies. Legionus, seeing what Arthur was about and correctly reading his intention shouted to Gelda to gather as many men as she could and follow the King's lead, whilst he remained in the thick of the battle. Despatching the two Saxons that she was engaged in combat with, she broke off, wheeled around, gathering those that were close to her and set off to join Arthur.

"Come my King," she urged arriving by his side, "lets do battle together and stop these Saxons once and for all."

With that she spurred her horse forward with the King, together with the group they had gathered and engaged the enemy. Arthur raised his sword and shouted 'Excalibur,' whereupon a brilliant white light burst forth from the blade and red fire poured from the serpent mouths of the guard, covering the whole area such was its intensity, taking everyone, including the King by surprise and instilling fear into the enemy.

The Saxon army faltered in disarray as fear gripped their hearts and had now split into two groups, those being attacked by Arthur and his troop and the main body that Sir Bors with Legionus were engaging. A Saxon leader shouted something intelligible to his troops and they fought with renewed vigour, determined to go down fighting to the last as they realised that there was only one end to this battle. An end that they had not expected, but was now a reality, as only a little over three hundred of them remained on their feet and able to fight, whereas Arthur still had well over five hundred of his cavalry still functioning. The end was not long coming, a few tried to escape but were chased and hunted down, then quickly despatched, one or two tried to surrender but Arthur's men had lost friends too and no mercy was given.

The sounds of battle had ceased and Arthur surveyed the scene, something he was getting used to, but it still caused him anguish that this was necessary. Many good men had died to uphold what they thought was right and he was proud of them for laying down their lives serving him for the good of the country, but it was still painful. Why was he the one chosen to tread this pathway and lead men to their death?

"Because many others would have died had you not been their leader," the voice of Berius answered from his side.

Arthur a little startled looked towards him unaware until then that he was there.

"Yes my Lord I read your thoughts, but that was not difficult, it was obvious what you were thinking by the look on your face. You were selected for this task because you were the best man for what needed to be done. It is good that you feel the pain of loss, you feel for others and your country and will always do your best no matter how you feel, sacrifices are often necessary to achieve the goals. Those that have fallen knew it could happen and accepted it as they strove to support you for the greater good of the country. Do not feel sad my Lord they gave their lives willingly, that others might benefit and they will continue their journey elsewhere knowing that they achieved what they set out to do and would have learnt much on their journey."

"Thank you for those words of wisdom Berius, I do understand much of what you say but human emotion often clouds the wider issue, a gentle reminder is always welcome to put life into perspective. Now I think we should do what we have to here, take the short journey to the villa and unwind, celebrate and toast our fallen comrades with hope that all this has not been in vain."

The wounded had been tended to and a cart would be sent to collect the serious cases, those that had fallen would be buried the following day, except the Saxons who would be gathered and burnt to stop the spread of disease. Arthur gathered his weary army for the short journey to the villa, men had already been sent there to make preparations for a feast which would help ease the tension of the day.

When Arthur arrived at the villa with his army he was surprised to find Merlin there waiting for him together with Taliesin. They said they had been chasing around the country trying to catch up with him, having gone to Cadbury and finding that he had already left. The King smiled and said they should have asked Berius then, in their strange way, it would have saved them the trouble of all the travelling. Merlin and Taliesin looked at each other in mock surprise, then grinned. Merlin said that they thought they would just drop in and see how things were, to which Arthur replied that they never just 'dropped in,' there was always a good reason behind it. Merlin smiled and said that whilst Arthur had been chasing the Saxons in the south other bands had been making a nuisance of themselves in the west. Persistent raiding in the land of the Cornovii and threatening the major stronghold of Viroconium Cornoviorum [Wroxeter] and Arthur's assistance had been requested by King Cadell of Powys. Arthur wanted to know where that was as although he had heard of it did not know its whereabouts, so Merlin drew a map in the dust indicating its location saying that it was less than seven days ride from Cadbury Castle, reminding him that King Cadell had supported him at the King making council. Arthur said that they would leave within the week unless the matter was very urgent. Merlin agreed that it should be satisfactory according to his information, besides he would accompany him for most of the way, then suggested that now business had been concluded they should indulge in a little celebration to mark Arthur's latest victory over the Saxons.

Chapter 13
A HAPPY REUNION

CARTS HAD BEEN ORGANISED to retrieve the bodies of their fallen comrades and a mass grave had been prepared for them in the grounds of the villa, with Arthur saying a few appropriate words of thanks for the laying down of their lives for the greater good of the country. He spoke to the congregation thanking them for their splendid efforts, saying there was still much to be done to rid the country of the tyrants, therefore they would shortly be travelling north to give assistance to King Cadell of Powys. The area was being plagued increasingly by raids from the Saxons who were trying to establish a base in the west. They would return to Cadbury first, when Andulus and his men had returned from destroying the Saxon keels, then within a few days head north and whatever lay before them.

It was three days later before Andulus and his weary band returned to the villa from a successful mission, although they had only managed to locate and destroy fifteen Saxon keels. None of them were guarded except one that was anchored mid stream, containing about twenty men, that escaped when Andulus and his men were spotted. That was probably just as well Arthur told him, the Saxon leaders would know that the rest were not likely to return, and that they were prepared for them. He then brought Andulus up to date on the battles that took place and the loses suffered. He went on to explain that he was taking the army north shortly, and as they would be away for a few weeks at least. He would like Andulus to stay and keep an eye on the villa, as well as Pilsdon Pen, as Sir Kay and Sir Bors would be going with him. Arthur told him that he would speak to both of them to find out if they had anyone that they would like to leave behind to assist him, but in the meantime to select forty men that could be split between the two locations, as that was all that he could spare.

King Esla, Lord Tryfig and their retinues took their leave with many thanks from Arthur for their speedy response in time of need, with the hope that the Saxons had learnt their lesson for awhile and would stay in their enclave, but to send word if help was needed. Sir Drustanus and Sir Sagremor who had enjoyed their forays with Arthur and respected him as a leader decided to join him permanently in his quest to bring peace to the country. Sir Kay and Sir Bors were just pleased to be in Arthur's company again as life had become too quiet, although much had been accomplished in their regions, with the local population reaping the rewards of a better and peaceful life.

Arthur gathered his commanders and outlined his plan of action. They would break camp in the morning and return to Cadbury Castle where they would stay for a couple of days before starting their journey northward. Taliesin was going to Glevum [Gloucester], travelling with them part of the way, but Merlin would accompany them for most of the journey as he had business in that region. Arthur stated that he did not have any knowledge of the area to which they were travelling but believed Legionus did, he received a nod in confirmation. So they would be meeting many new people and hopefully extending their influence. When they arrived at Viroconium Cornoviorum [Wroxeter] they would assess the situation with King Cadell and decide on a plan of action.

The journey to Cadbury was uneventful and as this time they took the direct route, arrived before the day had passed, to a warm welcome from Greyfus with news that all had been quiet and there was a feast awaiting, for those that were hungry. Arthur asked him how he knew that they would be returning that day. Greyfus responded that Merlin mentioned it when he and Taliesin had passed through several days ago, saying all would be hungry as dogs when they arrived. Arthur laughed and said that was typical of Merlin, always seemed to know what was going on, even when he wasn't around. He had best let the others know that there was food and wine to be had, that would please them. Greyfus replied that they had smelt it and most were already in the great hall, so Arthur had better hurry if he wanted any, before those hungry dogs eat it all. Arthur took off his sword and scabbard, giving it to Berius as they both headed for the great hall to join the others.

The feast did not progress into an all night session of eating and drinking as many were tired and drained from the vigour's of combat. Sleep and good rest had been sparse of late, now the adrenalin had ceased to flow they all felt it. Some had fallen asleep where they were, whilst others excused themselves to find a place of peace and quiet, as soon they might have to do it all again.

Arthur engaged Merlin and Taliesin in conversation to hear news from around the country and the state of things in general. There was still a feeling of unease in many regions with occasional clashes, but nothing significant except for the Saxon incursions into the land of the Cornovii, and they were increasing by the day. It was a hilly area and the population was widely scattered so it was relatively easy to penetrate deep inland, Viroconium was the major stronghold and whoever held it controlled a wide area, hence the Saxon interest. King Cadell did not have a large force at his disposal, like many of the kings in that region, therefore required assistance from elsewhere when trouble arose. There posed the problem because many of the surrounding kingdoms were still wary of each other and thought of each as a potential threat. Such had been the case for many years, and often justifiably so. Arthur could help in breaking those barriers down, by bringing them together, something that Merlin had been trying to do for a long time, with some success, but he did not have the authority like the King had, progress was therefore slow.

"King Caradog of Gwent," Merlin continued, "another that had supported you Arthur, would be a prime candidate to assist you and Cadell in flushing out the Saxons. They both rule over large neighbouring areas and could do with supporting each other against common enemies, not just the Saxons but the Irish and Picts as well. This is something that you should work on, and as it happens we are calling in to see Caradog Vreichfras first, so there is a good opportunity to enlist his aid and bring the two of them together for the common cause, under your command as King. A simple guarantee from you to protect each of their territories from any unwarranted intrusion should suffice. They supported you, now it is time to deliver and support them, encouraging them to work together to help bring peace and prosperity to the country. So simple when you think about it but so often outside the parameters of the human ego. Some people do make life so difficult for themselves, they never see the light. Thankfully there are people, like yourself Arthur, that have a wider vision and can help make the necessary changes in the way of life to move things forward."

* * * * *

Arthur's army moved out of Cadbury Castle two days later on the journey to Viroconium, making for Caer Baddon [Bath]. Then slowly descending from the higher ground to join the old Roman road as they headed northward towards the great expanse of the River Severn, as it narrowed gradually on the approach to Glevum {Gloucester]. Merlin had said that they needed to cross the river but the nearest point to cross on horse was ten miles below Glevum, but they could only do that when the tidal water was at its lowest, and with care due to the soft shifting sand. Taliesin left them at the turn for the old passage, as it was known, to continue his journey northward, wishing them well and parting with a cryptic comment of see them in a month.

This was a totally new area for Arthur as he surveyed the rolling hills and sharp escarpments that descended suddenly towards the river, with just a few small hamlets and villages scattered across the countryside in the valleys. He noticed that there were a greater variety of trees in that region, most spread across the hills with the lower ground being farmed, the crops spread out in a patchwork pattern and the cattle grazed near the banks of the river. *Well ordered and peaceful,* he thought, *but what problems were there lurking just beneath the surface, was it a false image that he saw? Even the air felt different - cleaner, fresher and with more vibrancy. Was there a different outlook on life here, or was it the land itself and the influence of the river? Did that create a dividing line of some sort, a natural bar-*

rier that gave protection from whatever was on the other side, or an escape route from trouble on this side? As they were going to cross to the other side he would be able to test his feelings there, and see if they were any different. He noticed Merlin watching him thoughtfully.

"You feel it don't you?" Merlin commented, "that difference in the air as we draw near to the river."

"Yes, it is most strange," replied Arthur, "I feel more attuned to the land, as if I was part of it and see things more clearly in my mind, but it is confusing, as I do not know if it is real or I am dreaming."

"It is real indeed," Merlin answered, "you are the bearer of the sword and water increases its potency, even without holding it Excalibur will bring you greater clarity when close to such a powerful river as this. It belonged to the sea people, as we were once called, and the vibrations of water are in its making, as they are in all living things. It is showing itself to you and connecting with you so that you will act as one in the task that lays ahead of you. The knowledge and wisdom that it contains will be available to you when it is needed to enable you to follow the right pathway in bringing light and life back to your country, as a stepping stone for far greater things in the distant future. Your small country will lead the way in many ways, as the peoples of your world move forward to their new and brighter future, such is the way all things evolve. It will take a very long time to get there, but you are the one that has been selected to start the process and lay the foundations. There will be many pitfalls on the way, not just for you, but for others that follow after. Hopefully the human race will make it this time, unlike previous attempts that failed because the timing was wrong, the people were not ready."

"That makes things much clearer Merlin but increases the burden on me to walk the right pathway, so much is expected of me I hope that I do not falter in my task."

"Trust in the sword and it will steer you to the right course if you are ever unsure of the direction to take, use its wisdom, it is there for you that is why you have started to feel the connection. The bond is growing, Excalibur has accepted you and is now willing to serve you for the greater good, listen to its wisdom, its knowledge is far greater than you or even I have."

The army had arrived at the river bank at the right time, with the water a small flow some distance out in the wide expanse of sand. A line of small rocks indicated the safe passage across, although some had obviously moved with the constant flow of water and hadn't yet been replaced in their correct position by the local people. Merlin led the way with instructions to follow in a single line as there was only a narrow path of harder sand on top of a now submerged stone causeway built a long while ago by the Romans. Either side there was soft sand that varied in depth that could suck a man down to his waist, and a horse would definitely be lost. The narrow belt of water in the middle was no more than a foot deep and everyone made it safely across, although a few of the horses were none too happy, but their riders kept them calm and at ease.

Merlin, as guide for the journey, rode beside Arthur and led them back up to the high ground as they headed towards Blestium [Monmouth] where King Caradog should be in residence. He travelled around his kingdom on a regular basis and Merlin said that he had been reliably informed that he would be there at this time, as he was every year. *Merlin always seems to know what is going on,* thought Arthur, *even before others do. His mystical powers are beyond my knowledge but most useful to have available in saving time and wasted journeys, not to mention his apparent knowledge of their enemy's intentions. It's almost as if he knows what is going to happen, even before it does, no wonder he is called a seer by those that know him.* His thoughts were interrupted by Merlin indicating that they were almost at their destination and should make camp, it wouldn't do to approach the town and fort with such a large army, without proper warning. Such mistakes had led to unfortunate battles in the past because the wrong impression had been created. Arthur gave the order to his commanders to pitch camp on the banks of the River Wye that they had been slowly descending towards.

Arthur and a small company of knights, together with Merlin and Berius, crossed the river near the town, approached the gates of the fort and requested entry in the name of the High King of Britain who sought audience with King Caradog of Gwent. The gates that had not long before been closed for the night swung open and a guard beckoned them forward and directed them to the central courtyard where they would be attended to. Caradog, who had been sent word, greeted them saying that he was honoured that the young King had found time to call on him and to alight and join him for some refreshments. Arthur thanked him and introduced his companions, some of whom were already known to Caradog Vreichfras.

General conversation ensued whilst they enjoyed the plentiful food and drink, then Caradog asked the purpose of their visit as it was not often that he was fortunate to have such an illustrious group of knights to entertain. Usually it was just that old troublemaker Merlin (said with a smile as he looked at him) who came on his own and disappeared just as quick, after he had emptied his kitchen and cellar. Everyone knew that Merlin ate and drank very little and this was a common jest that he had become used to. Arthur explained that the Saxons were causing increasing problems in Powys and had stepped up the severity and frequency of their raids, inquiring if Caradog had experienced similar problems. A few he replied, mainly in the west along the boundary of his kingdom, but he never seemed to be in the right place to catch them, they plundered and killed in the villages and moved on, disappearing into the hills.

"The situation in Powys is becoming serious as the enemy are now threatening Viroconium with frequent attacks, if that falls then your northern boundary also becomes very vulnerable." Arthur paused here for a moment to let the information sink in before continuing. "King Cadell does not have a large force and it is widely spread, as is yours I believe, this leaves you both vulnerable to a concerted attack in strength by the Saxons, or even the Irish raiders." Another pause by Arthur, "this is why I have brought my army here, not two miles away, to help crush our enemies."

Surprise passed across King Caradog's face as that was definitely news to him, no word had reached him of the army being so close, that was worrying. Arthur sensed the unease that his words had caused, the king was an intelligent man and saw the dangers that this lack of information could pose if it was not a friendly force. Continuing he reminded Caradog that both he and Cadell had supported him as the rightful heir to the Kingship of Britain and now he was here to support them both to rid the area of Saxon intrusion. Each had a right to govern their own region without interference from another and he as High King of Britain would see that this was upheld. Working together would help restore peace to the region. Fighting amongst themselves would play into the Saxon's hands and everyone would lose, just like happened with the Romans. Arthur stopped talking whilst Caradog mulled all this over and absorbed what had been said. After several moments silence, nobody else had said a word, all had listened intently, Arthur asked the direct question, would Caradog join him with whatever men he could spare, and go to the aid of King Cadell of Powys. King Caradog of Gwent looked at Arthur and replied that he now appreciated why he had supported him so positively at the King making council, yes he would support him and let any past grievances with Cadell be forgotten for the good of their country.

* * * * *

Three days later they set out. Caradog and managed to gather nearly eighty foot soldiers, that Arthur considered to be a reasonable number at short notice. Enough for his purpose of showing solidarity with Cadell in his fight against the Saxons and bringing the two kings together for the benefit of all. Their journey was uneventful and although the region was hilly the old Roman road that they joined headed directly to Viriconium. The sixty mile journey taking just over two days, Arthur letting Caradog's men lead the way so that they were not eating the dust that the horses threw up behind them. Caradog himself rode with Arthur and Merlin, as was befitting his status, allowing them to discuss events across the land and the recent troubles in the south with the Saxons. His respect for Arthur rose considerably as he listened to the King's exploits since his crowning, Merlin adding his comments when important issues were modestly brushed over. King Caradog was very impressed and said so to Arthur, observing that although he was young in years he had accomplished much in a short period of time, and grown in stature as a consequence. Arthur thanked him and replied that he was only doing what he felt was right for the people and the country, with a fierce resolve to continue in the same way as long as he could. That was the role he have been given in his life, he stated, his vision was for peace and stability for their land, showing the world what could be accomplished if the desire was there.

Their conversation moved on to what was happening in that region, the history and reasons for tribal conflict that periodically occurred. These seemed much the same as everywhere else - greed and power, the downfall of the human race. This was the biggest problem that Arthur had to face, irrespective of the quarter it came from, the only way to counter it was having the people behind him strong enough to influence those that wielded the power, keeping them in check or removing them, whichever became necessary for the common good.

The weather had changed as they approached Viriconium and a wet camp was pitched just two miles from the town, using the shelter of the trees on the lower slopes of the gently rising hills, close to where two small rivers joined. Merlin, perhaps due to an inner vision, suggested that they wasted no time and a small party of kings and knights should go forthwith and seek an audience with King Cadell. He felt time was now getting short, there was a different feeling in the air. Events were unfolding faster than he had anticipated, he confided to Arthur, which was why he had stayed the full journey with him. He had intended to leave once Arthur had convinced King Caradog to join with him, but the situation had been changing and they were needed urgently now. Arthur gathered his commanders and gave instructions for them to inform the men to be doubly vigilant and set extra guards as there was trouble in the air. Legionus was to stay behind in command of the army and to act as he saw fit if the Saxons appeared. If Arthur or a messenger hadn't returned by noon tomorrow then none of them were able to and he should bring the army to Viriconium at the gallop ready for trouble, before then if he felt it was necessary. Before they moved out Arthur spoke a few words privately to Legionus.

Arthur and his party approached the gates of the town, which to his surprise were wide open with people coming and going, commenting as much to Merlin, who was equally bemused. Nobody challenged them as they entered the town and few took any notice of them. Where were the guards and lookouts wondered Arthur, this place was wide open to a surprise attack, nobody seemed in the least perturbed, he could have brought his whole army in here and taken control in a matter of minutes without anyone realising. If he could do it, so could the Saxons and it would be a total massacre, men, women and children dead, because no one was on guard and able to raise the alarm. He would speak to King Cadell about this. Had they been brought here on a fool's errand, he doubted it as Merlin was always correct with his information, unerringly so in fact. They stopped at the far side of the square, Merlin saying that he would go and seek out Cadell and discover what was going on.

It was some while before he returned with a worried look on his face to report that the king had left earlier in the day with around two hundred soldiers, following reports that a large party of Saxons had been spotted about fifteen miles westward towards Cefn y Castell. That accounted for there being nobody on guard, Cadell had obviously taken all the men he had available in pursuit of them, Arthur commented. There was not much that they could do at the moment, except wait as dusk would be falling soon. They could not go searching as they did not know that area, but they could secure the gate and mount guard lest the Saxons should attack. He looked at Merlin and asked him if he could organise some food for them, as he was known there, whilst they made themselves comfortable in the gatehouse and awaited the out turn of events.

Dusk slowly darkened into the black blanket of night with just the tiny pin pricks of light from the vast array of twinkling stars in the clear sky. The full moon cast its pale glow across the land and created shadows that sometimes appeared to be moving forms of indistinguishable shape that made those on watch look twice to try and discern what they thought they saw. A time when the eyes and mind played tricks with each other, causing a nervous tension in the watcher. Creating something from nothing, just a shadow, a trick of the light, magnifying noise in the stillness, all very unsettling to those unused to night watching. Arthur was bristling with tension but Berius was totally unconcerned, just watching and listening, as they shared the first period of guard duty. He was used to this, having spent much of his time on earth working with the animals and the land, he understood the night life and the amount of activity that went on during this period, when the human race was asleep. Berius enjoyed the peace of the night and knew all the noises and what was causing them, especially the intrusive noise of people moving in the dark. He heard the band of men approaching long before their dim shapes could be seen and warned Arthur. The King inquired if he could gauge how many and what tongue they were using, Berius answered that there were over a hundred with several horses and were of his own tongue, definitely not Saxon. Arthur quietly summoned the others and said that he was going to surprise the approaching group by throwing out a challenge to identify themselves, that might make Cadell think twice in future about leaving his town unguarded.

The body of men drew closer and their outlines could just be seen when Arthur shouted out his challenge, "In the name of the King who approaches the gate by stealth undercover of darkness?"

The men totally taken by surprise stumbled to a stop and then came an answer from the leading horseman.

"Your king of course returning with his men from an encounter with the Saxons. Now open the gates."

Arthur was smiling to himself as he replied sternly, "I am the King, identify yourself if you wish entry, before I set my troops on you."

Merlin and the others were all smiling at this little charade that would hopefully teach Cadell a lesson as the reply came back with laughter in the voice.

"Welcome to my domain Arthur, High King of Britain, for it is only you that would have the audacity to challenge me at the gates of my own town, I am glad you have arrived. Might I now be permitted to enter? It has been a weary day and I believe all is not yet done."

Arthur laughed and opened the gates with the comment, "welcome back to your wide open town King Cadell, thankfully for you I am not a Saxon."

As Cadell rode through he looked at Arthur smiling, "the point is taken my lord, quite remiss of me," and seeing King Caradog standing behind him repeated himself, "yes quite remiss of me, it could have been a bad error of judgement, but thankfully all is well."

The gates were secured again and men left on guard as they all headed for the hall.

Arthur made the introductions and went straight to the point of King Caradog's involvement explaining that he had put the proposition to him that both had supported him as High King and it was now time to put differences aside and work together to defeat the Saxons and any other enemies. King Caradog seeing the benefits of that had accepted and brought eighty men with him, all that could be gathered in a short time. As High King of Britain he guaranteed the borders of the regional kings and would personally settle any disputes that arose. He looked at Cadell and asked him if he found favour with that and would accept that working together was the best for all. The king looked around at the stern faces watching him and realised that Arthur really did have that strength of leadership that was needed, they were all with him, he should be too and nodding, gracefully accepted.

Cadell then outlined to them all the events and attacks that the Saxons had been mounting in the region. Testing their strength he felt as they would carryout a raid then disappear into the hills, only to reappear a little later somewhere else some distance away. Arthur asked him to outline a map on the floor and indicate where they had attacked and when, which Cadell did. As he thoughtfully studied it he casually asked how many Saxons were in the raiding party? Nigh on five hundred from the sightings that they'd had, was the answer, but sometimes less and each raid getting closer to the town. What were the distances between those places? asked Arthur as he pointed to several points on the map in sequence, Cadell gave him approximate mileage for each and the dates for each raid again.

Arthur studied the map carefully and Merlin was pleased to see that he had a hand on the hilt of his sword, even if he wasn't aware of it, and the frown he wore spread into a smile at that moment. *Good*, Merlin thought, *he is using the sword because the situation puzzles him, the answer to his question will dawn on him in a moment.* Sure enough it did, as Arthur turned to face all of them and told his onlookers that there were three groups of Saxons raiding and probing and that they were making their way towards them there, where they would join up for an assault on the town. Once the Saxons had secured the town they would then bring in more men by sea, having swept the area from the coast to Viriconium for opposition, of which there was very little, then they would begin to spread south and east. That would isolate the western regions from the rest of the country and they could deal with them at their leisure, so gentlemen they should expect a concerted attack within days from around fifteen hundred Saxons, They had arrived just in time thanks to Merlin's warning.

The others, except for Merlin, were amazed at how Arthur had interpreted the details so easily, but it was so obvious now that he had pointed out what had been going on and the reasons behind it all. He would return to their camp in the morning and brief Legionus and the other commanders and catch the Saxons in the open as they approached the town.

Events however did not happen quite as planned. The town was woken shortly after dawn by the alarm being sounded, Saxons were approaching in large numbers just over a mile away and men were running to man their positions and to secure the gate properly.

"How many?" asked Arthur as he rushed outside nearly knocking Merlin over.

"Several thousand by the look of it," was the answer from Merlin, "more than you thought."

"No," replied Arthur, "exactly what I saw, but I didn't want to cause alarm last night so I reduced the number. There should be about three thousand."

"Near enough," answered Merlin, "but big trouble whatever the number, without your army here."

"On the contrary," replied Arthur, "if we can hold them for awhile then the Saxons will be caught between the two."

Seeing the puzzled look on Merlin's face, he explained that before they left camp he told Legionus to post scouts to watch the town and if there was trouble to come at once, not wait until noon. Merlin laughed, Arthur still managed to amaze him at times with his forethought and planning, a far better leader than his father was, and Uther was good, but not in the same league as this lad.

Arthur took command without a thought, it came naturally to him and was his birthright, his orders were obeyed without question, even by the two kings. His decision was to go out and meet the Saxons, but stay within a hundred paces of the gate, directing Cadell to have twenty men remain and keep it secure should they need to retreat quickly.

"We have to keep the Saxons engaged so that they do not hear or see the army under Legionus approach, until it is too late, and they are trapped between us."

Cadell inquired, "how long will it take for your foot soldiers to arrive. Can we hold the enemy at bay long enough?"

"We are Britons fighting for our land," Arthur answered, "we will hold them at bay for as long as it takes, my army is five hundred of the best cavalry that you will ever see, the Saxons will not stand a chance."

With that he swung his horse around, ordering the gate to be opened and led the small fighting force of less than two hundred out into the open to do battle. Caradog and Cadell rode beside Arthur with his other knights on either side whilst Berius and Merlin rode just behind the King. They stopped fifty paces from the gate as the foot soldiers fanned out behind them forming a solid wall of defence. The Saxons continued to advance and came to a halt a hundred paces away, six of them approached closer and their leader spoke in the British tongue with a very harsh guttural accent.

"We wish to take hospitality in your town as we have travelled many miles and are weary and look for a good place to rest for the day."

"You are welcome," Arthur replied, "but first you must lay down your weapons. Strangers are not permitted to bring them into the town, they must remain here."

"We cannot do that," replied the Saxon. "How can we protect ourselves if attacked?"

"Then you must remain here," Arthur answered and made to turn away, gaining a little more time.

"Then we must enter your town by force," was the answer, "and many of you will die, your women will become playthings for my men and your children will starve. Do you not wish to reconsider?"

"I have given you my answer," Arthur replied with finality, "the choice is yours, leave your weapons and enter, or stay and forfeit your lives."

The Saxon laughed, "that is grand talk from a boy sitting on a big horse. Why don't you dismount and come and take my weapons and show you are a man?"

Arthur knew he was being goaded and played with and smiled inwardly at such an obvious ploy, but he needed a little more time yet before Legionus would arrive and made his decision. He vaulted from his horse, taking everyone by surprise including the Saxon, landing within feet of him as he drew Excalibur. Quick to recover the Saxon chief drew his weapon. There was a clash of steel as their blades met in attack and counter attack and he soon realised that this was no boy he was fighting, but a skilled and knowledgeable swordsman and needed all his concentration to survive. Several times he tried to manoeuvre Arthur so that his back was to the other Saxons, but the King was too wise to let that happen, he didn't want a sword in his back.

They went backwards and forwards but the chief began to tire and shouted something unintelligible to the others and Arthur sensed another had drawn his sword and was approaching. Next minute Sir Kay was by his side shouting that he would deal with him. Merlin had understood what the Saxon had shouted, but Kay had acted even quicker, before he could shout a warning. Just like old times Arthur had shouted back as he wore the Saxon chief down and with a sudden thrust it was over as Excalibur found its mark and took the man through the body. Glancing round Arthur was aware that Sir Bors, Drustanus and Sagremor had joined the melee too and were engaging the others, but more than that the rest of the Saxons were in uproar and advancing rapidly.

Back to the horses he shouted, quickly before they were overtaken. Two of the remaining Saxons fell dead and the other two were badly wounded as Arthur and the others dashed back to their horses, just in time before the mass arrived. Raising Excalibur in the air Arthur shouted its name and immediately brilliant white light burst forth from the blade dazzling and blinding the enemy such was its intensity, causing them to falter in terror and awe.

The two opposing groups clashed and frenzied combat ensued and soon after Berius shouted to Arthur that he could hear horses, Legionus was on his way and not far distant. *How can he hear horses with all the noise of battle going on,* wondered Arthur. Sure enough Legionus and the cavalry swept into the Saxons from behind, splitting them into two groups as they smashed a wedge through them. Surprise was total and the slaughter brutal as they fell in their hundreds. From the centre of the formation Gelda appeared with her troop to secure the centre ground and relieve Arthur and his men, with the comment that once again she had arrived just in time to save her King, it was becoming a habit. He laughingly shouted back that it was a good habit.

The Saxons although vastly superior in number were no match for the cavalry and were soon put to flight, chased and hunted down until the majority were accounted for, none being left alive when caught. Arthur had lost few men, surprise again being the key to their success, and that night there was much merriment in celebration of another victory against the Saxons.

The talk of the night was Arthur taking on the Saxon chief in the way that he had, but as he said he was buying them time to enable Legionus to reach them before it became an all out battle, as there were so few of them. Cadell and Caradog had been greatly impressed by Arthur and his natural air of command and were talking quite amicably together about the events of the day, and how a small cavalry army could be devastating against far superior numbers of foot soldiers. So far their luck and good leadership under Arthur had served them well, would it last, only time would tell.

Merlin as usual was quietly contemplating his own thoughts and congratulating himself on what a good job had been done in educating Arthur in the right way, he was putting his knowledge to good use even without the additional aid of Excalibur and that was very encouraging. *We will give him a nice surprise on the way back to Cadbury if Taliesin had done his bit, which he knew he had as he had been in touch in his normal mystical way. Let him have a rest here for a couple of days and increase his knowledge of the area, then it will be time to leave. Arthur had done well with the two kings, Caradog and Cadell, bringing them together with the right words at the right time, he certainly knows how to read situations and turn them to an advantage. Our High King is becoming a very shrewd man indeed and a bold and valiant leader, that bodes nothing but good for the country. He treats everyone with respect and compassion, his reputation for being fair and just is growing all the time, the changes that he is making will last for many generations and maybe will help this world of theirs move forward to its ultimate destiny. The highest souls, of which the Elders were the physical interaction to support this evolution, waited in timeless patience for what one day would be the human transition into their true selves. A time of untold joy that would reverberate amongst all sentient beings across all dimensions of the many worlds scattered throughout the great and expanding cosmos. Worlds that had been through the same slow process across aeons of time to finally make that gigantic leap and reap all the rewards of the long journey. It would require many visits here by those such as the Elders, but at least the process had finally started and the more that Arthur could achieve in his time here the sooner it was likely to happen, albeit many hundreds of earth years would pass before that would be achieved. It would happen, as it had already been written.* Merlin emerged from his deep thoughts, a smile of satisfaction passing across his countenance as his gaze took in the whole relaxed scene before him, the laughter and joviality of men as they released their tensions after a hard fought battle.

* * * * *

Two days later, just as Merlin predicted, Arthur gathered his commanders and indicated that it was time to return to Cadbury and to get the army ready to move out. Caradog decided to remain in Viroconium for a few more days as the guest of King Cadell and develop a strategy for working more closely together. Both expressed their appreciation for the help that Arthur had brought in their time of need, and for laying the foundations for greater co-operation between them, they were at his service should it be requested, just send word. He replied that it was his duty and task as High King to seek peace and stability for the country but he needed the help of kings such as them, it was not possible to do it on his own. They could help by working together and with other neighbouring kingdoms. United they could defeat the enemy, but squabble amongst themselves and all would be lost, the choice was theirs, lasting peace or constant conflict. He hoped that they would chose wisely for the greater good of the people of this land. Arthur bade them farewell and to think on his words carefully, as he swung his horse around and led his commanders out of the gate to take his army southward and home.

They followed much of the same route on their return journey as before, except that they bypassed Blestium, heading further south and towards the River Severn. Arthur queried this with Merlin, inquiring why they had not headed towards the crossing point on the river that they had used before on their journey north, as he had said that it was the lowest point that they could cross. Merlin laughed and commented on his good observation saying that he wished to visit some good friends at a small hamlet not far ahead, ones that Arthur might remember. This intrigued the King who wished to know more. Merlin laughed and asked him if he felt any different, what sensations and feelings were running through him? Arthur thought about this for a moment and then replied that he sensed familiarity, as if he was going home after a distant journey. That was absolutely right, that's exactly where they were going, home to where he was born, to the healing sanctuary at Lydney. Arthur smiled, no wonder he felt so calm and at ease inside, such a peaceful place so full of love and harmony, he could feel it drawing him closer. Aloud he wondered if he would see the bears again. Merlin laughed at this and said it was doubtful, but he would see his mother, who was expecting them. Arthur called him an old rascal for keeping quiet about it and not even mentioning how close they had been on their journey northward. It wasn't the right time Merlin replied, besides Taliesin had to make arrangements before they returned so that they would be expected, He thought that they should stop now as it was only a mile further.

Arthur brought his army to a halt and indicated that they should make camp, informing his commanders that he and Merlin had some private business to attend to at the hamlet up ahead. Berius would accompany them to look after their swords as Arthur thought that it wouldn't be right to take them into the place that they were visiting, he looked on the sanctuary as more holy than a church - his birthplace.

The three off them rode the short distance, Arthur full of anticipation for seeing his mother again, well his second mother Gwendolyn, who had nurtured him and brought him up. Berius remained at the entrance to the grounds with the horses and the swords and Arthur and Merlin made their way on foot to the stone building set back amongst the trees. Taliesin was waiting for them and greeted them warmly and led them to seats in the garden. Recollection came back to Arthur of all those years ago, or so it seemed, when he sat in that spot with the healing ladies as they taught him many things about nature, the animals, flowers and trees. He could vividly recall the spot where he was sitting when the bears appeared and how he had removed the young one's pain. Was it that long ago now? He heard people approaching and turned to greet his mother and the ladies and found himself looking at both of his mothers smiling at him, Gwendolyn and his birth mother Lady Igraine. King or no King he moved quickly to them and embraced them both, lifting them off their feet, such was his delight at finding them both there. They marvelled at how he had grown, not just in size but stature too, no longer the boy King but a man in his own right. They moved towards a stone seat and sat either side of him as Merlin and Taliesin discreetly withdrew and joined Berius at the entrance.

Both of the women were eager to hear all about Arthur's adventures since they had last seen him, so he spent nearly two hours bringing them up to date, from the arrival of the Sarmatians to the recent defeat of the Saxons at Viriconium. They marvelled at how so much had befallen him in such a short time and he had obviously dealt with all of it in his stride. Their pride and joy at what their son had accomplished for his young years showed in the beautiful smile on each of their faces as they listened intently to him.

Arthur eventually paused and asked what had been happening in their lives since they last met, as it seemed an age ago now. The women looked at each other and Igraine nodded to Gwendolyn to tell her story first. There was not much to tell she said. She had returned to the sanctuary to assist the women and was made most welcome by them, as it eased their burden considerably in the good work they did. Life was full of love and peace there and she felt thoroughly at home, pleased that she had made the decision to return and be of service to those in need. They were always busy with people travelling great distances to them for healing many different ailments, as their reputation for unbiased and successful help had spread far and wide. Local folk as well as lords and ladies sought out their expertise and genuine caring. Everyone that came fell in love with the place, so peaceful and beautiful. Her one regret was that they had never seen or heard of the bears again, but perhaps that was a good thing as she felt that they had come there deliberately seeking out Arthur. A strange thing to say maybe but she had that inner feeling telling her that was how it was, because the animals knew instinctively that they could trust him, he would do them no harm, even though he was a human. She told Arthur that she would be happy to stay at the sanctuary for the rest of her natural life, however long or short that was, she knew that she was doing something worthwhile in serving others and it produced happiness and contentment within herself, what more could she ask for.

He asked Igraine what news she had to tell, inquiring as to the well being of Sir Cador and her two daughters, who must both be ladies of the court now. Igraine replied that Cador was handling the responsibilities of being the Duke extremely well but she felt that he was becoming a little bored of court life, just like his father had, and sought more action than the small amount of minor disputes that occurred.

"One day I'm sure he will travel to join you, especially after he hears of your adventures, its in his blood I'm afraid, but it is not for me to stand in his way if that is his desire. As for my daughters, Anna is still the quiet one and Morgause as ever the rebel, so much so that she got her hooks into

King Lot when she saw him and married him within the week. I don't think he had much to say about the matter, he was totally besotted with her. They already have two sons and I expect there will be more. I have a suspicion too that she was with child when they married, before King Lot arrived, but she refused to discuss the matter with me." Igraine looked pointedly at Arthur when she said this, but continued, "it is of no consequence however with the situation as it is, although I am sure that Lot was not aware of her condition, it is best left unsaid. News is much delayed from the north and as yet I do not even know the children's names, perhaps I should inquire of Merlin if he knows; talking of the dear fellow I think we should invite him and Taliesin to join us." Gwendolyn said that she would go and fetch them whilst Igraine concluded her news. "There isn't much else to tell, Sir Brastias continues to oversee much of the day to day running of the fort and Sir Ector still frequently calls. I will inform him of your adventures, I think they will please him, as he had a very high regard for you and your friendship with his son Sir Kay, who appears to have played a major role in the skirmishes with the Saxons."

Merlin and Taliesin arrived shortly after with Gwendolyn looking a little flushed complaining that the two of them had caused her a little embarrassment with the very handsome looking young man looking after their horses, but she wouldn't be drawn any further. Merlin and Taliesin just looked at each other and smiled without embroidering on Gwendolyn's flustered appearance, despite a questioning glance from Igraine. Arthur commented that the very handsome young man, as she called him was Berius, the guardian of his sword and closely associated with Nimue, Lady of the Lake, whose domain they were currently in. As he had not wished to bring their weapons into such a loving and peaceful place as the sanctuary, Berius had remained at the gate with them.

"We must see this wondrous sword of yours before you leave, and the handsome man of course," replied Igraine.

They all burst out laughing at this and Gwendolyn forgot all about her embarrassment as she joined in too.

They spent another hour together before Arthur said that they really had to go, although he would liked to have stayed much longer, that would have to wait for another time. He was grateful and happy that the two mystical old men had arranged the surprise for him and it would be something that he would cherish.

They walked slowly to the gate, Merlin and Taliesin leading the way and Arthur following with a mother on each arm, happy and content. They retrieved their weapons from Berius, who gave them a warm smile as he was introduced commenting to the ladies that even the animals and birds were happy there, they understood what the sanctuary provided and they felt the love emanating from it. The women looked at Berius in mild surprise and wonder until Arthur explained that he had spent much of his life with animals and knew their thoughts, another mystical man and good to have along.

Arthur showed them Excalibur and handed the sword to Igraine, who tried to unsheathe it from the scabbard to take a closer look, but to no avail, it didn't budge. Arthur apologised and told them that only he, Berius and the Lady of the Lake could draw the sword, as the bearer and guardians, nobody else could, not even Merlin. Neither could he hand it to them as it would not leave his hand until he returned it to the scabbard. The women were amazed commenting that it was truly a magical sword and would serve him well, they felt happier that he was so well protected. Arthur refrained from divulging any more of Excalibur's secrets, saying that it was time to take their leave of them, giving each a big embrace with a promise to see them when he could.

Igraine suddenly remembered that she had a message for him from her daughter, well more of a riddle, she didn't understand it but hopefully Arthur would. Morgause had asked her to tell him 'beware the fiery sun that rises in distant lands, give respect that is deserved, ignore at your peril.' He said that it did not mean anything to him at the moment but he would think on it. With that he mounted his horse and with a final wave the party moved off, heading back to camp and a continuation of their journey home to Cadbury.

The comment troubled Merlin but he didn't have an answer to it either, but would keep it in mind and give the riddle some thought.

Chapter 14
THE SAXONS INCREASE THE PRESSURE

ARTHUR DID NOT SLEEP WELL, his mind kept wandering to what Igraine had said, that she suspected that Morgause was with child when she married King Lot. His mother had given him a questioning look when she mentioned it, as if she knew that her son was the father of the child, which it seemed likely that he was. Morgause had seduced him with gay abandon without thought of the consequences and he had allowed it to happen, his own half sister, although he wasn't aware of their association at the time. Not just allowed it to happen but taken control of the situation and given her more than she had been expecting, turning the tables on her. The timing was about right according to what his mother had said, no wonder Morgause was in a hurry to marry Lot, she was trying to hide her condition and needed a man quickly, one that she could manipulate and make out that the child was his. A dangerous scheming woman, and what was the meaning of her riddle he wondered, was it a warning or a threat, you never knew with Morgause. All he knew was that she wasn't happy about losing the battle of words after their passionate encounter, going by the way that she stormed off.

He drifted off into a dream state, but that was no better, he had a feeling that something bad had happened in the south whilst they were dealing with the Saxons at Viriconium. Was he led that way deliberately? whilst the enemy attacked from behind. His dream was vivid as he saw great slaughter and death sweep suddenly, without warning, on a sleepy fort by the sea and continue inland. The pain and anguish on people's faces as they realised no help was at hand. He tried to concentrate, seeking to identify the location, but to no avail, all he could hear was the cries of the people shouting his name in desperation, but he couldn't reach them in time, he was too far away.

He awoke suddenly, bathed in sweat, with Berius shaking his shoulder asking him if he was alright, as he appeared to be having a bad dream and calling out. Arthur moped his brow and shook his head to try and clear it, answering that he was greatly disturbed and felt that something bad had occurred in the south of the country. Merlin appeared at that moment, attracted by voices. On hearing Arthur's words commented that he had felt the same vibrations and sent his vision out far and wide to determine the cause, what he saw was indeed bad news. The Saxons had landed in force that night using the clear night sky, illuminated by the soft glow of the full moon to steer their way safely to shore. The inhabitants of Bosham, close to the old derelict Roman Palace at Fiseborne, and right on the waters edge were taken totally by surprise and did not have chance to defend themselves. The slaughter was terrible, all were put to the sword as the Saxon horde swept through the village and other hamlets that they passed on the way, as they headed inland in a north west direction. The attack was so swift and unexpected that no signal beacons were lit, therefore no warning of their coming or arrival had been given, and the south slept unaware of the extreme danger that they were in.

"Indeed that is grave news," Arthur commented, "we are several days ride away from them, unable to bring help in their hour of need and too far to warn others of the impending danger. Merlin do you have contacts in that area that you could communicate with in your mystical way? Enough to at least give warning that a large Saxon army is on the rampage and to do what they can until we can reach them."

Merlin pondered this for a moment before replying, "I will do my best, but there are only a few that are receptive to our way of communicating, where they are and whether they will understand sufficiently is another matter. When I have done that Taliesin and I will take our leave of you and make haste south, we can travel fast when we have need. It puzzles me what the Saxons intend and what their objective is, other than to create as much turmoil as possible whilst you are being kept busy elsewhere."

"I had wondered that," answered Arthur, "I get the feeling that I was drawn north deliberately to allow them the advantage of establishing a stronghold on the coast, but why have they moved inland, thus making themselves vulnerable to attack from my forces. It is a puzzle at the moment but no doubt will become clearer as time progresses. I do not think it is just to cause dissent in the area because I am not there to protect the people, there is a deeper motive I am sure, but that alludes me for now."

Merlin made to leave, "I will waken Taliesin and we will be on our way, head for Glevum then take the old Roman road to Corinium and gather what extra men you need," he instructed the King, "any news that we have will be sent to Berius, mark his words carefully they should lead you in the right direction. Good luck."

With that Merlin melted into the night and soon Arthur heard two horses depart the camp as they set off on their errand. He realised that he hadn't challenged Merlin on his precise location of the attack being at Bosham, how could he be so positive, that was days away from there. Another of his mystical talents that he must ask him more about. How could he see that distance he was only human, or was he, did the Elders belong to a totally different race that was superior to the rest of them? He would enquire of Berius and see what he could glean from him as he was one of them, but then he would undoubtedly only divulge what was allowed and necessary, going by an earlier conversation with him. They appeared to operate by a different code of conduct, as if they should not overly interfere in events that were happening, just act as ambassadors and advisors when necessary. A quiet race were the Elders, just listening and observing most of the time, until asked for advice, then they would share their wisdom and knowledge as befitted the occasion, but Arthur wondered how much they knew that was never said. As Merlin had once said, they had the power to change the world but were forbidden to use it, that must be accomplished by the people themselves, otherwise they would never learn. Arthur was greatly appreciative of their help, without which he knew his task of uniting the country in peace and prosperity would be very difficult and prolonged, but there was still a great deal to do and a long way to go. He would have a few hours rest whilst it was still dark, then gather his army and follow the route that Merlin had indicated to him. He smiled to himself, more of a command than a suggestion. When Merlin spoke, you listened, whatever knowledge or insight that he had he was rarely wrong, it was as well to take notice and act accordingly. Arthur raised his eyes skywards sending a silent prayer of thanks that Merlin and the Elders were with them and not the enemy.

The journey to Glevum was short and Arthur and his commanders sought out the local lord, a Duke no less, and appraised him of the situation stressing that the Saxons, although some days away, were apparently heading in that direction and more soldiers than he had at his command might be needed to stop them. The Duke wanted to know how many of the enemy there were and how sure Arthur was that Glevum was their destination. The King told him that the information that he had was good and there were several thousand Saxons on the rampage. Although he was not sure of their ultimate target there were very few places en-route that were of strategic importance, other than there and Corinium, which was his next stop. The Duke pondered on the situation for a moment, then agreed to gather what men he could spare to join the King's army, but that he himself would not be able to join them as he was suffering from a malaise that prevented him from riding. He would however send a good commander with them as at times the men could be a little unruly, although stout at heart, all they needed was a firm hand to keep them in order. Arthur expressed his thanks as the Duke invited them to rest awhile and take some sustenance whilst he made the arrangements.

Several hours later Arthur and his commanders took their leave of the Duke with nearly one hundred and fifty foot soldiers led by a surly looking individual called Fergus, snarling his orders at them to watch their manners before the King. Arthur smiled to himself, *I hope he doesn't try to treat any of my men like that,* he thought, *he would bring on himself a great deal of grief if he did, but maybe it is time for him to learn how to treat people and not try and use fear as a weapon. It would be a good idea to keep an eye on him, lest he caused trouble amongst the men.* They rejoined the main army and headed out of Glevum following the Roman road as it climbed steeply to the top of the escarpment and then headed directly towards Corinium some ten miles away. The foot soldiers led the way as they were slower and would not have to continually eat the dust that the horses threw up behind them. It also gave Arthur the opportunity of keeping an eye on them and identifying those that might be the cause of trouble. He had learnt much in his short life so far, one of the most important lessons being that he could distinguish between those that were likely to cause trouble and those that would not, it had become an inbuilt instinct that had served him well.

They set up camp on the outskirts of Corinium and once again Arthur and his commanders set forth to enlist further aid, returning some while later with the promise of whatever men could be assembled by the morning would go with him. He could feel the underlying tension around the camp area of the Duke's men and resolved to go and speak with them before it spread to the rest of the camp. It was not good to allow that sort of feeling to grow as it eventually affected everyone and would diminish the effectiveness of his army. Sir Kay and Gelda said that they would like to accompany him and Arthur agreed, Sir Bors seeing the look Gelda gave him remarked that he had already seen the King in action, to his cost, when they first met.

The three of them silently approached the Duke's men and it was obvious a heated exchange was taking place by the raised voices. Fergus was giving a young lad a verbal onslaught, but several others were telling him to back off and leave the lad alone.

"He shouldn't be here anyway," one said, "with his mother being so poorly."

"That was none of their business," was the retort. "He's here because I told him to be."

"Threatened him more likely," came another voice from the crowd.

"Any more nonsense from you lot," Fergus exploded, "and I'll run someone through."

"Is that why you didn't give the lad a sword?" came another voice from deep in the crowd, "in case he ran you through."

This comment brought peels of laughter from the group and infuriated Fergus that much that he was on the point of drawing his sword when Arthur stepped forward into his line of vision.

"What's all this about Fergus?" Arthur inquired. "Why is the lad here if his mother is poorly? He should be at home with her, not here. What reason did you have for bringing him?"

Fergus was flustered, he hadn't realised the King had been listening and stuttered in reply, as he looked menacingly at the lad, "because he asked to come."

"Fergus you are not a very good liar (the crowd drew in their breath at this), you didn't even give him a sword. What's he going to do when we meet the Saxons, throw stones at them?" Arthur replied with a hint of sarcasm in his voice.

The crowd laughed nervously at this, knowing that Fergus had a short but vile temper and was likely to explode at any time, nobody had spoken to him like this before and got away with it, even the Duke was wary of him.

Arthur spoke gently to the boy, "come over here lad and tell me your story."

He led the young lad some distance away and heard how Fergus had wanted his mother but she had spurned him, not liking his violent temper. Fergus persevered, to no avail, then his mother became ill and refused to see him and he ranted and raved about all the nasty things that he would do to them both, and his mother's health declined even more. When Arthur arrived and Fergus was sent for he saw a way of getting even with the lad's mother threatening him that if he didn't go with the King he would see that his mother suffered a broken heart and a slow death. The lad did not want that to happen, so agreed, even though Fergus said he could not have a sword until he had learnt that it was not wise to upset him.

Arthur and the boy made their way back towards the group just as the action occurred. Gelda had moved closer to Fergus and was just staring at him, which unnerved him. He was wondering what a woman was doing with the army, then a smile broke across his face and he uttered a vile comment. Next moment he was doubled up in agony as she kicked him hard in the groin and then smashed her fist into his face, splitting his nose wide open so that blood spurted all over him, as she sent him tumbling back the other way to land flat on the ground with her sword at his throat. She asked him if he wished to repeat what he had called her? Through the mist of pain searing through his body he had the sense to shake his head as best he could. She relieved him of his sword and stood up to see the stunned look of amazement on the faces of the crowd.

"In my country," she said with a voice full of pride, "women fight alongside their King, and we are good, if you don't believe it come and test your pride against me," and with that comment she walked slowly away.

Arthur and the boy stood looking down at a very pathetic looking Fergus, cowering in the dust. "That is what happens if you insult one of my soldiers," the King said to him, "no matter who they are or where their home lies they fight for the good of this country and I have the honour of leading them as their King, do not trifle with them, you are not in their league." Turning to the crowd he said that Jonas, as the lad was called, had appraised him of the situation. "If any of you men have been threatened or coerced by this pathetic excuse of a man (indicating Fergus) to come on this journey, then you may return to your homes in the morning. I need men to help me with the fight against our enemies, but they must be willing and able, capable of using a sword and not afraid of dying if that be the case. If you cannot find it in your heart to put your life on the line for your country, then you will be a danger to yourselves and your comrades around you. There is no disgrace if you feel this way, I and your neighbours will not think any less of you if you wish to return home, whatever the reason that lies behind your decision, you are all free men and are entitled to free will and choice, that is universal law. However as your King, responsible for seeking to bring peace and prosperity to our country, I willingly forego that choice to accomplish my task. That my friends is my choice in life. Think on my words and those that wish to leave gather here at sunrise and return, like Jonas, to where you are needed the most." Looking down at Fergus, who was still moaning gently with the pain that refused to subside he said, "you, my little man will accompany us in our fight against the Saxons, with or without your sword, that depends on your attitude and behaviour before we encounter them."

Arthur bade them goodnight and returned to his own area taking Jonas along with him as he did not trust Fergus one little bit, that man was nasty through to the core and was unlikely to change.

The crowd were quiet for sometime, reflecting on the event that they had just witnessed and the speed with which it occurred. Instant retribution for Fergus, and by a woman at that, but what a woman, good figure, attractive and deadly, not one to pick an argument with. Neither had they heard a lord or a king speak in the manner that they had just listened to, a young lad himself, speaking with the wisdom of an elder and passionate about protecting his country from its enemies. This was indeed something new for these men and stirred their hearts, just as Arthur knew his words would do, creating that feeling of wanting to be part of the fight for freedom under a leader such as the King. The fear and apprehension that Fergus had fed constantly had subsided to be replaced by a personal pride and determination that they wanted to do their part in securing a good future for their families. It was in their hands to help if they so wished, and the majority did.

At sunrise only ten men appeared in Arthur's camp wishing to return home, their spokesman saying that none of them had ever used a sword or any other weapon. Listening to the King's words of the previous night they realised that they would be a liability to everyone. They felt awkward leaving their neighbours, some of whom they might not see again. Arthur raised his hand and told them that they had made the right decision, not just for themselves but all the others as well, he wished them well and asked them to see that Jonas returned safely to care for his ailing mother, and that there was no need to inform the Duke of their return.

Not long after the small group departed a contingent of eighty men arrived from Corinium headed by two knights on horse introducing themselves to Arthur as Sir Agranaut and Sir Bedwyr. Arthur extended a welcome to them and introduced his commanders to them. Their eyes rose a little at meeting the Sarmatians, for they had not encountered them before and even more surprised at seeing women amongst them, but they kept their counsel. Arthur told them that the Sarmatians were the best cavalry unit in the country, including the women. Then explained that they were hoping to intercept a large warband of Saxons that had landed on the south coast and made their way inland heading in their general direction, but their destination as yet was unknown.

Turning to Berius Arthur inquired if they had any more news yet and he replied that they should head slightly south east for Avebury as Merlin felt that they could be heading for The Sanctuary. A renowned spiritual and religious centre, close to the village, that was viewed by many as the heart and soul of this country. The energy vibrations that emanated from that site were like the beating of a strong heart uplifting all in its vicinity with an immense feeling of love and belonging to the spirit of the living Earth. No wonder it had a long history of being a very special place for the peoples of this country, it might be that the pagan Saxons wished to strike a blow at the heart of the Briton's culture and destroy it, claiming it was the will of the gods to punish the people for turning to the one God.

The name of Merlin intrigued Agranaut and Bedwyr as they had heard his name mentioned in many places but had not met him, thinking that perhaps he was just a myth. Certainly not a myth, Arthur corrected them, very much flesh and blood like they were and he was currently trying to locate them, along with Taliesin, and lead him to them. They looked at each other mystified and asked how the King received this information, as they were so far away. Arthur smiled and told them that they communicated news to Berius in their own mystical way. He ended the discussion by saying that it was time to move out, asking if any of them knew how far away Avebury was. Agranaut replied that it was about twenty five miles, following the Roman road towards Calleva Atrebatum then leaving it near Liddington Castle and heading southwest along the Ridgeway, they should make it well before the day was out.

The Romans had constructed many roads throughout the country to link the major administrative centres and they tended to run straight, taking the shortest route, and this one was no exception. The pace was slower than Arthur was used to as normally his army had just been the cavalry units, but now they had to travel at the speed of the foot soldiers who lead the way. Arthur had told a very subdued Fergus to stay at the back of them and just in front of the horsemen so that he could keep and eye on him, any trouble that he caused would be dealt with as swiftly and painfully as Gelda had done. Fergus was not a happy man and still in some considerable pain but Arthur had decided to let him suffer and experience what he had dealt out to others. He was aware that further trouble was likely to ensue at some point as Fergus was the type of person to harbour a grudge and seek his vengeance, but the King was prepared for that and willing to give him the chance to redeem himself.

The journey was without incident, the army resting briefly near the site of the old Liddington Castle, long since abandoned, before striking southwest along the Ridgeway to Avebury. Arthur felt the difference in the air as they approached the hamlet, calm and peaceful but with a vibrant energy about the place. He mentioned this to Berius, who as usual was travelling quietly by his side, and was told that what he felt was the great Earth energies coming together and meeting at The Sanctuary. Something that was understood by the Celt and Druid leaders and many others before them, and now appreciated by Christian followers. The place brought nature, the Earth and people together as one and would bring great dismay if defaced by the Saxons, it was embedded in the culture of the Britons going back through many generations, a sacred place. It could not be destroyed by man alone but the special nature of that area could be changed totally if violated by the Saxons and their destructive energy. The balance would be disturbed and the Britons would feel as if they had suffered a savage blow to the heart of their historical roots. As they came in sight of The Sanctuary Arthur sent a rider ahead to call the foot soldiers to a halt and make camp whilst he took his commanders ahead to survey the lie of the land.

Arthur could feel the energy increase as they came closer to the great stone circles, it seemed to draw him forward towards those giant stone megaliths, standing like silent sentinels in perfect array. Some parts partially roofed and the rest open, but all extending a warm welcome to weary travellers. *I wonder who built this, and what it was intended for. It bore no resemblance to a church of any kind and the openness of it all showed that whoever was responsible was not attempting to contain the energy but let it flow naturally in all directions. Perhaps that was its secret, just a marker to show the people that many different energies met here and combined into a greater force that then spread in all directions across the land. Just like a giant spider's web that reached out to other energy junctions spreading across the country, and maybe even further, linking up all the Earth energies as it expanded, thereby keeping the flow constant. The living Earth that survives and breathes because of it, that connects each and everything in our world, no doubt Merlin understands this and uses the energy for his apparent mystical ways, that would explain a lot. Where are these thoughts coming from?* he wondered, *is it because I am the bearer of the sword or because I have a hidden understanding of these matters, whatever the reason the feelings are good and I give thanks for this knowledge which eases my burden greatly.*

His thoughts were interrupted by Sir Bedwyr indicating the avenue of smaller megaliths that headed in the direction of the hamlet some distance away. Arthur led his troop along this to more stone circles, amongst which a few huts were scattered, pausing to enquire from an old gent, wrapped in a Druid robe and reclining against one, if what they saw was the extent of the hamlet or were there other huts further out. The old man replied that what they could see was all that there was, only those that tended the area lived there, most folk found it a strange place and would only visit at certain times of the year. Arthur thanked him and headed his troop back towards their camp with the feeling that surely the Saxons would not expend their effort there, as there was very little that they could do, other than kill a few people and pull down some stones. They would violate the energy, but Arthur felt that it was strong enough not to be permanently damaged, and how many people would realise that they had been there. Their real destination must be elsewhere, but not far away. He must gather what information he could from Agranaut and Bedwyr about the area and look for somewhere that would be of strategic importance to the Saxons.

Back in camp he gathered his commanders and put the problem to them, checking with Berius if there was any further news from Merlin. Not much, but it was encouraging in some respects as the Saxons were still heading towards them but they were deliberately avoiding the larger towns and any resistance that they might encounter that would slow them down, so they hadn't yet reached their target.

"What we have to decide gentlemen is what would be an important location for the Saxons in this area," Arthur began, "Merlin is sure that they are headed towards somewhere close to us and he is rarely wrong, Avebury was his first choice on his knowledge at the time because of its significance to our people, however it has no strategic value to them so gentlemen what can you tell me of this area." this last comment was directed to Agranaut and Bedwyr.

Bedwyr was the one who replied using his sword cutting into the earth to indicate the position of the various places that he mentioned.

"There is not much in this area, Littlecote, ten miles east of us was at one time an important Roman staging post, but is not much more than a quiet village these days. Going back along the Ridgeway we passed Barbury and Liddington castles, neither of which could be called important. Further along we have Durocornovium [Wanborough], a busy and sizeable town at the junction of the Roman roads to Cunetio [Mildenhall], Calleva Atrebatum [Silchester] and our own Corinium [Cirencester]. It is the last Vicus [a provincial non military settlement], used for watering horses before the long climb up the escarpment and out of the surrounding valley, and is not fortified and would be difficult to defend as the buildings were spread both sides of the roads. That is all that we have of any significance within a day's ride of here."

"Well gentlemen," Arthur began, "whoever holds Durocornovium controls the road to many important towns within the heart of our land and puts the whole region at risk. If we allow them to gain a foothold they could soon cut a large swathe of the south off from the rest of the country. They would also control Avebury and The Sanctuary and deny access to all, holding the people to ransom until they acquiesced. From the reports that we have from Merlin it appears that only a small part of the Saxon army, a few thousand only, are en-route to attempt to seize and hold the town. If successful they would then deploy a much larger force to the area to subdue it fully, its our task to stop them before that can happen. I will go and speak to the men now to prepare them for the approaching encounter, we will leave at first light and hope that I am correct in my assumptions. Berius will you inform Merlin of my intentions and reasons behind them and see if he has any better idea of the number of Saxons that we are likely to encounter"

Arthur spoke to his army and availed them of the situation, instructing them to get a good rest as it could be a hectic time soon. He noticed that Fergus was still very subdued but had that perpetual evil look on his face. Gelda had really given him a painful awakening, but he was still there and behaving himself and had not once asked for his sword back. Which was just as well as Arthur did not trust him with it, he would return it when they encountered the Saxons. The King returned to his area and sat leaning against a tree, staring up into the sky, letting his thoughts wander, back to Avebury and The Sanctuary and the feeling he had in his body and mind there, wondering if he had made the right decision concerning the Saxons. The tree was warm and he could feel the energy running through it and into his body, just as if it were talking to him, such a pleasant feeling just relaxing this way.

He awoke suddenly, Berius was gently shaking his shoulder and whispering quietly that Fergus was on the prowl, seemed like he was seeking out Gelda amongst the sleeping forms, but not to worry as she was awake and waiting for him.

"How can you be sure Berius?" he whispered back.

"Because I have been into her mind and awoken her, she is very receptive to that," he replied, "Fergus is going to get another nasty surprise."

They both watched in silence as Fergus hesitated and stopped by one of the sleeping bodies, having found his quarry. His hand raised in the air and they saw the glint of a knife blade caught in the moonlight. Arthur gave a sharp intake of breath and was about to leap to his feet, he should have thought of searching him for other weapons, when Berius touch his arm and whispered to him to wait. As Fergus brought his arm down and let his body drop the sleeping form of Gelda suddenly sprang to life, her sword flashed, taking him right through the body. He dropped like a stone, crying out in agony as the cold steel sliced into him, the knife falling from his hand as he clutched himself to try and stop the flow of blood. His face contorted into a mixture of unbearable pain and surprise. Gelda stood up, put her foot on his stomach and pushed him off her blade causing him to cry out once more at the terrible pain that seared through his body again as he dropped to the ground writhing. The noise had woken others, but seeing that Gelda was okay they rolled over and went back to sleep. Fergus took a long time to die and Gelda just stood there watching him impassively without a word, until he finally slipped away, then she returned to her bed, having wiped her sword on his lifeless body. Arthur expressed his thanks to Berius for letting Gelda know of her danger, he should have been more wary himself, but at least that was one less problem to worry about and he doubted if anyone would miss Fergus, except for the peace it brought them now.

The army moved out at daylight, Arthur despatched riders to scout the country ahead and on their flanks for signs of the Saxons. No reported contacts were made and they reached Durocornovium at noon, circling the town to pitched their camp to the north, but close to the junction of Roman roads. Their arrival had caused consternation amongst the townsfolk as they had been seen on their approach. A small party of horsemen had ridden out to meet them and discover what a large army was doing in the vicinity. They were the officials and elders and were introduced to Arthur by Sir Kay who had ridden out to meet them as they were observed approaching. They were honoured at meeting the King but what brought him to that region, all was peaceful and business was good. Arthur explained why they were there and that it wouldn't be peaceful for much longer, unless they were able to deal with the Saxons successfully, it was a large force, not just a wandering warband. They were currently approaching Littlecote, Berius had informed him of this earlier as the latest news from Merlin, and were making for there and could arrive before the day was out. The town's reception committee asked why the Saxons would want to attack their town, the military presence had ceased a long time ago, it was just a business community now. Arthur pointed out that they were in a strategic position at a major road junction and whoever held their town would have control over a large area, he had brought his army there to stop them gaining that control. He and his commanders would accompany them back to the town as they needed to see how it was laid out and how best to protect it as he believed none of it was fortified.

The town was laid out as Bedwyr had said, buildings on either side of the roads, not large but spread out all the same and difficult to protect, surprisingly it supported three churches. The town leader answered Arthur's query by saying one was built for each road which is why they were only small ones, but well supported. Arthur told them to gather all the townsfolk that night and to take refuge in the churches, bar the doors and remain there until he or one of his men returned to them, and to take water and victuals to last the day. It would be very dangerous to be outside and whilst there they could pray for the King's success as reports had it that they would be greatly outnumbered. His foot soldiers would be in town whilst his cavalry would intercept the Saxons before they reached there, and hopefully they could prevent them from breaking through. Having seen the layout of the town he sent his commanders back to camp saying that Berius and himself would follow shortly as there was something he wished to do first.

He went to the first church and entered, peering into the dim light and sought out the cleric and exchanged quiet words with him whilst Berius discreetly hung back. Finally the cleric put his hand on Arthur's shoulder and the other on his shield and blessed him. Arthur repeated the process in the other two churches and then rode back to camp with Berius quietly by his side, then gathered his commanders together to outline his battle strategy.

The foot soldiers would go to town at first light under the command of Sir Agranaut and Sir Bedwyr to protect the townsfolk in the churches should any of the Saxons break through. The cavalry would be split into the three groups as usual with Legionus, Sir Bors and himself as troop leaders and Sir Kay would accompany him. The troop under Legionus would be held in reserve as normal to give support where needed or contain any breakthrough, bearing in mind that there were likely to be more Saxons than they had encountered before. Each troop was to supply a scout to survey the land and establish the exact whereabouts of the Saxons and if they appeared to be in one group or several, as they did not want some of them circling around behind them. They would leave at the first sign of daylight before the enemy were upon them.

"At the moment the town should be between them, so even if they have scouts out themselves they should not be aware that we are here, and we will keep that cover as long as possible. The ground to the south comes down from the escarpment, then levels out so we should see them before they see us. We will wait for them to descend to the valley before we attack, but keep your eyes open that they do not go further along before they decide to come down. I have a feeling though that they might use the road from Cunetio as it follows the river valley and is easier going. Although they will be in the open a lot sooner they are not expecting a military presence here and therefore it might not bother them. We will meet again at first light and review the plan, by then we may have received more information."

It did not seem to Arthur that he had been asleep for very long when he was woken by Berius shaking him, it was still dark, dawn was some way off yet. He had received news from Merlin that the Saxons were no more than ten miles away and had begun to move forward again after a short camp, using the darkness to hide their movement. They were on the road from Cunetio and were about four thousand strong, led by four and twenty horsemen, animals that they had acquired during their attacks. Merlin believed that they might split into two or more groups as they moved closer and dawn started to break, a surprise attack on the town from different directions so that no townsfolk escaped to tell the story. To Arthur this was disturbing news, a change of tactics by the Saxons, moving during darkness in what was a strange land to them, unless they had prepared well for this and sent people previously to discreetly survey the land.

Time to move the army into position before they arrived and hopefully catch them before they had a chance to split into groups. Berius indicated that he was going to do a little scouting and see what he could glean from the animal kingdom and would be back shortly, slipping quietly away into the shadows as Arthur set about raising the men from their slumber. Arthur informed his commanders of the situation and sent Agranaut and Bedwyr to take the foot soldiers to town immediately, and to be wary of attack from more than one direction. The cavalry would try to contain the enemy, but some at least were likely to break through.

Berius returned at this point with news that the Saxons were just over five miles south of the town and appeared to be still in one group. Arthur wondered briefly how Berius had found that out in such a short space of time, he'd have to fly to cover that distance so quickly. He put it out of his head for the moment and returned to the business at hand. The plan of the previous evening would stand, Sir Bors and his troop to the left, the King's troop to the right and Legionus, with the most men, slightly back in the rear creating a funnel to draw the Saxons in. They would ride out to meet them a couple of miles from the town, whilst they were still grouped together, and just as dawn would be breaking. He looked around for any comments and as there were none gave the order to move out.

They passed around Durocornovium and joined the road to Cunetio with the King's troop leading, followed by Sir Bors and his men then Legionus with the Sarmatian cavalry, making their way slowly to keep the noise from the horse's hooves as quiet as possible. Arthur brought his army to a halt some two miles from the town and sat motionless on his horse, just waiting. The light began to gently increase as darkness lost its hold on the night. A bird began to sing, then another, two flew over their heads barely visible with their dark plumage, the countryside had started to wake up, a little early for some but they had been disturbed. Berius looked at Arthur and quietly commented that the enemy were less than a mile away and moving quite fast, he would hear their footfalls on the road soon shortly before he saw them.

The King waited, then he heard them and then all manner of things happened at the same time. Unusually dawn burst upon them suddenly, the Saxons stopped in total surprise seeing their way barred by a large host, then surged forward, spreading out, as Arthur gave the same commands to his army. He lead his troop to the right as Sir Bors moved to the left and the armies clashed with a multitude of noise of steel on steel and cries of anguish of those struck down or trampled by the horses. Those at the rear of the Saxon horde started to spread out to encircle Arthur's army, which was being pushed back by the concentrated weight of numbers at the front, forming a wall that was difficult to penetrate.

Arthur pulled his men back, turned and charged the Saxon wall repeatedly, making some inroads each time but steadily being pushed back at every attempt. Those that had tried to encircle Arthur's men were being dealt with more effectively as they were spread out, but several small groups had broken through the cavalry and were making for the town, the foot soldiers there would have to deal with them. The enemy were losing men gradually but they kept on coming, with their concentrated numbers still tightly grouped, and Arthur's army had suffered some casualties too, both men and horses. Where were the twenty four Saxon horsemen? They hadn't shown themselves yet, most likely at the back urging their men on.

The town was getting closer behind them all the time and Arthur realised he needed to change his tactics before it was too late, so shouted to his men to withdraw and fall back ready to regroup. They disengaged and galloped towards the town with the Saxons surging after them fanning out as they went thinking that they had Arthur on the run, but they had done exactly what he hoped they would and spread out. The King brought his cavalry to a halt just short of the town. Then following a thought in his head, without questioning why, he took his dagger and cut the binding that was retaining the plain looking cover on the shield that Eudaf Hen had given him, ripping it off. His men watched in astonishment at this strange act but were equally amazed by what was revealed. A red cross on a white background, but right in the centre over the lower part of the cross was a picture of a beautiful woman, the Virgin Mary, the image known to many of them. Arthur smiled and held it aloft shouting 'right and justice are with us,' then swung his horse around, drew his sword and held it aloft shouting 'Excalibur.' Bright light burst from the blade with such an intensity that it dazzled the advancing Saxons throwing fear into their hearts.

At the same moment several hundred horsemen appeared from the town, racing to join Arthur, King Esla's pennon leading the way followed by another and Lord Tryfig as well. This was a welcome sight indeed, just at the right time. Acknowledging them as he lead the charge against the Saxon horde, this time spread out and not bunched together, a tactical error on their part for which they were now going to pay dearly.

The battle was fierce, Arthur's men revitalised by the secret that his shield revealed and the arrival of some welcome help. The enemy however had become demoralised by the sight of Excalibur and its blazing blade as it cut them down in droves as the King rode into them. They were fighting for their lives and losing and they had nowhere to run. Arthur sought out their horsemen at the back of the Saxon army, still trying to push their men forward. Sir Kay was with him and Gelda joined them with several of the Sarmatians as they engaged them in combat. Several took flight as the rest stood their ground but Excalibur dazzled and confused them as eight succumbed to Arthur's determined onslaught, as the others dealt with their opponents with the loss of just one of the Sarmatians, who was caught between two Saxons. Gelda extracted her revenge very swiftly for that and both died with surprise on their faces at being bettered by a woman.

The battle was finally over, except for a few that had escaped, the Saxon horde lay scattered across the valley, dead or in the last throes of dying, no pity spent on them for the savage butchering of Bosham. Arthur's army had suffered casualties too but small in comparison to the enemy, his cavalry had proved themselves highly effective once again against superior odds. He sent a detachment of men to scour the meadow for any wounded men of his and give whatever help they could, the rest of his army he led triumphantly into the town.

More Saxons than he realised had penetrated the town but by the look of it had been dealt with by his foot soldiers and others that had arrived with King Esla. Arthur sent Sir Bors, Sir Kay and Legionus to the three churches to spread the good news that the local folk could safely return to their dwellings, the danger had passed.

They emerged from the dim interiors of their refuges, blinking profusely in the bright sunlight as they surveyed the multitude of the King's army passing through on their way back to camp to the north. Bodies of the enemy were scattered around the buildings where they had been dragged off the roads to clear a way through, but Arthur's fallen had been placed close to the churches as a mark of respect, as they would be given a proper burial later.

As more people emerged, smiles of relief on their faces, nervous laughter and ragged cheering broke out as they relieved their pent up emotions of fear on seeing such a welcome sight. Arthur raised Excalibur into the air and acknowledged them, the majority seeing their King for the first time and marvelling at his youthful appearance. He shouted to them that God had been on their side as he raised his shield so that all could see the cross and likeness of the Virgin Mary emblazoned on it, "he serves us well as I serve him and do the best for all my people."

A spontaneous cheer erupted from the crowd, all their fear now washed away as they started to chatter amongst themselves.

Arthur dismounted asking Berius to mind his horse whilst he revisited the clerics in their churches, going from one to another as before and spending some moments with each, taking his shield with him. All three asked him the same question, the origin of the shield with its holy emblem. To each he gave the same answer, that it had been given him by the spirit of Eudaf Hen with the instruction to remove the cover only when the time was right, his heart would tell him when that was. They were amazed at his revelation and observed that it was divine providence that he had been chosen as their King from an early age, to bring the country together as one. Arthur agreed that such was his task and he would carry it out to the best of his ability but there was still much to be done to bring harmony and justice to the country so that the people could prosper in peace. He thanked each of them for their prayers and blessings, not just for him and his army but for the people as well.

Arthur led the rest of his men back to their camp to review the days happenings with his commanders, and discover what brought King Esla and his entourage to arrive just when they were needed.

Some of the Sarmatians had gone hunting for game to supplement their meagre supplies and provide a good feast for the evening, which was still some six hours away, the battle with the Saxons had lasted most of the morning. Arthur was introduced to Lord Forrester from Calleva Atrebatum who had met King Esla en-route, both having had a visit from Taliesin warning them of the danger and requesting that they went to Arthur's assistance. Lord Tryfig was visited by Merlin with the same request, being advised not to use the road from Cunetio as that was the Saxon's likely route. All were told where to head for and when they needed to be there by, almost to the hour as it turned out. Each of the groups had arrived at the town within minutes of each other to be informed by Agranaut and Bedwyr the whereabouts of Arthur's army, not a moment too soon as it transpired. It always puzzled Arthur how Merlin could be so exact with his timing and now he had Berius disappearing in the dark, returning with information in such a short space of time that even a bird would be hard pushed to cover the distance involved. *What is it about these Elders that make them so different to us?* he wondered, *are they an ancient race that still have many mystical powers? There were stories told in some quarters of a race that were masters of this world once, in the long distant past, until something went terribly wrong. Do some of them still walk amongst us, it appears so, but why are they still here if they are not allowed to use the full extent of their powers, is it because of what happened back in their time? Merlin had often said that they were just ambassadors of peace and could not intervene directly, we had to sort out our own problems otherwise we would not learn, words of wisdom indeed. Who or what restricts them from full involvement, is it a higher authority or just their law that they abide by? When the time is right I will enquire of them, either separately or together.*

Berius interrupted his thoughts indicating that the huntsmen had returned with several good looking trophies that would produce a good feast later and looking directly at Arthur concluded by saying that he would learn more when the Elders decided that the time was appropriate. Arthur, startled, stared at him, then burst out laughing as he realised Berius had read his thoughts again, one of their many talents. Perhaps that was how he knew where the Saxons were, but then he wouldn't have had to leave the camp. The comment was valid, he would be patient and just watch and listen in the meantime, that was a good way to learn in life.

Chapter 15
ARTHUR RENEWS AN ACQUAINTANCE

THE EVENING TURNED into a merry feast for all as the huntsmen had excelled themselves earlier with their tally. Many of the townsfolk joined them, bringing along a cartload of excellent ale, which was greatly appreciated by the weary soldiers. They must have emptied all their cellars to find so much, which indeed they had, as a token of appreciation for their salvation and the timely arrival of the King's army. The singing and dancing carried on into the small hours until sleep finally caught up with them all, the horrors of the day having drained from them, with the help of the festive mood induced by good ale.

Late morning saw the camp gradually come to life, with a few sore heads, as the different groups prepared to move out and go their separate ways. The town elders and clerics arrived to renew their thanks once again. Men were already out in the meadow removing the Saxon carcases for burning and Arthur's fallen warriors would be given a proper Christian burial close to the churches to remind all of their ultimate sacrifice in defending the town. Arthur graciously accepted their thanks, but reminded them it was not just his army that had delivered them from the Saxons, the Lord was with them and had responded to their prayers, providing the help that they needed at the right time. They asked if they could have one last look at his shield before he departed, which he duly obliged, holding it up for them to see. There were gasps as one said, 'but the picture of the Virgin Mary has vanished.' Sure enough when Arthur looked all that remained was the red cross on the white background, he was equally puzzled for it had still been there the night before.

"Gentlemen," he confided, "we must conclude that it was a sign given to us to strengthen our resolve and put fear into the hearts of our enemies, and that is what it did, the vision will only appear when needed."

The words seemed to come into his head as he spoke them, as if coming from a higher authority, not his words, as he did not understand what had happened either. No wonder Eudaf Hen had told him that he would know when to remove the cover from the shield. It would be a voice or thought that would spring into his head that would prompt him to do it, and he would not question it.

Looking at the townsmen he told them that they had witnessed a miracle to remind them of the power of prayer. With that he bade them farewell as he gave the command to move out, taking leave of King Esla, Lord Tryfig and Lord Forrester. Sir Agranaut and Sir Bedwyr were returning to Corinium with their troop and those from Glevum whilst Arthur was making directly south west for Cadbury, intending to revisit The Sanctuary at Avebury before they finally left the area. He was drawn to it but wasn't sure why.

As the army neared Avebury, Arthur instructed Sir Kay to take command and continue in the same direction that they were heading, as he and Berius were taking a short detour to The Sanctuary and would catch up with them later. Sir Kay protested that he should take a troop with him as some of the Saxons had escaped and could be anywhere, but Arthur held up his hand to silence this warning, saying that it would not be necessary, they would be perfectly safe. The two of them rode away leaving Sir Kay a little bemused at the King's action and apparent disregard for his own safety and that of Berius.

They approached along the centre of a straight avenue of giant stones. Arthur noticed that there were two distinct shapes to them and they alternated as if they were meant to be in pairs, not just within each row but opposing each other too. He queried this with Berius who pointed out that the tall rugged ones signified the male energy and the smoother slightly rounded ones the female energy, a perfect balance. Whichever way you looked there was a pair, male and female, the living Earth joined in harmony. He said that the world was once covered with giant markers like those until man became destructive and tore many of them down, seeking to blame them on the demise of the human race and the golden age. They couldn't see that they only had themselves to blame, as greed and avarice took hold and spread like a disease amongst them. Luckily this little country of his had managed to preserve many of them, as the peoples' beliefs were strong, but even that waned to a degree and some fell into disrepair and were lost. Many however had survived, their energy as vibrant as ever.

They reach the impressive circle of The Sanctuary and dismounted. The air felt electric by comparison to the avenue, coursing through every inch of Arthur's body, his whole being alive with energy, strong and bold but at the same time warm and gentle. Waves of it flowed through him. Even Excalibur, swaying with his movement, was humming and vibrating softly by his side, as the energies melded together in unison. The sensation was something that he could not describe, it was beyond words, not unpleasant, just strange until the body adjusted to it, then it seemed quite natural. He was subconsciously pulled slowly towards the centre of the stone circle, without any effort on his part. It was as if he was gliding towards the middle, feet hardly touching the ground. As he came to a stop the energy changed, appearing to come into his body from all direction, running down through his legs and into the earth, his senses heightened, everything appeared in sharp focus, crystal clear and vibrant. Pictures sprang into his mind, but as if in front of his eyes, various scenes played out before him. It took some while before he could piece them together and understand their meaning, then they faded and he felt the energy within him subside to a gentler level, the connection broken.

He stood quietly for some time absorbing the detail of what he had just experienced and seen, understanding more now of the mystical powers of Merlin and the Elders. They knew how to use this energy, connecting to the vibrations of the living Earth and being in many places at the same time without moving. Their vision taking them to wherever they wished to be to see what they needed to know, as if they were actually there. It was all so real and had shown him a glimpse of where trouble would next occur, not in a vague hazy dream with shadowy figures that could not be identified, but sharp and perfectly clear as a bright summers day. Surprisingly he did not doubt what he saw, the strength within him accepting it as a divine vision without question. He knew now where the next major Saxon assault would raise its ugly head, but he had plenty of time to prepare.

He looked at Berius, smiling. "That was an wondrous experience to be given, I understand a little more now how you, Merlin and others of your kind use the living Earth energies, working in harmony with them to great advantage to see the way forward."

"My lord, you are shown these new things to help you, but only when the time is right, they cannot be rushed, everything happens when it should, and not before, you were ready for this revelation," he replied.

"Yes," Arthur answered, "I was drawn to return here, I knew something would happen, but knew not what. I feel a new energy after that experience and renewed hope that all will turn out well. There is still much that needs to be done, but by staying in touch with the energy of this land I can accomplish the task that I have been entrusted with, and my people will benefit for many generations to come. Let us rejoin the others."

* * * * *

Their return to Cadbury was met with jubilation as befits a King returning from a successful campaign. Merlin and Taliesin were already there to greet them and had organised the welcoming feast with Greyfus, knowing in advance, as usual, Arthur's arrival time. The King more aware now as to how they knew these things, something that had previously puzzled him, not all of the answer as their mystical talents were many, but hopefully he would learn more of their ways as time progressed.

The feasting lasted for two days during which Arthur spent considerable time with Merlin and Taliesin finding out the details of the slaughter at Bosham, and how the Saxons had caught them unawares. Apparently a local festival and been taking place and much ale had flowed, as was usual at such events. The Saxons had landed at night guided by a clear sky brightly illuminated by the full moon and caught them in their intoxicated slumber. Lookouts had either deserted their posts to join the festivities or fallen asleep, having acquired jugs of ale and over indulged, consequently no warning of the attack was raised until too late. Many were put to the sword where they slept, men, women and children, only a few on the out-skirts of the landing area managed to escape into the countryside and raise the alarm, but by then the Saxons were pushing forward inland. Their goal important enough that they did not dally on the way, just slaughtering all they encountered as they moved forward, surprise on their side. Speed was important to them, to reach their target before they encountered any major opposition, as once there they would be in a good position to control the area by holding the major road junction until further soldiers were sent for. Luckily with Arthur's intervention their plan failed and the Saxons lost yet another army in their attempts to expand their influence. This might make them rethink their strategy before attempting another thrust. It was a bold move on their part to try to penetrate deep into Arthur's territory, but was always fraught with danger for them if further troops did not follow behind them. Merlin indicated that this was what they had intended. Many more keels were to follow with a second army, but they got caught in a violent storm at sea and most of the ships were lost. The few remaining barely managing to return to harbour quite badly damaged.

Arthur was surprised at this news, he had not thought that there would be others following so soon, but in hindsight it made perfect sense. The situation could have been much worse had the second army managed to land, his thinking had been flawed on that occasion, something else that he had learned. Arthur asked Merlin why he thought they were heading for The Sanctuary initially, as on seeing the place it had no strategic importance. Merlin smiled at this and told him that it was a place that the King had to visit as part of his education, but it was necessary that Arthur worked out the details himself of where the Saxons were really heading and why, an-other aspect of his learning, and he had passed the test admirably.

Arthur confided in him about his life changing experience at The Sanctuary, how he felt and the visions that he had concerning the next danger spots in the country and when they would occur. How great the strength of the Earth energies were that flowed through him, even affect-ing his sword. Merlin was greatly pleased by these revelations and said as much. Arthur was coming into his own more now, that was a good sign and he was being rewarded accordingly, as he allowed his strong caring charac-ter to develop in the right way, always for the benefit of his people and not himself. The rewards matched the effort that he was putting into his task and would continue to do so provided he did not waver in his resolve, but continued to fight for the good of all, laying the foundations for a better way of life. It would take many generations and there would be setbacks along the way but the impetus would be moving forward, no matter how slowly at times, Arthur was initiating the changes that were needed, and he would be helped in his task in many diverse ways. The King was grateful for the confidence that Merlin inspired in him, the wisdom of the ancients was always worthy of note and their assistance and guidance was greatly appreciated, it made his task that much easier.

* * * * *

Life at Cadbury settled into a relaxed routine throughout the rest of the year, many visitors passed through, paying their respects to the King, a few travellers stayed on, offering their services including Bedwini, bishop of Gwent. All were gratefully accepted. Sir Agranaut and Sir Bedwyr arrived, having decided to join Arthur, bringing with them several other lesser knights looking for adventure, and a steady stream continued throughout the year. Arthur took a small troop out on a regular basis visiting hamlets and villages across a wide area to keep in touch with the people. Receiving a warm welcome wherever he went, as he listened to their problems and resolved minor disputes in his usual fair and just manner. The people were solidly behind him as he showed that he cared about their welfare like no other King had done before, and he delivered on his promises, something that they were not used to. His reputation grew greatly and word spread far and wide amongst the peoples of the land. Not just for his deeds and success in battle against the Saxons, but because he was concerned for their welfare, he treated them all as equals, not as King and serfs.

Summer began the slow transition into autumn and the vivid colours of the landscape began to fade into darker hues as trees began to shed their leaves in preparation for the dormant period of winter. The harvests had been successfully gathered and stored, leaving the land looking barren and brown as it rested until the next sowing. Those animals that took shelter through the winter months hurriedly made their final preparations of food stocks and shelter, whilst others that would see the cold months through as they were, continued to graze the meadows. Life began its gentle run down to the restrictions of winter and Cadbury was no exception. The stock of provisions, ale, oil and wood, had been organised and checked by Greyfus as usual, with plenty to spare should it be a harsh winter, or they had an unexpected influx of people. Feed for the horses had not been forgotten either.

* * * * *

Arthur was not expecting trouble, and none occurred, as one year faded and another blossomed, a year that would be fraught with trouble if his visions were anything to go by, but forewarned was forearmed and he was confident that he would be in the right place at the right time to counter the onslaught. Time to make preparations and think through his plan of action. It was going to be a busy year, that would make or break the Saxon menace for some time, or see his undoing and all the good that he had accomplished so far. Winter was the time for this careful thought and he spent much of his free time doing just that. Sitting quietly subduing his everyday thoughts and allowing his mind to connect with his innermost feelings, seeking guidance for the way forward. He felt his energy vibrations change as he allowed this to happen, as his whole being connected to those Earth energies around him. Not strong like at The Sanctuary, but sufficient to be noticeable as they permeated through him in his relaxed state, producing a calm and stillness that encouraged clear thought.

By the end of the winter he knew exactly what he needed to do and summoned his commanders to explain some, but not all of his thoughts, as to where they would be going and why. Merlin and Taliesin had for once wintered with them. Although Arthur had not asked for their assistance or advice yet, as Merlin had said he needed to work out much himself, he was sure that they would comment if they felt he was wrong.

* * * * *

Spring was not quite upon them. There was still a chill in the air as they sat in the Great Hall with several logs fires blazing away, feebly attempting to bring some warmth into the vast expanse, failing miserably, but the red glow and dancing flames gave a comforting feeling to those present. Arthur explained that he had brought them together now because he was convinced that the Saxons would make a concerted effort that year to attempt to gain a strong foothold in their land. It was up to him and his army to stop them at all costs and push them back to their own territory with such a force that they would not bother them again in a serious way for some time.

The Saxons had tried unsuccessfully to breach their defences in the south and had lost many men in their forays, he felt that they would now switch their attention northward and attack the east coast, thinking that the King had his forces waiting in the south for the next onslaught. His information was that the most likely area would be in the vicinity of the City of the Legion at Eboracum [York], an area that Legionus knew well. It was a strategic fortification well defended, within a day and a half by foot from the coast, but even less if approached from the wide river in that area. He suspected that the Saxons would land a force to the north first in an attempt to draw the army quartered there away from the city. Then their main force would come from the south, having sailed up the river, and attempt to seize Eboracum, which would be only lightly defended. They would be waiting for them and yet again take them by total surprise and they would start to wonder how this King of the Britons kept turning up to confront them wherever they went.

Sir Drustanus asked what they were all thinking, how did Arthur know that he was not being lured there deliberately so that they could attack the south again, knowing that the King's army was miles away chasing ghosts in the north. Arthur replied that he could never be totally sure but was guided by good information and his instincts, which so far had not let him down. Turning to Merlin he asked him for his comments and whether he had any information that was to the contrary. Merlin smiled at Arthur's rhetoric and how he had refrained from saying where his information had come from, and told the audience that his information was basically what they had just heard. The Saxons were most likely to attack Eboracum, probably at the time of the spring tides when there was more water in the river. Arthur continued by stating that they would travel first to the other City of the Legion at Deva Victris [Chester] and show the King's pennon there and enlist their aid. They would set forth in two weeks time. He asked if there were any questions and as none were forthcoming he concluded by saying they would meet again shortly before they departed to review the situation.

Merlin and Taliesin stayed behind with Arthur and Berius after the others had left and continued the discussion on the campaign plan, the King saying that he had a feeling that they might encounter some trouble at Deva Victris, but not necessarily from the Saxons. Merlin agreed saying that it was more likely to be Irish raiders that periodically attacked the coastal settlements in that area. Not in great force, but extremely disruptive none the less. He asked Arthur, even though he knew the answer, if there was anything that he required of Taliesin and himself whilst he was away. The King gave him a knowing smile as he replied that Merlin knew already, and that was for both of them to keep an eye on the happenings in the south and send their thoughts to Berius if anything major occurred that would require him to return immediately. If he had been mistaken in taking his army north when trouble was going to re-occur in the south. Arthur thought this unlikely although there was always a vague possibility, but needed to take every precaution to safeguard his people from the indiscriminate slaughter of the pagan Saxons. Merlin and Taliesin agreed and said that they would take their leave in the morning and go about their business in their normal way. Anything of note they would advise Berius of, otherwise they would see him on his return in a few months. They took their leave of Arthur, as he pondered those last words, both anticipated a long campaign, or other events would keep him away from there for that time, knowing too that it was going to be a busy year.

* * * * *

The King and his army left on time two weeks later, taking supply wagons with them on this occasion as they would be away for some while, too much for each man to carry individually. Greyfus had seen that they were well provisioned. They would follow the Roman roads where possible, heading for Corinium then Glevum before heading north to Viroconium Cornoviorum once again and finally Deva Victris. The journey would take nearly a week.

They made good time, arriving at Viroconium five days later where King Cadell elected to join them with thirty horsemen and a hundred foot soldiers as they continued their journey. As they made their way towards Deva Victris Arthur brought King Cadell up to date on the conflict with the Saxons at Durocornovium the previous year and the events that lead up to it. Cadell mentioned that word had reached them just before winter had set in, but there wasn't much detail. Just that the King's army had again defeated the enemy, after the unfortunate slaughter at Bosham. That was dreadful news, all those poor souls just mercilessly killed by the pagans, forgetting that British kings had done the same to each other in the past.

The day passed and the next brought them close to Deva Victris when Berius broke his customary silence and suddenly spoke to Arthur warning him of trouble ahead, the animal noises had changed and he sensed the tension in the air. The King immediately summoned two of his men with orders to ride ahead and seek the signs of trouble, but to do so without being seen if possible. He himself had begun to feel a slight sense of unease just before Berius had mentioned it.

The riders soon reappeared with news that the city was some two miles ahead and was being attacked by a large group of foot soldiers, but they were too far distant to ascertain who they were although their garments looked different to those of King Cadell's men. Irish raiders or Picts most likely commented Arthur summoning his commanders to him and advising them of the situation. The foot soldiers were to remain there and guard the supply wagons, They would break into their usual three troops as they got closer. Himself, King Cadell and Sir Kay with the lead troop, Legionus to the left flank with Sir Agranaut and Sir Bedwyr, Sir Bors to lead the right flank with Sir Drustanus and Sir Sagremor. The commanders gathered their troops and set off following Arthur towards the City of the Legion, ready to do battle.

As they galloped towards the city Arthur could see that the massive gate appeared to have been breached and hordes of warriors were fighting their way slowly in through the narrow entrance. The defenders giving way under the weight of those pushing forward, too many for them to keep at bay. Arthur gave the signal to his commanders to spread out into their positions as they thundered forward towards the enemy with their pennons flying, a mixture of Picts and other strangely garbed men.

The noise from nearly six hundred horses approaching at speed alerted those at the rear of the surging pack. Cries of alarm went up as they faltered, turning to face this unexpected threat. Arthur drew his sword and shouted 'Excalibur,' the blade immediately bursting into life cascading tongues of dancing white light towards the enemy. Shouts of dismay echoed at this phenomenon as their ranks broke and they began to scatter in fear,

GORDON ETHERINGTON

as Arthur and his army bore down on them. The troops under Legionus and Sir Bors spreading out to ensnare them. They rode into the scattering mass of bodies cutting them down at will as they tried to escape. Very few turned to fight, fear was consuming them, their only thought was of escape, but alas there was none, they were trapped.

Arthur's troop fought their way to the gate, slowed by the greater concentration of men, some still pushing forward not yet aware of the threat behind them, whilst others were trying to flee the King's onslaught. Arthur with Cadell by his side broke through the mass at the gate, his men forcing their way through with him and spreading out into the wide courtyard beyond. The city defenders had been pushed back to the buildings on the far side of the courtyard. Now with the arrival of Arthur the insurgents were trapped between the two factions, fighting for their lives. Arthur shouted to them to lay down their arms and go free, or die where they stood, Excalibur glowing brightly in his hand to reinforce his words. The High King of all Britain had spoken, they would not get a second chance.

Common sense prevailed as the clatter of many weapons falling to the ground confirmed. Arthur instructed Sir Kay to see that they were all searched for concealed weapons and to take fifty men and escort them several miles towards the coast, making sure that they did not retrieve any weapons from the battle field. If any tried to escape he was at liberty to put them to the sword. Arthur looked at the forlorn remnants of the enemy force and told them to inform their people that any further incursions into his lands would suffer the wrath of the King and be dealt with in a like manner. Sir Kay led them away, passed the hundreds of bodies of their fallen comrades that littered the battleground outside the gates, and the lifeless scattered bodies further out of those that had tried to escape. A timely reminder of the fate that awaited them should they return.

The commander of the city defences approached Arthur and identified himself, thanking him profusely for his timely intervention in what was a nasty situation that was rapidly turning against them. Arthur inquired how they had managed to breach the city gate which was more than capable of withstanding such an attack. The commander said that they had been caught unawares by deceit. Messengers had arrived supposedly from the King of Rheged requesting help as a large force of Irish had landed to the north. His lord, King Cadwallon Longhand of Gwynedd had responded and taken most of his forces to go to their aid, leaving just a small contingent to safeguard the city as it was well fortified. However they had been secretly infiltrated by several Irish supporters. When the enemy force arrived near the gate the guards were overpowered by five men and the gate opened to allow them in. Luckily one of the guards had escaped to give warning of this treacherous act and they quickly responded. It was too late to shut the gate and all they could do was to try and contain them but his men were losing ground when Arthur's army thankfully appeared on the scene. If the

Irish had taken the city then his king would have returned to a trap and paid dearly for it and the Irish influence would have spread.

Arthur asked if they had apprehended the infiltrators. The commander responded that three had apparently been killed as the King forced his way through the gate and his men were searching out the other two and they would deal with them accordingly. Arthur said that he would withdraw his men and rejoin their supply wagons and pitch camp within a mile of the city and would be pleased to receive King Cadwallon on his return as he required his aid. The commander thanked him once again and said that it would be done, it was likely that his lord would return on the morrow as he had already sent a rider to recall him. Arthur gathered his men, rejoining Legionus and Sir Bors just as Sir Kay returned with his small troop and they headed back to their supply wagons.

The next day Arthur used as a rest day for his army and just let them relax whilst he waited the return of King Cadwallon. It would take them another week to reach Eboracum, but his vision at The Sanctuary indicated that he had a few days in hand before the Saxons invaded there.

It wasn't until late afternoon that the king returned with his troops and shortly after rode out to meet Arthur, accompanied by his commander at the city. The King greeted him and invited them both to join his table as food had just been prepared and no doubt the king would welcome some after his abortive journey. King Cadwallon expressed his gratitude for Arthur's timely arrival and stated that it would be a pleasure to share a hearty meal with him, as they both dismounted.

A lively discussion took place as they ate, concerning the events that had led to the king taking his men to help King Merchiaun of Rheged. It was something that happened fairly frequently, each helping the other when the Irish raiders landed in force and this occasion appeared no different. Cadwallon started to suspect that all was not well when the messengers that had travelled with them disappeared during the night. Then the following morning a rider appeared from the city requesting his immediate return. It would have been too late by then but thankfully Arthur and his army had arrived on the scene unexpectedly, and just at the right moment to thwart the attack, but how did that come to pass he inquired.

Arthur explained that he had received reliable information that a large Saxon army was planning to attack Eboracum on the spring tide at the end of the following week, that was where he was headed. His source also indicated that there was much trouble from Irish raiders in the area around Deva Victris and that Arthur would most like encounter some where his timely intervention and assistance would be required. His journey would also give him the opportunity to enlist aid to help repel the Saxon attack. King Cadell of Powys had joined with them as they passed through Viroconium and his aid was most welcome. King Cadwallon responded that the least he could do after the events there was to offer his services and join with Arthur and show a united front to the Saxons. He would also send word to King Merchiaun of Rheged and request that he join them at en-route at Melandra Castle two days hence. Arthur welcomed his assistance and any additional help from the King of Rheged would swell their numbers to a sizeable force, as the Saxon army was likely to be considerable in strength.

Cadwallon took his leave of Arthur to make arrangements for departure the following morning, remarking that there was a good Roman road all the way to Eboracum that would make their journey easier. Although they would encounter the high ground at Melandra for awhile. The group broke up to make ready for an early start the next morning.

The journey to Melandra Castle was easy going and they made good time. Cadwallon, good to his word had joined them on departure from Deva Victris with two hundred horsemen, a hundred foot soldiers and two supply wagons. Arthur's army was beginning to look very formidable indeed. Even more so when King Merchiaun joined them at Melandra, with another two hundred men, as they began the long climb up through the valley between the massive peaks, before dropping down to the wide expanse of the dales the other side. Arthur took time to appreciate the rugged bleak beauty of the high ground and the total contrast as they dropped down into the lush green meadows stretching for mile upon mile into the distance. They rested frequently as the King knew that he had made good time and he needed his army fresh and fighting fit when they made their landfall. He felt it was going to be a difficult confrontation with the enemy in an area that he did not know.

* * * * *

Three days later brought them within sight of the massive fortified City of the Legion standing on a slightly raised plateau in the middle of the valley. Arthur stared in wonder at such a sight, it made Cadbury Castle seem insignificant by comparison. *How did the Saxons think they could take such a place without a prolonged siege by a large army. Where was its weak spot?* wondered Arthur. Legionus, as if reading the Kings thoughts had brought his horse alongside him.

"Impressive isn't it," he said, gazing at his former home, "but the river runs right through the centre of the city and a determined enemy could enter that way in small boats or on foot, it only comes up to a man's knees in most places. The archways over the river have to be high as the winter rains roar through the centre as the water pours down from the hills and would otherwise flood the whole city. The Saxons could bring their keels all the way from the sea up river as far as the village of Naburn, four miles south, as it is fairly deep and tidal up to that point, then rapidly shallows. However the city is surrounded by many marshy areas and they would need to be aware of those as they approached."

"That's very interesting Legionus," Arthur responded, saying that he was searching for the weak point in the defences, and the answer was in front of his eyes all the time. Then asked him to indicate safe ground to pitch camp for the moment, as it wouldn't be wise to approach the city in force, it might be mistaken for a hostile act. Legionus lead them half a mile off the road towards a gentle slope that was firm ground bordered by a belt of trees. Pointing out areas of marshy ground between them and the city that could be detected by their darker green colour and thicker grass and vegetation. No sooner had they stopped when Berius told Arthur that a group of horsemen were approaching from the direction of the city, no doubt to discover their intentions as they had obviously been seen by the city guards.

The horsemen brought their mounts to a stop before Arthur and the other kings and the one in the lead spoke.

"My lords I am Dubrovus of the Sarmatian legion, my Lord Peredur, Duke of Eboracum extends his welcome and wonders why such a large army camps close to the city. Do you travel far?"

"Thank you Dubrovus, I graciously return the welcome to Lord Peredur. I am Arthur, High King of Britain, King Merchiaun of Rheged, King Cadwallon of Gwynedd and King Cadell of Powys at your service," as he indicated the others, "We have arrived at our destination in preparation for a Saxon attack against Eboracum. I have brought my army north to thwart it and we seek counsel with your lord on this matter."

"My Lord I do not question your words or mean any offence but in these times we have to be careful, we do not know you in this region. My Lord Peredur would appreciate a sign of your lineage."

"Well spoken Dubrovus," replied Arthur, "I appreciate a man who is careful and diplomatic. Would you take the word of another Sarmatian?"

"Of course my lord, we are a people of honour," Dubrovus answered.

"Good," responded Arthur, "Then you would take the word of Legionus or any other of the two hundred Sarmatian cavalry that serve in my army?"

"My Lord Arthur, no words are necessary. If my old friend Legionus rides with you then you are indeed the High King of Britain, as he rode south with his troop to seek you out to offer his services." he replied.

"My commanders and I will join you on your return to the city, if me may, to avail Lord Peredur of the situation as we see it and to seek his counsel," requested Arthur.

"Indeed Sire, it will be my pleasure to enter the city in the company of four illustrious kings and their gallant lords. Lord Peredur will be greatly honoured to receive such a royal visitation," Dubrovus stated.

The group set off for Eboracum with Dubrovus explaining the features of the landscape around the city, at Arthur's request. The course of the river with its marshy areas and the great forest that lay a few miles to the north, extending from the centre of the country almost to the east coast. People stopped and stared as they passed through the massive gates, their sombre glances suddenly turning to smiles as they recognised the Sarmatians in the group and a few called out to them by name, bringing a raised hand in response.

The meeting with Lord Peredur lasted for several hours as Arthur explained the situation to him and the information that he had been given (but not how it was given). The Saxons would launch an attack from the north to draw Lord Peredur's forces after them before those that came up river in the south attempted to take the city. Peredur laughed at this saying it was nigh on impossible as the fortifications were designed to keep an army at bay, until Arthur pointed out that the weak point was the river running right through the city. A determined assault there might be difficult to contain. Once the Saxons had breached the defences they could pour into the city in vast numbers where it would be difficult to use the cavalry, it would be hand to hand fighting in the streets, they had to be caught in the open. Until they knew the size of the two Saxon armies it was difficult to plan a response so it was agreed to send scouts out in both directions to make visual contact with them and ascertain their numbers before drawing up a battle plan. Peredur suggested that Arthur move his army to a better position, one that Dubrovus would show him. A little more secluded and closer to the river whilst the King and his entourage accepted his hospitality there, ready to formulate a plan once the scouts reported Saxon movement. Sir Bors said that he would stay with the army and keep them in readiness for the signal to move, and so it was agreed. There were still three days before the spring tide and all they could do was wait, that gave Arthur time to see the city and check its defences and river exits.

* * * * *

If it hadn't have been for Sir Bors they might have been taken by surprise. He had ridden along the river bank passing the quiet village of Naburn on the east bank, travelling leisurely southwards. Just absorbing the tranquil beauty of the swiftly flowing water gurgling its way upriver, when voices came faintly to him on the gently breeze. Moving away from the river towards the cover of the trees that adorned the bank on either side and had followed the line of the watercourse for several miles, he moved slowly forward, ears straining for any sound and eyes darting about, alert for any movement ahead. The voices came again, stronger this time and not in his native tongue either, harsh guttural words of the Saxons, and rounding a slight bend he was astounded. The river had widened out considerably there and it was full of Saxon keels. Several had run aground on either side, sailing too close to the bank and swung out blocking the river. Downstream more were making their way slowly forward towards the others, twenty in all that he could see before the river curved away again around another bend. They were large keels that could easily carry two hundred men each. This was a formidable force and there could still be more that were out of his field of vision at the moment. The Saxons had arrived early as the spring high tide was not due until the next morning.

Sir Bors sat still on his horse, hidden beneath the shadows of the trees, quietly watching the scene unfolding before him. He noticed that the river was running downstream now, the Saxons would not be going any further today in their keels. Sir Bors stayed for another hour silently watching the activity, his well trained horse hardly moving a muscle, before the Saxons began to make a move. They appeared to be disembarking on both sides of the river, mostly on the east bank but a considerable number this side too. It was time to make a move and take the news to Arthur. He eased his horse slowly back into the trees before he turned around and keeping under cover quietly left the scene, putting some distance between him and the Saxons before he broke out into the open at the gallop. He stopped opposite the village at Naburn and shouted across the river to attract attention, warning them to make for the city straight away as a large party of Saxons were making their way upriver on both banks not ten miles away. It would not pay to be there when they arrived, with that he galloped off towards the camp to raise the alarm and to the city to alert King Arthur.

Arthur was slightly perturbed at the news, as none of the scouts had reported back yet with any sightings, possibly because they had taken a direct route to a point further downstream and the Saxons were already behind them by then. But what of the scouts that went north, why no news? Arthur pondered this mystery for a few moments, then realisation came to him as he automatically held the hilt of Excalibur. They had all sailed together and were only going to separate into two forces after they had landed. The coordination between the two armies would be that much better and the timing of the attacks more certain. No doubt they would send scouts forward to check that Lord Peredur took his forces out of the city to chase those attacking settlements to the north.

Arthur gathered the kings and lords together and outlined his plan to them. He would bring his army into the city away from the prying eyes of the Saxons and await their move. The foot soldiers would guard the weak points where the river flowed through the city and the cavalry would be split into two factions. Sir Peredur would lead his army, together with Legionus and Arthur's Sarmatians, northwards when news of the Saxon advance in that direction reached them. Arthur would wait with the remainder of his army, out of sight within the city, until the Saxons to the south made their move and tried to breach what they thought would be a sparsely guarded city. Most likely as the day faded gently into twilight and before darkness took a hold of the land. That was the time when men were normally weary and guards less observant. A good time for a surprise attack, and hours after the main army had departed on their fool's errand. So it was agreed and Sir Bors hurried off to camp to bring the army into the city. Then it was a question of just waiting and watching as a steady trickle of people arrived from Naburn and other outlying hamlets, seeking the protection of the great walled city.

Life began as normal the following day, people went about their business as usual, but there was an air of anticipation hanging over the city. All knew now of the threat that was hanging over them, many had been through this situation before, but they felt safe within the confines of the fortifications, built to withstand a siege. It was not until noon before there was flurry of activity as several horsemen arrived in quick succession, the scouts from the north returning with their news. A large Saxon army had been spotted just south of the ancient Galtres forest and they were headed towards the city, but did not appear to be in any hurry. Arthur decreed that it was time to put the plan into action and Sir Peredur gathered his mounted army and an hour later left the city at the gallop, the great gates booming together behind him as they were quickly secured. Arthur had directed that he did not engage them fully, whatever their strength, but to harry them and probe their ranks. Picking them off one by one before pulling away to repeat the action again, wearing them down slowly. Giving ground a little but containing them, until he could hopefully join the fray with the rest of the army, once he had dealt with the Saxons there.

The sun was beginning to fade before the first movement was detected on the landscape. The great ball of fire sinking slowly behind the rugged outline of the hills in the west, casting long shadows wherever its dwindling rays touched. The Saxons made their move, coming out of the shadows and advancing rapidly towards the city, along the line of the river. Arthur, waiting patiently with his cavalry gave the order for the gates to be opened and they poured forth to spring their surprise, and indeed it was. The Saxons had not expected to be confronted by such a large number of horsemen, their scouts had indicated that a major force had left the city hours earlier and had not returned. Where had these men materialised from? they wondered as the King and his men galloped towards them. The Saxon ranks wavering in indecision, should they stand and fight or proceed with all haste towards their goal where the river exited the city. Some turned to fight but their leaders were urging them forward, reminding them why they were there and that they had the strength of greater numbers. Their army was splitting into two, those engaging Arthur's men trying to hold him at bay, whilst the others made for the weak point in the fortifications. Only to be confronted by a determined force of foot soldiers barring their way. The water flowed red as Arthur and his men swept amongst the Saxons repelling their attack and pushing them across the river as they began to scatter and flee, heading northwards.

The sun had almost disappeared as they pursued them, sinking behind the hills, just leaving a red glow as if the Earth was on fire. An eerie feeling pervaded the landscape as the full moon started to exert her influence in response, bathing the scene with a pale luminescence that gradually grew in strength. Arthur and the cavalry had slowed their pace in the reduced light but continued to pursue the remnants of the enemy, who were making for the forest. Stragglers were quickly dealt with as they encountered them.

Fires began to twinkle in the distance, the other Saxon army or Sir Peredur, they would soon find out as they drew closer towards them, ready for an immediate response should it be the former. It soon became clear that it was Sir Peredur and his men, camped as if guarding the forest, into which the Saxon horde had disappeared. He was delighted to see Arthur and the others and indicated that there were several thousand of the enemy and they had taken refuge in the forest.

They had been almost reluctant to fight and slowly gave way as Sir Peredur and the Sarmatians had attacked them, retreating to the trees for protection. Arthur told him that they had deliberately done that to lure him away from the city until it had been taken, but they would know now that their guise had failed as the remnants of their other force had taken refuge there too. They would probably try to escape back to their keels in the dead of night when most of his army would be in their slumber, the difficult question was how to prevent that happening. He excused himself from the others saying that he needed to give the problem some thought and wandered off to a quiet spot with Berius, as usual quiet and unobtrusively by his side.

Arthur sat quietly on the remains of a fallen tree, struck by lighting at some point in the past. Not yet dead as it was still rooted to the ground, but its life force fading slowly over the years until it would soon give up, yet some of its energy would remain in the form of the young sapling growing tenuously close by. All this passed through Arthur's mind as he sat, his hands curled around the hilt of Excalibur as he allowed its energy to meld with his and bring clarity of thought, feeling warmth from the old tree that was surprising. The old in its wisdom giving way and nurturing the next generation. What did that remind him of from his younger days?

He turned to Berius suddenly and said without thinking, "are there any bears in this forest?"

"Yes my Lord," Berius answered. "This is an ancient forest that has been the home of bears for many generations, it is their ancestral home and although their stock has depleted over the years many still live here. Your name is known to them through the caring deed you showed one of their kind when you were a young lad, they do not forget such a rare thing from a human. Do you seek their help in this matter?"

"Yes Berius, it came to me sitting here that they can help by putting fear into the Saxons to the extent that they flee the forest. To force them out into the open before the night is out, right here so that we can deal with them and stop them escaping, just to return again. Do you think they will be willing to aid the King?"

The answer Berius gave surprised him. "I will go and ask them my Lord. I am sure that they will agree, you are a King in their eyes too, they know you are very different to other humans, I will not be long," with that he disappeared into the night without a sound, except that Arthur thought he heard the gently beating of a bird's wings in the distance, an owl or some other night creature perhaps.

Arthur sat in silence for what seemed an eternity before Berius suddenly reappeared, as silently as he had left, a smile on his face and with good news.

"The bears do not like the Saxons as they kill indiscriminately, they are willing to assist the King in removing them from their forest. As they remember the kindness that you showed to one of them in the past, in fact he is currently the elder here. It will take them four hours by my reckoning to call on sufficient of their number to make such a noise that it will strike terror into the hearts of the Saxons and make them flee the forest. Most of them appear to be in the vicinity of where we are, but the bears will cast a wide net to drive them this way. The dark of the forest will help generate fear in them and it will appear as if there are thousands of bears on the rampage."

"Thank you Berius, that is magnificent news, I must warn the army and have them prepare for battle."

Arthur returned to the camp fire and gathered the kings and commanders together and outlined what was going to happen and how they would respond. The group were astonished at those revelations and looked on Arthur and Berius in a different light from then on. Enlisting the aid of animals was something only spoken of in ancient tales, when many men had mystical powers and used them to great advantage. Now their High King and his sword keeper were making new stories to be told, ones that would generate new deeds and perhaps awaken that ancient knowledge once again.

"It is not ideal to fight at night," Arthur said, "but tonight the full moon is casting more light than is usual at this time of year, with a cloudless sky sparkling in a vast array of twinkling stars that it appears almost like a dull sunless day, we should take this as a good omen. The Earth and nature working in harmony with man, as used to be the way until the human race lost its direction. Tonight will show that we haven't totally forgotten how it should be and that we are willing to re-learn what the ancients always understood. We will mount up in two hours and spread out in a new moon formation with kings and lords to the fore to show we mean business and show our crests. Let the Saxons disgorge from the forest before we attack, Excalibur will be the signal."

The combined army of Arthur and the kings waited patiently, spread out in the agreed formation just half a mile from the edge of the forest, the night was clear and silent, not a breath of wind stirred the trees, their leaves totally motionless.

Almost to the minute that Berius had indicated the peace of the night was instantly shattered by a spine chilling roar, others followed immediately, then more, the ground seemed to shake, the noise was horrendous. Leaves rustled, trees swayed and the noise grew, startled birds took to the air, confused by the cacophony of noise that was emanating from the ancient forest, it was just as if all the trees had come alive too at that same moment. Even the normally docile horses of the cavalry were beginning to twitch and so were their riders, the noise was tremendous, something was bound to happen; it did. The forest suddenly disgorged hundreds upon hundreds of Saxons, fear etched deeply on their faces as visions of dragons and giants gripped their lucid imagination in the dark confines of the forest as they fled in sheer terror.

Arthur waited until the flow of bodies from the trees eased, then raising his sword boomed out 'Excalibur' in a voice that he didn't recognise as his own. The affect was instantaneous, brilliant white light burst from the blade, illuminating the whole landscape, darts of the light burst upon the enemy as tongues of red fire shot from the mouths of the serpents that formed the guard. The Saxons had fled from the forest consumed with terror, now they were petrified as they saw Arthur and the kings bear down on them, the blazing sword at the front striking down all that were in the way.

The fighting was fierce, the Saxons were hemmed in by the forest behind them that still reverberated with tremendous noise, a magical sword and cavalry to the front, and nowhere to escape, they were doomed. The battle lasted an hour. An hour full of sheer terror and death for the Saxons before they finally succumbed. A few escaped into the forest as the lesser of two evils, but none were seen again, and a handful managed to disappear into the night totally traumatised. The land was covered in blood stained bodies, not all were Saxons, the kings had lost men too, but few by comparison.

Arthur surveyed the scene, the bears had done a very good job, motioning to Berius to join him he rode towards the forest, stopping just short of the trees as several bears ambled out from concealment of the thick foliage.

"Berius can you convey to the bears what I am about to say?" Arthur asked.

"Of course my lord, although you could, just by thinking the words from your heart," Berius replied.

Arthur relaxed as he sent his thoughts out to them thanking them for their valour and help in removing the Saxons, their intervention was greatly appreciated and would be rewarded. Then turning around to face his army he raised his sword as he let his words carry to them.

"Now hear this, I Arthur, High King of Britain do declare that the ancient forest of Galtres is from this day forward and for as long as I live the sacred domain of the bears, they shall not be hunted or taken captive for any reason, upon pain of death. This is their domain and so it shall remain, under the King's protection, any that use this forest shall respect the habitat of the bears, they have full royal rights in its use and are answerable to no one except the High King, that is my command."

Berius had communicated this to the bears by his thoughts and as Arthur finished they gave a roar and thumped their chests in gratitude. Arthur saluted them with his sword and slowly turned his horse and moved away, stopping momentarily to turn, as he raised his hand to the majestic creatures in a gesture of peace and friendship.

Chapter 16

ARTHUR BREAKS THE SAXONS AT BADDON HILL

LIKE AN ARMY OF SHADOWS snaking their way across the landscape, under the pale fluorescence of the full moon, Arthur lead his men back to Eboracum. The men had never seen such a sight as Excalibur spewing out its dancing light by night before, nor the noise and commotion of so many bears striking fear into the hearts of brave men, making them flee in total terror. This night would stay in their memories for a very long time and be retold across many a warm fire during the cold winter months. How their King had, by some mysterious means, enlisted the aid of the bears to drive the Saxons from the forest so that they could deal with them. Rewarding them with his royal protection within the ancient forest, for their brave deed. The kings themselves had never witness such an extraordinary spectacle either, their respect and regard for Arthur and his leadership increased many fold, he was worthy of the High Kingship. A man that certainly stood apart from the rest, even commanding allegiance from the animal kingdom.

Arthur stayed at the city for two days, relaxing and enjoying the festivities that had continued unabated since their return, before indicating that it was time to begin their journey back to Cadbury. King Merchiaun of Rheged was staying on for a few more days to discuss with Lord Peredur how they could work together in combating the Irish raiders. King Cadell and King Cadwallon would travel with Arthur as far as Deva Victris before leaving him. He was invited to stay there for awhile with them, but graciously declined on the grounds that trouble might re-occur in the south, as it was sparsely defended at the moment, he should return there forthwith.

* * * * *

Two weeks later saw Arthur and his army back in familiar territory as they came in sight of Cadbury Castle, perched on the hilltop. Partially obscured by the shimmering haze from the watery sun, a welcoming sight indeed.

Life returned to normal very quickly, punctuated regularly by various dignitaries seeking the King's advice or paying their respects socially, and the Saxon menace soon faded from the forefront of their minds, except Arthur's. Occasionally riders appeared, seeking out the King to offer their services and a steady flow of young men arrived on foot from villages and hamlets in the region, some travelling many miles, wishing to serve Arthur. There was always a need for more men and women in the castle, not just to be trained as soldiers, but for the many services that the growing population required. All were made welcome and given tasks according to their abilities.

Life was settled, but Arthur knew that this was only a short respite. The Saxons had lost many men in their confrontations with him and it would take them time to recover, but they would return with a vengeance, of that he was sure. In the meantime the King was not idle either, seeking to replenish and grow his forces too, ready for the next onslaught. Greyfus was his normal busy self, arranging the stocks of winter food and fuel and securing more horses from the traders. Bishop Bedwini was organising the building of a church in the castle grounds, astounded that they did not have one, but as Arthur remarked there had been other pressing matters to keep them busy, though they were sorely in need of one.

Summer moved slowly on and much was accomplished before the days became shorter and the changing colours of the landscape to deeper, darker shades heralded the arrival of autumn. Merlin and Taliesin arrived to see out the winter in some comfort, stating that the signs were that it was going to be severe. Rivers would freeze in some parts of the country and the earth would become like solid rock, not a time to venture forth on the land. Berius nodded in agreement saying that the animals and birds had been preparing for a hard cold winter for some weeks. They understood the subtle changes in the earth and air, seeking better refuge deeper in the forests where the denser foliage would give greater protection. Arthur relayed this information to Greyfus as a matter of courtesy, knowing that the preparations that he had made would be adequate for even the most severe of winters, even the horses would not be forgotten. Greyfus was very proficient at what he did, borne of many years experience of catering for the unexpected.

* * * * *

The winter was indeed very severe, even the castle gate froze solid some nights and many cursing hands were needed to free the giant hinges in the morning, only to have them freeze again the following night. Fires were kept alight continuously in the Great Hall, the focal point of life for all during those terrible months. Most of the people ate, slept and spent the whole time there when they were not working, soldiers, servants and children. There was no distinction of rank, all were welcome, all were equal, this was a community that lived, worked and died as one, a philosophy that Arthur had encouraged and insisted upon. It worked exceedingly well, everyone pulled together looking to the needs of each other and although the winter was a depressing time as it was a period of inactivity, the general mood was jovial and relaxed.

Arthur spent much time with Merlin, Taliesin and his commanders, reviewing the various battles with the Saxons, and what they had learnt about their tactics, other than that they favoured weight of numbers above all else in their confrontations, and their leaders directed them from the rear. Discussions centred around where they were likely to attack next. Many suggestions were made and countered by others as Arthur, Merlin and Taliesin sat quietly listening to the debate, keeping their own counsel for the moment. Eventually Arthur was asked for his thoughts on where he felt trouble would occur next.

"A difficult question," conceded Arthur. "The Saxons have tried, and failed several times in the south, not venturing too far from their territory until our last battles with them. They know we are strong in the south and they failed disastrously in the north west and north east, that leaves the south west and western coast. The south west is perhaps too far for them at the moment and there is nothing significant there that would take them so far from home. However the west, especially in the region of the Severn estuary, is a different matter. There are many small forts that command strategic positions along the coast of Demetia, Gwent and Glywysing, that if they fell into Saxon hands would pose a major threat to our country. A short journey by sea across the estuary and they would threaten the whole area from Glevum to ourselves here at Cadbury. We would be fighting them both in the west and the east, if they also took the opportunity to break out of their land in the south east. It would be difficult to contain them, our forces would be stretched too much, even with three times as many men as we have at the moment. I feel that they will strike in the west, perhaps in more than one place at the same time, to divide our army. They tried once before but the weather turned against them, which was a blessing for us, I do not think we shall be as lucky the next time. When spring arrives I intend to take the army to Caerleon and speak with King Caradog of Gwent and organise the defence of the coastal region. Then my lords we wait for the Saxons to make a move."

He turned to Merlin enquiring if he had missed any detail that was worthy of a mention.

Merlin shook his head, "I think you have made an excellent case for your thoughts, there is nothing that I can add at this moment in time. It would be a good idea to visit Caradog again and enlist his aid and meet some of the other kings and persuade them to work together, there has been much squabbling between them in the past."

"Thank you Merlin," replied Arthur. "It pleases me that my thoughts have gone down well with you. Your teachings have been beneficial in directing me to follow my inner instincts, seeking answers from within."

"You are doing well," Merlin answered. "As you will have noticed I do not advise you as much these days, your own inner sight has developed well and my advice is not needed, but it is still there if you require it."

"I heed your words and they inspire me with greater confidence," Arthur stated, "now let us relax a little, spring is still along way off and there is little else we can do until nearer the time."

* * * * *

The freezing weather of the winter months passed slowly, little moved within the castle grounds or indeed on the landscape, unless it was absolutely necessary, it was a time for hibernation. Arthur spent much time in quiet contemplation, going within himself whilst holding the hilt of Excalibur gently in his hands. Many wondrous visions passed through his mind, of time long ago. The splendour of a previous age where people lived and worked peacefully together, a time of harmony and plenty that suddenly faltered as greed and power, sought by a few, raised their ugly heads and rapidly destroyed Utopia. Society disintegrated, the materialistic urge spreading like a plague, unstoppable by those that saw the danger, either being ignored or killed by those leading the downward spiral to self destruction. Mankind had sunk to the lowest level of existence, but there was hope. Some pockets of civilisation that had followed the old ways of the ancients had survived, and spread to many sparsely populated areas of the world to continue their way of life, in readiness to assist, at a point in the future, the revival of the golden age. Many generations would pass before the time was right and then it would take hundreds of years to rebuild, slowly, a little at a time, until the people changed their awareness and perception of life to as it should be. Arthur saw his task more clearly now, his small island nation had been selected by the Elders as the place to begin the restoration, and he was to lead them forward to start rebuilding. A process that would continue long after he was gone. An honour indeed for the responsibility to fall to someone so young as himself. The Elders had faith in him and he would do his best to see that he did not fail them, his confidence had grown of late, but he was also painfully aware that he was only human. He could only do his best, whatever the outcome. He saw that the role of Merlin and the other Elders was purely advisory, they could not intervene directly as he was already aware, their law forbade it. Mankind had to sort out its own problems, but guidance was there for those that would listen. Arthur had listened and learnt much, holding their wisdom in great regard and gave his thanks for their continued help, without which the struggle would be much harder. The gift of his magical sword, Excalibur, from the Lady of the Lake was a turning point in his battles with the Saxons. Since his visit to Avebury, feeling the Earth energies at The Sanctuary the bond between them had strengthened, its power more devastating than before, and its wisdom readily available. Arthur was at ease with himself, secure in the knowledge that he was blessed with help from many quarters, his leadership acknowledged without question. What more could he ask for?

* * * * *

The new year slipped in quietly and the icy weather began to ease its grip a little as the amount of daylight slowly increased each day. Colour started to creep back into the landscape as trees and flowers awoke from their slumber, and the birdsong took on a joyous note. People started to move around the compound again, grateful for chance to stretch their bodies in the air without the freezing breath that had surrounded them and seeped into their bones. The horses were able to exercise properly at last and general activity increased as the castle came back to life.

Arthur summoned his commanders and told them that they would be moving out for Caerleon at the end of the month if the weather continued to improve. He wanted to get the defence of that region organised as soon as possible, it was likely that they would be away for two months at least. As they departed about their business Gelda approached Arthur and said that she wished to see him privately that evening if she could call at his chambers, to which he readily agreed.

The King sought out Merlin to seek his advice on the history of the area around Caerleon, the lords and their ancient squabbles, the lie of the land and possible landing places on the coast that the Saxons might use. They were closeted together for several hours as Merlin took Arthur through the history of the region. Arthur asked him if he wished to travel with them this time as it was generally regarded as his homeland. He agreed it would be a good opportunity to visit old friends, as Taliesin would be off south again soon to keep his ear to the ground in case the Saxons had further aims there.

Their conversation finished Arthur went in search of Greyfus to check arrangements were in hand for the army's long period away and to advise Bishop Bedwini of the forthcoming journey, should he wish to join them. He declined on this occasion saying that it would give him the opportunity to see the church was finished in readiness for their return.

The day drew to a close and the clear, but dark sky, under the cold crisp light of the moon indicated another chilly night ahead as Arthur made his way to his quarters to await the arrival of Gelda and whatever problem she had. He was not surprised to find her already there, curled up under the covers of his bed, saying it was the best place to keep warm, Arthur smiling, told her it would have been easier if she had kept her garments on, pointing to them on the floor, to which, fluttering her eyes she agreed, but not so much fun. Arthur, needing no second bidding, quickly joined her and as he gently caressed her body asked what was troubling her, for it was obvious something was. Looking into his eyes she told him that she felt her time was getting near, that she would not survive the year. It had been growing steadily for months to the point that she was certain in herself that it was true. If that was the case then she wanted to enjoy herself as a woman again, before it was too late, she wanted him, she needed him, and Arthur responded to her wishes.

Their passion was relentless, continuing unabated long into the night as their bodies heaved and thrust in unison, exploding together with shouts and groans of pure ecstasy. Time after time, until exhaustion overtook them both and they slept, entwined in each others arms, still joined together in their lust.

* * * * *

Arthur lead his army out of Cadbury three weeks later with four large supply carts trundling slowly behind them, as they set off for Glevum before turning south to Caerleon. It would be too dangerous to cross the Severn at the ford they had used last time, adding less than a day to their extended journey. Merlin spent the time telling Arthur stories of the ancient kings of the area, almost as if he had known them personally, but that could not be possible surely. It would make him centuries old, perhaps he was just using his 'vision' to take him back to those times and re-live the moment. He let his thoughts wander. *The Elders were certainly a mysterious people, their knowledge stretched back aeon's, Their foresight proved to be uncannily right, they seemed to know, in great detail, what had happened in the distant past and also events that would unfold in the future. Where did they originate from and what brought them to this small island to begin with? Was it because the British people were somehow different to those throughout the rest of the world? The Elders sought no reward for their services or advice but never seemed to be without sustenance, travelling widely around the country on their 'business' as they called it. What was their business? Ambassadors certainly, often mediators between squabbling British kings. Apparent knowledge of Saxon intent and guidance to quell their advance. What was the real reason behind it all? Why were they so concerned that he made the right decisions and sought peace and prosperity for his land? Appearing when needed and then sometimes disappearing for months at a time, only to reappear just as suddenly when something was about to happen. Uncanny how they did that, bad news normally arrived with them.* Arthur was aware in himself of some of the answers, more so since his experience at The Sanctuary, but the real reason still eluded him, perhaps in time he would understand more, when he was ready to know.

Caerleon was a picturesque town, the substantial fort sprawling across the hilltop, overlooking the wide river valley sweeping away to the sea a few miles distant. King Caradog extended a warm welcome to them on their arrival, inquiring if this was a social visit or a sign of trouble brewing. Arthur laughingly replied that he hoped it was just a goodwill visit, but there was business to discuss as well whilst they were there, it did not pay to become complacent where the Saxons were concerned. Caradog agreed and suggested that they talk about it as they ate, as good conversation was not forthcoming on an empty stomach, his men would see to their horses. He had some guests visiting, Ogrfan Gawr and his beautiful daughter Gwenhwyfar, a fair sight indeed and fit for a King, he remarked pointedly at Arthur as he led them into a great stone hall, similar in size to that at Cadbury Castle.

Caradog performed the introductions to his guests. A fair sight was an understatement conceded Arthur, Gwenhwyfar was an extremely beautiful fair haired maiden and he boldly told her so, causing her to blush slightly as she graciously acknowledged his compliment. Small talk accompanied the food and wine until with a great belch Caradog finally asked the question that at been on his mind since Arthur arrived; the nature of his visit. Considering that he had brought his army with him.

Arthur explained his thoughts on where he felt the Saxons might launch another attack and the reasoning behind them. Nothing was known for certain, but it was as well to be prepared and make sure his good friend Caradog was aware of the possibility. They had tried to penetrate Arthur's forces many times, and each time had failed disastrously in the end, it was likely that they would try a different approach. They were more than capable of sailing this distance and could land on either side of the Severn Sea. Effectively coming around behind Arthur and his army, landing this side to draw his army here, then mounting another attack on the opposite coast where resistance would then be light. Arthur wished to make sure Caradog and other lords on the coast there were prepared, so that he could concentrate his army on the other shore in readiness. Caradog considered Arthur's words and agreed that they made sense, it was better to be prepared than taken by surprise. He would ride out with them on the morrow and introduce him to other lords along the coast that would need to be told of the possible threat.

Conversation then turned to other more light hearted topics and broke into small groups, and Arthur found himself talking with Gwenhwyfar, a knowledgeable lady as well as strikingly beautiful, and he found himself perfectly at ease in her company.

The following morning saw Arthur and his commanders, together with King Caradog, head out to take his warning along the coast to the lords and princes of the land, calling on King Glywys of Glywysing, a small neighbouring kingdom of Gwent. It was a fruitful day, all having heard of the deeds of Arthur, but most never having met the High King of Britain before, and he left them feeling more at ease afterwards, Arthur's bearing and manner instilling confidence in everyone that he spoke to, a man young in years maybe, but old in wisdom, a born leader.

For several days they roamed the countryside, calling on the local lords, stopping at hamlets along the way to speak to the people. Merlin travelled with them, as it was an area he knew well and he was recognised and spoken to by many along the way.

Each evening saw them back in Caerleon enjoying the hospitality of King

Caradog and his delightful guests. Arthur engaging in much conversation with the beautiful and voluptuous Gwenhwyfar, her father extremely pleased that the High King had taken more than a passing interest in her, a match there would be most beneficial. Arthur conveyed to all that they would have to reluctantly take leave of the king's hospitality in a couple of days as they needed to make their way back around to the opposite coast to prepare them for a possible Saxon attack. As he said that he experienced a strange feeling that events were already happening that would change his plan, that it was already too late to do more, except wait. Arthur glanced across at Merlin to find that he was gazing steadfastly at him, a slightly glazed look in his eyes as he asked the King if he had felt it, that change in vibration of the Earth energies.

"What is it Merlin?" Arthur asked. "It felt as if something was happening, that this journey would not be finished, that events were moving faster than I had anticipated."

"Your senses are sharper now, you have read the feeling correctly, a fleet of Saxon keels are already on their way, they have passed through the straights of Lyonesse during the day, unseen until then, they could be here within three days with a favourable wind." replied Merlin.

"I will send word out along the coast in the morning for lookouts to scan the sea for sign of them, lest they take us by surprise," stated Arthur. "We can only watch and wait, and hope their landfall is noted."

The mood of the feasting had changed, the light hearted banter replaced by more sober talk as the thought of approaching conflict spread amongst them. Gwenhwyfar excused herself as it was time for men to talk, asking Arthur to see her safely to her quarters, eliciting the reply that it would be an honour and a privilege. He escorted her from the great hall, her arm crooked in his, bringing a knowing smile to the group as they watched young love blossoming. Arriving at the guest quarters, she turned and thanked him, raising herself on tip toe and giving him a warm kiss, that as Arthur responded turned into one long passionate kiss.

"Go now, back to the others," she breathed heavily, "before I decide to keep you prisoner for the night."

"Yes I had better," he replied, as his body began to respond, "but if you need my assistance anytime, by chance, then I am in the next chamber."

With that he kissed her again and quickly returned to the hall. There was a bounce in his step and his body was still alive with excitement from the passionate kiss, his thoughts a jumble of beautiful possibilities, but alas there were more important matters to deal with first, Gwenhwyfar would have to wait.

His arrival back in the hall surprised a few, those that had read the signs of a successful union in the making, but Arthur soon brought the discussion around to their immediate problem. Where were the Saxons headed? Although it was a hilly region many rivers took the excess water down to the sea, creating an abundance of possible landing places for the enemy, and thus a potential problem for the King. Following advice from Caradog and Merlin various lookout points were decided upon, each being manned by four riders, ready to raise the alarm once the Saxons were spotted out at sea.

It was a long coastline but Arthur felt that they would sail into the narrower Severn Sea before landing, therefore the watchers would only extend to Merthyr Mawr, some forty miles distant, commanding a view of the open sea from there. As a precaution four watchers would go up the coast to Caerwent, to the mouth of the river, in case the Saxons managed to slip passed unseen and land behind them. Caradog marvelled at how Arthur made everything sound so simple, certain that the attack would occur on this side of the sea first, not the other, that he felt would come later. The watchers would need to remain vigilant and search for a second fleet of keels, following perhaps a day or two behind, these would most likely head for the other shore and a landing there, if that was the Saxon plan. Arthur felt sure that it was, it was in the vision that he had at The Sanctuary, but he did not enlighten the gathering what he felt and saw that day.

All through the discussions Merlin had sat quietly watching and listening, smiling to himself, Arthur had learnt much and was now following his inner feelings and instincts to a greater extent, he was doing well. Some of the knowledge of the ancients was resurfacing from the depths within, to aid him in his task. His new battles with the Saxons would stretch him to the limit at times, but he would succeed in taming them and quench their thirst for expansion for many years to come.

During the next two days little happened, the watchers had been sent to their destinations with clear instructions on what to do if they sighted the Saxons. Tension in Caerleon was at a height, little was said or done, the army was prepared, but all they could do was wait for news from the lookouts. Every time a horseman entered the gates, anticipation rose momentarily, only to dissipate as quickly on discovering that it was just another traveller.

The evening feast was a sombre affair with little conversation, even Gwenhwyfar failed to appear the second evening, having sent her apologise via her father that she was unfortunately indisposed. Most of those gathered in the great hall retired early, wishing time move on faster to allay the boredom of waiting. Even Caradog and Merlin muttered their excuses and departed, leaving just Berius and Arthur sitting quietly with their own thoughts. Eventually Berius broke the silence and told him to stop thinking and worrying about the Lady Gwenhwyfar, instead to go and see her and put her mind at rest concerning the forthcoming trouble. She was gravely concerned for the King's welfare and was waiting for him. Arthur smiled at this, he had forgotten that Berius could read his thoughts, as he unbuckled

Excalibur and handed it to him and set forth to comfort the lady. A difficult time for her with the uncertainty of what might happen.

She was not in her chambers but curled up under the covers in his bed. He stood watching her for a moment as the light from the oil lamp flickered across her face, looking even more beautiful in her slumber as the covers rose and fell gently with her breathing. Quickly removing his garments he slipped in beside her, delicately caressing her face, such beautifully smooth skin, with not a blemish to be seen. Slipping his hand beneath the covers, as he gave her a light teasing kiss, he explored her firm warm body. Sighing gently she opened her eyes, giving him a beautiful smile as she returned his kiss, her hand running slowly over his body, ending with a little squeal of pleasure as she found what she sought, the hard throbbing seat of his passion. Slowly they explored each other sending shivers of pleasure through their bodies as two lovers do with such intimate contact on their journey of discovery. Pure love, pure and total ecstasy, as they sought to please each other, until they melded together and let their passion consume them in violent eruption that seemed to go on forever. Before collapsing into each others arms with sweet words of endearment. Neither slept that night, tomorrow might turn their world into heartache and turmoil, this time was theirs, they enjoyed every sweet moment and word, nothing could take that from them.

It was not 'til late afternoon of the third day that word finally came to those waiting at Caerleon. Many keels had been spotted off Merthyr Mawr, sailing in mid channel. Not long after a watcher from Llantwit Major arrived with the same news, then another from the post at Cold Knap, followed by a rider from Llandough. All reported the Saxon keels still in mid channel, with no indication of where they were headed.

The light was beginning to fade when a lookout arrived from the Twrc estuary, below Caerleon, saying that they appeared to be going passed the river mouth, about two miles offshore, but that a sea mist was beginning to form in the channel, slowly rolling in from the open sea. This posed a dilemma for Arthur. Would the Saxons keep on going and make landfall further along, heave to and spend the night at sea, or head for shore before the sea mist closed in on them? He decided to send some of his men further along the coast, whilst keeping the main force at Caerleon until daylight.

Sir Bors took two hundred horsemen, including some of Caradog's men for their local knowledge, setting out for the coastal path and the many small inlets and bays upstream that the Saxons could use for landing their army. Desolate and uninhabited places that would be ideal for bringing a large body of men ashore undisturbed.

Sir Kay was despatched towards the Twrc estuary with a hundred men. Not much could be seen in the wet swirling sea mist that was also creeping slowly onto the land, creating ghostly shapes on all that it touched, but they might hear if the enemy landed. Sound travelled further in those conditions, although the direction that it emanated from could be confusing to the senses, making it difficult to pinpoint the exact location, they should hear them.

All that Arthur could do now was wait, the morning would bring a better idea of the Saxon whereabouts, once the mist had lifted. Gwenhwyfar was waiting for him again in his chambers, and they spoke at great length on what the future might hold for them, before their passion overtook them again as two naked writhing bodies exploded together in ecstasy, the outside world totally forgotten for the moment., Arthur, physically and mentally exhausted, fell into a slumber, Gwenhwyfar kissed him gently, dressed herself quickly and left him to the sleep that his body needed, tomorrow would be a hard day for all.

It was one of Sir Kay's men that returned to raise the alarm, the mist had vanished quickly with the morning light to reveal many Saxon keels in the Twrc estuary rapidly disgorging several thousand men onto the shoreline. Arthur and Caradog gathered their troops and set forth from the fort at a gallop, the gate clanging shut with a finality behind them, leaving few men behind in its defence.

The few miles to the coast quickly fell behind them and soon they saw the Saxon keels spread in an array about the river banks, the enemy soldiers moving to join together. Sir Kay and his men had already engaged the Saxons from four keels that were separate from the rest, as the main body of the enemy started to group together and head towards them. Arthur immediately saw Sir Kay's danger as he drew his sword, shouting out that magic name 'Excalibur.' The sword burst into life and its brilliant white light cut through the air, dancing menacingly towards the Saxons in a sign of defiance. The enemy faltered for a brief moment at this frightening spectacle, and the unexpected arrival of hundreds of cavalry bearing down on them and turned to face this new threat. Arthur and his men were quickly amongst them but they stood their ground, even though many fell around them.

The arrival of Sir Bors and his men tipped the balance and the Saxons began to fall back, their casualties increasing alarmingly until a harsh guttural command that emanated from the rear had the ones at the front try and hold their line. The Saxons were withdrawing men back to the safety of their keels as quickly as they could. Those concentrated at the front trying to give them time, the deep gullies and lie of the land now in their favour, restricting Arthur's cavalry assault to short probes on the narrow spurs.

The Saxons had lost many of their number in the conflict, but more were escaping, as first one, then another keel put out to sea, men scrambling aboard as they left. Soon there was only a few hundred left on land but Arthur still could not get at them with the full force of his cavalry. Suddenly they turned and fled, those that reached the water throwing themselves in to make for the waiting keels, the others being cut down by Arthur's army as finally they had the space to manoeuvre amongst them.

Arthur watched as the keels sailed out to sea, knowing that they would now head for the opposite coast and land there. Time was at a premium, he had to take his army to the other side as quickly as possible. They had no ships, it would be just over a two day ride, the Saxons would do it in less than a day, even with the tide against them. There was no time to lose. He had foreseen this at The Sanctuary in his vision, but did not have a large enough army to defend both sides at the same time. That was his reason for seeking King Caradog's help first and depleting the Saxon strength there. More Saxon keels would land soldiers on the other side, of that he was sure, but he had time, just, to take his army around there before they arrived. Arthur would be greatly outnumbered but his cavalry would have the space to come into their own.

He sought out King Caradog and told him of his intention, they would return to Caerleon and each man would have to take their own supplies, they could not take the carts with them, it would slow them down too much. Caradog said that he would join Arthur with as many horsemen that he could gather and send word to King Glywys advising him of the situation so that he could watch the coastline for any more Saxon keels. Events already unfolding however were to change Arthur's plan and test his leadership skills even more. Pressure was building up, life was not as simple as it appeared, the Saxons were aiming for bigger stakes, that was soon to become apparent.

Their arrival at the fort was greeted with relief. Three Saxon keels had landed a force at Cold Knap, possibly becoming detached from the main force in the mist, and they were heading along the coastal path, several hundred strong. Arthur called Sir Kay and told him to select a hundred men to go with King Caradog and deal with the enemy. When that had been done he was to bring whatever horsemen he could muster to join Arthur on the coast directly opposite to them. Use his instincts and follow the river until he found sign of them around Portus Abonae [Sea Mills - Bristol], he told him, if they were not in that area then to head inland towards Caer Baddon [old English name for Bath] that he believed would be their final destination.

Sir Kay and King Caradog left shortly after, taking their troop to deal with this other Saxon menace. Meanwhile Arthur despatched his other commanders to prepare the army, making sure that they each took sufficient food for a week and he went in search of Gwenhwyfar. She was in her chamber this time, quietly consoling herself and praying for Arthur's safe return. Her smile on seeing him was enough to make the King's heart miss a beat, but he quickly explained that he could not stay. There was more to be done yet before he could relax and spend time with her, enquiring after her father and his whereabouts. She directed him to another chamber, giving him a quick kiss and extorting a promise from him that he would return to see her when the trouble was over. His reply took her breath away as he looked her in the eyes and said that he would return to claim his Queen, taking her in his arms as he gave her a long lingering kiss. Then he was gone, off to inform her father of his good fortune.

Arthur and his army made good time, without punishing their horses, and arrived at the causeway on the River Severn, known locally as the passage, just as daylight was fading, pitching camp for the night as it was not advisable to cross in the dark. Frustration abounded the next morning as they had to wait for the tide to recede sufficiently before crossing and continuing their hurried journey southward along the river bank. Few people were seen on their travels, a deceptive peace and calm prevailed over the area as the water flowed swiftly down the river towards the sea. At any other time a pleasant ride, but theirs had a sense of urgency about it for they knew what lay ahead. No sign was seen of any Saxon keels, not that Arthur had expected to encounter any this high up, they would be further south, closer to Portus Abonae, though he felt sure that they would avoid the port itself as resistance might be encountered there.

The day drew on, the weak sun breaking through the cloud cover periodically. It was still early in the year and there was not much heat in the day yet, ideal conditions for a hard ride as the horses stayed cool and travelled well, with not many rest periods needed, for horse or rider. Berius, with his excellent vision was the first to spot the keels in the distance, beached and left stranded by the receding tide, devoid of any movement. The Saxons had long gone. The question was, how long ago and in which direction were they travelling, or were they perhaps still in the locale waiting for the second armada to arrive? Caution was necessary as Arthur let his thoughts have free reign in looking for inner guidance. His gaze was drawn to a small hill a couple of miles away at Cathbregyon [Catbrain Hill at Filton, Bristol], an ideal vantage point to survey the surrounding land for signs of the Saxons. He led his army slowly towards the solitary peak, standing proud like a sentinel in the surrounding flat landscape. His senses suddenly alert to potential danger, the feeling intensifying as they approached the hill. Drawing Excalibur he motioned to the others around him to do the same, the Saxons were close, he could feel them, although he could not see any sign of them.

Suddenly, rising up from a blind gully in front of him, they unleashed their assault, only Arthur's instincts saved them from being taken unawares in a trap. The cavalry spread out rapidly to better counter the attack and keep the enemy from surrounding them. Fighting was fierce, Arthur's men were greatly outnumbered, but the speed and agility of his cavalry countered this and they began to push the Saxons back towards the hill. Daylight was fading rapidly now as the day drew towards a close. The enemy ranks braking under the constant pressure of the cavalry charges, wavering in their resolve to hold firm and stand their ground. Their line had been broken into smaller groups from repeated attacks by the cavalry, driving wedges through their ranks, making it easier for Arthur's men to pick them off.

As darkness descended the battle suddenly ceased as the Saxons melted into the gloom of the starless night, the cavalry briefly giving chase. Darkness fell quickly and it became too dangerous to continue the pursuit, they would have to wait for daylight. The Saxons had suffered heavy casualties but there were still many that had escaped into the night. Arthur had lost thirty or so men and several horses, they had escaped lightly thanks to his instincts, it could have been much worse if they had been taken by surprise. All they could do now was tend to the wounded and wait for the morning to continue the pursuit, Arthur sure of the direction that they would take, his vision had been correct so far, there was no reason to doubt that it would let him down now.

Daylight revealed the full extent of the carnage, the battlefield strewn with bodies and limbs of the unfortunate souls that had perished. Arthur was always dismayed at those sights, why the human race had to descend to those levels because of their insatiable greed for power and domination over others, what a total waste of life. There was a better way of life if people would only explore all the other options for a peaceful co-existence, his task was to lay the groundwork for change. He could only hope that he would be successful so that others had the opportunity to build on what he had started and bring about the change in attitude that was needed. No time now to put these people to rest properly, the carnage would have to stay as it was, he needed to be moving to seek out the Saxon army and bring it to a halt once and for all. Arthur gathered his troops and with one last look at the battlefield and a quick prayer for the fallen they set off towards Caer Baddon.

He soon knew that they were headed the right way as once in awhile they came across the body of a Saxon soldier. Obviously escaped wounded from the battle but fallen by the wayside and succumbed through loss of blood, to perish alone and in a strange land. Not an ideal end for anyone, no matter who they were, in pain and without comfort as they relinquished their life in this world. Arthur felt his heart and thoughts go out to them, enemy they might be, but human all the same.

They came upon the Saxons on the hills above Caer Baddon and a running battle ensued, turning to fight and then breaking off continuing their journey as if they were making for a specific location. Indeed they were and Arthur was soon to discover the reason for their haste as they pursued them over the brow of the undulating ground.

It was enough to cause dismay even amongst the strongest hearted. Before them stretched thousands of Saxons. The second army that Arthur had been expecting to land, but far more numerous than he had anticipated. This time they were obviously intent on crushing Arthur's army once and for all and gaining control of the country. Sweet revenge for the many occasions in the past that the King had thwarted their aims, now led by their own kings. For once Arthur had to pause for a moment's thought, they were greatly outnumbered, even the advantage of cavalry would not suffice here. Berius interrupted his thoughts to suggest an alternative move.

"My Lord, Baddon Hill to our right has an ancient hill fort at the summit that is defendable against superior odds. If we can hold it for three days help is on its way, Merlin and Taliesin have been very busy."

"Thank you for those comforting words Berius," Arthur replied, "I was at a loss briefly as to the best course of action, your suggestion is most appropriate. If help is on the way so much the better."

Arthur shouted to his troops to follow him, as he turned his horse towards Baddon Hill, with the Saxon army rapidly bearing down on them, shouting and banging their swords on their shields as they perceived Arthur and his army on the run at last. It did not matter to the Saxons at that moment whether Arthur fought or fled, they knew they had the upper hand and sensed success in the air, driving them forward with renewed vigour as they pursued the fleeing army. Arthur led his men up the steep slopes of the hill to the narrow plateau on which nestled the old fort, still habitable and in reasonable condition for one that had not been used for some time. Defensible as well, with only one side easily accessible by foot or horse. The narrow gate still functioned after a fashion but importantly could be secured against attack.

Arthur and his army sought refuge in the compound with fifty horsemen on the narrow approach outside the gate to deter the Saxons on their initial attack. Attack they did, but they could not push many men forward through the narrow gully leading to the plateau. Arthur's cavalry cutting them down as they tried, some broke through but were dealt with by a second line fighting on foot. Time after time the Saxons attempted to break through, each time being repulsed by Arthur and his men until the bodies of the fallen mounted so much that the way was almost blocked. The Saxons were having to drag bodies out of the way to continue their assault but Arthur's men held firm throughout the day.

Dusk saw the hostilities cease for the night and an uneasy calm settled over the fort, guards keeping watch for any sudden move by the Saxons under cover of the darkness, but there were none. Bodies were removed from the plateau, the enemy being unceremoniously thrown down the gully whilst Arthur's fallen were moved to the confines of the fort, thankfully not many, others were being treated for wounds.

Arthur gathered his commanders and relayed what Berius had told him before the battle commenced, that help was on the way, but they needed to stand firm for three days before it could reach them. Who or how many he did not know, but any number would be most welcome. It would put the Saxons between two forces, and when the time came they would need to break out from the fort and attack. That would be a dangerous time until they could spread out lower down the hill, for now they had to hold the fort. His comments lifted the spirit of his commanders and they departed to relay the message to the rest of the men and give them some glimmer of hope that all was not lost. Stand firm and all would be well, the advantage was theirs now.

The attacks started again at dawn, the Saxons had removed all the bodies from the gully and were pushing forward hard. Arthur's men met them on foot this time, enabling more men to pour out of the fort to stem the incessant flow of enemy soldiers. Excalibur glistening with blood as it cut them down, glowing ferociously in the dismal light of another day. The battles were fierce as the Saxons tried all ways to break through and many men fell, mostly the enemy, but Arthur's men suffered casualties too, Sir Sagremor being one of them, a sad loss, he was a good knight, several of the Sarmatians were casualties too. Sir Drustanus and Sir Bors had both suffered wounds but luckily they were not serious, just glancing blows.

All day the attack relentlessly continued without respite, bodies again restricting the Saxon thrust, until they were removed. The intensity increasing as the day wore on until without warning the fighting suddenly ceased as the Saxons withdrew. A deathly hush descended over the plateau. What were they planning now, were they going to try a different approach somehow, a change of tactics? Their choice was very limited, there was only one way to approach the fort, or was there? Arthur sent some of his men to guard the walls in case the Saxons attempted to scale the escarpment, dangerous and difficult, but by no means impossible for a few determined warriors.

An hour later the attack resumed, even more Saxons attempted to force their way through the gully, but were again held at bay as Arthur threw more men into the counter attack. All of a sudden a shout went up inside the fort, the Saxons had penetrated the defences and scaled the escarpment and walls using ropes and ladders, not many as yet but enough to cause havoc within if not contained. Gelda, fighting close to Arthur, said she would go and see the seriousness of the situation, despatching her opponent with a quick thrust of her sword and disappearing into the fort.

Fighting was going on in several quarters as she surveyed the scene, not many had infiltrated yet, but the ladders must be removed before it was too late, sending soldiers to locate and push them over. Making for the horses she was surprised by three Saxon soldiers that had been attempting to untie them. She realised instantly that they were trying to turn them loose ready to herd them through the gate and stampede them through the King's men. Gelda set about them, killing one at the first thrust and slicing the arm of another. Her third adversary circled her warily, she might be a woman but she was dangerous. They clashed blades as he tried to force her back amongst the horses. She slapped the rump of the horse nearest her and it lashed out with its hind legs catching the Saxon squarely in the body as she followed through with her sword. Aware too late from the look in her enemy's eyes of the danger behind her. She felt tremendous pain as the blade entered her body and passed through it as she half turned to confront her assailant. The sword wrenched from his hand by her movement as she started to buckle at the knees as well. With her strength fading fast she drove her sword into his body, as she sank to the ground, killing him instantly, a look of total surprise on his face.

Arthur found her there a little later, worried by her long absence he had gone to search for her and seen her legs protruding from amongst the horses, dead Saxons surrounding her. He gently cradled her in his arms, she was still breathing but not for much longer, it was a fatal wound, the blood gently seeping from her body forming a crimson pool on the earth. She opened her eyes and smiled at him.

"My King, I said my time was nigh," she barely whispered. "Take me home with you so that I might stay close to you, now kiss me one last time, I am fading fast, god bless you Arthur, my King and lover."

Arthur bent over and gently kissed her trembling lips, tears running down his face as she slipped away. For a long while he just sat there holding her, overcome with the loss of one so close to him. A beautiful woman in all respects, who had shared with him her thoughts, her life's desires and his bed, he would miss her dearly. He removed the sword from her body and carried her to a small archway nearby, laying her down gently, as if in a deep slumber, stepping back and saying a little prayer for the joys of her life and a speedy journey across the mystical divide between there and the afterlife.

The problems in the fort had been dealt with, no more Saxons had penetrated their defences, but the battle still raged outside. He used Excalibur with a vengeance, a new strength and resolve in his being, Gelda was not going to have died for nothing. All the Saxons fell back under his withering onslaught, nothing was able to touch him, his sword more brilliant than ever and now spouting fire from the serpent mouths of the guard. The enemy were dismayed that one man could decimate them so thoroughly and remain unscathed, a demon unleashed.

Suddenly the fighting ceased, the Saxons had retreated, leaving behind many dead, but still not enough to replace the loss of Gelda, that could never be done, she was unique, her memory would live on with all of them. Arthur told Legionus of their loss and took him to where he had laid Gelda out, saying that her last words were that she wished to be taken home with them and laid to rest at Cadbury, close to her friends. That would be done once they had dealt with the Saxons.

Arthur appeared at dawn next morning differently attired, as well as his shield bearing the red cross he now wore a white tabard emblazoned with the red cross.

"Men," he shouted, "this tabard once belonged to Eudaf Hen as did the shield and was passed to me to wear on a special occasion. That day is here, for today we will defeat the Saxons once and for all and banish them to their own lands. Help is on its way, when we see a sign of it drawing close we will leave this fort, our benefactor of the last few days, and we will descend on the Saxons with such ferocity that they will be annihilated. Good luck and God be with you all."

An hour after dawn and the Saxons had still not attacked, the lookouts reporting that there did not seem to be much movement yet, looked like they could not decide what to do. Berius was on the walls too scanning the horizon for sign of the promised help and watching the birds in the sky, Arthur had joined him and enquired why the interest in the birds, Berius replying that they would give him the answer.

Nothing stirred for the next two hours, then one of the lookouts shouted that there was movement in the Saxon camp at the same time as Berius saw what he had been looking for, indication from the birds. He called to Arthur to rejoin him on the wall, pointing out the dark clouds growing in the distant sky,

"A storm?" queried Arthur.

"Ravens," Berius corrected him, pointing in three different directions. "They are bringing your help, another debt repaid by the animal kingdom for the kindness and healing you gave to a raven many years ago, in that terrible storm that you and Sir Kay were caught in. They should be here in less than an hour."

"That is good news indeed Berius, help from three directions too, I'm amazed," replied Arthur.

"You shouldn't be sire, your reputation as a fair and just leader is widespread, even with those you have not met. Word spreads rapidly, you are known throughout the country, your command in battle is renowned."

"Time we went and told the men Berius, that will be heralded as good news indeed," replied Arthur as they left the vantage point on the wall and rejoined the troops.

Arthur lead his army out of the fort a short while later and made the slow descent to the meadows below. The red cross on the white background of his tabard and that on his shield glowing boldly in the rays from the early morning sun. Excalibur unsheathed in his hand, catching the light as if slowly smouldering, the serpents forming the hilt and guard representing the caduceus. An awe-inspiring sight, filling his army with pride and hope, and the enemy with fear. The Saxons were waiting on the plain below the hill, unaware of the danger they were in from approaching forces coming to aid Arthur, all they saw was a small force of cavalry opposing their several thousand foot soldiers. Their kings were smiling.

Arthur raised his sword shouting its name, the light bursting from its blade instantaneously, in such intensity as not seen before, enveloping the Saxon horde in brilliant blinding light as the cavalry gathered speed to meet them.

Many things happened all at once. The sun seemed to disappear and the sky became black as tens of thousands of ravens filled the air, squawking and diving on the enemy, throwing them into total confusion at this sudden airborne attack from nowhere. Several hundred horsemen appeared from the north bearing down on the Saxons, more were streaming in from the east and another group from the south west. The armies clashed as the cavalry tore into the Saxons from all directions. Their kings no longer smiling at what seemed an easy victory, they were now fighting in earnest for their lives on all fronts. Arthur's combined armies, still vastly outnumbered, mounted attack after attack against the Saxon wall, breaking it down and penetrating it each time. The Saxons had nowhere to run, they had to stand and fight to try and break through Arthur's net closing in around them. Arthur, Sir Bors with Legionus and his Sarmatians were attacking in one quarter. Sir Kay, together with King Caradog and King Glywys and their men were attacking from another direction whilst Sir Cador, Duke of Cornwall had arrived with many men from the south west. As the battle became fiercer more help for Arthur arrived in the form of King Cadell of Powys and King Cadwallon of Gwynedd with a several hundred strong cavalry army. The Saxons were losing men rapidly as the pressure increased again with the arrival of King Esla and several hundred more cavalry from the east.

Arthur was fighting his way relentlessly towards the Saxon kings, Excalibur cutting down all in his way. Sir Bors, Legionus and the Sarmatians trying to keep up with him and give him some protection, not realising that Excalibur was the only protection that the King needed. Arthur finally broke through the guards surrounding the Saxon kings, Aelle and Oesc. Dismounting from his horse to fight them on foot as befits one King against another. He took both of them on simultaneously, thrusting, ducking and weaving as they tried to out manoeuvre him. Excalibur flashing and dazzling them as they both took wounds to the body, they could not penetrate his defence, no matter how they tried. It was if Arthur was playing with them, goading them into making a false move, watching their fear increase as they realised this was their last battle. He was wearing them down slowly, his energy and strength were tremendous but Aelle and Oesc were weakening, their moves becoming slower and more erratic. Arthur only had eyes for them, what was happening around him he had no idea, but he needn't have worried. His men had thrown a ring around the kings fighting so that no others could interfere, this was Arthur's fight alone and they respected that.

The end came swiftly, Aelle made a mistake, leaving his body exposed for a moment. Excalibur struck deeply and Aelle died instantly to a thrust through the heart. Oesc seeing his chance made a move on Arthur, only to find Aelle's sword protruding from his body, as Arthur had swiftly grabbed it as the Saxon king fell dead and thrust it deeply into Oesc, unable to use Excalibur at that moment.

The battle was all but over, the Saxon army of nearly ten thousand had been annihilated by Arthur and his combined armies of less than twelve hundred well trained cavalry. Those Saxons that tried to flee were chased and dealt with swiftly and without mercy to crush their expansionist endeavours once and for all.

The carnage had been horrendous, the dead and wounded littered the plain, the earth was stained red. *What a total waste of life. Maybe this will be the end of it*, thought Arthur, as he surveyed the scene. *The country needs peace, time to rebuild and move forward towards a better life. Let us now hope that we can do that, and leave all this behind us. Perhaps this battle at Baddon Hill will be looked back on as the turning point in our history, where we shrugged off the current way of life and connected again to the ways of the ancients with their knowledge and wisdom and how to live in harmony.*

Chapter 17
THE COUNCIL OF ELDERS

THE WOUNDED WERE TENDED TO, then Arthur led his victorious forces back to the fort, a place of safety where they relaxed and shared out their meagre rations with their additional guests. Tomorrow he would lead them all back to Cadbury for a King's feast and much merriment. The tide had finally turned in their favour, the Saxon armies had been totally destroyed, hopefully peace would now prevail in the years ahead.

The kings and lords discussed the battle, Arthur was interested to know how it came about that help had arrived at a very opportune moment. All had much the same story, either Merlin or Taliesin had visited each of the kings requesting aid for Arthur, giving the location to head for and to follow the ravens when they saw them gathering in the sky. Much debate arose on how the two Elders could be in so many places in such a short space of time, even a horseman could not cover the distances involved in that time. Arthur reminded them that the Elders were of a very ancient race and could do many mystical things that appeared almost impossible for the rest of them to do.

"Their knowledge and wisdom of many ancient crafts is far superior to our understanding of things, we have lost that knowledge over the ages, whereas they have not. It would be in all our interests to listen and learn from them, so that one day we may regain that understanding and develop a better life for ourselves."

Arthur's words stilled the talk for awhile as each digested the import of what he had said, then conversation resumed and veered towards different aspects of the battle and who had fallen and in what circumstances. The King said he would send word to Caer Baddon in the morning to secure several carts to transport some of their fallen friends to Cadbury for burial. Unfortunately there were too many to take all of them, the others they would bury there, as a reminder to all of their great victory.

Sir Kay left the fort shortly after dawn to secure three carts and to visit the bishop of Caer Baddon to inform him of what had occurred and request that prayers be said for all the unfortunate souls that lost their lives in the battle. Arthur delegated others to see to the mass burial of the rest of his men in the valley where they had fallen. The Saxons mass would be seen to by the people of Caer Baddon, one of the requests Sir Kay had for the bishop, the people could keep whatever valuables that they found as their payment.

By the time Sir Kay returned with the carts the burials had been completed and Arthur had spoken a few words of thanks over the mass grave. The King gently carried Gelda's body to a cart, whilst Sir Bors brought the lifeless form of Sir Sagremor. Two Sarmatian commanders, Elfinus and Gotlebe. were also being taken to Cadbury. The other two carts contained others from all parts of the army that the kings had decided upon, all were represented by those of note that had fallen in battle. The procession, led by Arthur, his kings and lords set off for Cadbury Castle, a journey that would not be completed until dusk.

The welcome that they received was rapturous, the news of their victory having preceded them. Strange how news often traveled faster than men, but then Taliesin was there to greet them. He had received the news from Berius by way of their mystical thought process. Greyfus had already seen to the preparation of the feast, even excelling himself with the vast array of food, wine and ale freely available to all.

The merriment carried on right through the night as everyone finally relaxed and enjoyed the hospitality of the King's table. Arthur sad that Gelda was not there to share in the joyous celebration, but he knew she was there in spirit if not in body, a loyal friend that knew her days were numbered. She died happy knowing that she had served her King well, and he her, all her dreams fulfilled. She would be celebrating with them on this joyous occasion in the realm of the departed, alongside her comrades in arms that passed over with her.

The following morning saw their fallen comrades laid to rest in the meadow below the castle, near to where Arthur's father, Uther, was buried. Bishop Bedwini carried out the moving service and all the castle inhabitants turned out to pay their respects. Arthur himself placed Gelda in her grave, facing the castle, just like all the others that were laid to rest there, facing her King as she would have wished, and gave her forehead a last kiss before he lowered her into the ground. He could have sworn she smiled briefly at this, but that was probably just the memory of her lovely smile that had stayed with him when she slipped from this life into the other world.

Nobody wanted to leave Cadbury with its atmosphere of celebration, but eventually after several days King Caradog indicated to Arthur that it was time he took his leave. There were arrangements that needed to be made, were there not? Arthur laughed in agreement, it would soon be time to go and claim his Queen, Gwenhwyfar, as he had promised. May day would be an appropriate time for the ceremony, he would bring Bishop Bedwini with him to perform the rites, if that was appropriate. It was agreed.

King Caradog departed the next morning with King Glywys, their depleted forces smiling at the thought of going home, but a slight reluctance to leave the party so soon and the new friends that they had made. The other kings began to make their move soon after, all with an invitation to Arthur's nuptial celebrations at Caerleon, culminating in his marriage to Gwenhwyfar on May day. All readily accepted, barring unforeseen events.

* * * * *

The next few weeks passed quickly, the energy in the castle more vibrant than ever, the joyous mood continuing unabated. Bishop Bedwini had seen the completion of his church, shortly after Arthur's return, conducting a service to consecrate the building and the successful campaign against the Saxon menace. He was a little disappointed that the wedding was not taking place at Cadbury, but delighted to perform the service at Caerleon. Arthur had spent his time visiting his soldiers and conveying his personal thanks for all their efforts, as well as speaking to all those that had remained at Cadbury, their work was just as essential. He spent some time with Taliesin, finding out more of what had happened prior to the recent conflict with the Saxons, and if he thought that peace would now reign for some time. Taliesin felt that it would, in that quarter anyway, they had lost many men in their battles with Arthur and it would take them years to build up their strength again. Only a small number came from their homeland now, their armies depleted there as well as in Briton. It would be wise however to look towards his own kings, localised trouble was still likely to occur, especially over border disputes. He would need to be a mediator on more than one occasion to preserve the internal peace. Arthur thanked him for his advice, his own thinking had been the same, but it was always good to hear another viewpoint, there might be something that he had missed. After his wedding he would give some thought to travelling around the country, this time on peaceful missions, taking his Queen with him to meld the country together more and encourage peaceful co-operation between neighbours. Instead of violently reacting to petty disputes, like had been the scourge of the past. Taliesin agreed that his idea would bring beneficial results over time, acting as ambassador and mediator as well as the High King.

* * * * *

It was time for Arthur to leave for Caerleon, he was taking his lords and commanders and fifty men. Bishop Bedwini was travelling with them, the rest would remain at the castle under the command of Greyfus. They passed through the gate to the cheers of many that had turned out to see him leave. Word had spread rapidly that he was off to marry his Queen in waiting. Taliesin had given Arthur a message from Merlin, that he was to call at the healing sanctuary at Lydney in passing, where his mothers were both waiting to join him for the last leg of the journey. Arthur admitted that he had forgotten all about inviting them, thank goodness that Merlin had remembered, they would not have been too pleased otherwise. It did not pay to upset one's mother, King or not, and he was blessed with two, life would have been unbearable.

Merlin greeted them at the healing sanctuary at Lydney, saying that they could set up camp for the night in the spacious grounds. Igraine and Gwendolyn would join them a little later after the evening prayers, in the meantime a little light conversation would go down well. They gathered around the camp fire, and of course the 'light' conversation centred around the battle with the Saxons and Merlin's part in securing help from the other kings, that arrived just at the right time. He was not forthcoming on how he managed to cover such distances in a relatively short period of time, other than to say that as one of the Elders he had knowledge of many things outside their realm of understanding, but that his machinations proved successful, that was what mattered. The Saxons would not bother them again for a very long while, their defeat had been humiliating and the loss of men unsustainable, they had learned their lesson.

A lull came in the conversation just as Igraine and Gwendolyn emerged from the sanctuary, giving Arthur a big hug, saying that they could only stay briefly, as they had much to do before the morning, a woman liked to take her time when choosing the garments she needed for a special occasion. A few moments later they took their leave and let the men continue their conversation, with the promise to be ready to leave soon after sunrise.

Caerleon was only twenty miles from Lydney and they arrived in the middle of the afternoon, after a leisurely ride. Having left a little later than planned as the women were not ready until two hours after sunrise. Gwenhwyfar was there to greet Arthur, waiting patiently with her father. Arthur alighted from his horse, courteously acknowledged Ogrfan Gawr and waited to be formally introduced to his daughter, taking her proffered hand and giving it a gentle kiss, as if this was their first real physical contact.

The King escorted them over to a little group that had gathered with King Caradog, introducing them to Igraine and Gwendolyn as his two mothers. This caused a little confusion at first until Arthur explained the difference between them, although he looked on both as his mother, albeit in different respects. Gwenhwyfar said that she would show the ladies to their quarters, so that they could have a proper womanly discussion and get to know each other, and maybe share their secrets that they kept from the men, women's talk. She smiled at Arthur mischievously as Igraine and Gwendolyn followed her, with two soldiers carrying the bags that had been strapped on to the packhorse that had accompanied them. Caradog escorted his guests to the great hall to indulge in a little pre-celebration drink to quench their thirst and wait for the ladies to return, which was some hours later.

* * * * *

The days before the ceremony were a hive of activity, final preparations were being made. New guests arrived continuously, keeping Arthur busy as Caradog introduced him, so much so that he saw very little of Gwenhwyfar in that time, or his two mothers. Merlin was kept busy being the King's Ambassador, with old friends and new, as Arthur recounted, on request and many times so it seemed, the annihilation of the Saxons at Baddon Hill. The kings and lords that had been invited had all arrived, each with their retinue. Luckily the fort was large enough to accommodate them all in the manner expected of their status. All was ready.

May day arrived, the celebrations beginning early, building up throughout the morning to the pinnacle of the day, the marriage ceremony. Gwenhwyfar looked exquisite in a lilac robe over a white and gold flowing dress, her long fair hair blowing gently in the breeze, whilst Arthur was resplendent in his white Tabard. The red cross on the white background vibrant in the midday sun, no trace of the battle remained on it. The service, conducted by Bishop Bedwini, was held outside in the central courtyard to accommodate the masses that attended, followed by a short private service in the chapel for honoured guests.

As they left Merlin raised his voice and shouted, "Behold, Arthur, High King of Britain and his beautiful wife Queen Gwenhwyfar, the fairest of all."

Arthur acknowledged the cheering crowd, raising his sword and calling out its name, 'Excalibur,' the blade responding by showering the onlookers with a dazzling display of dancing white and gold light. Gasps of awe rose from the crowd, many had never seen this phenomenon before, least of all Gwenhwyfar, although they had heard tell of it. Arthur sheaved his sword and the magik of the moment was broken, leaving a brief interlude of perfect peace and quiet. Then the chattering started as each turned to their neighbour with comments on what they had just witnessed. Arthur and his Queen led the way to the great hall and the feasting began, lasting long into the day and throughout the night. It was the biggest social gathering at Caerleon for many years and was remembered long after.

At last Arthur and Gwenhwyfar were together, the last few days of their enforced separation behind them, their pent up passion unleashed in a night of untold joy and total ecstasy. Uther Pendragon would have been proud of his son that night, surpassing even his great appetite and stamina with the ladies. Dawn was hinting at its arrival before they both succumbed to exhaustion, falling into a deep slumber in each others arms, the outside world totally forgotten. This was their time; the period of exceptional bliss when nothing else mattered, or even existed outside the four walls of their chamber. The earth could have swallowed them up and they wouldn't have known, or cared, their love had been fully expressed, that was all that mattered.

* * * * *

The festive spirit continued unabated for a week before the guests began to drift away, kings and lords excusing themselves to return reluctantly to their own domain. Each expressing genuine gratitude to Arthur and Gwenhwyfar for their invitation and to Caradog for his excellent hospitality. Merlin had left several days previous saying that he had urgent business to attend to, but would not be gone long and would return before Arthur considered returning to Cadbury.

Caerleon slowly began to return to normal and Arthur and his Queen at last managed to spend some precious time with Igraine and Gwendolyn. It had been a long while since they had been able to relax and talk at length, life had been a little busy for the King.

Merlin reappeared a few days later, smiling and looking very pleased with himself as he announced to Arthur that the Elders were shortly to hold a council meeting and that he had been invited to attend as an honoured guest, something never before allowed. It was being held near Blestium [Monmouth], they would leave on the morrow and be away three days, just the King, Berius and himself, there would be no need of an escort. Arthur accepted the invitation with pleasure, a grin spreading across his face as he replied that no doubt Merlin had a hand in persuading them, the wily old sage that he was. Gwenhwyfar would remain with Igraine and Gwendolyn, happy with that arrangement as they still had much to discuss, and as Queen she would have to become accustomed to Arthur going off without her on occasion. Secretly pleased too that she could have a rest from his insatiable demands in her boudoir, not that she objected in any way as she was a very active participant, but she did need her rest occasionally, she couldn't match his stamina.

The three of them set off late morning to journey the twenty miles to the council meeting, a secret cave hidden deep amongst the trees close to the river, difficult to find unless its location was known. This was one of many caves spread throughout the land that the Elders used, rarely frequenting the same one twice for a full council meeting, although they were used at other times. Merlin led the way through the trees until they came to a small secluded valley with a little stream running through the middle of it, four horses were already tethered there on a long leash. Leaving their own horses with the others they climbed the slight embankment and disappeared into the trees, turning this way then that, first up then down until they came to a thick growth of bushes that Merlin carefully led the way through. In front of them was a rocky outcrop and the cave entrance, a gentle glow of light emanating from the interior, as if in welcome.

As Arthur followed Merlin into the cave he suddenly felt a surge of energy pass through him and fill him with a beautiful sensation of peace and love, and his eyes beheld a most amazing spectacle. The cave had widened out and it was full of beautiful light emanating from many crystals positioned at intervals on what looked like stakes in the ground.

The Lady of the Lake welcomed Arthur, High King of Britain to the Council of Elders, introducing him to the others standing by her. Ganeida of the islands, Lailoken of the north, Radast of the east, and the three that he already knew, Taliesin of the south, his frequent companion Merlin of the west and last but not least Berius, the keeper of his sword Excalibur. She told him that her name was Nimue, but also had many other ones in different areas, and explained that they were the Elders of this land, once known as Albion [Great Britain], a name bestowed on the islands by their own people in the far distant past. How that name came about he was most likely to learn during the council as Merlin had persuaded them to break their unwritten law of excluding outsiders from a full council meeting. He felt that the King had earned the right, and rightly so, to understand more of the task before him. The Elders were extremely pleased with the speed that Arthur had learned and the wisdom that he had attained in a short period of time, it had been thought initially that it would take much longer, but events unfolded even quicker than even they had anticipated and he had responded as they had hoped he would. Seeking guidance when necessary, but mostly following his own inner instincts, quickly and decisively, connecting with those Earth energies that were there to help him, without even realising it until recently.

"Come my Lord Arthur, and sit beside me," the Lady of the Lake commanded. "It will be a long night as there is much for the Council to discuss, each will have their say concerning what is happening in your land in their particular area of observation. Then we shall discuss the merits of what we have heard and come to a decision on what needs to be, or can be done, in the light of the information shared here tonight. Much will interest you, and even astonish you, with the depth of knowledge that the Elders have of the pulse and the direction in which your country is heading currently. Please be patient with the questions that you will undoubtedly have, there will be time for those when our main business is concluded. We will endeavour to answer them as fully as we are allowed. Our laws on disclosure of information are subject to Council agreement, but there are some things that are sacrosanct and can only be divulged with the agreement of our High Masters. If that should occur then we will seek their guidance on the matter. Now My Lord enjoy the dialogue and learn more of the peoples' feelings in your land, and what is currently happening."

"Thank you my Lady for your gracious welcome, and this honoured invitation from the Council. I will listen with interest and endeavour to keep my counsel until the appropriate time," replied Arthur.

The hours flew by as Arthur listened to each of the Elders describe what was happening in their regions, amazed at the amount of knowledge that each possessed. Not just about troublesome barons and kings, but likely areas of conflict, and more surprisingly, what the underlying current of feeling there was amongst the people. No two areas were the same. Lailoken indicated that the north suffered from intermittent infighting, usually family orientated, as well as periodic raids from the Picts and the Irish Celts. Ganeida reported just localised disputes in the islands with occasional raids during the summer months from Vikings and Danes. Whilst Radast said the east was slowly being infiltrated with Jutes and Angles, they were much less hostile than the Saxons, seeking to settle peacefully in new land, escaping from the ravages in their own homeland. The west was fairly settled according to Merlin, other than King Mark of Cornwall, who periodically upset his own people through erratic governing. The rest of the area was peaceful since Arthur had arrived on the scene. Taliesin reported that the Saxons had apparently ceased hostilities since their overwhelming defeat at Baddon Hill and he felt that this had set them back many years, according to his sources.

Having given a resume of events each then discussed in more detail the relevant factors underlying the main events. What surprised Arthur was that his name was brought up many times, right throughout the country. Word of his deeds had spread far and wide, not just amongst the nobles but the people were singing his praises as a true High King. Some of the lesser kings were not so enthusiastic however, but recognised that he would be a formidable foe if crossed. His exploits with his blazing sword, Excalibur, had become well known, his 'magik' was to be feared. If he could defeat a Saxon army of many thousands with scarcely twelve hundred cavalry, despatching two of their kings single-handedly and at the same time, then he was a force to be reckoned with.

At last the individual reports were finished and they all took a little light refreshment. Nimue asking Arthur, with that beautiful smile that was always radiating from her, heightened by the glow from the crystal lights, if he felt a little more enlightened as to the well being of his country. Arthur nodded in astonishment at the amount of knowledge the Elders had, at the same time taken by her overwhelming radiant beauty, more so than on their previous meeting when she presented him with Excalibur. Her whole aura emanated total unconditional love for all those present, including himself. No mortal man could ever do her justice by word or thought to describe her, if there was such a thing as perfection in every aspect, then the Lady of the Lake was it. Her presence, and the loving energy that she radiated touched the soul totally, as if joined in unison. Arthur glanced around the cavern, although a fair size the soft glow from the crystal lights reached every nook and cranny filling the whole place with gentle radiance, he wondered how they worked and made a mental note to ask later. The energy there seemed to be heightened to a degree that allowed clear thinking, not obtrusive, just sufficient to be noticed by those with an awareness of such subtleties.

As he looked at the Elders he was aware that they all had an air about them that was different to ordinary people. Strikingly obvious when gathered together, much less so when dealing with them individually, the wisdom and ancient lineage apparent in their bearing and manner. Many questions ran through his mind concerning their history but he was recalled from his thoughts as they were ready to continue the meeting.

The second half of the Council meeting concerned the overall direction that the country was moving in and whether any actions were required on their part in their adopted roles as ambassadors and mediators, to help maintain the momentum towards peace and stability. The conclusion agreed upon was that Arthur was sufficiently accepted now, having proven himself by word and deed. That he now needed to build on that by travelling his land and laying the foundations for the future. The Elders would take a less active role than previously but still be available should the King need guidance, and they would continue to monitor the feelings in the country.

Arthur found it quite strange to hear himself spoken about as if he was not there, yet realised that their discussion would normally be like this. He had been privileged to join them on this occasion and considered it a great honour to be invited to their inner sanctum. Their support and belief in his ability to carry out his task of laying the foundations for a lasting and prosperous peace was on the one hand very comforting, but on the other magnified the enormity of what lay before him. Defeating the Saxons was only the beginning, the easier solution, now he had to mould the country together for the benefit of all, and hope that he had the strength of will and character to prevail. Arthur could only do his best, and that he was determined to do, he knew that he had the backing and support of the Elders and he did not wish to let them or the people down. He was made High King for a reason, and meant to see it through to the end. The Council meeting wound down to its completion and agreement. There was a slight pause and then the Lady of the Lake turned to Arthur and spoke directly to him.

"My Lord Arthur, you have been privy to our inner most thoughts, something never previously allowed to an outsider; access to our inner sanctum. A special dispensation was allowed in your case. You have performed above and beyond our highest expectations, a rare case indeed for one of your race. In your life so far you have learnt much and responded well, yet there is still much for you to accomplish. I hope you have discovered much of interest from our discussions and I know that you have many questions, we will endeavour to answer as much as possible as reward for your patience. Where would you like to begin?"

"Thank you my Lady for your generosity in allowing me to be an observer here today, it has been very informative and rewarding, even if a little strange hearing myself spoken about. My first question concerns Excalibur, such a wondrous magical sword. I would like to know more of its history and how it came to be? Which might also answer other questions. Who or what are the Elders, where do you come from and why are you here? Your wisdom and knowledge far exceeds any that I know of in these lands, your mystical abilities are those spoken of in tales of the ancient ones, it is most intriguing."

"Your questions are good Arthur, I will do my best to answer them," replied the Lady, "but I will start with who we are as that leads to the forging of your sword, it is a long story and will stretch your imagination."

The Elders came to this Earth many thousands of generations ago seeking a new life after their own world, Atlae, suffered terrible turmoil and near catastrophe from battles with peoples from another star in the Sirius constellation. They were not a warlike people by nature, preferring to live in peace, but had the capabilities and will to defend themselves, which they had done several times in their long history. Peace eventually was restored, but many sought a new world in which to rebuild and knew of the Earth. It had been studied for a long time as it was known to be a water world similar to their own. The Atlanteans, as the Elders were properly called were a sea people, and that was how they were known here for a long time. Living on a chain of islands in the middle of the great sea that stretched from the top of his world in the north to the bottom in the south and which they named the Atlantic Sea.

The islands were large and numerous and well away from the indigenous peoples of his sparsely populated world. However before they left their homeland to travel there the Atlantean master smith created and forged a sword using all his knowledge of metals and mystical craft to create an archaic symbol of hope and peace. It was to remind the people of the futilities of war, but unknown to all but a few, he crafted in the knowledge of the Atlanteans, a history of their achievements and their wisdom. It would only be accessible to a chosen few, and then just sufficient information that was needed at the time would be released to the bearer of the sword. His four children he made keepers of the sword, even though only two were making the journey at that time to the new world. They would guard and protect the sword, even when passed for awhile to a new bearer. It was their responsibility to safeguard the knowledge and wisdom of the Atlantean race for future generations, in the hope that one day peace would reign amongst the star systems generally and harmony between different peoples would prevail.

As Arthur was aware, the current keepers of the sword were herself and Berius, and together with the bearer of the sword were the only ones who could draw Excalibur from its sheath, it would not give to any other. The two other keepers who had not made that initial journey could also draw the sword, but none could use it as a weapon, save the bearer. Not many had been privileged to be the bearer of the sword, not even the Elders gathered there. The last in his world had been the great Alexander, who bore it for many years until disease unfortunately took him. The bearer of the sword was a great ambassador for peace, even though at times it had been needed as a weapon of war to accomplish that aim. The Atlantean Elders, of whom those gathered there belonged, had taken it upon themselves to promote peaceful co-existence between peoples and worlds, but that could only be accomplished if each world was peaceful within its own confines.

The Earth was one of the few places where it had not yet happened. A change in the way of life was necessary, which was why they gave all the help that they were allowed. Their High Masters forbade them to interfere directly, as that would not accomplish anything. The people of Earth had to do it for themselves, otherwise it would not last. One man or group would assume total dominance and that was not the answer, it would create more greed and lust for power because of the human ego. The answer was to relearn the wisdom of the ancients, working together with nature and each other, then, and only then would peace and prosperity last. The other star worlds had learnt that and were just waiting for his world to catch up before revealing themselves, to become as one with them.

Her story finished for the moment, the Lady looked to Arthur for a comment, seeing that he was struggling to comprehend much of what she had told him. The King sat quietly for some moments letting it all filter through his mind. It was like some enormous child's fairytale plucked out of the air, yet his instincts did not doubt any of it for one moment, within him it felt right, he had seen and felt things too. The devastation that Excalibur could cause, and at other times the clarity of thought he had when holding the hilt. Giving him guidance to make the right decision, so mystical and yet so believable, he did not doubt anything that the Lady had told him.

"My Lady, that has stretched my mind beyond what I thought were its limits, into virgin territory, yet inside I have an understanding of all that you have said, and that is most strange. I do not understand however how this small country, and my leadership, will influence the rest of this world to such an extent that peace will spread so far afield."

"It is good my Lord that your inner feelings are such, it shows that your ego does not control you, that you are in command of your senses and inner instincts. As for influencing the rest of your world, this little island of yours is a powerful energy centre, you felt some of it at The Sanctuary at Avebury. There are many more such places in your land. In fact Albion, the name we gave to it, signifies just that, these islands of yours are one of the main confluences of energy on Earth and as such what happens here is sent right around the world, influencing all it touches, even though many do not realise it. These energy lines are emanating from our sunken lands of Atlantis, deep below the sea, and they are still very active now just as they were before. Your little island as you call it is very powerful and with your leadership will lay the groundwork for the future. The tide will wax and wane just like the moon, but you will always bounce back, the ancient peoples here understood the significance of this energy and its widespread effect."

"Thank you my Lady for those comforting words, it will be an honour to work with this energy and lay those strong foundations for the future. It explains much as to why such a small area of land is so important in moving us forward. May I ask how you became to be known as the Elders instead of Atlanteans?"

"For many generations after our arrival here we had very little contact with the indigenous peoples. Those that we encountered called us gods because we were tall and slim, fair skinned with blonde hair and blue eyes, whereas most of them were darker skinned and smaller. Over the years we began to be called Elders because of our wisdom and longevity of life, our lifespan then was many times yours. That name was sometimes shortened to Elds and then to some people we became Elves and many stories were made up about us, but we prefer to be known as the Elders, it signifies knowledge and wisdom accumulated across many years. Do you have more questions my Lord?"

Arthur smiled. "You are aware that I do my lady, many questions that would help me understand more of your people. What happened on your world? What went wrong here on your islands? The location of other energy centres in this land and around the world and how Merlin and Taliesin appear to travel great distances in a very short space of time? Those are but a few. The lights in here fascinate me and although I do not understand their workings, something inside tells me that they are utilising the Earth energies."

"We must confer and seek authority from our High Masters before we answer those questions," the Lady replied. "You are commended for the accuracy of your insight regarding the crystal lights, they are indeed using the Earth energies to illuminate this cavern, one of the many things that we learnt in our early days."

Silence reigned for nearly half an hour before the lady spoke again. Arthur could feel the tingling of extra energy throughout that process as they conferred telepathically, however no stray thought came his way to give any indication of what was going on.

"It seems you have found great favour with our Masters," the Lady said. "They have agreed unreservedly for us to tell you those things that you wish to know, as it will help you understand the importance of all that has occurred and will happen going forward. The small but very necessary contribution that you will make to the process, without which it could not start as the time is now right. As I have spoken at great length, Merlin has agreed to continue, his knowledge of events is more comprehensive than mine and will probably save you further questions at the end. It is a long story and at times tragic for our race, hopefully it will show you what to be wary of as well as giving you guidance for the future. As a world we have been through many of the things that you on this Earth are now going through, and have done for many centuries, but eventually we learnt, and that is our hope for your people. That you might finally reached the plateau that we have arrived at; the stars will rejoice when that happens."

Merlin spent many hours recounting the history of the Atlanteans. What caused them to come to Earth, how they came, what they did here, what eventually led to the demise of their islands of Atlantis, and what happened after [*the story is told in a separate tale*]. It answered many of Arthur's questions, but not even Merlin could answer categorically who was orchestrating the whole scenario, other than that they were all part of it, and it was all part of everyone. Whatever each person regarded 'it' as.

GORDON ETHERINGTON

Chapter 18
ARTHUR'S PEACE

THE COUNCIL MEETING eventually wound down and came to an end. Arthur's mind literally buzzing with thousands of thoughts, generated by the story he had just listened to. Much of it was beyond his immediate comprehension, yet he had no reason to doubt any of what he had heard. It was astounding how much had gone on thousands of years ago on his small world, a way of life far more advanced than even the old tales hinted at.

The Atlanteans had lived through the fourth age of Earth, as Merlin had referred to it, the golden age. Until everything started to go wrong, as the human disease of greed and power took hold spreading like a plague. Culminating in the catastrophe that took place. Affecting not just the Atlantean people but all the indigenous peoples of Earth as the world tilted, land disappeared and the sea rose, washing everything clean in the process. The full force of nature unleashed to cleanse the land at the end of an era, and prepare the world for the coming of the fifth and current age. Giving humanity another chance to make good and learn from the mistakes of the preceding ages. Arthur's understanding of his task had become clearer, the peoples of Earth had not really moved forward in seeking a better life, lethargy and stagnation had become the order of the day. The old ways with the wisdom and knowledge that they had generated long forgotten. It was time to reawaken what was buried deep inside everyone, and show the people the way forward. His task was to rekindle those innermost thoughts and feelings, laying the foundations for a better society, that others following him could build on. He sat quietly contemplating his thoughts before he finally spoke.

"My Lady, I thank you and the Elders again for the invitation to join you here, never did I realise that so much had taken place here on Earth across the aeons of time. That our history stretched back that far. I have learned a great deal, a lot beyond the boundaries of my understanding, but an amazing insight into how things once were, and could be again if the right road is taken. My overwhelming gratitude is also extended to your Masters for allowing me the privilege of hearing your story. For their gracious trust and faith in my ability to bring about the change necessary in society that will enable us all to move forward in peace, harmony and prosperity. I will endeavour to do my best as a human to honour these expectations and fulfil my task."

"Lord Arthur, I extend the appreciation of all here for what you have accomplished so far. We have waited a long time for you, the chosen sword bearer, to arrive and begin the rehabilitation of your race. There is a very long way to go before the peoples of your Earth can aspire to the magnificent spectre of the sixth age of your world. Many out there throughout the heavens await that transition. It will happen at some point, and there will be much rejoicing and the sound of their singing will be heard across all time and space. We know full well that you will honour your commitment, yet we also appreciate that you are human. To fall by the wayside will not be failure, because much will have been achieved, and others will follow. It will not be easy and there will be many setbacks along the way in the future, long after your time. But what you accomplish now will help steer others through these periods of turmoil and back to the correct road. It is time now for us to part and go our separate ways. We will continue to support you in the background, but this is your time now Arthur, what you begin will last many lifetimes. Stories will be told about you and what you have left as a legacy. However, like as with us there will be an air of mystery and magik about the tales, that people will never be sure of who you were for many hundreds of years, but eventually it will become clear. Good luck Arthur, High King of Britain in all you do, and always remember the covenant of the sword."

"My Lady, your wondrous beauty and words of wisdom will forever be in my heart, giving me comfort and guidance along the way. May the light continue to shine brightly from you and never fade."

Arthur and Berius arose and headed for the exit. Merlin was staying with the other Elders for awhile longer and would return later. Before they reached the outside Arthur turned to face the Elders and going on one knee uttered in a clear voice.

"I salute the Elders of Atlantis, whose lineage is far older and greater than mine and bow to your superior knowledge and wisdom, may your visions be fulfilled."

The return to Caerleon was a quiet journey, Berius aware that Arthur was deep in thought, turning over in his mind all that he had heard. Things that he had never dreamt were possible, expounded in great detail by Merlin. A story beyond the realms of his knowledge, but with an inner understanding that explained many of the mystical occurrences that had puzzled him about Merlin and Taliesin, it all fell into place now. A unique and far more advanced race than any other on Earth, yet it appeared that they were not the first to visit his world, and possibly not the last. Many had stayed and were now helping the human race, a frustrating task, but they felt it worthwhile. *There was hope for us yet,* thought Arthur.

* * * * *

Gwenhwyfar had learnt much about the King in the few days that he had been away. The discussions with Igraine and Gwendolyn had been most informative, and all that she heard pleased her greatly, a man to be proud of.

On his return Arthur spoke at length with King Caradog on his vision for the country, and how he was going to initiate changes throughout his kingdom. The appointment of magistrates to uphold the King's law and release the local lords from that irksome task, respected men of integrity and wisdom. It would be a difficult task to find the right people, but it was necessary to bring law and order to the country. Where everyone, whatever their standing, had a right to a fair and unbiased hearing. Caradog agreed that it would not be an easy task, but there were men of that ilk, provided that they could be found. One or two in the locality that he could think of would be acceptable for such a position. Arthur suggested that he arrange their appointment and instigate a regular day for attending to minor disputes and set aside a time less frequently for more serious matters.

He himself was going to travel around the country and set things in motion in the different regions to start building a proper framework of magistrates to oversee the King's law. In some quarters he was expecting some opposition, but would deal with that as it arose. Through diplomacy if possible or royal command if necessary, backed up by his army. His aim was to set up regional centres that he would visit periodically and hold court there himself, being seen by the people to fulfil his promises. Caerleon would be his court for that region, where all could approach the King with their problems or grievances, and have them resolved in a fair and just way.

Caradog indicated that he could see the benefits of such an arrangement. Agreeing that some lords, and even kings, would consider this to be unwarranted intrusion into local matters and would rebel against it initially, but the might of the King should persuade them otherwise.

A few days later Arthur decided that it was time to return to Cadbury with his new Queen, Merlin would not be travelling with them, he still had many friends and acquaintances that he wished to visit. Igraine and Gwendolyn were returning to the healing sanctuary. Sir Cador was due there in two weeks to escort his mother home. Arthur promised that if everything stayed quiet he would come to Tintagel and visit her and call and see his old friend Sir Ector, bringing Sir Kay with him.

Arthur expressed his gratitude to King Caradog for his marvellous hospitality and the friendship and solidarity that he had displayed, and would return to hold court there once the magistrates had been set in place. With that the King escorted his Queen as they led the small troop out of Caerleon on their journey home. Saying farewell to his two mothers at the healing sanctuary as they headed for the river crossing and the ride south.

* * * * *

The hot summer passed quite slowly as Arthur and Gwenhwyfar enjoyed the peace of normal life. Bishop Bedwini had held another short service for them in his new church at Cadbury, for those that had remained there and missed the big day. It became a focal point where all gathered at least once a week, with Arthur often invited to speak. Which gave him the opportunity to express his thoughts and vision for the country and how everyone could help by consciously expanding that feeling of wellbeing amongst themselves and any that they came in contact with.

Arthur appointed Greyfus as his chief magistrate for the region, a man liked and respected by all, with a wealth of experience and wisdom to match. He was given free reign to appoint others he considered suitable, that could traverse the region and establish a formal system of justice. Greyfus would continue as custodian of Cadbury Castle but would look to relinquish more of his responsibilities to his assistants. It was time he relaxed a little, his years were catching up on him slowly. Let the younger ones do the hard manual work, whilst he passed on the benefits and wisdom of his experience.

There was much planning to be done during the winter months as Arthur prepared an itinerary of the places he wished to visit to establish greater contact with the people and to re-establish a uniform system of law and order. The Romans had created such a method that worked well under their administration, but it had fallen apart when they had left as there was no longer any central control. Each region began to do things their own way, as dictated by the local king or lord. This had led to the country falling into anarchy, with minor disputes escalating out of control into often violent clashes, as there was no coherent system of mediation or judicial control. Every region had become autonomous, the law, such as existed, was at the whim of the local lord and was inconsistent in its application. Arthur's first task was to bring it all back together in a unified system. He knew that it would not be easy, there would be much opposition in some areas, but he was confident that he could accomplish his task without undue bloodshed. His reputation for being fair and just had become well known, and he was backed by a loyal and formidable army that had proved itself many times against superior strength. It would be a long slow process, but the benefits would be far reaching and enable the country to settle, and enjoy the peace and prosperity that it would bring to all. The next few years would be a busy time as he established the foundations for a better way of life. That hopefully would become cemented into the social structure of the country, and would be viewed by other nations as a model to be incorporated into their own culture.

* * * * *

Arthur started his mission the following spring, accompanied by Gwenhwyfar and half his army as they set forth northward into what was for him virgin territory, stopping at many hamlets and towns along the way. There was no rush this time as they were not pursuing Saxons, just getting to know the people and their desires. Stopping in appropriate places for some while to initiate the appointment of magistrates, in conjunction with the local lords or elders. His reputation preceded him and the welcome he received from the people was genuine. Although the same could not be said for some of the nobility, who saw it as an unwarranted intrusion into their domestic affairs. Arthur had become a good diplomat in his short years and his reasoning and persuasion carried the day on most occasions. Not often did he have to explain the consequences of ignoring or interfering with his directive, and when he did the obstinate ones were under no illusion as to the consequences. In many of the towns he visited he held court and listened to the tales of wrong doers, gathering information from all sides before deciding on suitable punishment. Sometimes the matter was trivial and resolved through his words of wisdom, at other times more serious and an example was required.

At all these sessions Arthur would sit holding the hilt of Excalibur as he deliberated on what should be done. Seeking guidance when it was required, before delivering his answer. He was always fair and just, with a tendency to be lenient towards those that had erred, but with a warning that should it happen again then the consequences could be dire. However if the crime was of a serious nature, perhaps resulting in a death, then Arthur would respond according and match the punishment to the crime. Provided that it was absolutely clear that the person was guilty. He taught and appointed magistrates by example so that there would be consistency in the process of establishing and maintaining law and order. No one was immune from the law, it applied to lords as well as the people. This encouraged those with a dispute against their lord to bring the matter to court to be resolved in a fair and just manner. The ruling of the court was with the authority of Arthur as High King and should be obeyed accordingly by whoever was at fault. If the person felt that the court was unjust or misguided, and it was a serious matter, then it could be referred to the King himself for direction.

Arthur sat through many sessions and listened to many tales, from the theft of a loaf of bread, to disputes over land and boundaries, the occasional murder or rape of a young girl, to supposed acts of witchcraft. The most common grouse of the people however seemed to be the ever increasing amount that they were expected to pay in taxes to the local landowner, for use of land from which to scratch a bare living. Some lords were fair in the treatment of their tenant farmers but others were greedy, squeezing them for all they could get, and those were the ones that Arthur had most problem with initially. He would send for them to attend the court and explain themselves, but often had to despatch some of his men to physically fetch them, as they had ignored his command. On occasion they even rebelled at this and drew their sword in defiance, only to be killed or wounded in the process and delivered to court in this condition by Arthur's men. Whereupon their lands and worldly goods were forfeit to the King, if dead. However, if they were only wounded and repented their actions Arthur would allow them to keep their personal effects but forbid them from collecting taxes from any of their landholdings for two years and thereafter only one tenth of their tenants gross yield or income per year. Any that did not apologise for their action would be stripped of all their land and cast out to make their way in life as best they could with their ill-gotten gains. With a warning that should they attempt to create discontent or foster rebellion then they would be sought out and dealt with most severely. This tough stance increased Arthur's standing with the people even more, as it proved to them that nobody was above the law, not even the lords and barons. He was not just another King out for what he could get, but a man of the people.

Sometimes the situation was a little more involved, as in the case of the ferryman who provided a service for travellers crossing the river that was the boundary between the land of two lords. Both were taxing him on his income and he had been withholding monies due, so that he and his family could live. The lords had quarrelled between themselves over this and brought the ferryman to court for not paying his taxes, so that Arthur could give his direction. The ferryman charged different amounts according to whether it was a foot passenger, horse and rider or a cart and driver. To complicate matters, on market day he would only charge for the cart on the return journey when the driver had money from his sales. The two lords were taxing him on his total earnings, that left him very little to support his family, so he had withheld some monies to buy food for the winter as trade was very quiet then.

Arthur considered what he had heard from all parties before giving his directive. The ferryman was to keep his earnings in two separate jars, one for each side of the river. Monies collected one side would go in one jar and monies from the other in the second jar. Each jar represented one side of the river and each lord would receive tax from their jar. In the case of the money for the cart only being collected on the return journey, then the money would be divided between the two jars. Arthur enquired of the ferryman how much of his income he paid in tax and was told just over half, which left him very little to survive on. If he didn't eat well then he hardly had the strength at times to operate the barge, then there were new ropes and wood that required replacing frequently. Arthur directed that for every ten groats he collected in each jar one groat would be the tax he would pay to that lord whose side of the river it belonged too.

The lords protested loudly as that was much reduced tax on what they would normally collect. Arthur countered, explaining that the ferryman was providing a service for trade between their lands and as such was helping to provide goods and revenue that they would not have if the ferry was not there. It was a long way to the nearest ford and too wide for a bridge to be built. The ferry also needed to be kept in a good state of repair and so did the health of the ferryman, otherwise all would suffer, including the lords. Their protestations ceased as they realised the sense of what Arthur was saying. The ferry was a major route for trading, both ways, as market days were at different times. They would lose more in income than the relatively small amount of tax that they would forego from the ferryman if he was not able to provide the service. Arthur told the ferryman that he understood the difficult position that he had been in, but hopefully it was now resolved and to make sure that he paid his taxes on time and correctly in future, If a problem should occur to bring it back to court for direction and resolution before it escalated out of control. The ferryman thanked Arthur and scurried off to tell his family the good news, and what a fair King they had now.

During his travels Arthur discovered that there were pockets in the country where anything that was out of the ordinary in people was looked upon as witchcraft by the local baron. Many peasants, nearly all women, had been burnt at the stake because of it. Usually there was no shred of evidence that they had been dealing in black magik or anything that was detrimental to another. It was a lack of understanding that came from a narrow mind. Healing with the hands or herbs, as well as prophecy, was something that the ancients knew about and used frequently. Although the art had declined there were still many people with those abilities. In some areas they were accepted as gifted people but in others they were hounded as devils and burnt if so much as a whisper was heard of anything strange. Arthur was determined to stamp out this abhorrent and unnecessary persecution.

He encountered such a situation at Ratae Corieltauvorum [Leicester], a once thriving Roman fortified civitas, now in decline, with a relatively small population compared to the military presence that was once there. Lord Fergus was the baron and his word was law, although his dwelling was some way out in the surrounding country, as he preferred the quieter life. He was a small minded man that thought he was surrounded by evil deeds and plots against his person. In truth he was frightened by his own shadow, all his misgivings came from within himself and represented his own failings. But as is normal with this type of character he could not see that he was creating his own misfortunes. It was all a plot by others he vehemently declared. Unfortunately he could not name or identify who those others might be, if they existed at all. Therefore he strove to eradicate any that he perceived as a threat, and those with the gifts of the ancients he considered to be the main cause of his demise, and he declared them witches and had them burnt at the stake.

The majority of people cursed him but none would stand up to him for fear of being his next victim, and so had allowed him to decimate the community over the years. As there were some who would sell their own children for a few groats to curry his favour. Arthur could feel the foreboding amongst the people on his arrival, the gloom and despondency showed in their faces and their bearing and he began to inquire as to the reason. It took a little while, as many were reluctant to talk, but a cheeky young lad of about eight asked him if he had come to watch the witches burn. Asking him about it Arthur discovered that they would be paraded in the large hall next to the derelict church the following morning where Lord Fergus would deliver his verdict and then they would be taken out the back and burnt at the stake.

Next morning, Arthur, Gwenhwyfar and Sir Tristan, suitably cloaked to hide their obvious nobility, entered the hall along with many others. Whilst six of his men had hidden themselves around the back of the building in case of trouble. Lord Fergus was already in attendance, impatiently pacing up and down, wanting to get on with the proceedings, but also wishing to have an audience as he dealt out his form of justice. Four women of varying ages were dragged out from a side room by guards, and paraded in front of the audience, as Lord Fergus citied the charges against them. Various acts of witchcraft directed against his person indirectly via a third party. All had been caught in the act and would therefore suffer the consequences of being burnt at the stake for their crimes. The sentence to be carried out immediately at the rear of the building.

Arthur interrupted him, "if this is a court of law my lord, then where is the evidence that says they are guilty? None has been laid before the court."

Lord Fergus was taken aback, no one had dare challenge him before, and people turned to see who had spoken so boldly, words that they had in their minds but dare not say.

"Sir," he replied, not knowing who had spoken, "there is no need of evidence as I caught them in the act myself, and that is sufficient in the circumstances."

"My Lord Fergus, this is not a court of law, and your word is not sufficient to carry out such a barbaric act."

"Do you doubt my words sir, whoever you are? What right have you to challenge my authority? Fergus retorted, as muttering began in the crowd and people turned to look for the source of the voice.

"Yes my lord, I doubt your words. The King has given everyone the right to a fair hearing in law and to speak against what is not right, let the women speak for themselves." said Arthur in response.

The crowd were really getting noisy now, wondering who it was who dare speak to Lord Fergus in such a manner, and Fergus himself realised he was losing control and needed to do something quickly.

"Strong words sir from someone who is hiding in the crowd. Come forward so that we can all see you and discover what mischief you are attempting here to thwart justice from being carried out." tempted Fergus.

Arthur spoke quietly to his two companions and they all moved forward towards Lord Fergus as people moved apart and gave them room. Stopping just short of him, still cloaked, their hoods covering their heads.

"There is no justice here Lord Fergus," Arthur said. "You make a mockery of the King's law."

"Ah, so there are three of you, more witchcraft no doubt, and who are you to cast doubt on the King's law?"

"I do Lord Fergus, I Arthur, High King of Britain, at your service," saying which he removed his robe and let it fall to the ground. "My wife, Queen Gwenhwyfar, and Sir Tristan, Knight of the Realm, and behind your guards are my men. You see we came prepared knowing your treacherous reputation."

There was a stunned silence from the gathering, never did they envisage that the High King would visit their humble town in such a manner. Lord Fergus was lost for words, the plot against him had succeeded, the witches had finally won, despite all that he had done to stop them. He turned to flee, but there was no escape, he was trapped.

"If these women are witches Lord Fergus so am I, watch carefully," Arthur said as he drew his sword slowly and holding it aloft called out, "Excalibur." The blade burst into brilliant tongues of light that danced around the hall, bouncing off the walls and heading straight for Lord Fergus. It was too much for him, his internal fear finally consumed him totally, his eyes open wide in terror as he dropped to the floor, writhing for a moment. Then stillness as his heart gave out, unable to cope with the terrible fear within him. Arthur sheathed Excalibur, it was strange how men that went by the name of Fergus appeared to be of the same ilk, casting his mind back to the ruffian from Glevum, that Gelda had dealt with. Perhaps it was a way of marking them in the world. Gwenhwyfar and Sir Tristan were untying the women who were crying uncontrollably as the pent up emotions from their ordeal were released. The crowd had been stunned into silence, so much had happened so quickly, they still could not believe what they had just witnessed. This was their King and his beautiful wife, who had brought salvation to their town in such a miraculous way.

When the four women had ceased their crying, Arthur approached them and asked what their 'crime' had been. Two had helped a relative recover from illness by the love and care they bestowed upon them, one had healed using her knowledge of herbs. The last had prophesied, jokingly, what would happen to a man that was pestering her, unfortunately it had. Arthur then addressed the congregation and explained that the four women were just normal people helping others. Their lord had a fanatical obsession and fear of so called witches terrorising him, but it was all in his rather narrow mind, and that led to his downfall at the end.

The King went on to explain that his purpose in this visit was to meet the people and establish a fair system of law and order that would apply to all, even the lords and barons. He would be staying for some days with his army to sort the mess out there and was available in the hall every morning to listen to any problems that they might have. He asked why the church next door was derelict, and someone in the gathering shouted that the cleric had been put to the stake as a heretic by their departed lord. Arthur replied that he would try and find a replacement for him as soon as he could, it was not good to be without a man of the cloth. They had all seen what they considered a miracle today, it was a sign that had been given to show that there was good in people, and those that were bad would suffer their own downfall in due course.

Arthur stayed for several weeks making arrangements for the appointment of magistrates and resolving the issue of the late Lord Fergus's land, which as there were no known heirs he gave to Legionus for his help and loyalty throughout the campaign against the Saxons. Legionus didn't know what to say, it was something he never expected. Arthur told him to select fifty men to stay with him and to appoint a new commander to take charge of the Sarmatian cavalry. They would no doubt still remain in close contact, it was a legacy for him to leave for his family, if he had any, or whoever else he thought deserving of it. The land was his to do as he wished, he new Arthur's vision for the country and the King knew that the good work that they had started together would continue. He was leaving in a few days to visit King Cadell at Viroconium Cornoviorum [Wroxeter] and would enquire if there was a holy man in that area that would like a challenge in developing the derelict church, left vacant since Lord Fergus had put the previous cleric to death. Legionus expressed his thanks to Arthur and would endeavour to fulfil his obligations with honour, in the manner that the King had shown by his own example. His sword was ready should Arthur have need anytime.

Arthur, his Queen and a reduced fighting force travelled slowly to Viroconium, stopping at small hamlets on the way, engaging the local populace in dialogue, explaining the purpose of his visit. Many had heard of his exploits, not just in assisting King Cadell, but his other battles against the Saxons too, and received him with a genuine welcome, eager to catch sight of his new Queen. By the time that they reached King Cadell's stronghold they had travelled for nearly a week. Their arrival was expected as word of their coming had preceded them, and they received a warm welcome from Cadell, who had arranged a celebration feast in honour of his guests.

They stayed for several weeks, enjoying the hospitality and seeing more of the surrounding country, including a visit to King Cadwallon of Gwynedd. In each case Arthur explained the reasons for his visit and sought their help in establishing a common legal system of appointed magistrates. Both were supportive of his vision and agreed to help in anyway that they could in furthering the quest for peace and stability. Although they both agreed that it would not be easy and would take some years to bear fruit, as Arthur had rightly said.

The King informed them of the recent events that led to the demise of Lord Fergus, and that he had bequeathed the vacant lands to Legionus for his loyalty and valour. A man from a distant land that had fought for his adopted King and country as if it were his own. Cadell and Cadwallon agreed that this was a magnificent gesture from Arthur and well deserved. The Sarmatians were very loyal to those they served and this recognition would do the King's reputation nothing but good by showing that loyalty was well rewarded, no matter who they were or where they came from. Arthur mentioned the problem of the lack of a cleric or holy man at Ratae Corieltauvorum [Leicester]. Their help and suggestions as to a candidate for this vacant position would be most welcome, as his knowledge of those in the area was very limited. It was a reasonable sized town that could do with some spiritual guidance after the traumatic times that the people had lived through under the previous lord. They both agreed to give careful consideration to the matter and come up with a solution between themselves and put the proposition to a suitable candidate, of which they had one or two in mind that might relish the challenge, young men seeking to advance themselves.

The conversation moved to many other topics and Gwenhwyfar was asked her views, to which she answered that all this was very new to her, that she was listening and learning. Not just the duties of the Queen, but the whole aspect of royal life. There would come a time when she felt able to contribute, if asked, but that was some way off, in the meantime she was happy just to listen and learn.

Eventually Arthur decided that it was time to head south whilst the summer was still upon them as he wished to visit many places en-route and engage with the people, including those at Glevum [Gloucester] and Corinium [Cirencester]. They took their leave of King Cadell and Arthur said that he would return the following year and hold court, which he would begin to do on a regular basis. Cadell replied that it would be an honour indeed and looked forward to the King's return, when they would continue the celebrations for a new beginning.

* * * * *

Their journey south was very enterprising and much was accomplished with little difficulty at all the places that they frequented, until they came to Glevum. The Duke had met Arthur previously when his help was requested against the Saxons and he viewed this visit with suspicion, his men had not been the same since they had returned from battle. Their attitude towards him had changed and he had lost the services of the bully Fergus, killed by a woman of all things. Now his instructions were often ignored, he was a Duke in name only, his authority diminished to the point of defiance by the people. Arthur was aware immediately that not all was what it should be, it was patently obvious that the Duke exercised no control whatsoever, he was treated with contempt, even by his own men. This situation would require a degree of diplomacy beyond what had been needed so far, or the iron rule of the King, depending on the Duke's attitude and response to what would be laid before him.

The people had welcomed Arthur and his Queen, the exploits of the King well known as their returning soldiers had told many tales, including his handling of Fergus, and they had a high regard for him as a man of and for the people. Arthur had much dialogue with many of them, learning a great deal about life in the town and surrounding district and the ineffective rule of the Duke, whose only passion was hunting. In fact the reason that he did not accompany Arthur against the Saxons was that it would interfere with his pastime, as well as putting his person at risk, something he would never do. He had others do the dangerous tasks for him, but these days none would take on this role, not since the death of Fergus, attitudes had changed, even his own son refused to respond to his requests, preferring to lead his own life.

Arthur sought him out to discover more of his life and the role that he had taken on and was pleasantly surprised by the result and his passion for life. Antonious was his name and of a very similar age to Arthur, totally different to his father. A young man who saw what was happening around him and strove to better himself by learning from life and what it had to offer. The King explained his vision for the country and the reason why he was travelling around the country and what he aimed to achieve by it.

Antonious listened intently and when Arthur had finished commented that the King was to be commended for his brave vision. It was no easy task he faced, especially with his father's thinking, he would not give it a moment's thought, it would interfere with his lifestyle too much. That was what Arthur suspected from all that he had felt and heard, and responded that the Duke had a choice, to listen and implement the changes or lose his title and possibly his lands if he refused. Antonious was surprised at how strongly Arthur believed in his vision and the lengths that he would go to in seeing it come to fruition. The King had a strength of character that belied his youth, his father would not be a happy man, but there was not much he could do as he lacked support from those around him. Arthur was shortly going to confront the Duke with the reason for his visit and what he expected from it, and it was up to him to decide whether he was for or against it. Antonious wished him luck, saying that his father was not a bad person, just that he was at the stage in life that he only considered his own enjoyment. That had been the case since he had lost his wife in a hunting accident some years before. It was as if he was punishing himself in some way by continuing hunting, perhaps blaming himself for what happened. Although it was nobody's fault, just an unfortunate event. Arthur promised to be as diplomatic and kind as he could be in the circumstances but change must happen.

The audience with the Duke was difficult, his mind did not seem to take in all that was being said, and repeatedly asked questions as Arthur explained his vision and the reason behind his visit. The Duke was adamant that it could not be accomplished, it was far too difficult and he did not have the time to oversee it, being far too busy with other matters. Arthur told him that it was necessary that these things happened and if the Duke felt he did not have the time, then he should consider his position carefully. If he felt that those other matters were more important than the rights of the people, then he should give himself more time for these pursuits and relinquish his title and authority to his son. He would not have to bother then with those every day important issues that detracted him from his desires, but could enjoy life and let his son deal with the mundane tasks.

The Duke was not wholly convinced, worrying that his lifestyle would change without the income to support it. Although it was a pleasant thought to be able to concentrate on his hunting without having to worry about anything else. Arthur said there was no need to worry on that score, he could still draw a modest income from his estates that would provide for his every need. However it needed to happen for all concerned, with or without his approval. It would put the Duke in good stead if he willingly passed the title to his son without the King having to intervene, which he had every right too, but would prefer it to be a gesture from the Duke himself. He understood exactly the meaning of Arthur's words and was secretly pleased that he had been manoeuvred into that position, he could enjoy life better without the hassles of court. His son was quite capable of taking control and dealing with those matters, he had done it discreetly several times before when the Duke was 'indisposed,' when he wished not to be involved with something. It was agreed that the Duke make a proclamation to the people the following day, handing over his title and control of his estates to his son, allowing him to retire from public life to pursue his other interests. He would summon his son and make him aware of the situation and sort out the financial details of the estates and the amount of income that he would require to continue in the same lifestyle.

The proclamation was duly made in the town square and there was much rejoicing by the populace, many suspecting that Arthur had a hand in the announcement, although it was never publicly acknowledged. Antonious was pleased that Arthur had won the day in a gentle way for his father, releasing him to pursue what he liked best whilst retaining his honour and dignity. Arthur's vision, which he supported could now be slowly implemented as Antonious was much respected in the town. Being his father's son had not been held against him, they were totally different characters, he was more like his mother, who people still remembered with sadness at her loss.

Before Arthur left for Corinium he sought out the young lad Jonas, who had been coerced by Fergus to leave his sick mother and travel with Arthur in their foray against the Saxons, inquiring after her health. The lad was overjoyed that the King remembered him and said that his mother was fine now but had difficulty walking still. It would be an honour for her if she could meet him. Arthur willingly obliged and spent some while with her, listening to her story and explaining his quest. She expressed her gratitude at his kindness in sending him home to her when she had great need of him. Arthur left them, smiling and happy that the King had seen fit to put himself out and visit their tiny home and spend a little time with them, expressing genuine interest in their welfare and talking to them as equals.

Corinium was a surprise, it was still run very much on the lines that the Romans had established, with a stable administration and well administered law and order, and Arthur found it refreshing that many of the good aspects had survived. It was a bustling town and they were well received, but as much was already in place Arthur only stayed a week. Sufficient time for him and his Queen to meet the people and local lords and establish a rapport. Then it was time to move on, stopping at the villages and hamlets on the way, taking ten days for the last leg of their journey home to Cadbury Castle and a well earned rest before they embarked on their travels again the following year.

* * * * *

During the years that followed Arthur and his Queen, with part of his army, made frequent trips around the country building the foundations of his vision. In many areas he was accepted gracefully, but in a few there was sometimes discontent and occasionally rebellion. Arthur dealt with it all in his stride, peace and calm, for the most part, settled over the country for many years. Kings and lords changed but the structure of the country continued to evolve and prosperity grew. Arthur held court in many regions on a regular basis during this time, and kept his promise to visit his mother, Igraine at Tintagel, renewing his friendship with her son Sir Cador, and his new wife and son. Sir Kay accompanied him on this journey from his base at Rockbourne, from where he had frequently visited his father and it would be good to be altogether again for awhile after the turbulent times.

The reunion was quite an emotional time, seeing old friends again after so long and there was much to discuss. Sir Ector was still looking as young as ever, but he replied jokingly that the same could not be said of Arthur, who had grown in size and stature those last few years since he had last seen him, but was better for it. Arthur and Gwenhwyfar stayed for almost a month before they took their leave, with a promise to return again when circumstances allowed. They wished to travel the south west peninsular and call in to see Sir Bors at Pilsdon Pen before they made the trek home.

Their parting was just as emotional as their arrival, as none wanted to leave, but there was much still to be done and time moved on. So with reluctance they said their good byes and headed south west. Arthur had hoped to meet King Mark but he was over the water in Armorica, where he had other estates, which was a little frustrating as he had heard varying reports about him, and none were good. He had hoped to meet him and judge for himself, but that would have to wait for another time, in the meantime he would make himself known to the people of the region.

* * * * *

Several weeks of travel through this ancient land, with its many historic monuments and old tales that reinforced its rugged beauty, enabled him to meet many people. As he listened to their stories Arthur was convinced that King Mark was a man of many moods, that swung from one extreme to another. He was a man the King needed to meet, sooner rather than later, as he appeared to have a very disruptive influence with his contradictory directives, a possible source of trouble.

Sir Bors was in trouble, as Arthur approached Pilsdon Pen, he could hear the shouts and the clash of swords as if a battle was in progress. He commanded ten men to stay with Gwenhwyfar and led the rest of his force forward at the gallop. As they arrived in the village square he brought his men to a stop in amazement. There before his eyes were twelve grown men, brandishing swords which they clashed together with another, shouting at the same time as they danced around in a circle, Sir Bors was one of them. Arthur roared with laughter at the sight of his portly friend doing a jig, his men couldn't contain themselves either as smirks and laughter echoed around the square. The group came to an embarrassed stop aware for the first time of their audience, then the rest quickly disappeared leaving Sir Bors on his own.

"Just a new dance," he muttered, his complexion turning red.

"And we thought you were in trouble with all that clashing of blades," laughed Arthur. "You must think of better places to do it than in the village square, next time."

"Sorry to disappoint you my Lord, it was practice for a little tournament we were organising," confessed Sir Bors. "Something to amuse the villagers. It's normally done with sticks, but we thought swords were better."

"I think they will be greatly amused, as we were." replied Arthur.

The Queen and her guard were sent for and all headed for the old place on the hill. No longer old, it had virtually been rebuilt and extended since Arthur had last seen it and was now a worthy place to reside.

Their stay was pleasant and much was discussed in the days that followed, how far things had come and what was still to be done to bring the country together. Arthur mentioned his concerns about King Mark and Sir Bors said that he had heard strange stories too about his erratic behaviour, which seemed to be getting worse. There was likely to be trouble there he thought. The King agreed, it was a situation that he needed to keep his eye on, lest it got out of hand and ruined the good work that was being done elsewhere.

Chapter 19
ARTHUR BREAKS THE COVENANT OF THE SWORD

ON THEIR RETURN TO CADBURY Arthur discovered that three new knights had arrived during the time of his absence, Sir Drydwas, Sir Hector de Maris and Sir Liwlod, all from the western regions, all offering their services to the King. He graciously acknowledged them, accepting their offers and welcomed them to Cadbury, inquiring if they had been well looked after during their wait, receiving a positive response from each. Nothing much would happen during the winter months Arthur explained but in the spring they would be off on their travels around the country and were welcome to join him and learn about his vision for the country at first hand. They were delighted and accepted his invitation.

* * * * *

Arthur continued to travel the land each spring, holding court and attending tournaments, where the prowess of the knights was on public display. Many came from far and wide to join in, or just experience the jolly atmosphere. The tournaments normally lasted three days and were a time when ordinary people could mingle with the nobility. Arthur made the most of the festivities to wander at will with Gwenhwyfar, speaking to as many as possible, listening to their tales and woes and giving out his eagerly sought advice. Word had spread over the years that the High King was approachable and in touch with his people. Concerned about their welfare and interested in their views, always willing to listen and give direction when needed. On occasions Arthur would encounter one whose lot in life had been full of one problem or catastrophe after another, suffering anguish almost daily, and at a loss as to know what they could do to improve their life. The King and his Queen would sit with these people, listening to their woes and giving guidance to resolve these issues. Most of which were brought on by the people themselves and their attitude towards others. Arthur would gently point this out, showing them where they had erred and how this had created their problem. Indicating how they could alter their ways, leaving their woes behind them and enjoying a better life. He ended up telling them that if they did not try to change their ways or attitude, then life would always be difficult for them. The choice was theirs alone, the King could only advise, if they did not try they would not know, ignore his advice and nothing would change. Most listened and heeded his wisdom, thanking him for his concern, others did not, or would not, unable to accept the fact that they created their own misfortune by the way they acted and thought.

The tournament at Cadbury was always held after the harvest had been gathered by which time Arthur and Gwenhwyfar had returned from their many visits across the country. Many knights came to this festival to test their abilities against others, some of them staying afterwards and offering their services to the King, including Sir Goreint and Sir Grifflet. Even young and inexperienced ones such as Sir Medraut from the north, were accepted, although in his case Arthur was a little reluctant at first, the lad's temper was a bit volatile, but then that of Sir Bors was initially, but soon matured with the right handling.

* * * * *

As the years passed Gwenhwyfar became a little weary from the constant travelling and was becoming concerned that she had not produced an heir for Arthur, despite their long winter nights of passion. She expressed her concerns to her husband, that the constant riding might be the cause and suggested that she remained behind the following spring. Arthur surprisingly had not considered this previously, although he had noticed that his wife was looking a little weary of late, readily agreeing to her proposal, her good health was his prime concern. Merlin had paid them a surprise visit at the last tournament and at Arthur's insistence had agreed to stay for the winter and rest his weary bones and catch up on all the news. A surprising comment from him as he always seemed to know what was going on all around the country. Arthur had a better appreciation of how he did this now, since his attendance at the Council of Elders, and that made his comment even more mysterious. There was more to his willingness to stay than met the eye, it would be made known, no doubt subtly, when Merlin felt the time was right.

Greyfus passed over that winter, his age had finally caught up with him, slipping away during his sleep. He was buried the next day, alongside the grave of Uther, a mark of respect for his unswerving loyalty and devotion across two generations. Bishop Bedwini performed a moving service in the chill wind and Arthur sang his praises for being ever dependable, no matter what was asked of him, a man of exceptional qualities that would be sorely missed. His assistant, Nightmar, spoke on behalf of all the people that had worked for him, a kind and generous man, tough with his expectations, but always willing to assist and pass on his knowledge to others. A celebration in honour of his life was held afterwards in the Great Hall and all were invited to attend, especially the servants that he had commanded so well. Arthur and his knights waiting on them with ale and food on this special occasion, as a sign of appreciation for all that went on in the background. Never before had it been known for a King to wait on the servants, and it was remembered long after as word of this unique gesture filtered through the land.

Arthur and Merlin spoke at great length during the bitterly cold dark days of the winter, reviewing all that had happened and what had been accomplished so far, looking to the future and what still needed to be done. The King broached the subject of King Mark and the stories that he had heard of his erratic behaviour and felt that he needed to visit him and confront him on these matters. He was causing upset and confusion amongst the people. Merlin agreed that he needed to be dealt with sooner rather than later, as he appeared to be becoming worse each year, he felt it was an illness that had taken hold and was affecting his mind. However a more pressing concern was King Cadwallon of Gwynedd, his health was failing and he was losing control of his kingdom. Maelgwyn, a young upstart, was pressing him to step aside in his favour, and was creating much unease in the area. Ambitious and power hungry with his eye on the neighbouring regions, this young man was destined to be very troublesome if not contained, and even then would be a thorn in Arthur's side.

Merlin eased the conversation around to ask about the knights that had been arriving over the last few years, inquiring of Arthur what his views on them were, their background and character. Arthur considered this for a moment before giving his opinion. Most were young seeking to better themselves and show their prowess as knights, a mixture of characters that could be moulded over time to become good ambassadors. There was one however that caused him a little concern, Sir Medraut was a bit like Sir Bors in his younger days, boisterous and a little arrogant, but this young man seemed to have a fire in him that was not altogether good. He expected much, but was not always prepared to work for it, almost as if he felt it was his right, and he was very reticent about his background, not wishing to discuss it. Arthur knew only that he had come from the north and arrived there after a long and arduous journey. He spoke very little about himself but always sought favour with the King, although he was want to complain much about trivial matters. A capable knight but with few friends, he alienated others too frequently to sustain any relationship, not that he was despised, mostly just ignored and left to his own devices. Arthur felt that there was something in his background that troubled him, but Medraut was not willing to bring it out into the open and discuss it at the present time, although the King had given him the opportunity to do so. Merlin thought carefully on this, Arthur was a good judge of character, following his instincts, that were extremely good and rarely wrong, but felt that a warning would not be amiss in the circumstances. He spoke his thoughts suggesting that Arthur kept a wary eye on him, as he was apt to cause trouble with those close to Arthur if not held in check. Merlin knew who he was, but it was not his place to mention Medraut's lineage, that would become apparent at the right time, so he kept his own counsel. He was pleased that Arthur had read his character correctly, that was all that was important at the moment, the rest would unravel over time.

Their conversation turned to other topics, including the health of the Queen, and her request to remain at Cadbury for awhile to rest and recuperate, Merlin agreed that it would be wise in the circumstances. Arthur asked him what the true purpose was of his prolonged visit, other than to winter in the warmth, which he could do at many places. Merlin smiled, indicating that he wished to see if the King was noticing the subtle changes that were happening in a few places, that could create discontent and eventually lead to trouble. By their long conversations he apparently was aware, that was a good thing, Arthur was still as sharp in his observations.

* * * * *

The dismally cold winter passed quite quickly, the trees and flowers began to spring into new life and return from hibernation, much the same as the people did, and the landscape became populated with bright fresh colours under the growing warmth of the sun. Merlin said his goodbyes and took his leave of them to continue his travels, whilst Arthur began his own preparations for the coming year, a few things needed to be sorted out. He would start with King Mark as Merlin had advised that early in the year he was normally found in residence at Tamaris [Launceston] before relocating to Isca Dumnoniorum [Exeter] for the summer.

Arthur started his journeys a little earlier than usual as there was much that needed to be done that year. His instinct served him well as he found King Mark already making preparations to leave Tamaris for his summer retreat. The meeting was not a cordial one and Mark became very belligerent, overstepping protocol by drawing his sword on Arthur, amidst thinly veiled threats. The King responded to this challenge and quickly disarmed him, though not before inflicting a superficial wound on his side. Mark was taken aback that the King had stood firm in his resolve and not backed down, which he was used to people doing, being renowned for a very volatile temper. Arthur informed King Mark that he had forfeited his lands and kingship and would be escorted to Isca Dumnoniorum [Exeter] and put on a ship for Armorica [Brittany], where he would be allowed to retain his estates. Any attempt to return there would be dealt with most severely. King Mark's protests fell on deaf ears, Arthur had spoken, it would be done, he had one day to gather his personal belongings, escorted by Sir Medraut and four men. The following day Arthur and his army would take him to the coast to secure a ship and see that he departed those shores. Having sent King Mark into exile, Arthur needed to appoint another to replace him, and he knew just the man, one who was able and of the right calibre to look to the welfare of the people of this kingdom.

* * * * *

Three days later Arthur brought his army within sight of the fort at Tintagel and set up camp in a nearby valley, leaving Sir Hector de Maris in charge and taking Sir Drydwas, Sir Liwlod, Sir Medraut and six men to pay a surprise call on his mother, Igraine. They had been recognised on their approach and Igraine and Sir Cador where waiting to greet him, pleased to see him return again. Although it was already some years since his last visit, they knew how much he had to do around the country. His mother looked to have become a little frail since they last met, but she wore her years well and was still full of life and greeted him with a firm hug, suggesting they all go to the inner hall and take some refreshment and hear the current news. The air had a chill about it as the day waned, it was still early in the year and there was a warm fire inside to give them comfort. Arthur told them both of all that had happened in recent times and about his current errand to see King Mark, from where he had just come. Not a happy man and without a kingdom on these shores. Igraine and Cador looked at each other in surprise, as they were well aware of Mark's temper, and promptly asked Arthur what had happened.

The King explained about the stories that had come to his ears and had journeyed to Tamaris to confront Mark with them, only to be attacked by him personally, whereby he wounded him, stripped him of his lands and kingship and exiled him to Armorica, taking him to a ship and seeing that he left. They had just returned from that errand; Dumnonia [Cornwall] did not have a king at present. That was the reason for his visit, to appoint a successor and he would like it to be Sir Cador, relinquishing his role of Duke to his son and taking on the mantle of kingship. There was silence for a moment as all in the hall took import of what the King had said. Sir Medraut arose and left the gathering without a word, but not unnoticed. Igraine and Cador both expressed their surprise and gratitude together, as Arthur waited for a reply. Sir Cador, a thoughtful expression on his face, arose and requested a private word with Arthur in the cool evening air, Arthur nodded and they proceeded outside.

Sir Cador expressed his gratitude to Arthur for such an honour, but felt he needed to decline, their mother Igraine was not getting any younger and he felt that it was his duty to look after her. Arthur had much more important work to do and did not have the time to give her the care that she would soon need, whereas he did, and knew that if their roles were reversed the King would do the same. Arthur agreed that in the circumstances he would do the same as his half brother, it was a commendable display of care and devotion for the one they both loved dearly, putting her before personal gain. Sir Cador suggested that Arthur should consider offering the kingship to his son Constantine, who had also been instructed by Sir Ector and was old enough to assume the responsibility. He was currently with Sir Ector, but both would be returning in the morning and that would allow Arthur to make a judgement on the matter. Should he be found wanting Cador would reluctantly accept the honour, but only for a short time, until other arrangements could be made.

"That is a fair proposition brother," Arthur commented, "we will wait until the morning and make our decision then. Now let us return and explain that we are sleeping on the matter, we need not go into details."

Sir Ector and Constantine returned mid morning, the lad had certainly grown since the King had last seen him, fairly tall like his father, the same features in his face, with a confident air about him. Arthur's instincts told him that it would be a good choice, but he would speak to Sir Ector first. Taking him to one side Arthur explained the situation and sought his advice on the appointment of Constantine as king, saying initial instinct said it would be a good choice, but was he ready. Sir Ector smiled and agreed, there were far worse choices that could be made and Constantine was as ready as Arthur was at the time he became King, but a little bit older and certainly capable. Sir Cador had made a good choice by stepping aside for his son, and with very honourable motives that he should be commended for. Most would have taken the opposite course and accepted for selfish reasons. Arthur thanked Sir Ector for his sound advise and suggested they both go and speak to Cador and Constantine privately before any announcement was made and see if the lad was willing to accept.

A little later Arthur called the gathering together again and made his proclamation that Sir Cador had passed over the opportunity, for commendable personal reasons, in favour of his son Constantine who had agreed to rule as King of Dumnonia. Sir Cador would remain as Duke and support his son. A cheer went up from those gathered, except Sir Medraut who just rattled his sword, seemingly in frustration, and a celebration was called for to 'mark' the occasion. There was laughter at this apparent inadvertent jest, and it was used frequently thereafter by the court jesters in many of the local festivals and became an accepted turn of phrase throughout the kingdom.

As Arthur was about to leave the next morning, Igraine thanked him for what he had done, saying that this might be the last time they met, age was catching up on her now and she often felt weary. To take good care of himself and beware of Sir Medraut, he was likely to be trouble just like her daughter Morgause was, they had the same traits and look in their eyes. Arthur gave her a hug and wished her well, saying that Cador would take good care of her as he couldn't, and she smiled in reply that she knew in her heart that was why he had declined the kingship, that the two of them had agreed between themselves that it would be so.

"Take care son," she whispered as she gave him a parting kiss, "just do your best, nobody can ask more."

With a wave to Cador and Constantine, Arthur took his little group back to camp to gather his army and set off for the next town on his itinerary.

* * * * *

Their arrival at Isca Augusta [Caerleon] was eagerly awaited at this time of year, and was none too soon, as a delicate situation had arisen that could escalate into all out war between two neighbouring kingdoms. King Glywys of Glywysing had passed over and had been replaced by King Gwynllyn. He had carried off Princess Gwladys of the small kingdom of Brycheiniog and refused to return her to her father, despite repeated requests. Threats of force had recently been sent, if she wasn't returned. Arthur wasted no time in taking fifty of his men to go and speak with King Gwynllyn and discover the reason for this abduction, and act as mediator between the two factions, to avert a likely war. He was received cordially by the new king, and when Arthur pressed him about the abduction, was told a different story to that which was circulating freely. Princess Gwladys and he were lovers who wished to marry and had contrived the little ruse to be together, as her father was against their association and forbade it. She had come of her own freewill, although unknown to anyone else that it was prearranged. Her father, King Rhigeneu had threatened to march on Glywysing to secure her release if she was not returned within the week, whole and unharmed. Princess Gwladys confirmed the story and asked Arthur if he would intercede on their behalf and prevent unnecessary bloodshed. The King agreed, but insisted that she would need to accompany him to speak to her father so that he heard the truth from her own lips. Arthur would give support and argue her case on her behalf. They left the following morning with the princess guiding them to her father's stronghold, some miles distant.

King Rhigeneu greeted them with relief at the sight of his daughter, returned unharmed, but his pleasure was short lived when he found out the true nature of the visit. Becoming very vocal, castigating his daughter and threatening all kinds of violent endings to King Gwynllyn. Arthur let him air his frustrations until his temper began to subside, then gently asked him the reason for his displeasure, the couple were well suited and obviously in love. Rhigeneu replied that there were suitable candidates in his own kingdom that would be a good match and that his daughter should be looking to one of those. Lords that would be honoured to take her as a wife. Arthur replied that surely the princess had a say in the matter, she was of age to make her own decisions. Did the king not look to her happiness, instead of his own? She had found her love and was entitled to make her own life, however it turned out. Rhigeneu had calmed down, seeing the wisdom of Arthur's words, he was very fond of his daughter and had not wished to lose her, seeking only her happiness. If he persisted then he would alienate her and probably lose her for good, because of his own stubborn attitude and being over protective, as fathers often were of their daughters. He finally agreed to let matters be, but as she had returned spoiled, as she had obviously lain with King Gwynllyn then they must marry, and soon, lest there be issue, he would make the arrangements. Arthur commented that he had made a wise choice, it would also strengthen the bond between the two kingdoms and could lead to a merging of them in the next generation, which would be a good thing.

The King left the princess to spend some time with her father and strengthen their bond again and returned to King Gwynllyn to tell him of the good news. He was none to happy at first, seeing Arthur return without Princess Gwladys, but on hearing the news he was overjoyed and expressed his gratitude for the King's timely intervention and mediation. Arthur wished him well and took his leave of him and returned to King Caradog at Caerleon to continue the business of holding court there.

* * * * *

A week later Arthur took his small army northward again, stopping briefly at the healing sanctuary to pay his respects to Gwendolyn, as he usually did on his yearly visit. Then onwards, stopping at many towns and villages to review the progress of the measures that he had instigated over the years. His reception was always welcoming and his advice and ruling on diverse matters was often sought, and usually acted upon. Rarely did he find disagreement, where there was it was quickly resolved in an acceptable manner. Kings, lords and the people themselves showed him great respect and sought his favour, requiring great diplomacy on Arthur's part at times to excuse himself from one village to pass on to the next. Consequently his travels around the country were slow and not all places could he visit every year, so he varied his route between the major towns and forts each time to encompass as much of the country as possible over time.

The first outward signs of unrest and dissent came from the kingdom of Gwynedd where Maelgwyn had taken over as king on the death of Cadwallon. A power hungry individual that saw himself as a great warrior and leader with designs on becoming High King of Britain. Unfortunately for him he did not have the support that was necessary to further this aim, but that did not contain his belligerence. Resorting to force in the vain belief that it would strengthen his position. Word reached Arthur that Maelgwyn was marching towards Demetia [Dyfed] with the intention of securing the kingdom for himself, aided by an army of Irish warriors. He set off with his small army of cavalry to intercept him and go to the aid of King Cyngar of Demetia, whom he had met briefly once, shortly after he had succeeded the old king. Arthur headed for the fort at Caer Myrddin [Carmarthen], King Cyngar's residence and the reported home of Merlin, which was a journey of several days across a vast undulating and sparsely populated landscape.

Arthur was surprised that they were expected, until he found that Merlin himself was there, and that explained it. Using his visionary skills and probably drawing Arthur there, as instinctively he had headed towards Caer Myrddin without a second thought. King Cyngar had assembled what men he could to defend the region and Arthur suggested that they leave forthwith and meet the opposing army in open country, where his cavalry would be the most affective. They marched towards the western coast, at Merlin's suggestion, and encountered King Maelgwyn and his Irish force in the Teifi Valley near Cenarth. Arthur rode out, pennon flying from his spear, to confront the king, with six of his knights as escort. The advancing army halted as Arthur approached and Maelgwyn and his escort moved forward to meet with them, surprised to find The High King leading them, but relishing the encounter.

Arthur challenged Maelgwyn. "Why are you travelling this land as if prepared for war my lord?"

"Because I claim this as part as part of my kingdom," Maelgwyn replied, "either by agreement or by force."

"You will not have it either way," Arthur said quietly. "This kingdom is not yours to have, by right or force, turn around and take your men home, you go no further."

"And if I refuse?" retorted Maelgwyn angrily, "you are outnumbered two to one, do you think that you can thwart my plans so easily?"

"I am used to fighting for right with a small force, as the Saxons know to their peril, numbers mean very little my lord," Arthur responded. "You can return home now, with honour, or suffer the consequences."

"Why not let our champions decide the fate of our encounter?" Mealgwyn conceded, "much bloodshed would then be spared and our honours retained."

Sir Medraut quickly intervened and offered his services, which Arthur declined politely and speaking to Maelgwyn again, replied, "I fight my own cause and do not give that to another, no matter how able they are. If you wish to settle this honourably then you will have to draw swords with me personally."

King Maelgwyn had not expected this reply, it was not expected of a king to fight his own battles unnecessarily, that is why he had a champion, they were expendable and could be replaced, whilst a king retained his honour, even in loss. He declined the offer and rode back to his army, waving them forward, it would have to be settled by force, then he could humiliate Arthur for his defiance.

The battle was ferocious, but short lived, Arthur's cavalry, small in number maybe, decimated the Irish and put them to flight. Those that withstood the initial onslaught had King Cyngar's foot soldiers to contend with, containing them, whilst the cavalry rode through them, cutting them down in droves. King Maelgwyn was aghast that his army and his portentous ideas had so easily been destroyed and fled the battle scene, but Arthur was in pursuit with Sir Medraut and Sir Liwlod. The cavalry horses that Arthur's men rode were used to being hard ridden when required and Maelgwyn and his two companions were soon overhauled and challenged to stop.

Self preservation being uppermost in his mind, Maelgwyn knew to continue fleeing would only court disaster, and reigned in his horse, shouting that he yielded, knowing Arthur's wide spread reputation for chivalry towards an adversary. Sir Medraut, being headstrong, wanted to take his sword to them and Arthur had to verbally restrain him, indicating that he would strike him first should he try.

The King commanded Maelgwyn and his two companions to alight from their horses and place their weapons on the ground and to start walking back to Gwynedd. They complained loudly at this, Maelgwyn saying that it was not fit for a king to travel in that manner. Arthur replied that he was not fit to be a king and might learn the error of his ways on the journey. The alternative was to pick up his sword and fight for his honour and dented pride, the choice was his, to start walking or to fight. Maelgwyn turned, his face twisted in humiliation and began to walk.

Sir Medraut, wanted to know why Arthur would not let him deal with them, and was told that it was about time that he learnt the code of chivalry if he wanted to make his mark as a respected knight. His current hot head would be his downfall if not moderated. Listen, and learn from those around him and see how they carried themselves, the benefits that came their way by compassion and understanding of situations, a good knight did not just prove himself by the sword, but by other deeds as well.

They gathered the spare horses and weapons, returning swiftly to the army, as Maelgwyn and his two companions disappeared into the distance, leaving Arthur in no doubt as to the probable trouble that this episode would cause at a later date. Maelgwyn was not the sort of character to learn easily, he had powerful ambitions and would not let those lie dormant if he could see a way to further his lust for power.

The armies of King Cyngar and Arthur returned in triumph to Caer Myrddin and Merlin was one of the first to greet them and hear about the confrontation and battle. He warned Arthur that he had made an enemy there that would cause further trouble if not contained. The King realised this and said that he hoped to keep him in check by isolation, without support from any others, except perhaps the Irish. That notion was fraught with danger as they had their own designs on parts of that land, Maelgwyn might find that he had created more trouble than he could handle alone, if he went that route. Merlin agreed, but it would pay to keep a careful watch on him, he was a devious character and his craving for power consumed him, he would use any opportunity to further his ambitions.

* * * * *

The rest of Arthur's travels that year were peaceful by comparison, with only the odd minor dispute to resolve as he continued the process of rebuilding. At last they were on their way back to Cadbury and the harvest time tournament, that was growing larger each year. Gwenhwyfar was pleased to see him return safely and they spent many a long winter's night showing how much they had missed each other, but she was concerned that she was still not with child as spring rapidly approached again. Arthur himself was feeling a little weary, he was not as young as he used to be, the passionate nights took more out of him these days so he decided to restrict his travels to the major towns that year and spend less time travelling. He rotated the knights and men that he took with him, so that the ones that went with him one year, remained behind the next and could be with their loved ones, whereas he was travelling every year. It was taking its toll and sapping his energy.

Sir Medraut was not pleased that Sir Hector de Maris was given command of Cadbury, he considered that it was his turn for the honour, but Arthur told him he still had much to learn and needed to moderate his temper still before he was given that privilege. A knight had to earn respect before he was considered for such an important task, a commander who lacked the trust and respect of others would fail in his duty as guardian, creating all sorts of problems. When Sir Medraut was ready he would be given the opportunity, in the meantime he should look to alter his behaviour and become more amenable to others and seek their guidance, not aggravate them.

* * * * *

Arthur reduced his travelling for the next few years, King Maelgwyn had become worryingly quiet and Gwenhwyfar became more concerned that she had not produced an heir for the King. Sir Medraut had taken to disappearing for weeks on end when he was left at Cadbury and Arthur began to wonder what he was up to, as he would not say where he had been, other than 'growing up' as the King had instructed.

Parts of the country started to develop an unhealthy undercurrent as old kings died and new ones replaced them. Arthur spent much time in visiting those areas to re-establish the goodwill and repair the cracks that were undermining his foundations in places. It was not a serious matter yet, but had to be dealt with quickly before they spread, and in many areas he had success, others still required much of his effort and diplomacy.

Gwenhwyfar took to frequenting more with some of the ladies in an endeavour to discover the reasons why she was still childless. On one of these occasions a lady known to her whispered that perhaps she should take a lover, there were always many virile men left at the castle who would accommodate her. She exclaimed that she couldn't do that, what would the King say if he found out. The lady replied that if she timed it right and very discreetly the King would never know and perhaps she would bear him a child that he would think was his. She told Gwenhwyfar to think about it, she knew a young man that would be ideal for her, and such stamina too, she would enjoy the experience. Maybe her husband, the King, was doing the very same thing whilst away on his travels, comforting the ladies.

Gwenhwyfar let the suggestion fade from her mind, but every so often it would return to haunt her and over time she thought that the idea had a certain fascination about it and might solve her problem if handled correctly. She would not really be unfaithful to the King, as it would only happen briefly and was designed to please Arthur with a child, not for her own pleasure. Perhaps, as the lady had mentioned, Arthur was doing the very same thing and maybe had a child by someone else, because she had not delivered. They had never spoken of the problem and it did not seem to bother the King that she had not been with child. Maybe that was why, he already had one elsewhere. The thoughts subsided and she continued with her normal social life until Arthur's return a few months later. She had noticed that Sir Medraut was talking to people these days, especially with the women, and had more of a confident air about him, less prone to his temper outbursts.

Arthur returned, somewhat weary from his travels and Gwenhwyfar asked if he was feeling unwell, to which he confessed that he was just tired from all the incessant travelling. As he was doing it every year without fail, whereas his men had a break from it. It was a burden of command he told her, doing what he thought was right as High King and being available to his people. She mentioned the change she had noticed in Sir Medraut, how more affable and friendly he had become this time, talking to people and laughing. Arthur replied that it was about time.

That winter was not such a passionate one this time and Gwenhwyfar began to have some doubts about the faithfulness of her husband, the thoughts coming back into her mind regularly. She asked him if he minded that she had not produced a child for him, let alone an heir, and her thoughts raced away again when he replied that he hadn't given it much thought. It would be nice but not absolutely essential, events he felt would take their own course. She made a mental decision to take the lady's advice and seek a lover and if she had a child perhaps Arthur would stay more at Cadbury instead of travelling so much.

* * * * *

Spring arrived in its usual splash of vibrant colour and melodious sounds as Arthur prepared once again to travel the country without Gwenhwyfar. Sir Medraut had asked if he could remain behind so that he could observe how Sir Tristanus commanded the castle in Arthur's absence, to further his learning. Arthur agreed and commended him on his progress the past year, and what a difference it made. He would soon be in a position to take control himself, if he carried on in the same way, Sir Medraut replying that was his intention. Arthur was not sure, but he thought he detected a slight undertone with those words but shrugged it off as his imagination, ignoring his first instinct, which was unusual and was something he would come to regret later.

Arthur and his army left a week later, to travel the country once again, to hold court in the major towns and visit more of the villages that he hadn't been too for some while. Gwenhwyfar sought out the lady that had spoken to her the previous summer about taking a lover. She had about three weeks in which to be with child, if nothing happened she would have to wait until a few weeks before Arthur was set to return, otherwise it would be obvious that any child she conceived would not his. The lady was delighted for her, saying that she would arrange a discreet meeting with the young man, and she would not be disappointed, he had a beautiful body and knew how to please a lady. Gwenhwyfar, with only a single thought in her head did not think to question how the lady knew so much about the young man, otherwise she would have seen her danger. The meeting was arranged for that evening and the lady would escort her to the gentleman and make the introduction.

Not since her first few years with Arthur had Gwenhwyfar experienced such wanton abandonment and pleasure as this man gave her as he thrust into her from all angles. Taking her to new heights of ecstasy for long periods before his passion exploded within her with such power, causing her to cry out in complete fulfilment. For several hours he kept this up before she indicated that she was exhausted and must go to her own chamber and sleep so that she was not missed, but would like to continue the following evening. It was agreed that the lady would escort her whenever she wanted to visit, it would be discreet that way, and she could return to her own chambers afterwards. He dressed and fetched the lady to escort the Queen so if she was noticed it would be assumed that the women were returning from a ladies social gathering.

The secret liaison continued for nigh on three weeks before Gwenhwyfar called it to a halt for awhile as her monthly respite was due. That would be the testing time, had anything happened, she did not feel any different at the moment, but only time would give her the indication. If not she would resume the passionate encounters before Arthur's return, a last try.

The lady kept asking her if there was a result yet, and each time Gwenhwyfar had to say nothing had happened, but she must wait until August before she tried again and if the young man's virility did not work then, perhaps nothing would. The lady agreed and said she would remind Gwenhwyfar nearer the time, so that such an important issue was not forgotten.

* * * * *

Life continued as normal, Gwenhwyfar lay awake at night sometimes, wondering if she was doing the right thing, convincing herself that what she was doing was for Arthur's sake, to provide him with child that could be passed off as his, an heir. Not accepting that she had fallen into the trap of doing it for her own pleasure and enjoyment. The young man's agility was amazing with the different ways that he had taken her to new heights, things that not even Arthur had attempted. She still did not see that she had been deliberately led astray for another's sexual gratification and was just being used, a temporary plaything that would be discarded at some point in favour of another. It would not have bothered her if she had realised, in her mind it was a short term encounter with one aim in mind, to be with child, nothing else.

The weeks dragged by slowly until finally August was in sight and Gwenhwyfar's last chance that year to accomplish her dream, and so her liaison with the young man started again. Up until this point she hadn't realised how much she had missed the deep thrust and rhythmic motion of his loins as her whole body screamed with extreme pleasure as their volcanoes continually erupted in unison until fatigue overtook them.

Their secret meetings continued for two weeks until finally Gwenhwyfar said that the following evening would have to be the last as her husband was shortly due back. The young man responded that they would have to do something special that she would always remember. This intrigued Gwenhwyfar, but he would say no more, she would have to wait in anticipation until the following evening to experience the extreme emotions he had in store for her.

The day passed very slowly for Gwenhwyfar, wondering what new delights the evening would bring, the young man had been very mysterious as to his intentions. She suddenly realised that she was thinking of him more than the purpose of the liaison, that was worrying. Her sexual pleasure had become her dominant thought, it was as well that this was the last night, and still she did not feel as if she was with child. Perhaps that was the way it was meant to be, still, enjoy the evening of ecstasy then put it all behind her and get on with life.

The evening eventually arrived and she was escorted as usual to the young man's chamber. Clothes were quickly discarded and the passion began and the air soon became charged with the electricity of their writhing bodies thrusting at each other as they sought their climax. Suddenly the door flew open and in burst Sir Medraut closely followed by Sir Tristanus, swords in hand. Wanting to know what was going on, seeing the two naked bodies in their frenzied movement of total passion as they exploded together, and instantly recognising the woman as the Queen. They dragged the young man off Gwenhwyfar, and he darted naked for the door, but not quick enough as Sir Medraut ran him through with his sword before he could reach it. Sir Tristanus looked at the distraught Gwenhwyfar and suggested she dressed quickly and they would escort her to her chambers, where she would remain until the King returned to deal with her foolishness.

* * * * *

A week later Arthur and his army returned to a very subdued welcome, as word had spread concerning the Queens confinement, for reasons not disclosed. Sir Tristanus, with Sir Medraut by his side appraised the King privately of the situation concerning Gwenhwyfar, and what they had stumbled upon in the chambers. Arthur wished to know the full details of how the Queen's liaison with the young man was discovered and who were the informants.

As the story unravelled Arthur could sense that Gwenhwyfar had acted naively and been lured into a trap to get at the King. He had a distinct feeling as to who was behind it, he should have listened to his instincts more at the time. Sir Medraut indicated that the Queen had committed a very serious offence bringing dishonour on herself as well as the King's name and that was tantamount to treason. Sir Tristanus was appalled at that suggestion, and said so, but Arthur indicated he had every right to bring a charge of that nature, if he saw fit. Sir Medraut said quietly that it would be the best way to bring the truth out into the open, for people to judge for themselves.

What a devious person you are Medraut, thought Arthur, *I should have watched you more carefully, I wonder what your motives are in all this, the only way to find out is to let you have your head, and hope that you lose it.* Arthur agreed to hold court the next morning to hear the charges and listen to what the witnesses had to say, if Sir Tristanus would kindly arrange it. All were welcome, nobody should be excluded. Justice had to be seen to be done by all the people, no matter how painful it might be for the Queen or himself.

The King spoke privately to Sir Tristanus and asked him to find out all he could from the Queen as to how her misdemeanour came about. It was best in the circumstances if Arthur himself did not see Gwenhwyfar until the court sat the following morning.

Sir Tristanus returned some hours later and related to Arthur the whole sorry story as told to him by the Queen. She was beside herself with angst at what she had done, bringing shame on the house of the King through her stupidity and naivety and sent her deepest apologies for her actions. Placing herself in the King's hands, whatever the outcome. Arthur thanked him for his help, confiding that he was sure Sir Medraut had a hand in what had transpired, directly or indirectly, and he was determined to get to the bottom of it. The lady who had provided the introduction could be the key, if Sir Tristanus could find out more about her.

The court sat at noon and Sir Tristanus had been busy seeking information concerning the lady prior to this, and advising Arthur of the outcome of his inquiries. The story was intriguing, apparently she had arrived a few years ago in the company of Sir Medraut and several others, when he had returned from one of his impromptu excursions. Nothing much was known about her since, except that she had many lovers, one of whom was the young man that was introduced to the Queen. She frequently attended the social groups held around the castle but had not tried to coerce any others into taking a lover, although she often spoke of her own exploits. The lady appeared to be of good birth but was looked on as a lady of ill repute that gave her favours too easily. She had been seen in the company of Sir Medraut on more than one occasion, although they were always discreet. Arthur was very thoughtful as he listened to all that was said, complimenting Sir Tristanus on the wealth of information gathered in such a short time. It would be very useful in court.

The great hall was filled with people, many more than was normal for a court sitting. All waiting eagerly to hear what misdemeanour had befallen the Queen, who was sitting impassively waiting to hear her fate. Sir Medraut stated the charge and proceeded to outline the course of events that led to the discovery of what he considered to be a treasonous act. He spared no moment in blackening the Queen's name as she sought a lover for her own gratification, thereby bringing the King's house into disrepute and undermining his authority.

As he listened Arthur realised that Sir Medraut had been planning it for a long time. Just waiting for the right moment to spring the trap, in an attempt to destroy the King's authority and the respect that he commanded.

Sir Medraut introduced Lady Marge, who in her own words said that the Queen had approached her for help in seeking a suitable lover, one that would be extremely discreet and know his place, available when Gwenhwyfar desired his attentions. There would be no complications involving an issue as the Queen it appeared could not be with child, therefore she could lay with the young man as often as she desired whilst the King was away, and indulge her own fantasies at will. The young man became bored with her increasing demands, as men are want to and wished to end the relationship, but the Queen refused, he pleasured her too well. There were arguments and threats made and he turned to her to seek a way of ending the association and she agreed to speak to the Queen on his behalf, but before that was possible other events occurred that led to their discovery.

Sir Medraut continued the story, how he had heard much noise and fierce argument coming from one of the bed chambers. As he did not wish to investigate on his own he sought out Sir Tristanus and both entered the room together swords at the ready, to find the Queen and a young man completely naked in the throes of frenzied passion. Not knowing if she was a willing party they hauled him off Gwenhwyfar, but he tried to escape and Sir Medraut had no choice but to strike him down with his sword, unfortunately the blow was fatal.

Arthur had listened intently, it was a well thought out devious plot. Perfectly believable but contradictory in many places to what the Queen had told Sir Tristanus the previous evening. He hoped that she would be as open and honest with recounting her story here. Looking at Gwenhwyfar, still with love in his heart, he pointed out that it was a serious charge that she faced, but she had a right to put forward her story so that the court could determine the truth before reaching a conclusion.

Gwenhwyfar took her time as she gathered her thoughts and looked at all those in the gathering that would judge her in their own way and began by saying what they had listened to was only partly true. She had committed a sin, that she did not deny, but her story and reasons differed to what they had just heard. With all the travelling with the King she had become weary and believed that it was the reason why she had not produced an heir. The resting did not seem to improve matters and it seriously concerned her that nothing had changed, and that she was failing in her duty as a wife and Queen. In seeking advice from the other ladies, Lady Marge suggested that she should take a lover for a few weeks after the King had left on his travels and shortly before his return, any issue would then appear to be his. She would not entertain that idea, as she had no wish to be unfaithful, but the thought kept returning as she became more depressed at not being with child. Lady Marge kept asking her if she had changed her mind, as she knew a virile young man with a gorgeous body who would be ideal as a lover and very discreet. She still refused to entertain the idea, it would be wrong. Eventually in a fit of depression of thinking that she was failing to be a proper wife she succumbed and Lady Marge made the introduction to the young man, who was indeed exceedingly virile, but still she did not become with child. What she did was wrong she realised now, but was just to please her husband as she thought she had failed him as his wife. Although he did not appear to be concerned by the lack of an heir, but as Lady Marge said perhaps he already had one in some other part of the country, a man had his desires too. She did not believe that, but nevertheless the thought persisted and eat away inside her and became unsettling. Realising that her desire to be with child was becoming less important and that her mind was thinking more of the pleasures of the flesh, she decided that she must end the relationship, telling her lover that the following night would be the last. As it turned out it was, for it was that night that they were discovered together and the young man was shamefully killed, when there was no need for such drastic measures. She stated that she had brought shame on her husband and King that was inexcusable, let alone upon herself. Gwenhwyfar asked forgiveness for her foolish and naïve actions in thinking that it would bring him pleasure by having an heir by her desperate act. She placed herself at the King's mercy and was ready to accept her punishment as the court thought fit.

The crowd had been totally silent as they hung on every word of her story, their hearts going out to her for such an honest display of her feelings whether she was guilty or not, and by her own admission she was.

Sir Medraut had jumped up. "My lord, by the Queen's own words she is guilty of this treasonous act and should be punished accordingly."

"Sir Medraut," Arthur replied, "the Queen has admitted taking a lover, but is it not strange that her story does not match that of Lady Marge. A friend of yours I believe?"

"I do not have the acquaintance of Lady Marge my lord, except through this court," Medraut replied.

"Strange that you arrived here together after one of your absences a few years ago, and that you have been seen together since. Or had that slipped your memory?" Arthur stated.

A little surprised at Arthur's knowledge, he replied, "I said that we were not acquainted my Lord, not that I hadn't spoken in passing to the lady."

"You play with words Sir Medraut, your conversations with Lady Marge were of some duration, not just passing pleasantries. Are you also a lover of hers, like the young man you so conveniently slew? Would his story have been different? He could not have gone far naked, yet you took such drastic action, why?"

"My lord, my reaction happened in an instant and I regret now that it was so drastic, as for Lady Marge we have indeed spoken on occasion, she wished to get to know me but I was not interested and didn't ask her name."

There was a slight commotion amongst the gathering as a Lady near the front stood up and shouted that it wasn't true, Lady Marge had confided with several that Sir Medraut was one of her frequent lovers, even before she had arrived here.

"Well Sir Medraut, how do you answer that?" inquired Arthur, a smile on his face. "What tale will you tell?"

"Just talk amongst the ladies my Lord," he replied feeling a little uncomfortable at Arthur's probing.

"Lady Marge, what was your reaction when you discovered that one of your virile lovers had been slain by Sir Medraut so unnecessarily, was it jealousy between rivals do you think, or maybe something else?"

"Greatly upset my Lord, he was a beautiful young man, very active and knew how to please a lady, it shouldn't have happened, whether it was rivalry or not" she replied.

"Your words, my lady, seemed to indicate that they were both your lovers at some point, and that the young man was not supposed to be killed." queried Arthur. "Perhaps his story would have been different to yours?"

"His story would have been the same my Lord," Lady Marge replied, "but he shouldn't have been killed, there was no need, my lovers are not rivals they know their place. They need resting occasionally."

"I take it that is your way of saying that Sir Medraut was indeed another of your lovers?" Arthur replied.

"I have nothing more to add my Lord," Lady Marge answered, "it is a private matter between two people."

"Yet you willingly discuss your conquests amongst your lady friends, how contrary," Arthur answered.

"Sir Medraut, do you have anything further to add before I make my deliberations?" queried Arthur.

"No my Lord, all that has been required has been said, we await your judgement," Sir Medraut replied.

The Great Hall was totally still and quiet as they all waited for the King to give his verdict. At last he spoke.

"This is a difficult moment for me, I preside here as your High King and must make judgement on my own dear wife and Queen. By her own admission she has made a serious error not becoming of her position, by taking a lover. Bringing shame on herself and the house of the King and breaking one of the commandments of our Lord. She has expressed her deepest regret at her foolish actions in seeking to please her King in the most inappropriate manner. I accept her sincere apologies, but she is not solely to blame for the situation she finds herself in. I must take part of that blame on myself. Being High King is not easy and I have endeavoured to carry out my duties to the best of my ability for the good of the people. In the process I have neglected my duties as a husband somewhat, and not looked to the needs of my wife, not the physical needs, but being there for her and listening to her worries and concerns and supporting her through these difficult times. On reflection it would probably have been better for me to pursue my daunting task of restoring the peace and pride of this country without the aid of a wife. Although the help and support that she has unselfishly given to me over the years has been truly magnificent, it has been one sided. However we cannot dictate who we fall in love with or when, it just happens, and although this is a traumatic time for both of us my love is still there for her, but we must make recompense for our errors and spend quiet time in reflection. My judgement therefore Gwenhwyfar, my wife and Queen, is that you must go and do penance in a convent until such times as you are cleansed and made whole again. Bishop Bedwini will make the necessary arrangements."

"Thank you my King and husband for your understanding. My love will stay with you whilst I spend time in repentance and reflection, that some day we might be joined together again in harmony," she replied.

Sir Medraut jumped into the air astounded and in a temper at the outcome, "My Lord, your judgement is a farce, the Queen is guilty of a treasonous act and should be sentenced to death."

"On the contrary Sir Medraut," replied Arthur, "the treasonous act is yours and Lady Marge's, the falsehoods that you have both uttered in an attempt to destroy the credibility of myself and my wife. Taking advantage of the Queen when she was vulnerable, to drive a wedge between us and further your aims by leading her astray. It has become obvious by your own words that you plotted this between you. What for? Do you seek to become High King, or is there some grudge from the past that you seek to correct? I should have you both put to death, that is what treason warrants is it not, according to your demands?"

"It was all Sir Medraut's idea my Lord," shouted Lady Marge, suddenly fearful for her life.

"Quiet woman," replied Sir Medraut, seeing his plan fall apart around him.

"Sir Medraut, Lady Marge, I am a just and fair King. You have plotted against me and my wife, but not my life, therefore I spare yours. You are both banished from this country during my lifetime, return is punishable by death. You will be escorted to the nearest port and passage secured for you on the first available ship to foreign parts. Your sword Sir Medraut please."

He duly handed it over and they were both escorted from the Great Hall to their quarters to collect their possessions. Sir Tristanus detailed a troop to escort them to the coast and place them on a ship. The Queen had left with Bishop Bedwini to discuss a suitable convent that she would be taken to in a few days.

The crowd had began to disperse from the Great Hall with much chatter about what they had just witnessed and how sorry that they felt for the King and Queen, but it was a fair judgement, and how Sir Medraut had been uncovered as a traitor and got his just rewards. That day was spoken about for many years and some felt that it was the turning point for everything that happened afterwards.

* * * * *

Time passed and Arthur gradually came to terms with not having Gwenhwyfar around, it did not seem the same at Cadbury without her presence there, he missed her. Sir Medraut had not been heard of, but Arthur felt that he had not seen the last of him. A strange man that was pursuing some unknown goal that was likely to cause trouble somewhere at some point. Sir Kay put in an appearance to let Arthur know that his father, Sir Ector has passed on during the winter and was sad also to hear about Gwenhwyfar and the treachery of Sir Medraut. Sir Bors arrived whilst he was there and not long after Merlin and Taliesin appeared for a brief visit and they all helped cheer the King up and put his life back together again. Even the atmosphere at Cadbury was subdued now, the laughter was missing as people went quietly about their business with many thoughts straying back to that fateful day.

Arthur prepared for his travels and although the Queen had not travelled with him in recent years, his heart was not really in it at the moment, although he pushed himself hard to get on with his task. It was probably for that reason that he failed to notice and appreciate the subtle differences in some of the lords and kings around the country, an undercurrent for change was creeping into some areas. He was spending that much time listening to the people that he was ignoring the signs at the top, or just not seeing them clearly as he sought to put his life back together without his wife Gwenhwyfar. Minor disputes started to occur that required much diplomacy on Arthur's part to resolve, and he seemed to be chasing around the countryside, going from one problem to another. Each year seemed to be producing a few more than before, nothing serious as yet, but worrying to Arthur that he could not seem to keep up with them.

* * * * *

Merlin returned again the following spring with more bad news and a heavy heart. Sir Cador had asked him to come on his behalf and advise Arthur that their mother, Igraine, had passed away in her sleep after a short illness, but that was not the only grim news, Sir Medraut was on the move in the country, gathering support and an army to challenge Arthur's authority. Some of the new kings were not happy with Arthur's leadership, they felt that their own authority was being undermined and restricted by what they deemed as interference in their own internal issues. It was going to be a difficult time for Arthur, there was likely to be bloodshed again before it was resolved, and not against the Saxons this time, but his own kings. It was the same problem that Uther faced initially but eventually managed to overcome, and he had to do it by force as well. Merlin advised Arthur not to travel that year, but instead send word to those that he trusted and would support him and gather an army there in readiness. Sir Medraut would come to Cadbury, the seat of his humiliation, in an attempt to seek revenge, and would probably bring his army in from the west, the least likely direction that Arthur would expect trouble from, sometime during the summer. Arthur knew not to disregard anything that Merlin said, as he was always right, his insight aided by his visionary prowess. The King asked him why it was starting all over again, after many years of peace, and Merlin responded that it was because those young upstarts knew nothing of what it was like before. Their egos were controlling them as they sought the power they thought they needed, it was the same with each generation until they learnt, if they lived that long.

"Who is Medraut Merlin, I am sure you know?" Arthur asked

"He is the youngest son of King Lot and Morgause, your son and heir in fact," replied Merlin. "She conceived him, much to her consternation, on the occasion that she seduced you just before you left for the King making ceremony, and before you knew that she was your half sister. She has never forgiven you for that, but to this day King Lot believes that he is his son. Although he will not have anything to do with him nowadays, more so since he became aware of his involvement with the Queen's misdemeanour. His mother however has seen that he harbours a hatred for you by leaving her when she was with child with him."

Arthur recalled the cryptic message that Morgause had sent him through Igraine, 'beware the fiery sun in distant lands, give respect that is deserved, ignore at your peril,' not sun as he thought at the time but son. It all made sense now, she was letting him know that she would have the last word.

Well maybe not, he had no feelings for him as a son, they were totally different characters. He mentioned his thoughts to Merlin, who remarked that he had worked that riddle out himself some while ago, and then set about confirming it, but it was not something he could mention until the time was right, and that time had arrived.

Merlin left the following morning and Arthur gathered his knights and commanders and despatched them to various parts of the country with twenty men each to seek support and men from those that he knew he could trust and return as swiftly as possible. Summer would be upon them in a couple of months and Arthur wished to be prepared. He had told them all of the situation, with the instruction to make it known to each that they were visiting of the seriousness of the situation, that Sir Medraut was gathering an army to march on Cadbury.

* * * * *

Over the next month many men led by kings and lords gathered at Cadbury for the coming conflict with Medraut and parties of scouts were sent out twenty miles to give early warning of an approaching army. All they could do now was bide their time and wait for the scouts to return with news. Day followed day and still no indication of any large army. The weeks passed slowly and they waited, and then one hot summer's day several scouts returned with the news that they had been waiting for. Sir Medraut's army had been seen approaching the small hamlet of Somerton, almost due west and some fifteen miles distant, mainly foot soldiers with a few horsemen.

Arthur rallied the men and set forth, seven hundred cavalry and three thousand foot soldiers, leaving just a token force to guard the castle. They marched swiftly to make the most of the remaining daylight and within a couple of hours found a suitable place to camp where several rivers and waterways merged creating an unusual curved shape in the riverbank, as they swerved around some unseen obstacle that altered their direction briefly. Arthur did not expect trouble during the night but he posted guards anyway, it was better to take precautions with the likes of Medraut. He commanded that no fires be lit, he did not want their location known just yet. Some while later as evening closed in fires sprang up about a mile away, indicating the location of Medraut's camp, close enough to observe but far enough away not to pose a problem.

The night passed without any incident and as dawn approached Arthur summoned the kings and lords and said his intention was to ride out and meet with Medraut and see if bloodshed could be avoided. He doubted it, but he was not expecting to encounter Arthur there and it was worth a try. Arthur with Berius by his side, and eleven others mounted up and rode towards Medraut's camp, the Pendragon pennon fluttering in the gentle early morning breeze. They rode half way and stopped, dismounted and waited, soon a group of riders left the other camp and approached, reigning in their horses and dismounting also.

"Well if it isn't the High King himself," mocked Medraut. "What brings you here my lord?"

"I was seeking rodents for an early morning feast," replied Arthur, "it is said that just after dawn is best for such a sport, when they are only half awake."

"You have been misled as usual my lord, besides thirteen men would soon be overwhelmed by a large body of rodents if cornered," retorted Medraut with a smile.

"I banished you from this country Medraut, why do you disobey me?" Arthur asked. "I could kill you now."

"You could my lord, but you would not live very long, if you hadn't noticed my army behind me."

"Do you think I do not travel with mine," replied Arthur turning and waving his hand that brought all his men into view half a mile behind him. "You see we have been expecting you and thought we would give you a warm welcome here, before you spoilt the countryside around Cadbury."

Medraut was taken by surprise, thinking that the King was just part of a hunting party, not backed by several thousand men and his temper began to rise. How did he know that he was coming? The aim was to take him by surprise at Cadbury, not here in open country where his cavalry would decimate his army.

"I said you had much to learn Medraut, you should have listened to King Lot more than the poisonous tongue of your mother, she couldn't stand to be a loser either, just like you she was always scheming to get her own way, without regard for anyone else." Arthur continued. "Why have you returned, do you still seek to punish me son, or would you have my crown? Answer so we all know where we stand."

Medraut was getting very irate, how did Arthur know that he was his son, more to the point how long had he known, and kept quiet about it. Medraut lost it completely.

"You did not give me the standing that I was entitled too, always to someone else, saying that I needed to learn more, passing me over every time. You are not fit to be High King," he blurted out, "you lay with your own sister and conceive me, only to leave us, and your wife acts like a whore whilst you are away, neither of you is fit to lead the country."

Arthur had listened to this rhetoric unmoved until Medraut called Gwenhwyfar a whore. Something snapped inside him and a red mist filled his vision, the hurt welled up inside him, then anger at this young man consumed him. He swiftly drew Excalibur and thrust it through Medraut's body in one precise move. As he withdrew the sword it fell from his hand. Realisation at what he had done passed through him like a cold chill, he had killed his son in anger and broken the covenant of the sword. Medraut did not die instantly, he drew his own sword and brought it crashing down on Arthur's head as he stood frozen to the spot, splitting his helm wide open as he slowly collapsed slowly to the ground from the fatal blow. Arthur sank to his knees, blood streaming from his head. It had all happened so quick that nobody else had moved. Realisation finally sank in and everyone went for their swords, but Arthur, still conscious held up his hand and spoke.

"Gentlemen, stay your hands, there has been enough bloodshed today. Medraut is dead and I am wounded, there is concern in some quarters about my continued leadership, we will meet here tomorrow at dawn and vote on the matter. If I do not receive sufficient support then I will relinquish my crown and you may choose a new High King. How say you all?"

Looking at Arthur many thought that he would not last to morning and it would settle the issue in many of their minds without further bloodshed, some of them might not even survive a battle, so it was agreed. Medraut was placed on his horse and led away as Arthur's severe wound was tended to and he was lifted on to his horse.

Berius recovered Excalibur, totally aware that its protection had been removed from Arthur as soon as he broke the covenant, it did not look good for the King. Arthur's last battle had taken place and there were only two casualties. Nobody won, but the country would be the biggest loser.

Chapter 20
THE FLIGHT OF BERIUS

ARTHUR LAY ON HIS BED, mortally wounded but still in control of his senses, cradling Excalibur across his body. Berius was seated quietly in thought by his side, communicating silently with the Lady concerning the events that had just happened and that Arthur would not likely survive his wound. The other lords and knights were gathered around, unsure of what to do as Arthur had never suffered such a severe wound.

"My Lord, shall we send for Merlin?" Sir Kay asked, concern in his voice.

"There is no need," replied the King, "he will be returning from his business in a few days, I can inform him of the recent events then, by which time I will be on my feet again with nothing but a scratch to show. Remember gentlemen the power of the sword and the protection that I have from it."

There was a general muttering of agreement, even though all had seen fatal wounds like this many times before, they almost believed in the invincibility of Arthur. Luckily none had heard the covenant attached to Excalibur that the Lady of the Lake had brought to Arthur's notice at the great gathering, when she had presented him with the sword.

"Now gentlemen, if you would be so kind as to leave me to rest, Berius will inform you of any change to my condition as he will stay and look to my needs." With that dismissal the lords reluctantly left Arthur and Berius alone.

Arthur lay still and quiet for some while before he spoke. "You know my time is near don't you Berius?"

"Yes my lord I am aware," was the gentle reply.

Arthur continued, "I have let the Lady of the Lake and myself down as I have succumbed to my ego and struck out in blind anger when I shouldn't have. The covenant of Excalibur has been broken and I have suffered the dire consequences."

"My Lord, you are only human and it is a trait of your people that you allow the ego and emotions to take over at times and lead you astray from your path. Do not be hard on yourself."

"But I have let everyone down Berius," replied Arthur, "and the Lady most of all for the trust and faith she had in me."

"No my Lord," Berius answered, "the Lady was always aware that this could happen at some point, that is why she left me in your charge."

"Thank you Berius," said Arthur quietly, "you are too kind. Your people do not suffer from the ego or emotions of anger or jealousy, do they?"

"No my Lord," replied Berius, "but those of us that had dealings with men in the Elder days, and return periodically to help, could start to acquire those traits, if we return often or stay too long each time. We have to be careful."

"Yes I understand your caution," murmured Arthur. "You realise that once I am gone that some of the lords will squabble and fight amongst themselves for the right to the sword, and all that we have accomplished will be undone. You must take Excalibur Berius, whilst I am still alive, tonight as the lords sleep, for I feel that they are not totally convinced that I will recover. Time is short and you will need a good start as I fear that they will send men after you as soon as they realise that you and Excalibur are gone. Some of them will want it for themselves for the power that they think it brings. Not realising that you have to be the chosen one to use its power of wisdom and light, with the protection that goes with it. They will squabble and fight amongst themselves and much bloodshed will ensue – for what – nothing, as Excalibur will not give them what they expect. Therefore you must go soon and take Excalibur with you, but do not go straight to the Lady of the Lake, it will be too dangerous and I fear you will not make it. You must go in the opposite direction to gain time and hide it in a very secure location that I will describe to you, one I found many years ago that is not known of and impossible to enter unless you know how. Before I give you directions I need a moment to gain some strength, as mine is fading quickly now, and I need to last most of the night. Take a walk outside so that you are seen, because I guarantee that we are being watched. If challenged say that I am well and sleeping comfortably, you have just come out for some air for a moment. Stay outside for a little and then return and I will give to you the location of this hiding place."

"Very well my Lord," Berius said, and disappeared outside and was instantly challenged for news of Arthur, whereupon he relayed what Arthur had said. Let them know the minute there was any change was the reply from the darkness. He acknowledged that he would. Berius drew back into the shadows, and shortly thereafter returned inside.

"Come close Berius," whispered Arthur, "I do not want other ears to hear." whereupon Berius moved close to him as Arthur relayed the direction and location of the hiding place, including how to locate the entrance, and more importantly how to gain entry. It was many days travel and close to the sea where they had been before. Arthur described many landmarks en-route and that he would see his journey's end about 10 miles distance from the last landmark, if approaching from the direction given.

"The last bit is a fairly steep climb and the rock is surrounded by thick thorny bushes. Don't try and force your way through as you will get ripped apart by the spikes. Locate one of the animal runs and crawl through on your stomach until you are able to stand up and see the rock in front of you. Make your way around the rock until you find a crack in it that extends from the ground to above your head and is as wide as your fist. This is the entrance, just that, but you will need to do something next to widen it, which is why it is totally secure, as you will see. You have no doubt heard from Merlin or the Lady how I removed the sword from the stone to claim the right to be King. Well the principle is the same and as you are descended from the high order of old, you should have no trouble. With the sword in the stone I could see the vibrational energy of each and using my thoughts to re-align and match the energy to each other I was able to withdraw the sword from the stone with ease. Now here with the entrance to the cave, the same applies. Observe the vibrational energy around the crack in the rock and concentrate and match your own energy vibrations to it. If you are not used to seeing energy fields it is best done in the half light as your eyes will focus much better. When your energy field is aligned with that around the crack in the rock just gently push your arm, then your body into the opening and you will glide through effortlessly. Once inside, pause for a moment to allow your eyes to adjust to the dim light that is in the cave and you will gradually become aware of the many strange and beautiful objects that are around you. Some of these things you might recognise as belonging to your people at some point in the past. Do not be surprised if you are spoken to, it will be the spirit of Eudaf Hen, who is the guardian of the cave. Everything in there seems to give off vibrational energy in many colours and after a short while your eyes will adjust and it will seem like daylight. There are many places in there that you can leave the sword, either in view or hidden. The choice is yours because you will have to return at some point to retrieve it and return Excalibur to the Lady of the Lake. When you leave and make your way back to Cadbury Castle I suggest you do it by a circular route so that you approach from the direction where the Lady is known to frequent. By doing this everyone will assume that you have returned Excalibur to her for safe keeping. Merlin by this time will undoubtedly have arrived and he will have advised the lords that this would be so according to the covenant. This will ease the tension, but some of the lords will be wary of you and you will be watched for some time. I suggest that you wait until the following spring before you attempt to go and recover the sword and deliver it to the Lady, but only if you consider it safe to do so then. In the meantime the Lady might wish to go and retrieve the sword herself by following your instructions. I would advise against that as it would still be too dangerous, even for one so powerful as her. She would not have the same protection as afforded her as in her own environment. Now having told you all this, do you understand and have you any questions Berius? My energy is now almost gone and I need to rest so that you have a good start."

"I understand perfectly my Lord and agree that this is the best option to save Excalibur from falling into the wrong hands. I could summon the Lady but that would put her at risk and I will not contemplate that at any time. Does Merlin or anyone else know of the cave my lord?" Berius inquired.

"No, only you and I know of its existence," replied Arthur, "that is why I know it will be safe there until you have the opportunity to retrieve it. Now take Excalibur and leave me your sword. Put it across my chest and cover it with my cloak so that it cannot be seen, but the shape of a sword will be visible, and hopefully this will give you more time in your flight from here. Now go Berius before it is too late, god speed and give my apology to the Lady when you see her, for my failings. May your skill and the sword protect you. Go now."

"Very well my Lord. It has been a pleasure to serve such a noble and wise King. Rest in peace now Arthur, High King of Britain, the once and future King," with those parting words Berius vanished into the dark of the starless night, and due to his skill, totally unseen.

Some while later and many miles from the camp, Berius paused and listened. All was quiet, good, he thought, my departure has not yet been discovered. He sent out his thoughts to the Lady of the Lake advising her of what had taken place, and the journey he was making to place Excalibur in a place of safety until he could return it to her. Her thoughts came back to him agreeing that it was the right course of action to take in the circumstances and it wouldn't have been safe or prudent to have taken the sword directly to her. She wished him a safe journey and to inform her when his task had been completed. Berius acknowledged her thoughts and carried on his way at a fairly good pace, his vision almost as good in the dark as the light. Meanwhile the Lady had sent her thoughts to Merlin advising him that Arthur would shortly depart this world, and to meet her at his earliest convenience. Merlin promptly agreed and hurriedly completed his business and set off to meet her.

* * * * *

The camp was still and quiet. Arthur was managing to hang on to the threads of life, but not for much longer. Dawn was rapidly approaching and so were the King's last moments. The sky was beginning to change colour as the first glimpse of the false light took hold, heralding the full dawn of another day. Suddenly in the far distance a cock crowed and Berius, many miles away, came to a stop for a moment. Arthur had finally slipped from this world and passed over. Berius felt it, so did the Lady of the Lake and Merlin, each stopped in total stillness for a moment. Remembering a great and compassionate King who had accomplished more than they had hoped for, as they gazed up at the sky in its full glory of a new day beginning. The animal kingdom were aware of it also, even the bears in the north felt his passing, a tremendous roar of sorrow reverberating through their forest.

The birds did not sing that day. It was the end of a era for many things and the Elders were aware that their time there on that occasion was now limited. Their respective tasks having been fulfilled it would soon be time to move on. A new era was dawning, others would come now to help mankind move forward, albeit slowly, but they would return again when the need arose.

Pandemonium had broken out at the camp as the crowing cock had woken men early from a disturbed sleep and Berius was nowhere to be found. Soon it was realised that Arthur was not sleeping and had slipped quietly from the world and that the sword across his chest was not Excalibur. A cry of anguish reverberated around the camp at their loss as men searched all around the area for Berius and the sword. Lords from Medraut's camp had arrived, hearing the commotion and noting that Arthur had not appeared as he had promised. They were angry that Berius had been allowed to disappear with Excalibur and quickly organised small parties to go in pursuit to recover the sword. There was no knowing which way he had gone, so men were sent in all directions with instructions to seize him and the sword and bring them back to the camp.

At last the search had started in earnest but by then Berius had been gone many hours. Although on foot he came from a race that was swift and silent and had travelled many miles, but there was still a long way for him to go yet. Sir Kay and the rest of Arthur's kings and lords that had been close to him were not a party to this frenetic activity, but watched in disdain at this forlorn scrabble for power. They knew that Berius was the keeper of the sword and would be returning it to the Lady of the Lake, from whence it came, and out of reach of these power hungry lords.

* * * * *

As the morning progressed Berius decided it was time to look for a suitable spot to rest and headed for a little copse on top of the hill that he was drawing close to. This would give him a good view back over the way he had travelled and would give him the opportunity to check for any telltale signs of pursuit. Over this hill, in the valley below, he should see his first landmark, a diamond shaped wooded expanse with a large cleared area in the centre.

So far his journey had been without incident, with not another soul in sight, but that would obviously change as time progressed. On reaching the copse near the top of the hill Berius relaxed against an old tree that had been there for many years going by its height and girth. He surveyed the route that he had travelled, nothing stirred, all was quiet other than the gentle sounds of nature that came to his ears. The tree seemed warm and friendly and its gentle vibrational energy that he could feel sent him into a relaxing sleep.

With a start he awoke, feeling a different vibration in the earth and realised that he was feeling the disturbance caused by the pounding of horse's hooves. He surveyed the grassland below and sure enough two horsemen were galloping along, passing the hill on which Berius was resting. Too far away to make out much of their detail even with his good eyesight. He was aware that he must be more watchful now as they were undoubtedly men from the camp searching for him, and there would be others. He listened as the sound faded into the distance and the vibration that he had felt ceased.

Feeling rested Berius opened the small bag that he had crammed a few items of food into before he left. Knowing that Arthur did not have long and that he would need to travel swiftly and light. There was not enough food to last the whole journey but that would not be a problem as he was used to living off the land. He washed the small amount of food down with a mouthful of water from the skin that he always wore on his belt. Surprisingly it was cool and refreshing and he enjoyed the moment, but it was time to make a move as the light would start to fade soon and he needed to check his landmark over the hill. He bade farewell to the tree and thanked it for its warmth and friendliness, such was the way of those of the elder blood.

Berius made his way to the top of the hill and just over the rise there lay before him a large valley. A long way off to the left was a small hamlet hugging the banks of a winding river, but there in the centre of the valley was his landmark. The diamond shaped wood with the large clearing in the middle, with what appeared to be a jumble of rocks in the centre of it. The ruins of some long forgotten dwelling perhaps thought Berius looking at how overgrown it appeared from this distance. To the far side of the wood the river slowly meandered, at times disappearing into the trees, and at other times moving away from them as it followed the lie of the land. *What a glorious and peaceful sight, but somewhere out there could be lurking danger,* thought Berius as he recollected the two riders that had disturbed the peace earlier. With that he started to run effortlessly down the hill towards his next goal with Excalibur cradled gently in his arms. The breeze was slight and warm on his face, and although the light had started to fade he knew where he was aiming for and his step was firm and confident.

In no time at all he was entering the half light of the wood and slowed his pace. As his eyes adjusted to the dimmer light he noticed that the trees were well spread out with not much undergrowth between them. Obviously a well used place by animals and men alike, a good hunting wood so he must be alert and careful. He slowed his pace even more as the trees became more densely populated and the undergrowth thickened. A noise made him halt for a moment, but it was only a deer that had not noticed him, such was his quiet skill of movement.

The darkness descended quite quickly, but his keen eyesight picked out the way easily. He slowed even more as his nostrils picked up the trace of wood smoke ahead. As the density of the wood had increased he had strapped Excalibur across his back so that it would not be in the way and snag the undergrowth. The smell of wood smoke had become stronger and faint voices came to him on the evening breeze.

The wood started to thin out again as he neared the open area in the centre and he saw the glow of a fire ahead, around which men sat talking and laughing. As Berius stealthily moved closer to the edge of the clearing he saw that there were only two of them, and nearby their horses were tethered. That was not what he wanted so early on his journey, but as he listened their voices came clearly to him on the still of the evening. They were laughing and joking about their lords sending them on a fool's errand, as no way would they find Berius or the sword in that direction. They might as well enjoy themselves and stop at the hamlet away to the south and see what fun they could have with the women there. Berius watched and listened for some while until the men started to tire of their conversation and eventually both fell asleep and the fire died down.

When he was sure that they were firmly asleep he silently made his way passed them, pausing for a moment as he considered taking their horses, then decided that doing so would make his whereabouts known. Berius continued his journey through the wood for some while until he could hear the river not far in front of him. It would be too dangerous to cross in the dark, going by the noise that the water was making. He looked round for a suitable dense area of undergrowth that would conceal him till dawn and having found what he wanted he crawled in, and after checking the night noises fell asleep.

The night passed without incident and as dawn began to break Berius opened his eyes and listened to the morning noises of the wood. He was used to these wake up calls of the animals and birds, but it was not that which had awoken him, a different noise had disturbed him. Laying quite still he waited to detect the sound that was out of place. There it was, the faintest whisper of a mans voice not too far away. 'I told you he was here' floated quietly to him, and Berius tensed ready to spring into action. 'Who' came a slightly louder reply, 'quiet' was the command in response, 'not who you idiot, that great granddad of an elk' was the soft retort, 'I said he was in the woods around here, I can smell him.' Berius checked that Excalibur was still securely fastened across his back and quietly began to move away until he could stand up.

What had looked a good hiding place during the dark of the night afforded very little concealment in daylight. Stooping low Berius pushed gently through the undergrowth leaving just the barest whisper of leaves that the breeze might have caused. Next minute he emerged into a clearing and came face to face with an enormous elk, what a magnificent specimen the creature was. The deer was more surprised than startled and did not move, but stood rooted to the spot with less than an arm's length separating both of them. There is danger my friend Berius sent via his thoughts to the elk, you must go quickly and quietly. The deer blinked, bowed his head showing the magnificent spread on his antlers and moved off quickly. Berius moving swiftly in the opposite direction, aware that he was in the open and easily seen.

Next moment there was a shout and the elk came crashing through the undergrowth almost running into him. As he passed Berius saw a short throwing spear sticking out from the fleshy area above the shoulder of the animal and quickly grabbed it, pulling it out as the frightened deer sped away. With a snort the elk disappeared from sight leaving Berius between him and the hunters, who still hadn't seen him. He took off fast towards the trees on the other side of the clearing, not worrying about any slight noise that he might make. It would be drowned out by the sound of the deer disappearing through the undergrowth. Thankfully it was only a small clearing and very quickly the trees and bushes closed around him concealing him from sight. Not wanting to stop until he had put some distance between himself and the hunters Berius kept on at a good pace.

Suddenly the ground began to drop away and he began to slow, but too late. One minute there was ground underneath his feet, next minute nothing and Berius was half falling and half sliding through bushes down a very steep bank, with the sudden realisation that he could hear the roar of water below him. Then there were no more bushes, he was out in the open with the water in the gorge rushing up to meet him, or so it seemed. He tried to slow himself with his feet but to no avail except to send him off in another direction, but always downwards. His eyes took in the sight of the rushing water and his mind noted that it was not very wide there but obviously deep as the flow was fast, though he could see no rocks or white water. He noted a tree hanging down towards the river, slightly off to his right and tried to dig his heals into the earth so that he could steer towards it. However he dug too deeply in a soft patch, his knee bent and next minute he was hurtling through the air straight for the tree. Putting his arms in front of his face he crashed through the slim branches and managed to grasp hold of one, and with great strength of grip hung on. The branch bent almost double with his weight and forward momentum such that Berius thought it was going to break under the strain. Instead with an almighty crack the whole tree became dislodged from it's slim footing on the bank and Berius carried on his descent towards the water. Still hanging on to the branch but now with the whole tree bearing down behind him.

He hit the water feet first and disappeared beneath the surface feeling the cold engulfing him. His descent stopped with a jerk and he found himself shooting back upwards, still tightly gripping the branch. As he broke through the surface the main trunk of the tree caught him a glancing blow on the side of the head, as it reached the water. He felt as if he was floating on air as he slipped into unconsciousness and relaxed his grip on the branch. The tree sank into the water pushing Berius back under, then rolled over as the weight of its roots tipped it. Berius was trapped in the branches underwater, totally unaware of what was happening as in his dream state he felt as if he was on a ship floating out to sea. But it was dark and he couldn't see anything, or get his bearings. As the tree started to settle in the water it rolled again dragging Berius half out the water, trapped in the branches by Excalibur strapped on his back, as it was quickly swept into midstream.

The tree was taken rapidly through the gorge swaying this way and that in the turbulent water with Berius totally oblivious of the danger he was in. The river slowed a little as the gorge widened and the narrow end of the tree became wedged between some rocks jutting out from the bank. For some while it remained firmly stuck with Berius trapped amongst the branches, half in and half out of the water. Oblivious to all except his dream state of seeing himself and Excalibur floating out to sea. Never to be seen again and being unable to fulfil his vow to return to the Lady of the Lake the Sword of Wisdom and Light, Excalibur. The momentum of the water and the weight of the roots slowly swung the tree around freeing it from the projecting rocks and it continued its journey downstream.

As the river started to widen more the flow of the water gradually slackened as it began to meander across the valley and the tree drifted away from midstream and moved towards the far bank. On the next sharp bend of the meander the tree was pushed slowly into the shallows by the flow of water and with a jolt ground to halt not far from the bank. Berius, hallucinating on his 'boat' thought that they had hit rocks and that they were sinking, as he could feel the cold wet water lapping round his feet. This was where it all ended he dreamt and slipped into a deeper state of unconsciousness due to the cold that had finally taken hold. With visions of his vow unfulfilled and never seeing his Lady of the Lake again.

* * * * *

Many hours later Berius began to stir and consciousness began to seep through his body. He couldn't understand at first why he felt so lovely and warm as he drifted in and out of awareness. His head was pounding and warm water seemed to be trickling down his face and into his eyes, as well as running down his neck. He tried to move his arm to brush away the water on his face but he had no co-ordination. A soft voice came to him as if in a dream telling him to lie still as he was in no condition to move yet. He opened his eyes gently and saw a blurred vision of a pretty young woman bending over him, apparently doing something to his head. That feels good, it must be a dream, then he heard a lovely soft voice commanding him to go back to sleep with the promise of some steaming hot broth when he awoke properly. Berius slipped back into his unconscious state dreaming of hot food and a pretty woman or was it a pretty woman with hot food, he wasn't sure, but it did not matter as it was a very comforting dream.

The crackling of a fire, the smell of wood smoke and food finally brought

Berius back into the land of the living, Opening his eyes and laying still for a moment listening to the noises around him, before identifying them as safe sounds and relaxing. The light was dim, but gently moving his throbbing head he could see that he was in a hut with a fire going in the middle around which busied the pretty young woman, definitely not a dream he thought.

"Where am I?" croaked Berius. "Where is my sword, what is your name, is there anybody else around?"

"One question at a time sire," said the startled girl, as she had not realised that he was awake. "We are by the bank of the river in which you had your fight with the tree. I am called Tess, but my proper name is Megan, and there is nobody else around for many miles. Does that satisfy you sire? Your sword is by the fire and its lucky you had it strapped across your back and that it got tangled in the tree, otherwise we would not be speaking now."

Berius muttered his thanks, becoming aware that he was covered in animal skins that had kept him lovely and warm. Realisation suddenly hit home that he was completely naked under these skins, surely she hadn't stripped his clothes off him he thought, but she had indicated that she was alone. He asked where they were and was told that they were drying by the fire as they were in such a bad state that she had to wash them thoroughly. Seeing the look on his face blushed and confirmed that she had stripped them off him.

"Do not worry sire I have two brothers that I have to look after and tend to their wounds so I am quite used to seeing a man's body, but I have never seen one as beautiful as yours. I wanted to hold you and cuddle you to keep you warm but a man such as you must already be spoken for and it would not have been right."

Berius was quite taken back by her honesty and intuition. "Thank you," he replied, "your clear speaking and wisdom are a joy to behold in one as young and pretty as you, but alas I am not spoken for in the way that you mean. There is someone very close to me but we are of the same bloodline and have the same task in this lifetime."

"Now you are making me feel embarrassed sire," she answered.

"My apologies," muttered Berius, "but I only say what is true. May I have my clothes and sword please?"

"Not until you have eaten some hot broth, I'm not having your nice clean clothes spoilt," and with that she proceeded to ladle some into a large bowl. "Now you get this down you sire and I might let you have your clothes, but maybe I'll hide them and keep you as my prisoner," she joked.

"I'm not sure that your brothers would appreciate that. Where are they by the way?" asked Berius.

"On the way south to the hamlet for the market there," she replied. "They will barter what we have for what we need and they will be gone for about five days, so I have you all to myself," she teased.

Berius ignored her teasing as he demolished the broth, whereupon she refilled the bowl despite his protests, telling him that he needed to regain his strength quickly for whatever business he was about. Berius acknowledged the truth of this as he willingly tucked into the second helping.

"That was the best broth that I have tasted in a long while," stated Berius. "You certainly know how to look after a man Tess."

"Thank you sire, sometimes I'm not sure that my brothers appreciate me and how I feed them so that they are strong for the work they do. I know they do in my heart, but it would be nice if sometimes they said so, but I suppose it's so easy to take people and what they do for granted, but a little thank you occasionally would be reassuring."

"I said you were wiser than your years Tess. Showing appreciation, in whatever way, makes people feel good, but if they don't say anything we always know if it is meant by the way they treat us."

"That's enough talking now sire, you need more rest whilst I get on with my chores."

Berius agreed but asked for his sword to be brought close to him, just in case. With that Tess retrieved it from near the fire and laid it close by him noting that it was a truly magnificent sword and that he must be someone of great importance. He told her that he was no more important than she was, that they were all equal in importance for the tasks that they faced in life. With that he fell into a deep sleep and dreamt of Nimue the beautiful Lady of the Lake and young Tess, the Princess of the River, as he referred to her. How alike they were in many ways.

His ordeal had been terrible and a chill had crept into his body through the long immersion in the water, the warmth of the broth and the heat from the fire helped to bring out the fever lurking in him. He began to shiver as a cold sweat broke out and began to disturb his sleep. Tess knelt and moped the sweat from his brow as she talked to him gently. Coming to a decision, she swiftly removed her clothing and slid in beside him, telling herself that it was okay, he had said that he wasn't spoken for, she would help him through his fever. She embraced him, gently pulling his naked body towards hers, holding him close to give him extra warmth and comfort. Slowly his shaking subsided and his breathing became slow and rhythmic again and she began to caress him very delicately so as not to disturb him, all the while quietly whispering to him whatever came into her head.

She felt very good inside, this man did something to her just by his presence. Berius rolled closure towards her, and still in his deep slumber put his arm around her waist. Tess kissed his brow and murmured that his touch was delightful as she continued her slow caresses, exploring his beautiful body. Whether he was dreaming or half awake, Tess was not sure, but she felt his passion start to rise and push hard against her body and pulled him even closer as she enjoyed the intimate contact. Her own feelings were beginning to well up inside her. She wanted this man, whom she didn't even know, the wonderful glow deep in her essence was something that she had not experienced before. Tess could not hold back much longer, she wanted his child, a son and this might be her only chance, whether he was fully asleep or not, tomorrow he could be gone. She made her decision, gently rolling Berius on his back she eased herself on to him and with a gasp of pleasure slowly guided his passion into her fire. What an indescribable feeling, as she paused to experience the intense sensations that passed through her body. Unhurriedly she began to move her body with slow deliberate thrusts, Berius murmured in his dream sleep and his body began to respond and move in unison with hers. Gradually the motion increased as desire rose in them both, unable to keep control as finally she felt him explode inside her at the same time as her body released all her pent up passion. Collapsing on top of him she gave him a long passionate kiss, which finally woke him. Looking her in the eyes he said that he thought he was having a wonderful dream, but how much nicer to know that it was real and not a dream at all.

"I do not treat all my wounded soldiers the same way sire, but my desire for you was that intense I thought that I might not get another opportunity. Something inside of me wanted to bear you a son, even if I did not see you again, it was that strong that I couldn't go against it. How is your fever sire? It seems to have passed, you should rest again after all that activity, otherwise you will miss the morning meal and not have the strength to do anything," she said laughingly as she made to remove herself from him.

Berius put his arms around her saying, "not so quick my Princess of the River, I am not sure if that was a dream or not, but there is one way to find out."

He eased her over and began to kiss and caress her as he took the dominant role this time and caused her fire to burst into uncontrollable desire once again. as their bodies pounded together. A million stars exploded through her whole being as a cry of unbelievable ecstasy escaped from her mouth. They fell asleep curled in each others arms and slept many hours, by which time the sun was high in the sky.

Berius felt much better after his long rest and knew that he must be on his way, he had to place Excalibur in the safe cave that Arthur had described, to dally any longer could be dangerous. He mentioned to Tess that he had to leave, as he had an urgent errand to complete, but he would return to see her when it was done. She realised that he must be on important business and would look forward to his return, but did not know his name and if he was delayed would not know how to call the son that she would bear him. He told her that he was Eru of the Elder race but was called Berius at this time, the choice of name would be hers, whatever she felt appropriate for him. It would come to her in a dream, but he would be back before then.

Berius headed off into the woods, heading back up river to the ford where he should have crossed. Higher up than the place where he had entered the river with the tree for company, but caution was necessary as there was a small hamlet close by, another marker that Arthur had given him. It took him some hours to reach that point, he hadn't appreciated how far he had travelled downstream lodged in the tree, and sought shelter for the night amongst the seclusion of the woods. Tess had insisted that he take plenty of food with him to keep his strength up, as he hadn't fully recovered from his ordeal and he gratefully accepted her offer as the little he had before had been ruined in the water. His mind wandered back to their brief time together. There weren't enough wise and thoughtful people like her, but times were changing, and so were the people, thanks to Arthur and all that he had managed to accomplish, much of which would last many generations. One day there will be many more people like Tess in the world, more like his own people, loving, caring and wise, with a willingness to speak openly and truthfully from the heart. That was why he allowed his feelings to show for once, he related to her and was pleased that she wished to bear him a son, and he knew she would. She had followed the instincts of her higher self, just like Arthur had done, they were there for a reason, nothing happened by chance.

All the Elders had known that Arthur would succumb at some point to his negative human emotions, it was the way of his people, but he had accomplished much more and for far longer than they had dared hope for. Now was the time of change again and to move forward in a different way. Much of the foundations that Arthur had laid would remain in place, especially in the attitude of his people. Kings and lords would come and go, but the way of the people would continue to develop and evolve for the better, that was what it was really about, the many, not the select few. Berius fell into a relaxing sleep, dreaming of his sister, the Lady of the Lake and the lovely personality of the Princess of the River.

Well rested, Berius moved on the following morning after viewing his surroundings and taking note of the animal sounds. All seemed peaceful, there were no indications of human activity in the vicinity, the morning noises told him that. He made his way silently through the wood and emerged the other side to a spectacular view of the rolling countryside in all its vibrant colours. The many greens blending with the browns and yellows, the pinks and reds interspersed with splashes of blue, it was a marvellous sight. Way off in the distance he could clearly see his next landmark, three huge stone megaliths standing like silent sentinels on a bare hilltop several miles away. In between he could see one or two small hamlets. Those he would avoid, as he did not wish to make contact with anyone unless it was unavoidable.

Carefully selecting his route in his mind he broke into a gentle run, using the lie of the land as much as possible to hide his movement. Excalibur was secured across his back beneath his cloak, almost invisible, except by close inspection, it was best that he was seen to be unarmed if noticed by anyone. A few people were dotted about the landscape, tending their fields or animals, but he made a wide detour around them and the hamlets, although it added a few miles to his journey.

He covered the distance to the hilltop fairly quickly and was certain that he had not been noticed by anyone. Resting for awhile in the shade of a few trees at the base of the hill, as he had not fully recovered his strength yet. He ate some of the bread and fruit that Tess had insisted he took with him and surveyed the area, the hill stretched before him, tall and proud and completely bare of any cover. He would wait until the light began to fade before making his way to the top, otherwise he might be seen from a distance.

Berius let his thoughts wander over the recent events, some of the kings and lords would not have been very happy when they had discovered that he and Excalibur were missing, but those close to Arthur would know why he had left suddenly and bear him no grudge. They knew that Berius was the keeper of the sword and that he had not taken it for his own benefit, but to return it to the Lady of the Lake and place it out of reach of the tyrants until such time as a new bearer was selected, and that might not be for many hundreds of years. That would depend on the Masters and their view on the evolution of the indigenous peoples that inhabited Earth. If they were ready to move forward again and search for that elusive peace with determination and free will.

The light had faded sufficiently now and Berius made his way slowly up the hill towards those giant megaliths, he could feel their energy pulsating gently, drawing him to them. There had been four standing stones at one time but only three remained standing now, one had fallen, or more likely been pulled down and lay flat on the ground. Berius settled down to rest for the night amongst the stones, letting the Earth energy permeate through his body with soft and comforting vibrations, revitalising his own energy, like waves on the shore, gently cleansing and renewing. The energy did not feel complete with the fallen stone torn from its original position and Berius stared at it for a long while as he recollected the ancient way of moving them to build the magnificent stone structures that his people had left as a legacy. Concentrating on the stone, the energy field around it began to glow slightly and Berius moved his thoughts to his own energy field and slowly brought them into harmony with each other, holding out his arms he made a lifting motion. The stone rose into the air without any difficulty and Berius guided it into the hole where it had stood, moving his arms to raise it perpendicular, letting it down slowly so that it stood upright again. At no time had he touched the stone, but their energies were joined in unison and it responded to his actions as if an extension of his arms. Light as a feather with no feeling of weight the giant megalith was now standing tall and proud again in its rightful place, the energy of the stones was complete again, and the difference was noticeable. Arthur had done the same thing, without knowing it, when he had removed the Sword of Britain from the stone to become High King.

The new day brought sounds of activity to his ears, far off in the distance as he awoke and listened to all the noises that came on the soft breeze, alert for any sound of danger. A small hamlet, nestling on the banks of a meandering river two miles away looked as if it was preparing to hold a fair and travellers could be seen making their way towards it from all directions. *That is a little inconvenient,* Berius thought, *I will have to be very careful and avoid that area and take a long journey around it, as that is the direction in which I should be headed, to seek my next landmark. Well if they use this hill for part of their celebrations, then they are going to be in for a surprise, finding four standing stones now instead of three, that will pose them a riddle.* He smiled to himself as set off to find a way around the hamlet that would keep him hidden as far as possible.

It was a long day and many times he had to conceal himself as best as possible as he detected the sound of approaching people. Luckily they were engrossed in idle talk about the fair and not paying any heed to their surroundings. But as often happens when many people are about the unexpected occurs, suddenly and without warning. Berius was making his way along a narrow track through the woods that appeared little used, when there was a flurry of movement as several birds, sounding their alarm call, flew out of the trees in front of him. In the same instant three riders came in sight, travelling much too fast for the path that was barely wide enough for one horse, as if they were in a race to the fair. Berius just had time to throw himself to safety into the undergrowth as they thundered past, unsure whether they had seen him or not, but hearing the pounding of hooves fade into the distance. That was too close for comfort, he must be more careful and keep his wits about him, they could have been soldiers on the lookout for him, but in this case he didn't think so. He had to stop thinking about Tess and concentrate on his journey, when his task was completed then would be the time to relax for awhile. The rest of the day passed peacefully and he did not see another soul as he made his way towards the next landmark.

For the next few days he travelled warily, making detours around the villages and hamlets that he encountered, occasionally needing to take cover as he spied horsemen travelling in the vicinity. Unsure if they were searching for him, but not wishing to be seen anyway. At last he came within sight of the last marker, a tall slender peculiar shaped rock, that stood out in the landscape, a stones throw from the fort at Tintagel. Still ten miles distant, he needed to proceed with caution as there were likely to be many more people about. The fort was a busy place with much trade taking place and although they had a great regard for the King, Arthur had not wanted them to be aware of why Berius was there, it had to remain secret from all.

It took him the best part of the day to carefully negotiate the remaining miles. The light was just beginning to fade as Berius located the rocky outcrop that was the end of his journey and the tall gorse bushes that surrounded it. Remembering Arthur's advice he followed the line of bushes until he found a suitable animal run close to their roots that was wide enough to take his body. Long sharp barbs threatening ominously as he lay on his stomach and slowly crawled through the narrow opening. Once or twice he snagged his clothing but finally emerged the other side unscathed, and managed to carefully stand up in the narrow space between rock and bushes. He sidled unhurriedly around the rock, which rose some way above his head, looking for the crack that Arthur had mentioned. Only finding the one he studied it carefully, partially closing his eyes in the dim light to change his field of vision. Slowly the energy aura of the rock became visible to him and he began to mentally change the pulsating vibrations to match his own, until they were both in tune with each other. Then unlike when he had lifted the giant stone megalith in place, he gently pushed his fist into the crack in the rock, feeling it soft and supple, then his arm and shoulder, and finally his body. He was standing in a dimly lit cave and could see small patches of many different colour lights in the murkiness around him that very slowly increased in intensity as a voice spoke in his head and a lengthy conversation by thought ensued.

"Good evening young man, welcome. How can I be of service to one of the Elder Race?"

"Thank you Eudaf Hen for your gracious welcome. I have come on an errand of great importance and seek your assistance for a short time," replied Berius, "I am Eru the Elder, King Arthur directed me to you."

"Ah Eru, you know my name, that is good. What has befallen the King that he sends you to seek my aid?"

"Alas the King has passed over," replied Berius. "He was given the mystical sword Excalibur by Nimue, Lady of the Lake, and I as keeper of the sword need to return it to her, it has special significance to our people and this world. But it is sought by others in their greed, not realising that it will not help them, and it is not safe at the moment to take it straight to her. Many are searching for myself and the sword. I seek your help in hiding it here until the search has died down and I can safely return it to the Lady. Our late King described this cave to me on his deathbed and said that it would be safe in your guardianship until I could return. He also asked me to extend his gratitude to you for the shield and tabard that you gave him, he used them as instructed and they were of great benefit to him in securing peace for his people. The tabard I return, as Excalibur is wrapped in it, but it was not possible to bring the shield as I needed to travel light."

"It was a pleasure to help young Arthur, I am sorry to hear that he has passed over. He only visited this cave twice," replied Eudaf Hen, "but great things were destined for him and I am sure that he did his best. It will be an honour to look after the sword with all the other ancient treasures that are here, until such time as you return, but I fear that it will be much longer than you think, but I cannot say more. No other shall enter this cave until you return Eru, however long that takes. I will increase the light so that you can select a place for Excalibur, a sword whose name I heard mentioned in ancient tales when I walked this earth."

The light increased and Berius was amazed at all the ancient treasures that he saw hidden in this cave. Items that had been there for many hundreds of years probably, as its existence was not known about now. He saw a long protrusion on the rock face to his left and unstrapping Excalibur from his back laid it there, still wrapped in the white tabard with the red cross.

"Night has fallen outside Eru," stated Eudaf Hen, "it would be best if you rested here for the night and left just before sunrise and you can tell me tales of your people. My knowledge is a little limited, although I was privileged to meet some in my time and I learnt much from them."

They communicated by thought for several hours, until Berius became tired and fell into a peaceful slumber and the lights dimmed.

Feeling rejuvenated after his short sleep Berius took his leave of Eudaf Hen, with a promise to return as soon as it was safe to do so. Leaving the cave in the same way as he had entered, the dim light sufficient for him to see the internal rock face. Outside dawn was slowly arriving, the air was still and quiet and not a sound disturbed that peaceful time. Berius did not have long before the land awoke and animals and humans alike began their day. Quickly he crawled back through the gorse bushes and as all was clear set off at a steady run to put as much distance as possible between himself and the cave before the daily movement of people began.

He put many miles behind him before seeking a place to rest, following the same route and landmarks that he had used to find the cave. Caution was still necessary as Berius did not want to be seen in that area. It would not be a good idea, as if discovered it would be obvious that he had not returned Excalibur to the Lady of the Lake, but hidden it elsewhere, and that could create a great deal of trouble. Luck or divine guidance was with him and he travelled for several days without any problems. Seeking shelter to rest and sleep at the end of each day, enjoying a little food from his dwindling supply. He was heading for the ford in the river some miles upstream from where Tess was busying herself with her daily routine. Happy and content with a permanent smile on her face, as her thoughts strayed to him, wondering where he might be, but knowing that he would return. Once across the river Berius was going to make a long detour to approach Cadbury Castle from the direction of Lydney, as it was common knowledge that the Lady of the Lake resided in that locality, although nobody knew exactly where.

There was a change in the air that he was not happy with, a feeling of impending trouble that was increasing as he moved closer towards the river, still two miles away, his senses finely tuned for the first hint of danger.

Suddenly a little way ahead he saw the reason, a large band of warriors, Irish raiders by their dress, heading for the ford, no doubt to kill and plunder. If he was quick he could make a detour around them and reach the ford first, give the villagers warning and reach the safety of the opposite river bank and disappear into the woods. Berius started to run, the light was beginning to fade and that would help him.

He almost succeeded, making his way around the raiders without incident, but then he was spotted and with a shout they gave chase, knowing that he would warn the village. They were only half a mile behind him as he ran into the village shouting his warning, urging everyone to disperse into the woods. There was no time to dally and collect anything, just run and hide. Panic ensued as people grabbed their offspring and headed for the trees. Many made it but others didn't, being cut down in their flight. Berius could do no more, he had no sword and there were too many of them. He had stopped too long in trying to help and ran towards the river, a few of the raiders in pursuit. Berius did not have time to cross the ford now, danger was too close, but he had spotted a small boat downstream and headed for that.

Untying the little craft he jumped in and began to paddle for all he was worth, the raiders close behind him shouting and cursing. Short hunting spears began to hit the water around him as he headed for mid stream, desperately trying to get out of range. The spears fell behind him as the river started to take him downstream and he breathed a sigh of relief. Then disaster struck. He felt the pain as a long throwing spear penetrated his body, embedded deeply, then another struck him and he fell forward as he began to lose consciousness, the paddle slipping from his hands. The little boat floated down the river, taken by the flow, with Berius mortally wounded oblivious to what was happening. Through the gorge where he had entered with the tree many days before, spinning around on the rocky outcrop before continuing several miles until the boat finally came to rest.

Tess found him the next morning, still clinging to life in the little boat that had grounded in the same shallows as the tree had previously. She summoned her brothers to help her carry Berius to the hut where she gently removed the spears and tended to his wounds, knowing that he was unlikely to survive, he had lost too much blood. She did her best, with sorrow in her heart that she had not discovered him earlier when there might have been a chance. Whatever had happened to him? she wondered, he did not have his sword with him now.

Berius regained consciousness some hours later, the warmth having revived him. Tess was sitting quietly beside him with tears in her eyes as she held his hand.

He smiled at her, "I came back," Berius whispered, "but not the way I had hoped."

"Quiet sire," she replied, "conserve your strength, they are bad wounds."

"I am sorry Princess, but I do not have time unfortunately. I have not long left, but I need you to do something for me, my energy is going fast and I need yours to send a message to my sister, the Lady. Place your other hand on my brow, relax and let your energy flow into me."

Tess did as she was bade and Berius summoned all his reserves and communicated with the Lady of the Lake, telling her that the sword was safe but that his life was ebbing away, describing the events to her. She would not be able to recover the sword as Eudaf Hen would not allow any other entry to the cave, other than himself. It would have to remain there until he returned again. She acknowledged him and expressed her sorrow that they would not meet again in that life, but that they would be needed again and perhaps it was best that Excalibur was well protected until it could be recovered in a future time.

Berius spoke again, "thank you Tess. How is my son, is he growing yet?"

"It is too early for that sire," she replied, "but I know he is there, and for that I am grateful and will name him after you, your ancient name Eru, I like that, and I shall tell him all about you, even though I know little."

"Undo what is round my neck Tess and give it to him when he is older," Berius instructed her.

"Its beautiful sire," she said holding it in her hands, "I have never seen such a magnificent fish."

"It is not a fish," Berius barely managed to answer, "it's a Delphis [Dolphin], a sea mammal and it's the sign of my people. They are the guardians of this Earth. Kiss me Tess as I am now fading fast, take care of my son Princess of the River."

Tess kissed him gently, with tears running uncontrollably down her face as Berius quietly slipped from this world and made his transition.

Excalibur, the Sword of Wisdom and Light, Eru the Elder and Arthur, High King of Britain, all lost to this land; for now.

EPILOGUE

THE ANIMAL KINGDOM was silent again that day. The Elders mourned the loss of one of their own and were rarely seen for many a year after that, although they did return a long while later. But no one other than the Elders saw the Lady of the Lake again, she did go to the cave, but was denied entrance by Eudaf Hen.

* * * * *

Tess and her two brothers buried Berius by the riverbank and put a large mound over the grave, and every year in spring it was a profusion of many colours as the wild flowers carpeted it, lasting well into winter long after all the others had died off. Tess gave birth to a son and named him Eru in honour of her love, the lad was the very image of his father. As he grew up she would take him for a walk along the river bank and both felt the presence of Eru the Elder walking with them and they would send their thoughts to him, and feel his love and joy returned. When the young lad grew older he learnt to hear the answering thoughts from his father, especially if he held the Delphis that hung around his neck. That way he was instructed in the ways of the Elder Race and acquired much knowledge that he shared with his mother. Tess was happy, she had fulfilled her mission in life, the painfully brief physical love that she had experienced was replaced by something much stronger and more beautiful. She could never put the feeling into words but their son Eru understood, the Atlantean blood of the Elder Race flowed strong in him.

* * * * *

King Constantine of Cornwall was made High King, assisted by the diplomatic manoeuvres of Merlin, as one of his last acts before he faded from the scene. King Maelgwyn of Gwynedd failed to get the support he thought he deserved and was forever a thorn in everybody's side as he vent his anger wherever he could, but stopping short of all out war, which he would of lost very quickly.

* * * * *

Queen Gwenhwyfar was totally distraught on hearing of Arthur's death, taking blame on herself for her naive indiscretion that undoubtedly was the cause of it, and she died soon after from a broken heart. Her body was taken to Avalon, which was her request, and buried in the church grounds at Glasteining [Glastonbury], so that she could be close to Arthur. His body had been removed from the camp where he had died by three woman dressed in black, who had arrived on a small barge from upriver. Saying that they were taking him to Avalon to heal his wounds. Nobody had stopped them as they were more concerned with the whereabouts of Berius and Excalibur.

It was not until long after did some wonder how they knew what had happened to Arthur, by then it was too late, they had disappeared. Arthur had gone and so had Excalibur, would they ever return, some referred to him as 'the once and future king,' but what of the sword. Would Eru the Elder one day come again to retrieve it as Eudaf Hen had hinted.

* * * * *

The year following Arthur's death there was a catastrophic 'near miss' by a comet that caused the planet to wobble as the Earth energies were disrupted momentarily. Creating a widespread chain of volcanic activity, resulting in rapid climate change. The sun was screened by ash in the atmosphere, crops failed and plagues manifested, causing the death of a great many people, not a single country escaped. Was this the displeasure of Mother Earth and another lesson for humanity?

* * * * *

Nearly fifteen hundred years on we move towards another major cosmic shift as the sixth age rapidly approaches, as predicted by the ancient civilisations that were instructed in the knowledge and wisdom of the Atlantean Elder race. Much of what Arthur started still lingers on, in some cases much improved, in others conveniently forgotten as over time the human ego came to the fore again.

However in recent years enlightenment has spread to many people throughout this world of ours and the way of life is beginning to change. But is it enough, or will the human race fail again to make that transition to a peaceful and harmonious way of life?

Only time will tell, but as Merlin would say, 'time is not on our side.'